ONCE UPON TIME,
THERE WAS A WIZARD...

THEN IT ALL
WENT TO.

CURSE WORDS VOLUME #5: FAIRYTALE ENDING, FIRST PRINTING. JANUARY 2020. Published by Image Comics, Inc. Office of publication: 2701 NW Vaughn St., Suite 780, Portland, OR 97210. Copyright © 2020 SILENT E PRODUCTIONS, LLC. All rights reserved. Contains material originally published in single magazine form as CURSE WORDS #21-25 and the CURSE WORDS SPRING HAS SPRUNG SPECIAL. "CURSE WORDS," its logos, and the likenesses of all characters herein are trademarks of SILENT E PRODUCTIONS, LLC, unless otherwise noted. "Image" and the Image Comics logos are registered trademarks of Image Comics, Inc. No part of this publication may be reproduced or transmitted, in any form or by any means (except for short excerpts for journalistic or review purposes), without the express written permission of SILENT E PRODUCTIONS, LLC, or Image Comics, Inc. All names, characters, events, and locales in this publication are entirely fictional. Any resemblance to actual persons (living or dead), events, or places, without satirical intent, is coincidental. Printed in the USA. For information regarding the CPSIA on this printed material call: 203-595-3636. For international rights, contact: foreignlicensing@imagecomics.com. ISBN: 978-1-5343-1397-2

CURSE WORDS

VOLUME FIVE: FAIRYTALE ENDING

CREATED BY
CHARLES SOULE &
RYAN BROWNE

COLORS BY
ADDISON DUKE & **RYAN BROWNE**

LETTERS BY
CHRIS CRANK

SPRING HAS SPRUNG SPECIAL DRAWN BY
MIKE NORTON

BOOK DESIGN BY
RYAN BROWNE

PRODUCTION BY
DEANNA PHELPS

LOGO BY
SEAN DOVE

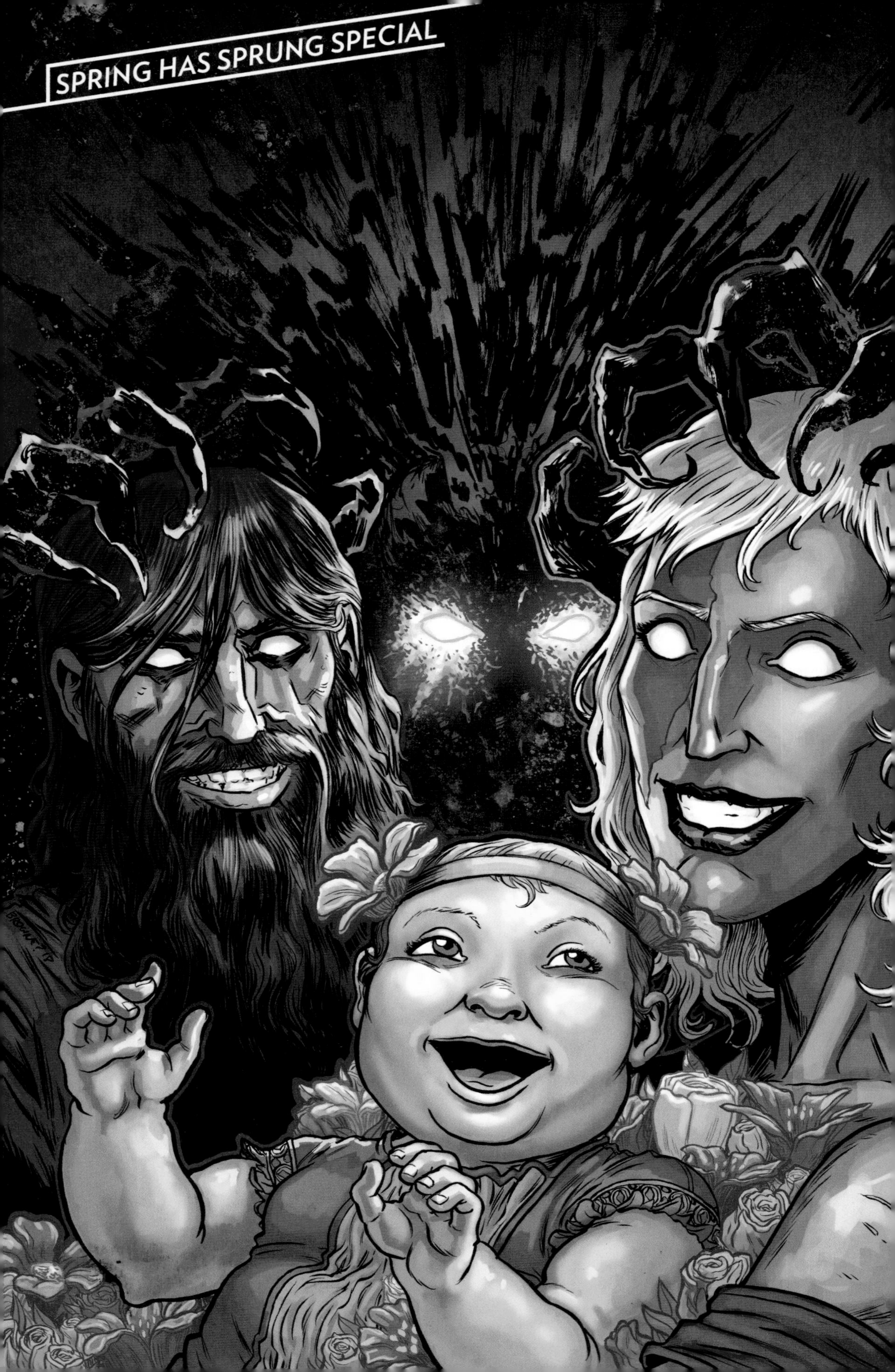
SPRING HAS SPRUNG SPECIAL

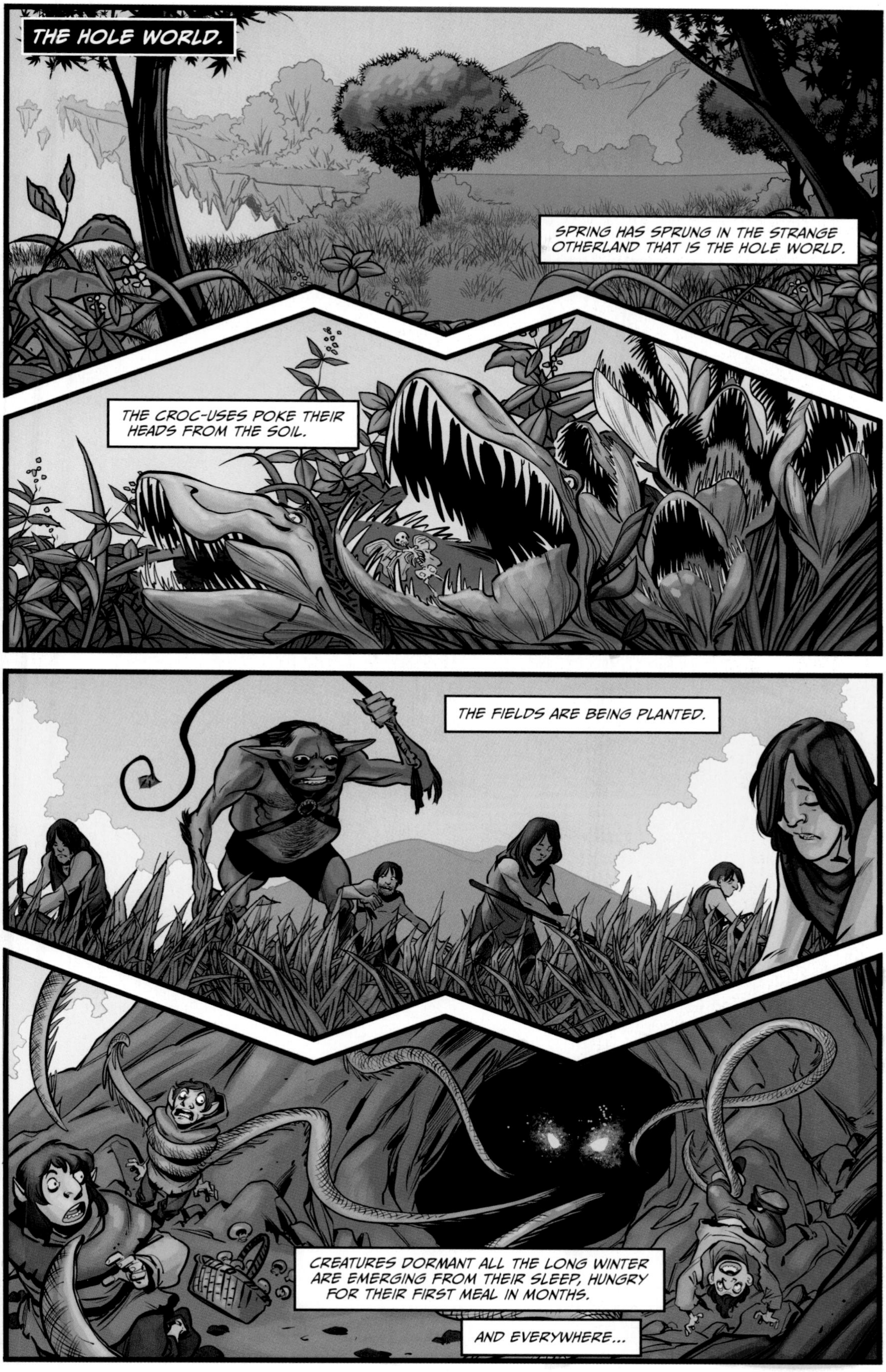
THE HOLE WORLD.
SPRING HAS SPRUNG IN THE STRANGE OTHERLAND THAT IS THE HOLE WORLD.
THE CROC-USES POKE THEIR HEADS FROM THE SOIL.
THE FIELDS ARE BEING PLANTED.
CREATURES DORMANT ALL THE LONG WINTER ARE EMERGING FROM THEIR SLEEP, HUNGRY FOR THEIR FIRST MEAL IN MONTHS.
AND EVERYWHERE...

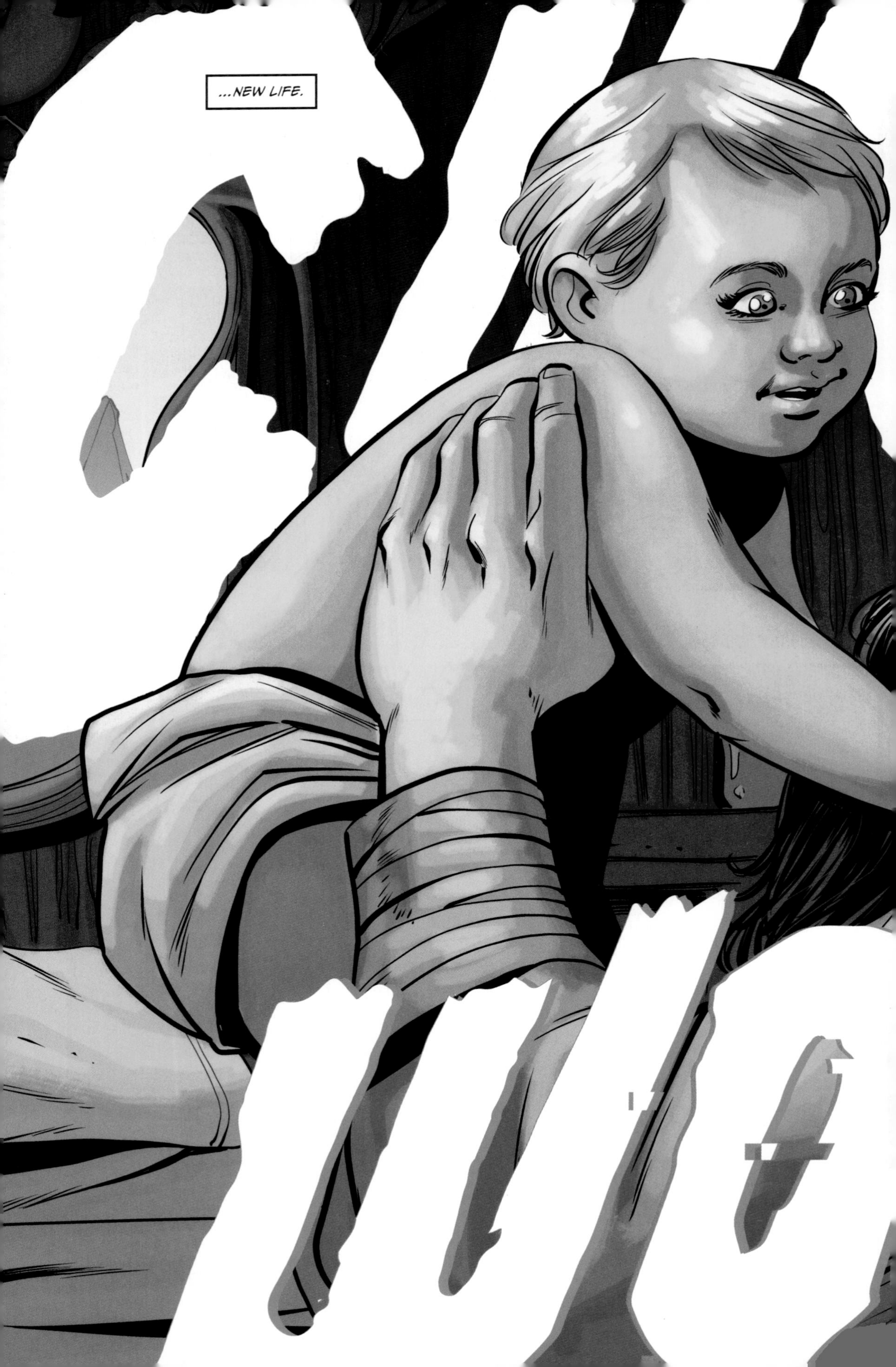
...NEW LIFE.

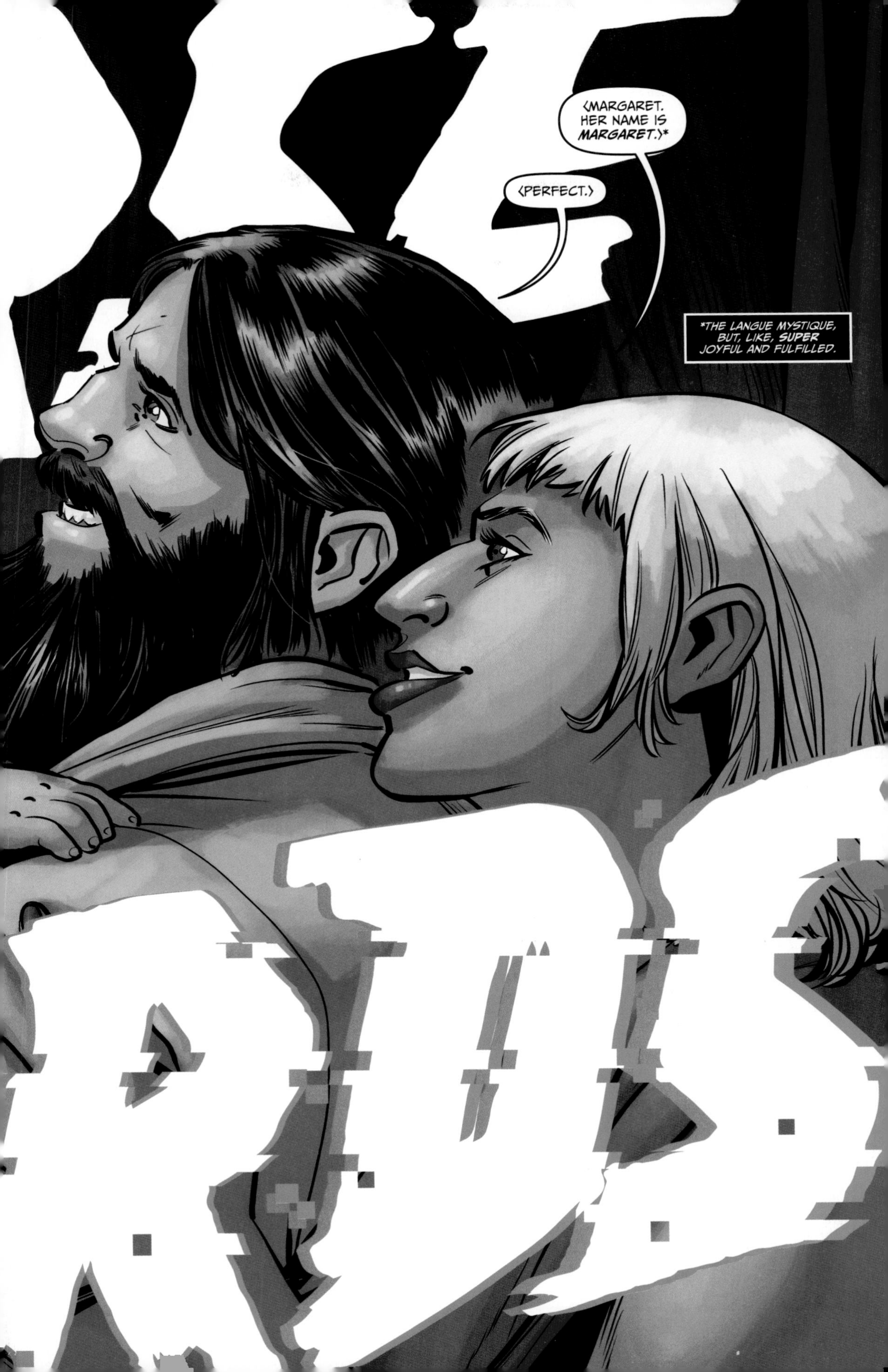

⟨MARGARET. HER NAME IS MARGARET.⟩*
⟨PERFECT.⟩
*THE LANGUE MYSTIQUE, BUT, LIKE, SUPER JOYFUL AND FULFILLED.

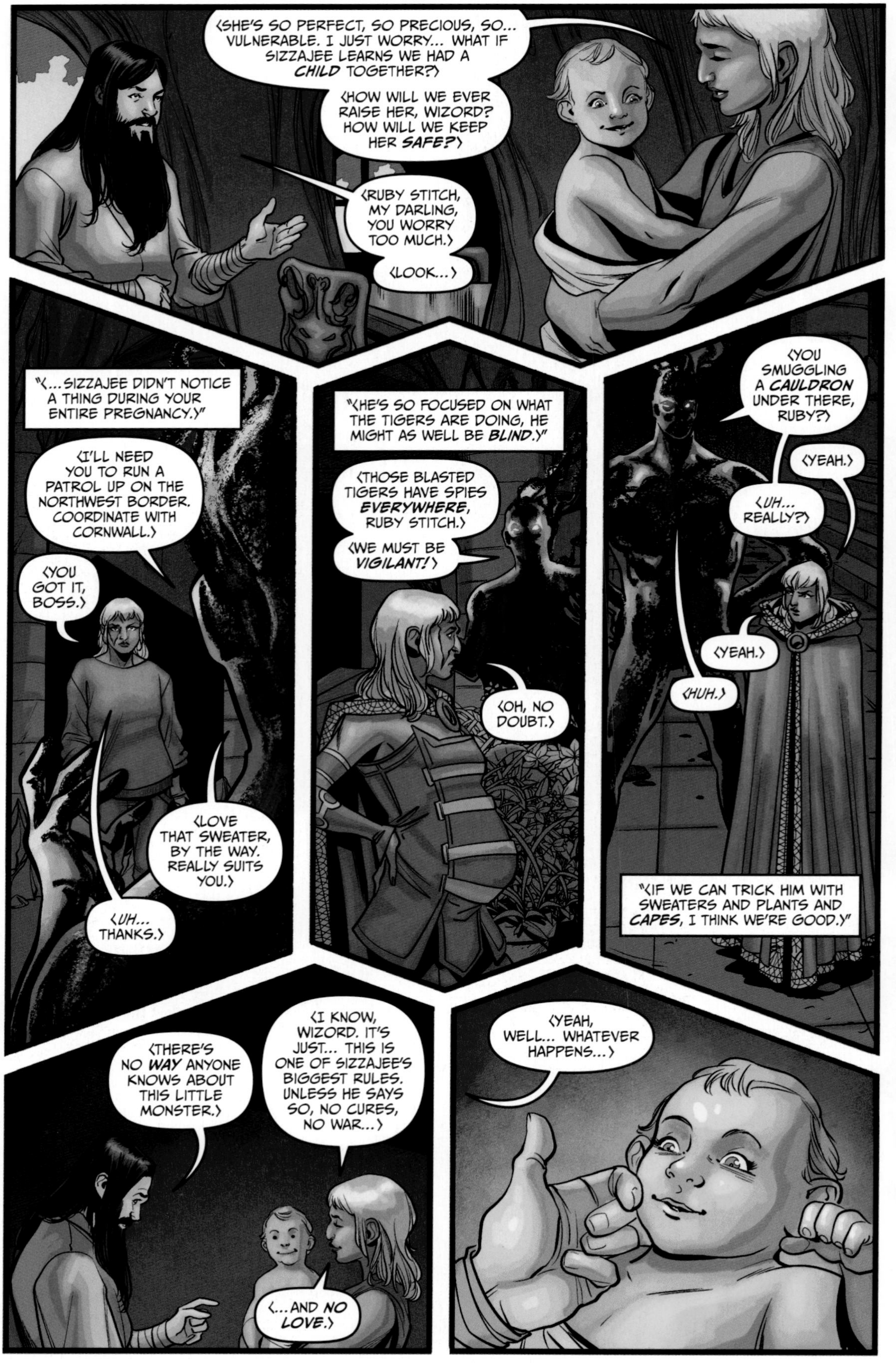

‹SHE'S SO PERFECT, SO PRECIOUS, SO... VULNERABLE. I JUST WORRY... WHAT IF SIZZAJEE LEARNS WE HAD A CHILD TOGETHER?›
‹HOW WILL WE EVER RAISE HER, WIZORD? HOW WILL WE KEEP HER SAFE?›
‹RUBY STITCH, MY DARLING, YOU WORRY TOO MUCH.›
‹LOOK...›
"‹...SIZZAJEE DIDN'T NOTICE A THING DURING YOUR ENTIRE PREGNANCY.›"
‹I'LL NEED YOU TO RUN A PATROL UP ON THE NORTHWEST BORDER. COORDINATE WITH CORNWALL.›
‹YOU GOT IT, BOSS.›
‹LOVE THAT SWEATER, BY THE WAY. REALLY SUITS YOU.›
‹UH... THANKS.›
"‹HE'S SO FOCUSED ON WHAT THE TIGERS ARE DOING, HE MIGHT AS WELL BE BLIND.›"
‹THOSE BLASTED TIGERS HAVE SPIES EVERYWHERE, RUBY STITCH.›
‹WE MUST BE VIGILANT!›
‹OH, NO DOUBT.›
‹YOU SMUGGLING A CAULDRON UNDER THERE, RUBY?›
‹YEAH.›
‹UH... REALLY?›
‹YEAH.›
‹HUH.›
"‹IF WE CAN TRICK HIM WITH SWEATERS AND PLANTS AND CAPES, I THINK WE'RE GOOD.›"
‹THERE'S NO WAY ANYONE KNOWS ABOUT THIS LITTLE MONSTER.›
‹I KNOW, WIZORD. IT'S JUST... THIS IS ONE OF SIZZAJEE'S BIGGEST RULES. UNLESS HE SAYS SO, NO CURES, NO WAR...›
‹...AND NO LOVE.›
‹YEAH, WELL... WHATEVER HAPPENS...›

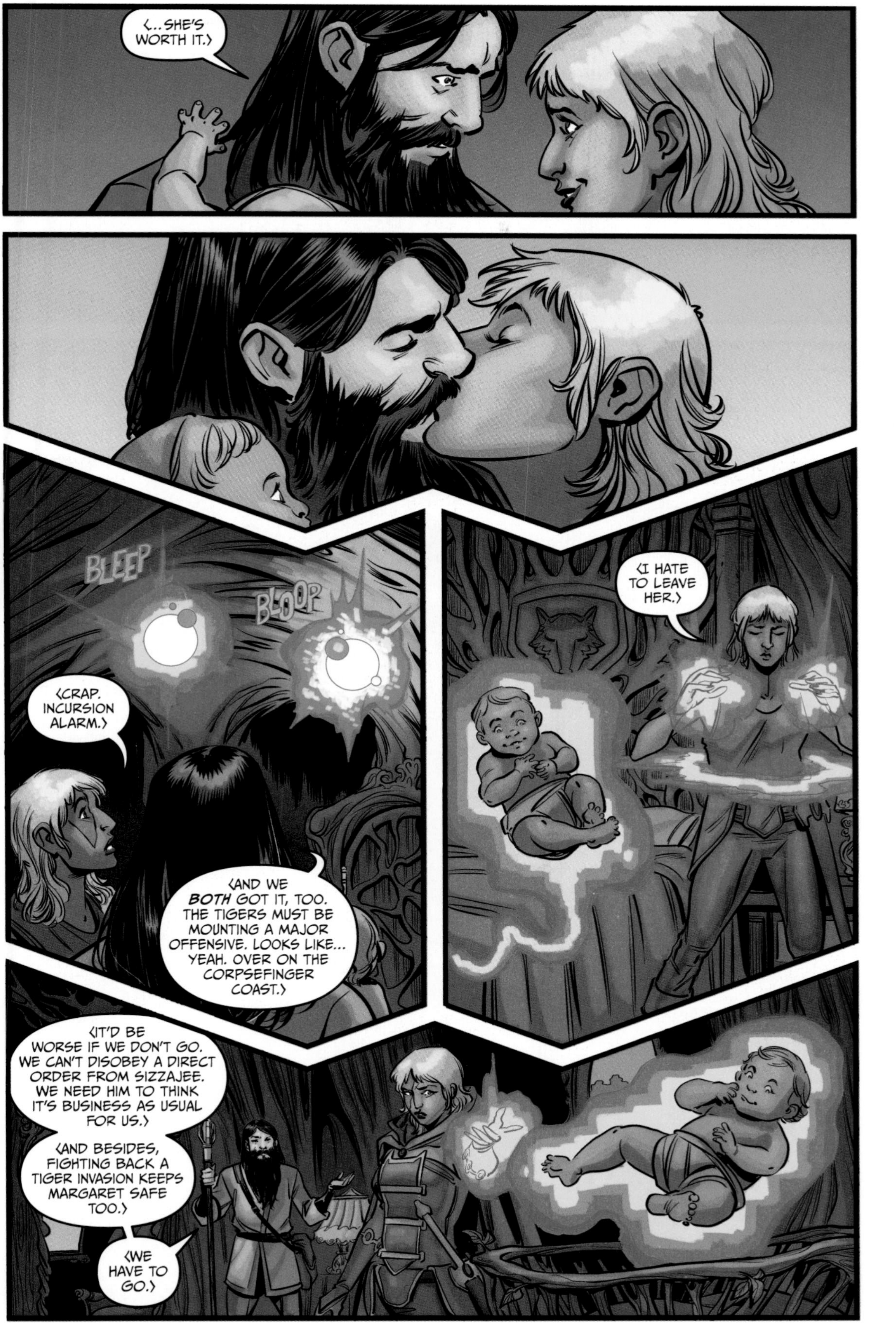
‹...SHE'S WORTH IT.›
BLEEP
BLOOP
‹CRAP. INCURSION ALARM.›
‹AND WE **BOTH** GOT IT, TOO. THE TIGERS MUST BE MOUNTING A MAJOR OFFENSIVE. LOOKS LIKE... YEAH. OVER ON THE CORPSEFINGER COAST.›
‹I HATE TO LEAVE HER.›
‹IT'D BE WORSE IF WE DON'T GO. WE CAN'T DISOBEY A DIRECT ORDER FROM SIZZAJEE. WE NEED HIM TO THINK IT'S BUSINESS AS USUAL FOR US.›
‹AND BESIDES, FIGHTING BACK A TIGER INVASION KEEPS MARGARET SAFE TOO.›
‹WE HAVE TO GO.›

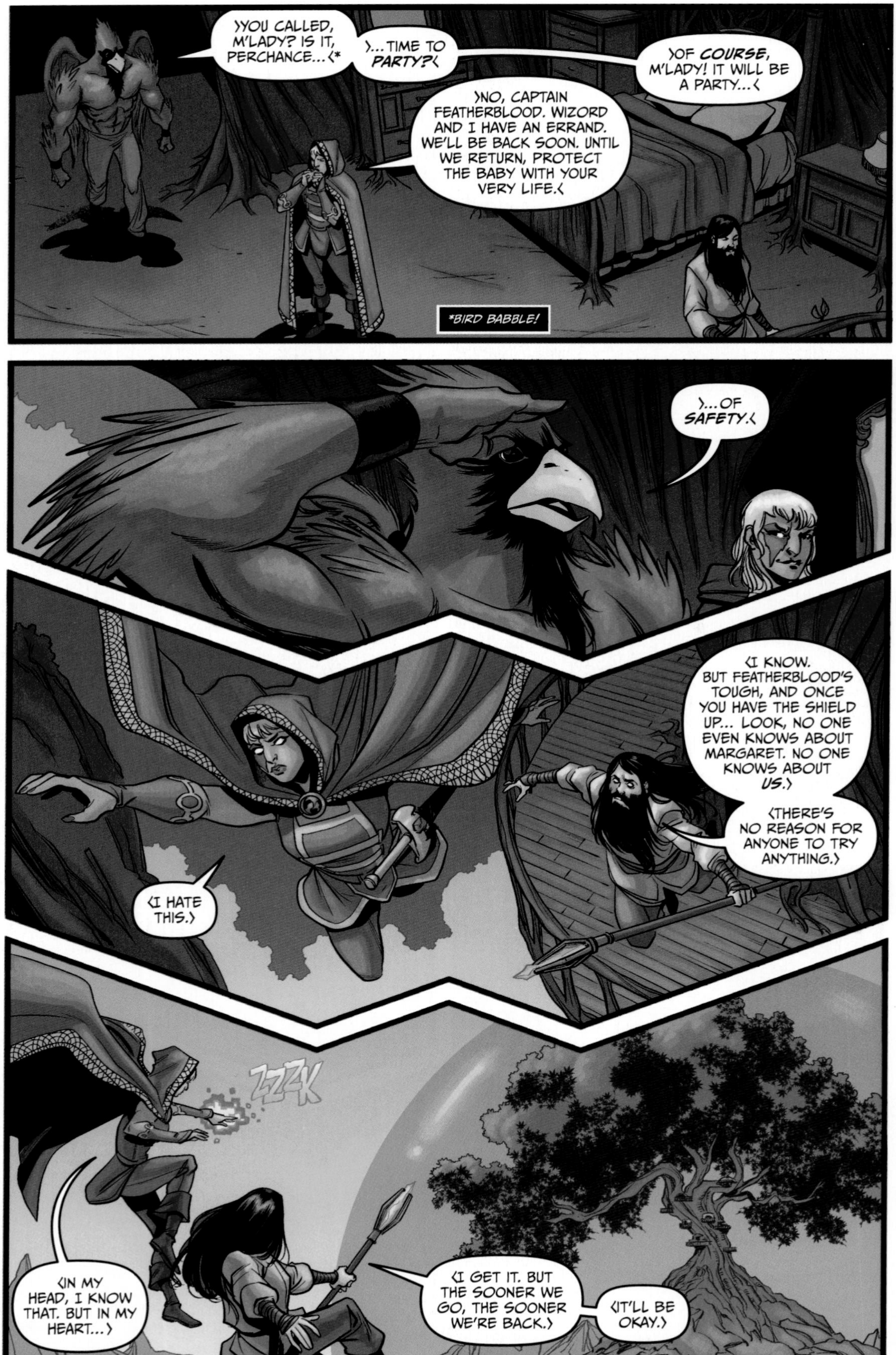
›YOU CALLED, M'LADY? IS IT, PERCHANCE...‹*
›...TIME TO PARTY?‹
›NO, CAPTAIN FEATHERBLOOD. WIZORD AND I HAVE AN ERRAND. WE'LL BE BACK SOON. UNTIL WE RETURN, PROTECT THE BABY WITH YOUR VERY LIFE.‹
›OF COURSE, M'LADY! IT WILL BE A PARTY...‹
*BIRD BABBLE!
›...OF SAFETY.‹
‹I HATE THIS.›
‹I KNOW. BUT FEATHERBLOOD'S TOUGH, AND ONCE YOU HAVE THE SHIELD UP... LOOK, NO ONE EVEN KNOWS ABOUT MARGARET. NO ONE KNOWS ABOUT US.›
‹THERE'S NO REASON FOR ANYONE TO TRY ANYTHING.›
ZZZK
‹IN MY HEAD, I KNOW THAT. BUT IN MY HEART...›
‹I GET IT. BUT THE SOONER WE GO, THE SOONER WE'RE BACK.›
‹IT'LL BE OKAY.›

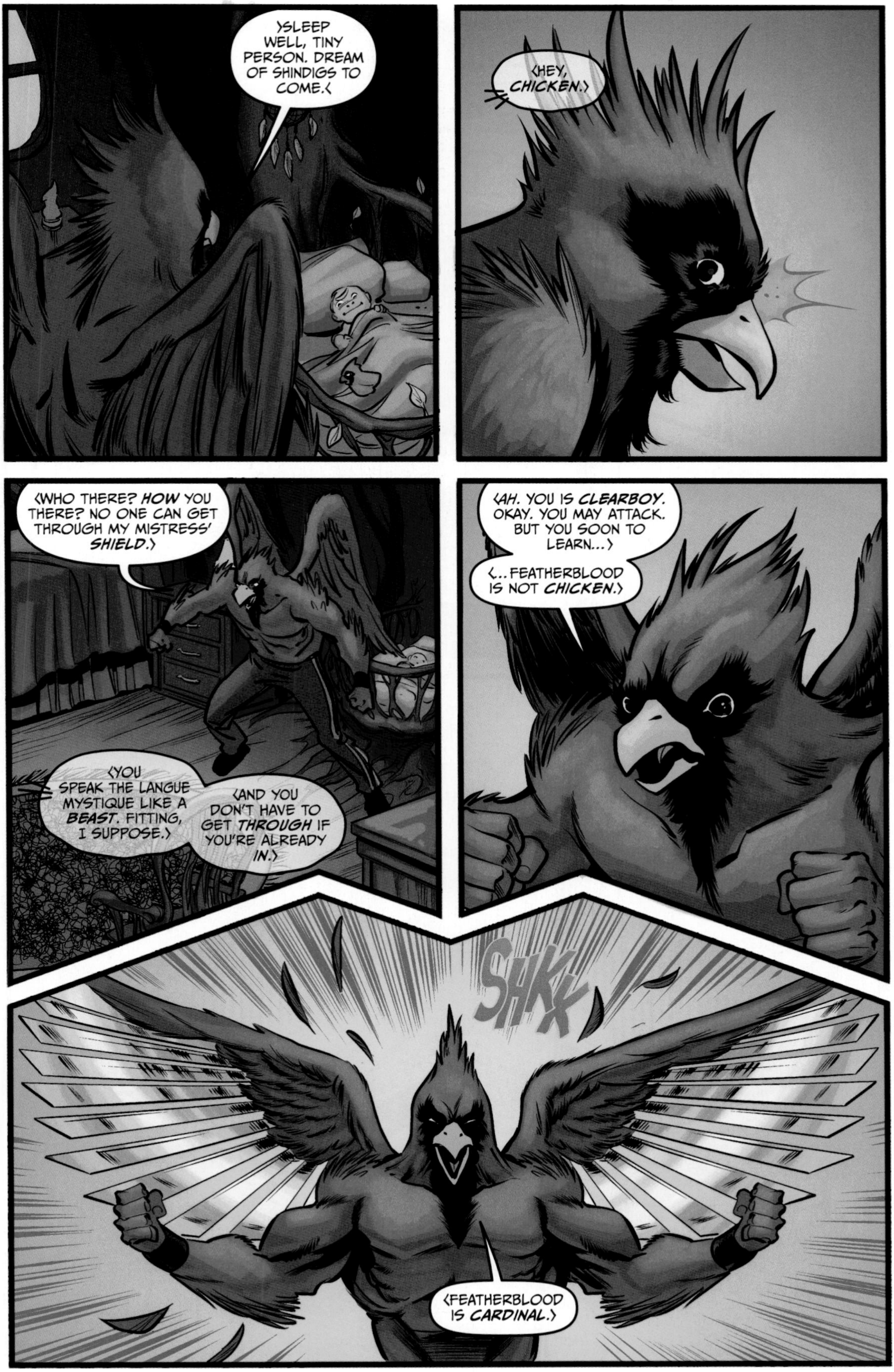
›SLEEP WELL, TINY PERSON. DREAM OF SHINDIGS TO COME.‹
‹HEY, CHICKEN.›
‹WHO THERE? HOW YOU THERE? NO ONE CAN GET THROUGH MY MISTRESS' SHIELD.›
‹YOU SPEAK THE LANGUE MYSTIQUE LIKE A BEAST. FITTING, I SUPPOSE.›
‹AND YOU DON'T HAVE TO GET THROUGH IF YOU'RE ALREADY IN.›
‹AH. YOU IS CLEARBOY. OKAY. YOU MAY ATTACK. BUT YOU SOON TO LEARN...›
‹...FEATHERBLOOD IS NOT CHICKEN.›
SHKK
‹FEATHERBLOOD IS CARDINAL.›

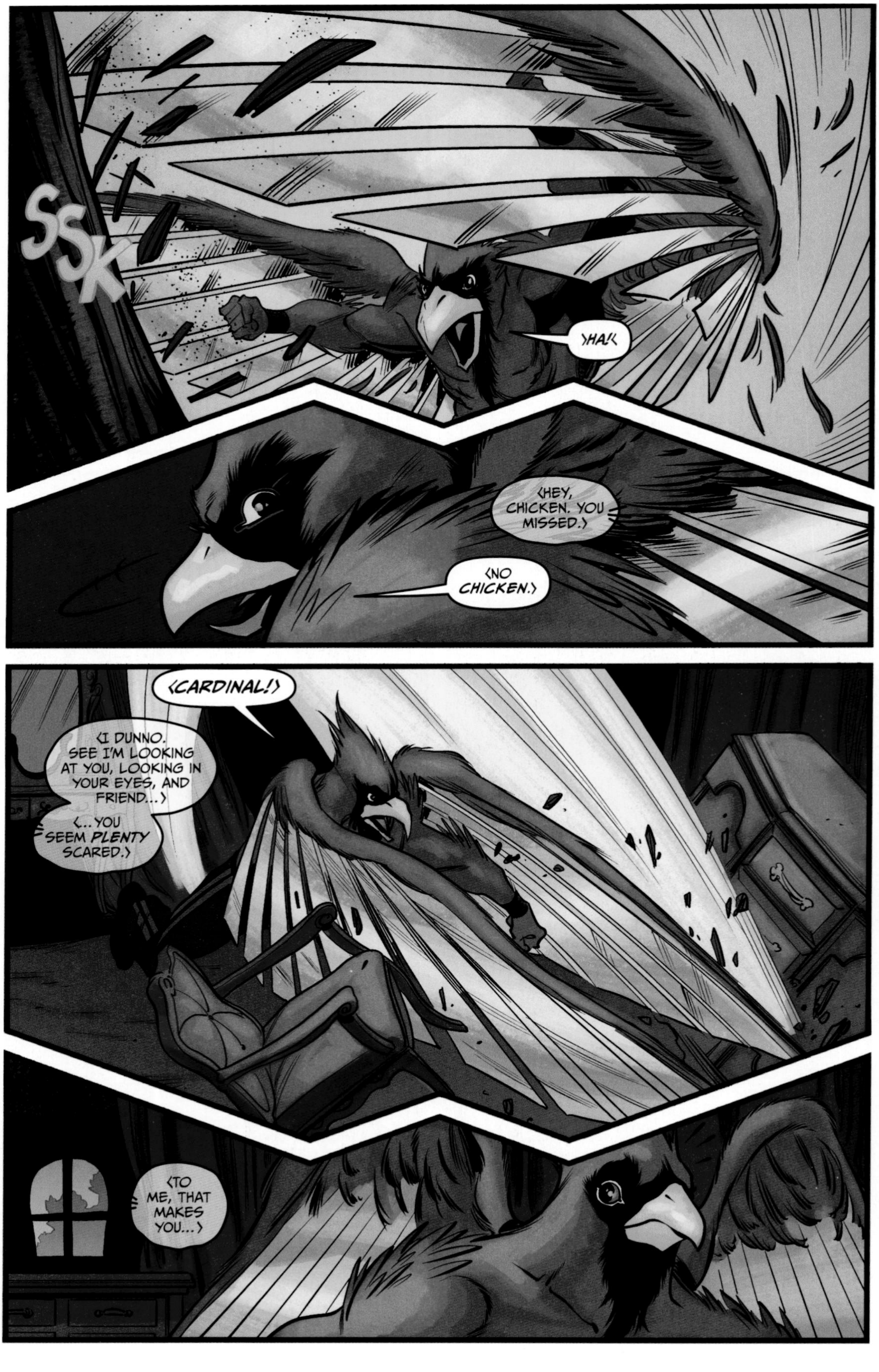
SSK
›HA!‹
‹HEY, CHICKEN. YOU MISSED.›
‹NO CHICKEN.›
‹CARDINAL!›
‹I DUNNO. SEE I'M LOOKING AT YOU, LOOKING IN YOUR EYES, AND FRIEND...›
‹...YOU SEEM PLENTY SCARED.›
‹TO ME, THAT MAKES YOU...›

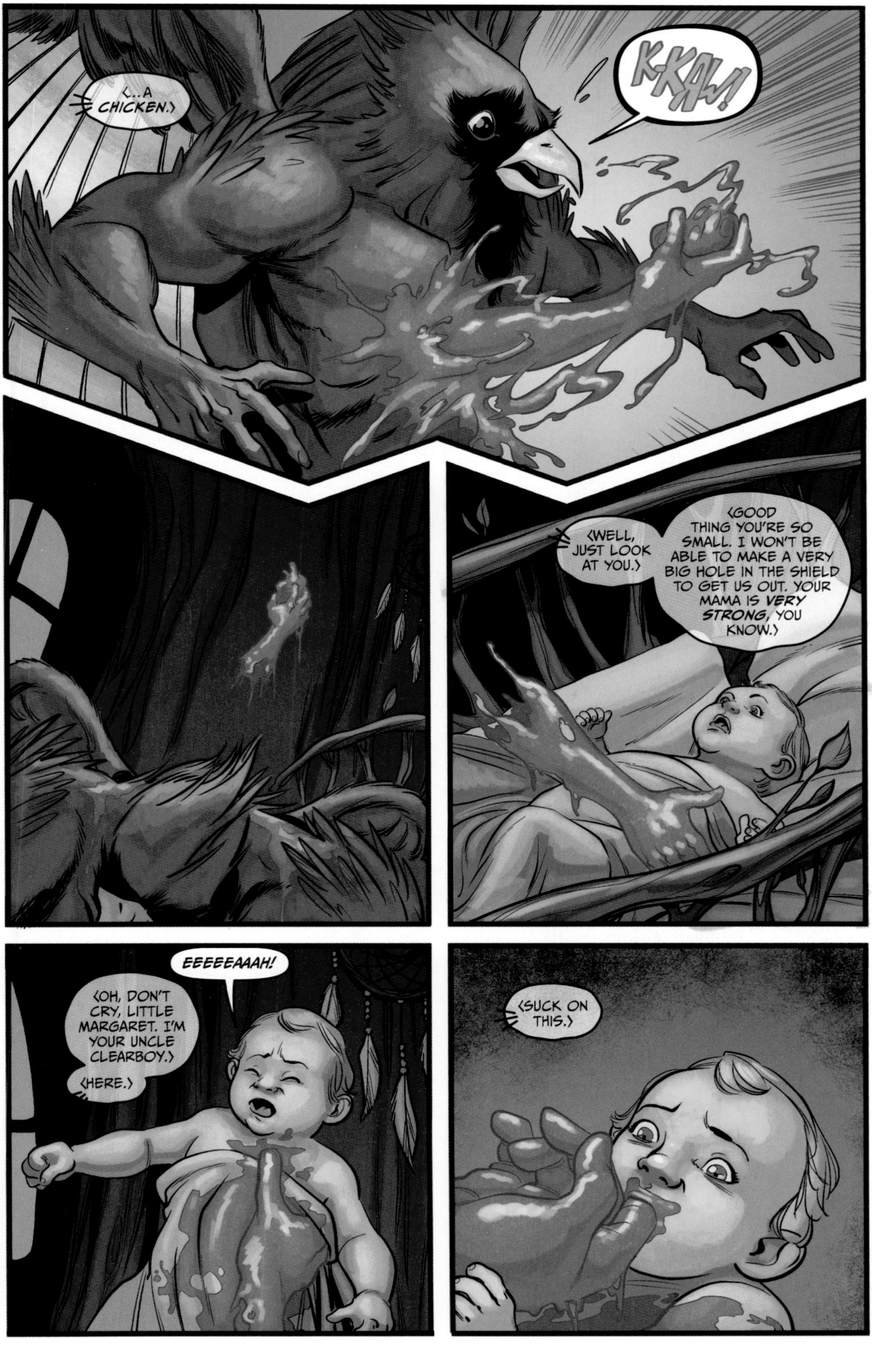

‹...A CHICKEN.›
K-KAW!
‹WELL, JUST LOOK AT YOU.›
‹GOOD THING YOU'RE SO SMALL. I WON'T BE ABLE TO MAKE A VERY BIG HOLE IN THE SHIELD TO GET US OUT. YOUR MAMA IS VERY STRONG, YOU KNOW.›
EEEEEAAAH!
‹OH, DON'T CRY, LITTLE MARGARET. I'M YOUR UNCLE CLEARBOY.›
‹HERE.›
‹SUCK ON THIS.›

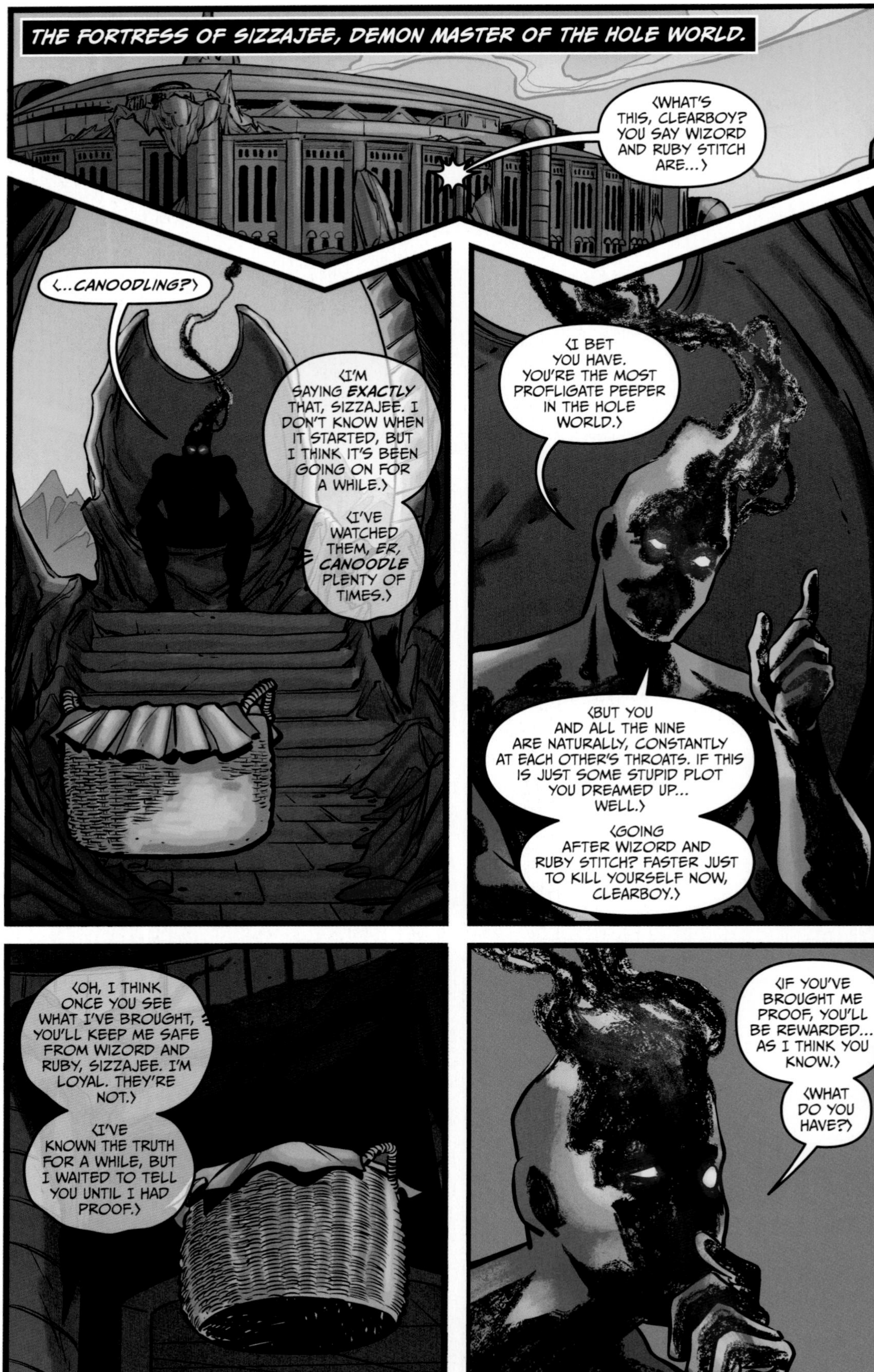
THE FORTRESS OF SIZZAJEE, DEMON MASTER OF THE HOLE WORLD.
⟨WHAT'S THIS, CLEARBOY? YOU SAY WIZORD AND RUBY STITCH ARE...⟩
⟨...CANOODLING?⟩
⟨I'M SAYING EXACTLY THAT, SIZZAJEE. I DON'T KNOW WHEN IT STARTED, BUT I THINK IT'S BEEN GOING ON FOR A WHILE.⟩
⟨I'VE WATCHED THEM, ER, CANOODLE PLENTY OF TIMES.⟩
⟨I BET YOU HAVE. YOU'RE THE MOST PROFLIGATE PEEPER IN THE HOLE WORLD.⟩
⟨BUT YOU AND ALL THE NINE ARE NATURALLY, CONSTANTLY AT EACH OTHER'S THROATS. IF THIS IS JUST SOME STUPID PLOT YOU DREAMED UP... WELL.⟩
⟨GOING AFTER WIZORD AND RUBY STITCH? FASTER JUST TO KILL YOURSELF NOW, CLEARBOY.⟩
⟨OH, I THINK ONCE YOU SEE WHAT I'VE BROUGHT, YOU'LL KEEP ME SAFE FROM WIZORD AND RUBY, SIZZAJEE. I'M LOYAL. THEY'RE NOT.⟩
⟨I'VE KNOWN THE TRUTH FOR A WHILE, BUT I WAITED TO TELL YOU UNTIL I HAD PROOF.⟩
⟨IF YOU'VE BROUGHT ME PROOF, YOU'LL BE REWARDED... AS I THINK YOU KNOW.⟩
⟨WHAT DO YOU HAVE?⟩

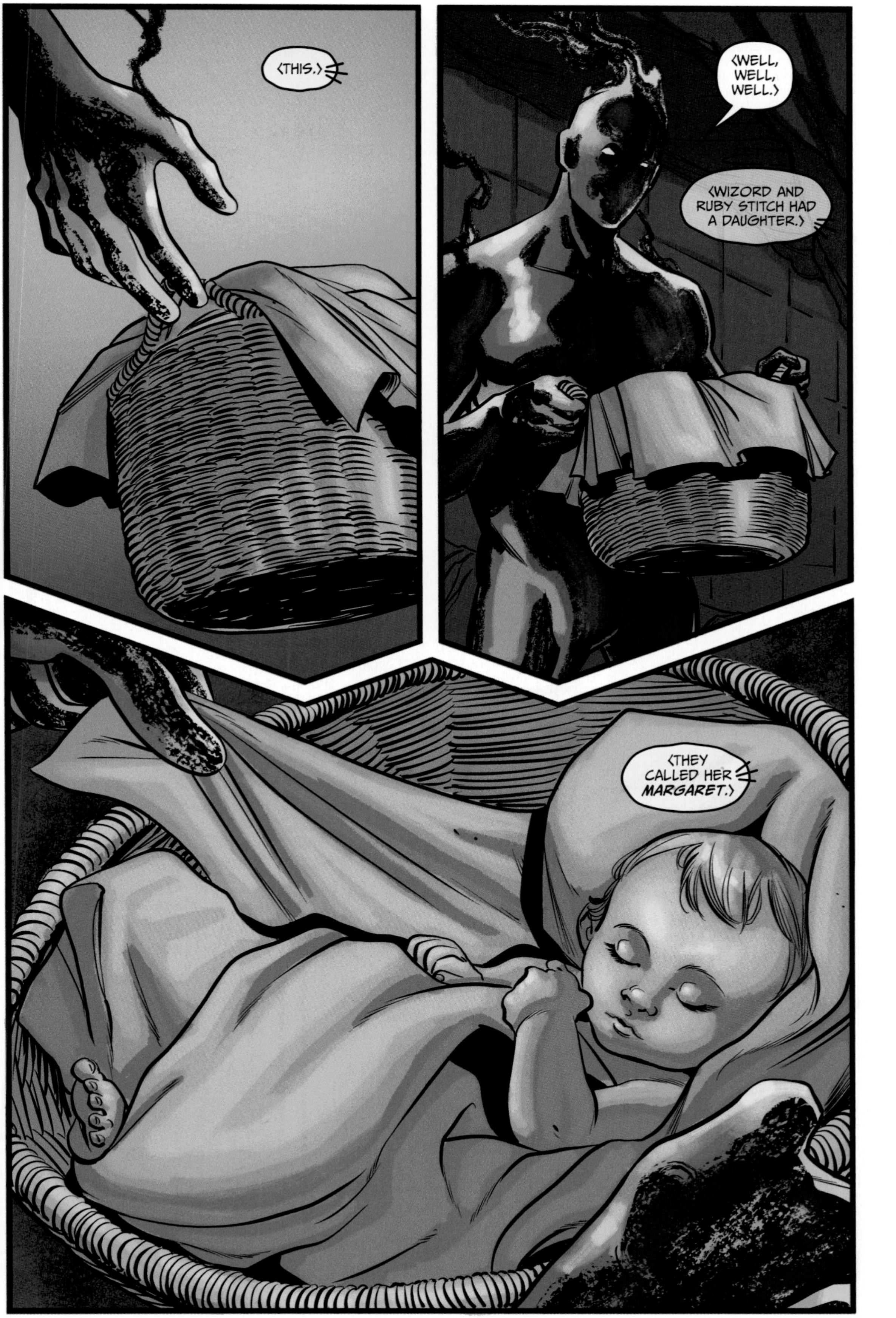

⟨THIS.⟩
⟨WELL, WELL, WELL.⟩
⟨WIZORD AND RUBY STITCH HAD A DAUGHTER.⟩
⟨THEY CALLED HER *MARGARET*.⟩

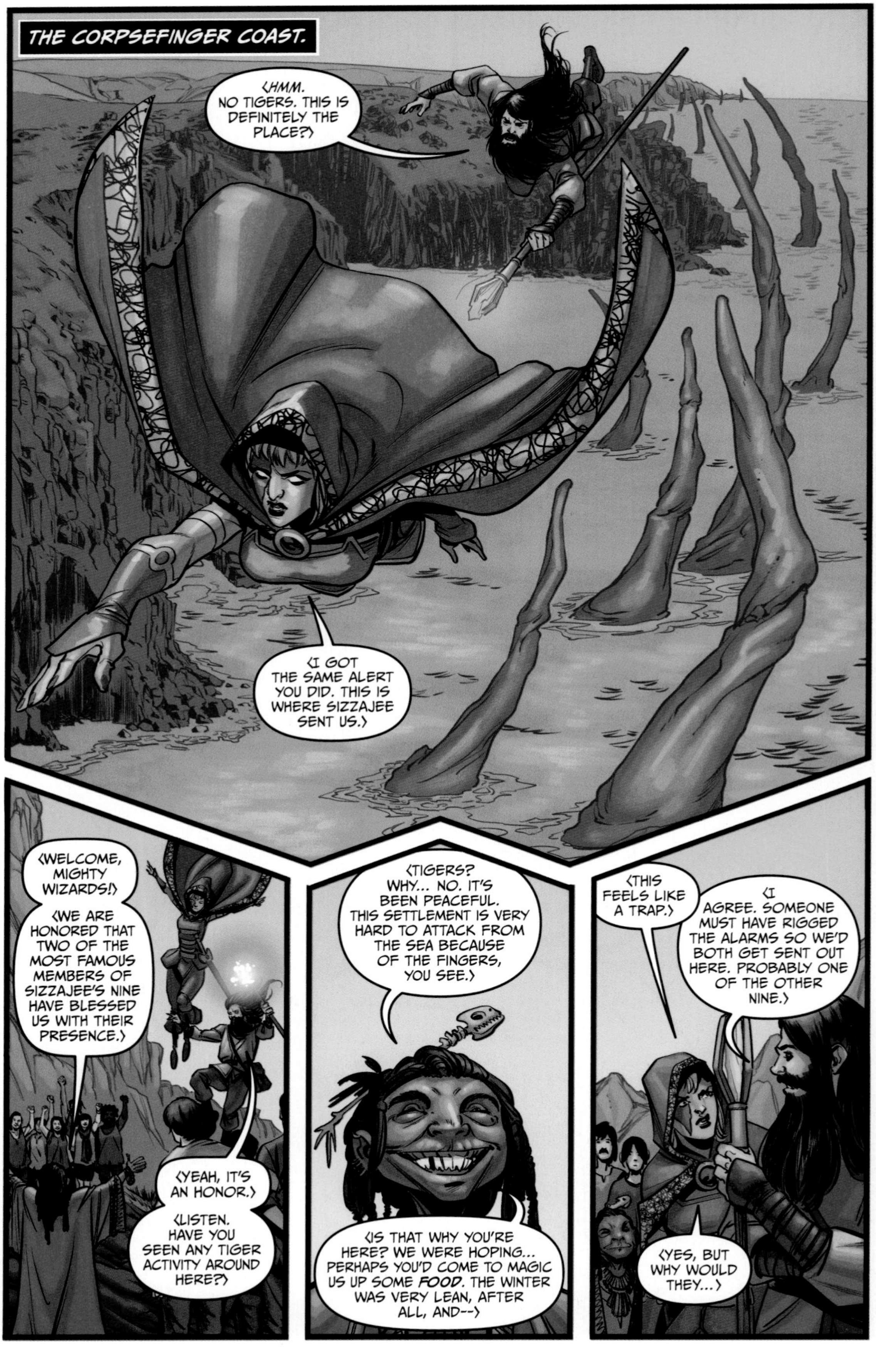
THE CORPSEFINGER COAST.
‹HMM. NO TIGERS. THIS IS DEFINITELY THE PLACE?›
‹I GOT THE SAME ALERT YOU DID. THIS IS WHERE SIZZAJEE SENT US.›
‹WELCOME, MIGHTY WIZARDS!›
‹WE ARE HONORED THAT TWO OF THE MOST FAMOUS MEMBERS OF SIZZAJEE'S NINE HAVE BLESSED US WITH THEIR PRESENCE.›
‹YEAH, IT'S AN HONOR.›
‹LISTEN. HAVE YOU SEEN ANY TIGER ACTIVITY AROUND HERE?›
‹TIGERS? WHY... NO. IT'S BEEN PEACEFUL. THIS SETTLEMENT IS VERY HARD TO ATTACK FROM THE SEA BECAUSE OF THE FINGERS, YOU SEE.›
‹IS THAT WHY YOU'RE HERE? WE WERE HOPING... PERHAPS YOU'D COME TO MAGIC US UP SOME FOOD. THE WINTER WAS VERY LEAN, AFTER ALL, AND--›
‹THIS FEELS LIKE A TRAP.›
‹I AGREE. SOMEONE MUST HAVE RIGGED THE ALARMS SO WE'D BOTH GET SENT OUT HERE. PROBABLY ONE OF THE OTHER NINE.›
‹YES, BUT WHY WOULD THEY...›

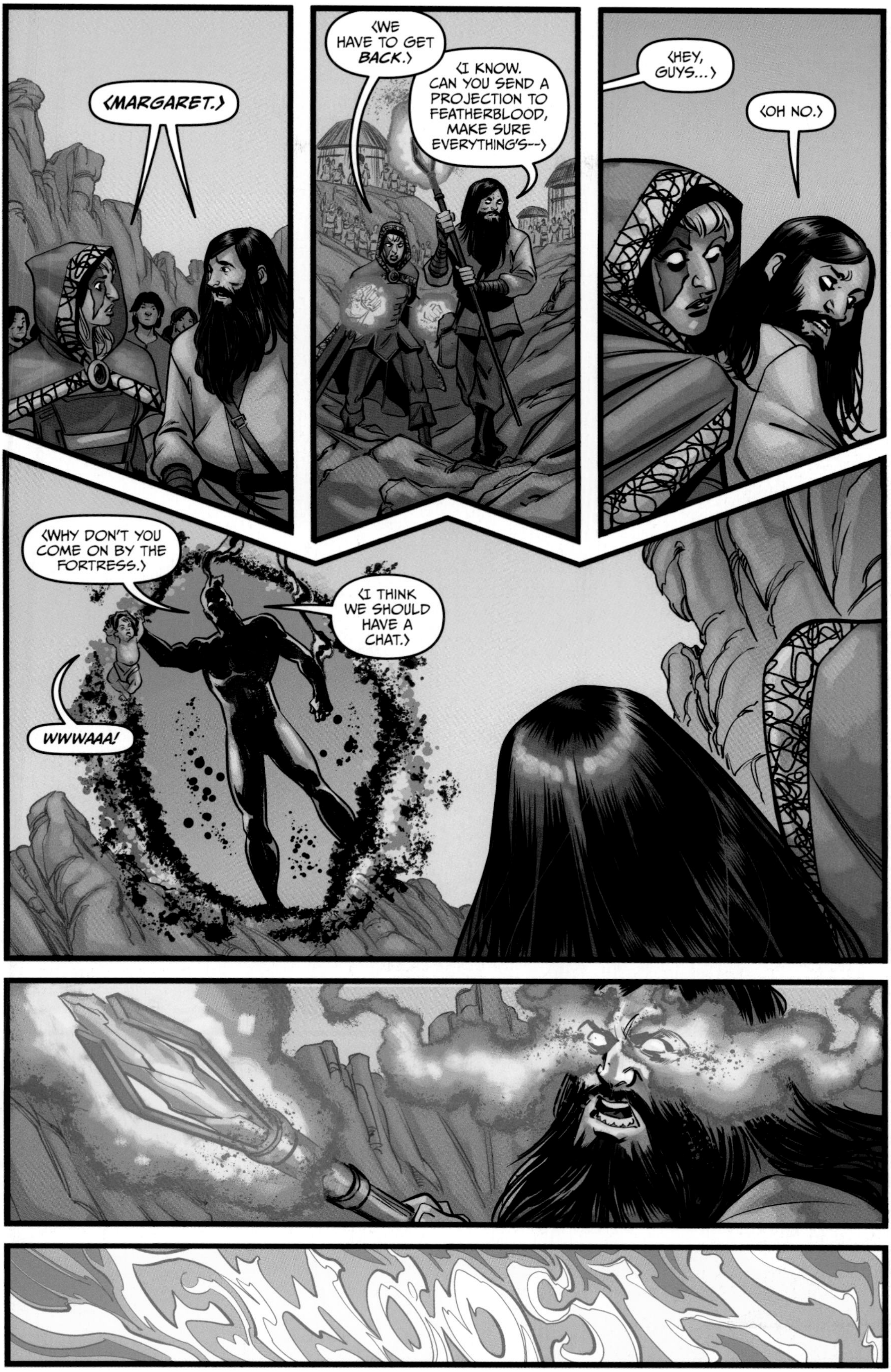
⟨MARGARET.⟩
⟨WE HAVE TO GET BACK.⟩
⟨I KNOW. CAN YOU SEND A PROJECTION TO FEATHERBLOOD, MAKE SURE EVERYTHING'S--⟩
⟨HEY, GUYS...⟩
⟨OH NO.⟩
⟨WHY DON'T YOU COME ON BY THE FORTRESS.⟩
⟨I THINK WE SHOULD HAVE A CHAT.⟩
WWWAAA!

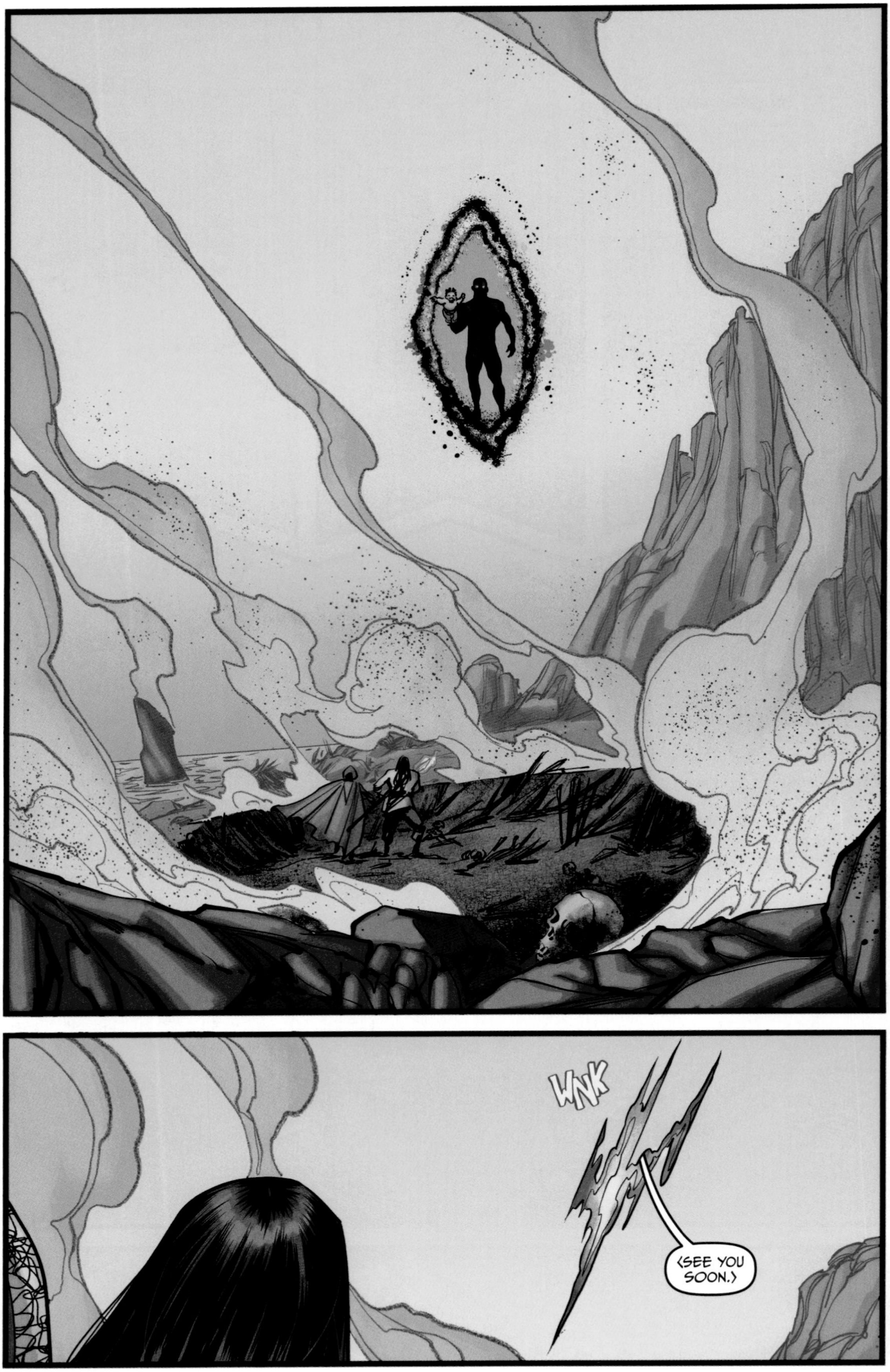
WNK
‹SEE YOU SOON.›

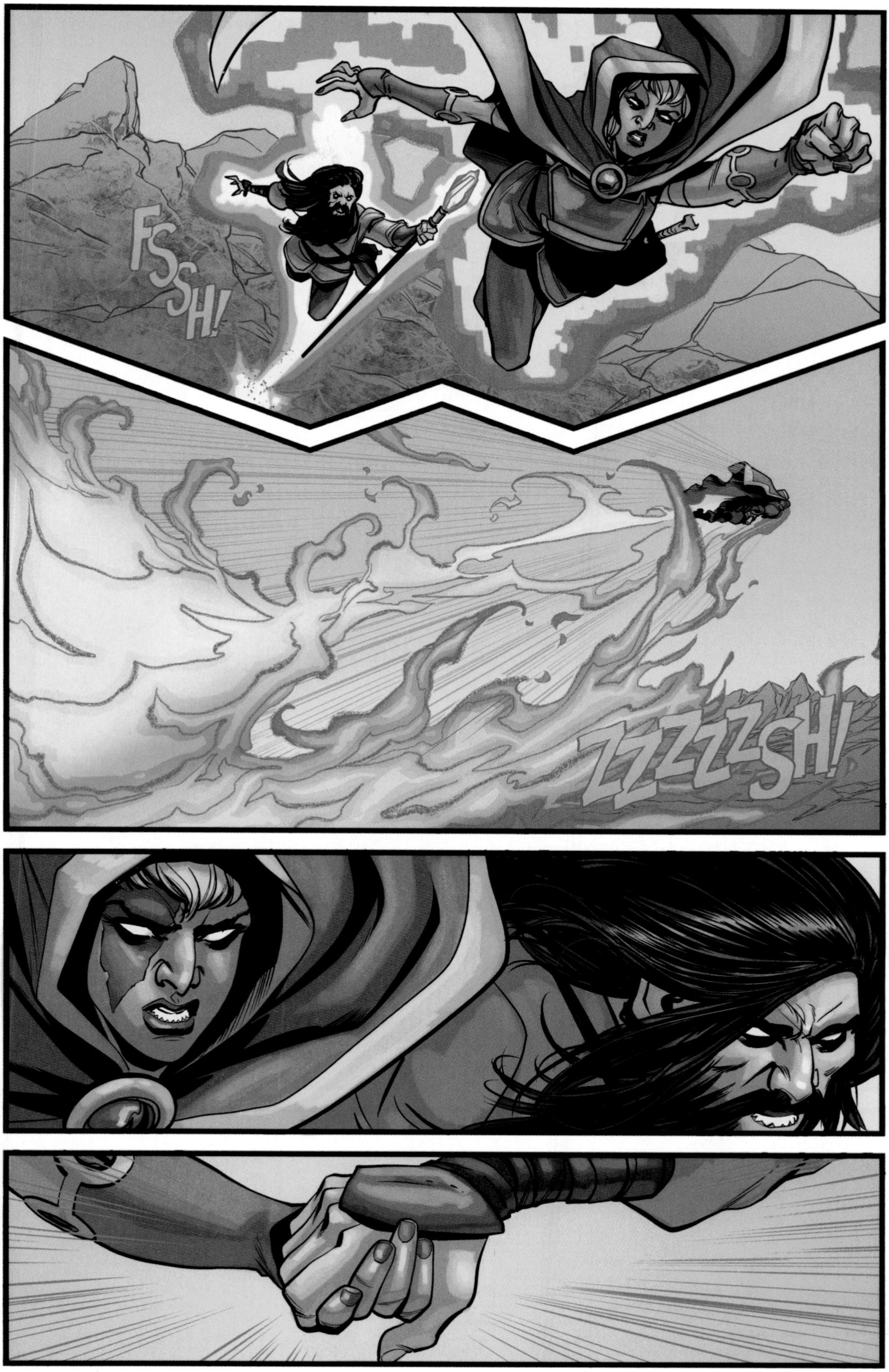
FSSH!
ZZZZZSH!

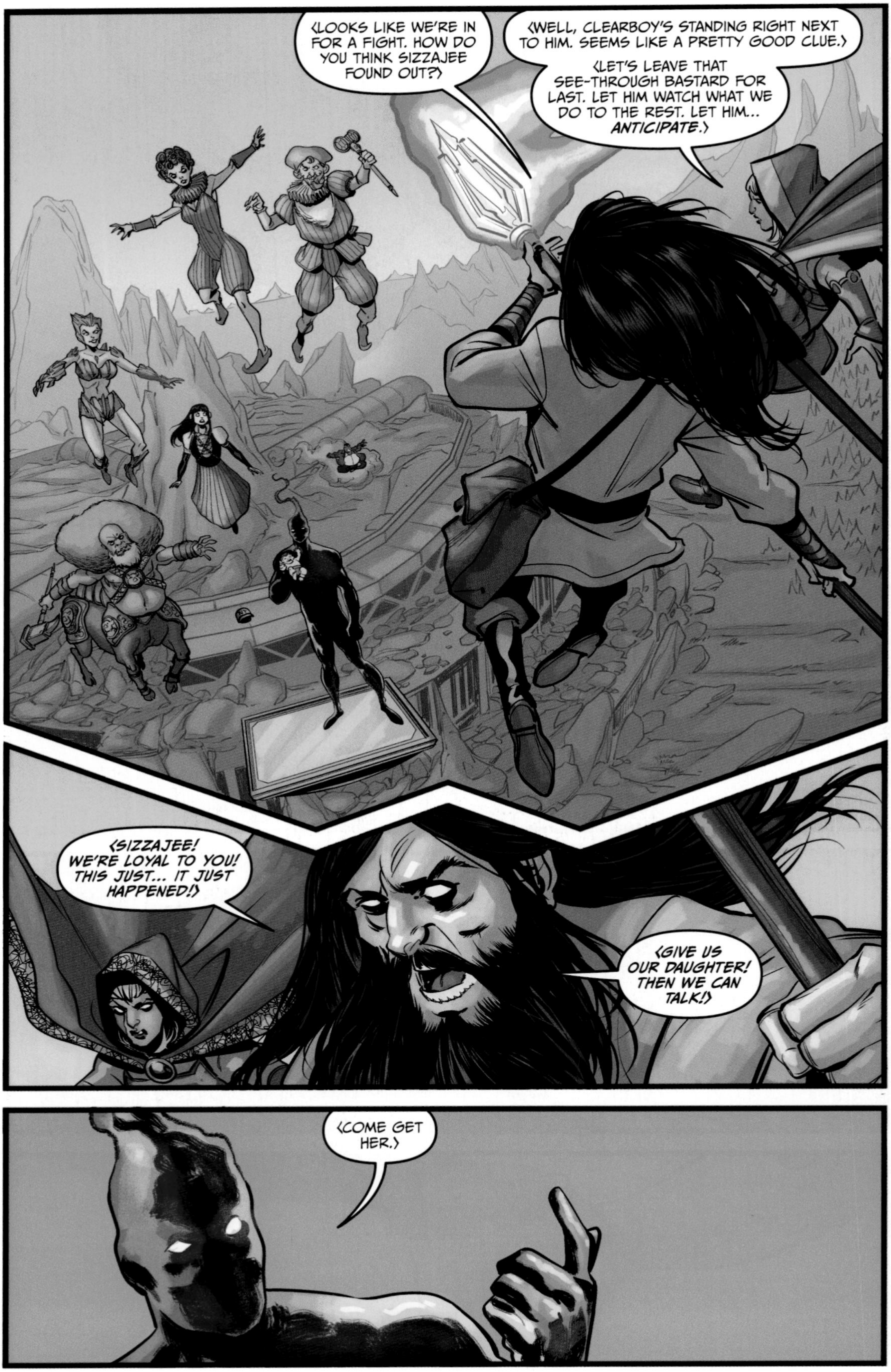
<LOOKS LIKE WE'RE IN FOR A FIGHT. HOW DO YOU THINK SIZZAJEE FOUND OUT?>
<WELL, CLEARBOY'S STANDING RIGHT NEXT TO HIM. SEEMS LIKE A PRETTY GOOD CLUE.>
<LET'S LEAVE THAT SEE-THROUGH BASTARD FOR LAST. LET HIM WATCH WHAT WE DO TO THE REST. LET HIM... *ANTICIPATE*.>
<SIZZAJEE! WE'RE LOYAL TO YOU! THIS JUST... IT JUST HAPPENED!>
<GIVE US OUR DAUGHTER! THEN WE CAN TALK!>
<COME GET HER.>

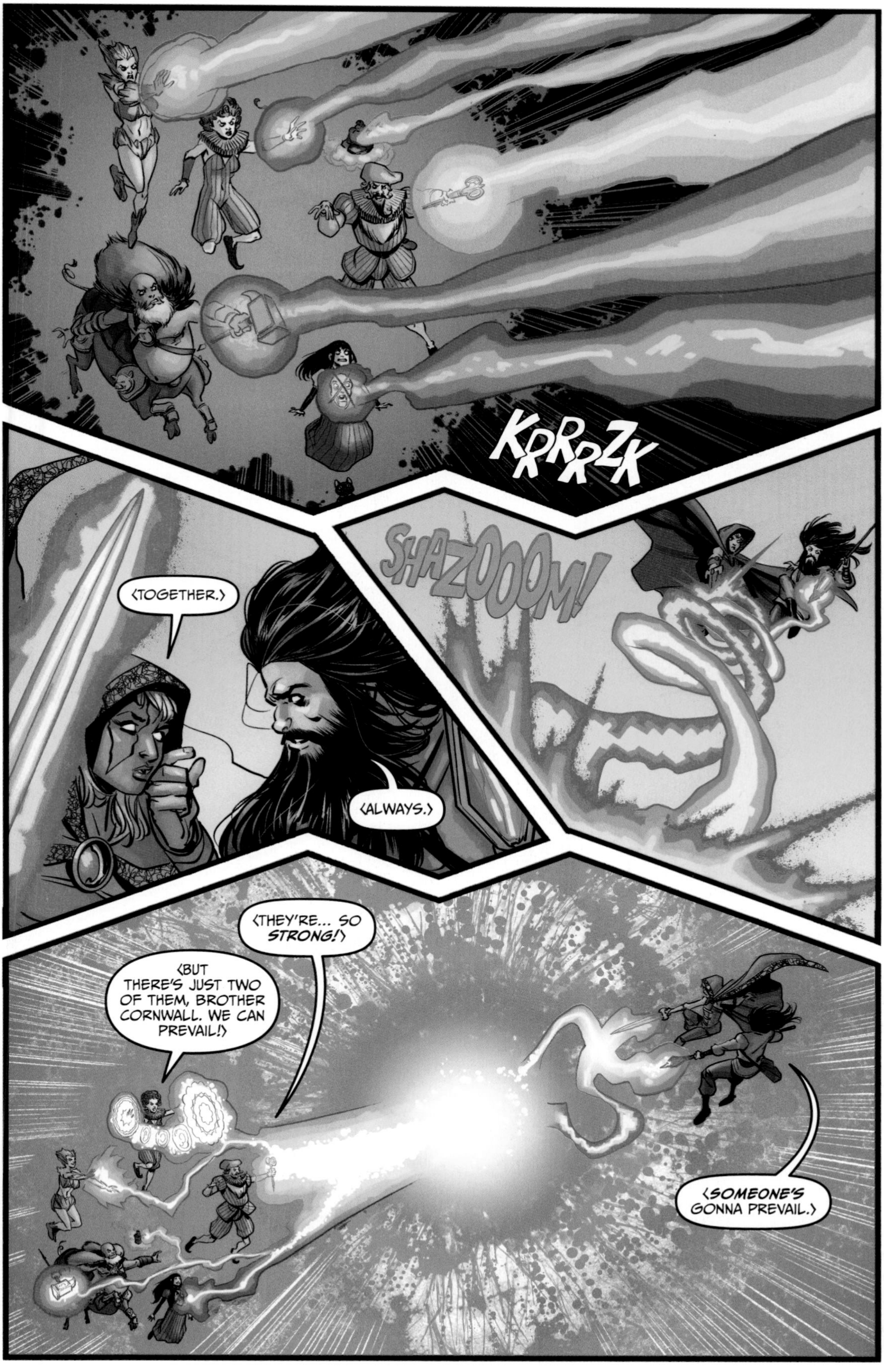
KRRRZK
⟨TOGETHER.⟩
⟨ALWAYS.⟩
SHAZOOOM!
⟨THEY'RE... SO STRONG!⟩
⟨BUT THERE'S JUST TWO OF THEM, BROTHER CORNWALL. WE CAN PREVAIL!⟩
⟨SOMEONE'S GONNA PREVAIL.⟩

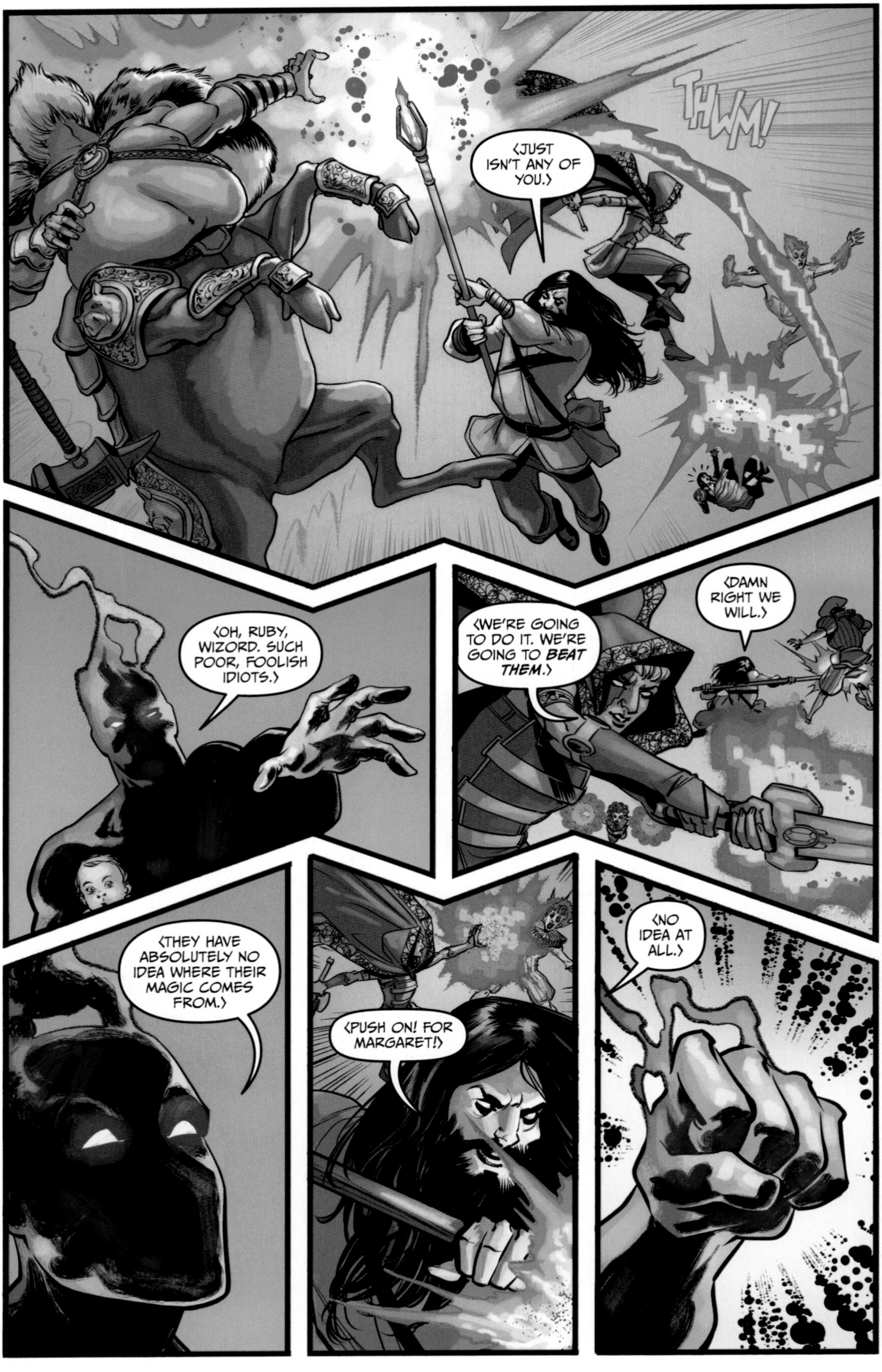
THWM!
‹JUST ISN'T ANY OF YOU.›
‹OH, RUBY, WIZORD. SUCH POOR, FOOLISH IDIOTS.›
‹WE'RE GOING TO DO IT. WE'RE GOING TO *BEAT THEM*.›
‹DAMN RIGHT WE WILL.›
‹THEY HAVE ABSOLUTELY NO IDEA WHERE THEIR MAGIC COMES FROM.›
‹PUSH ON! FOR MARGARET!›
‹NO IDEA AT ALL.›

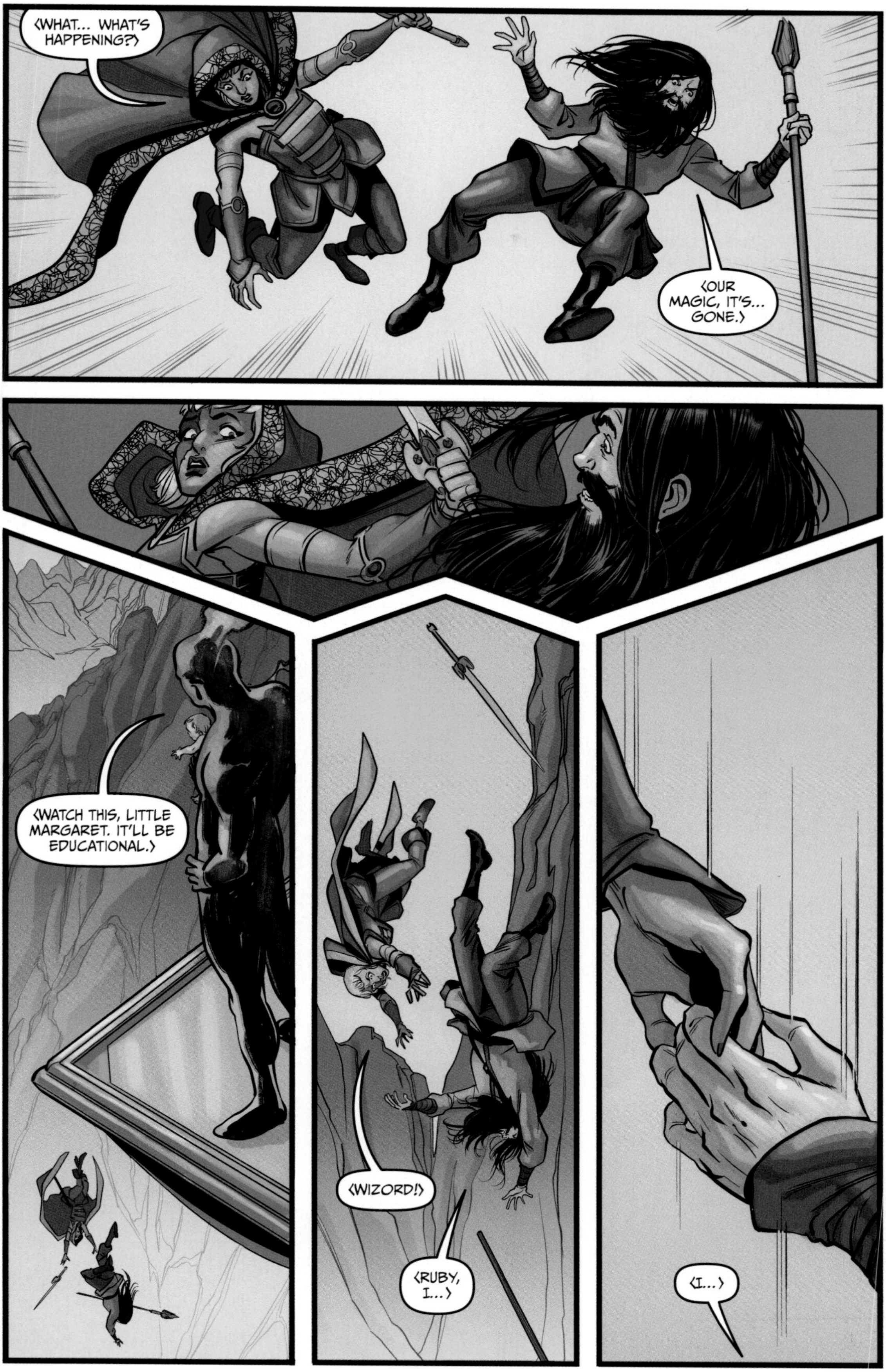
‹WHAT... WHAT'S HAPPENING?›
‹OUR MAGIC, IT'S... GONE.›
‹WATCH THIS, LITTLE MARGARET. IT'LL BE EDUCATIONAL.›
‹WIZORD!›
‹RUBY, I...›
‹I...›

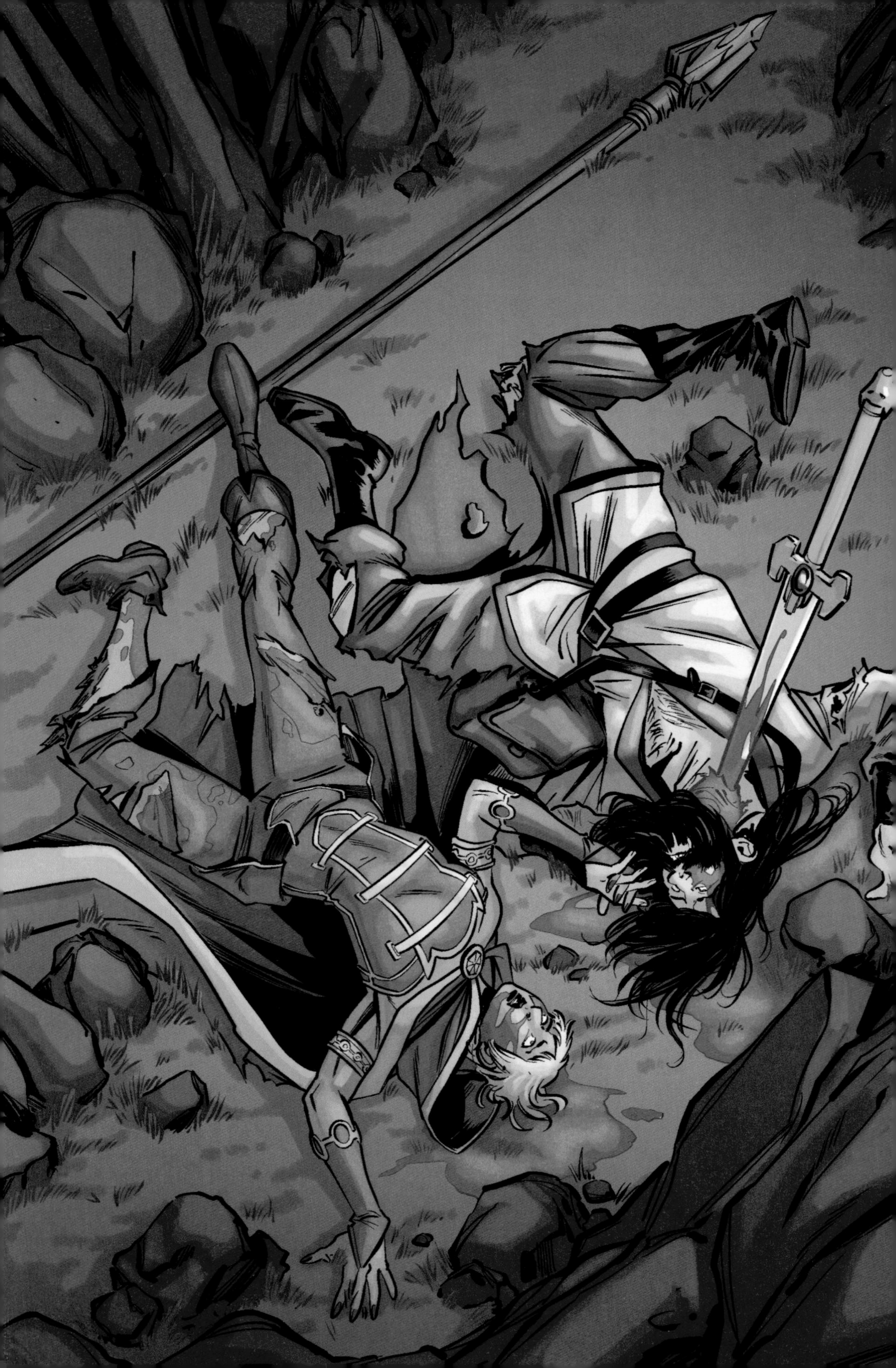

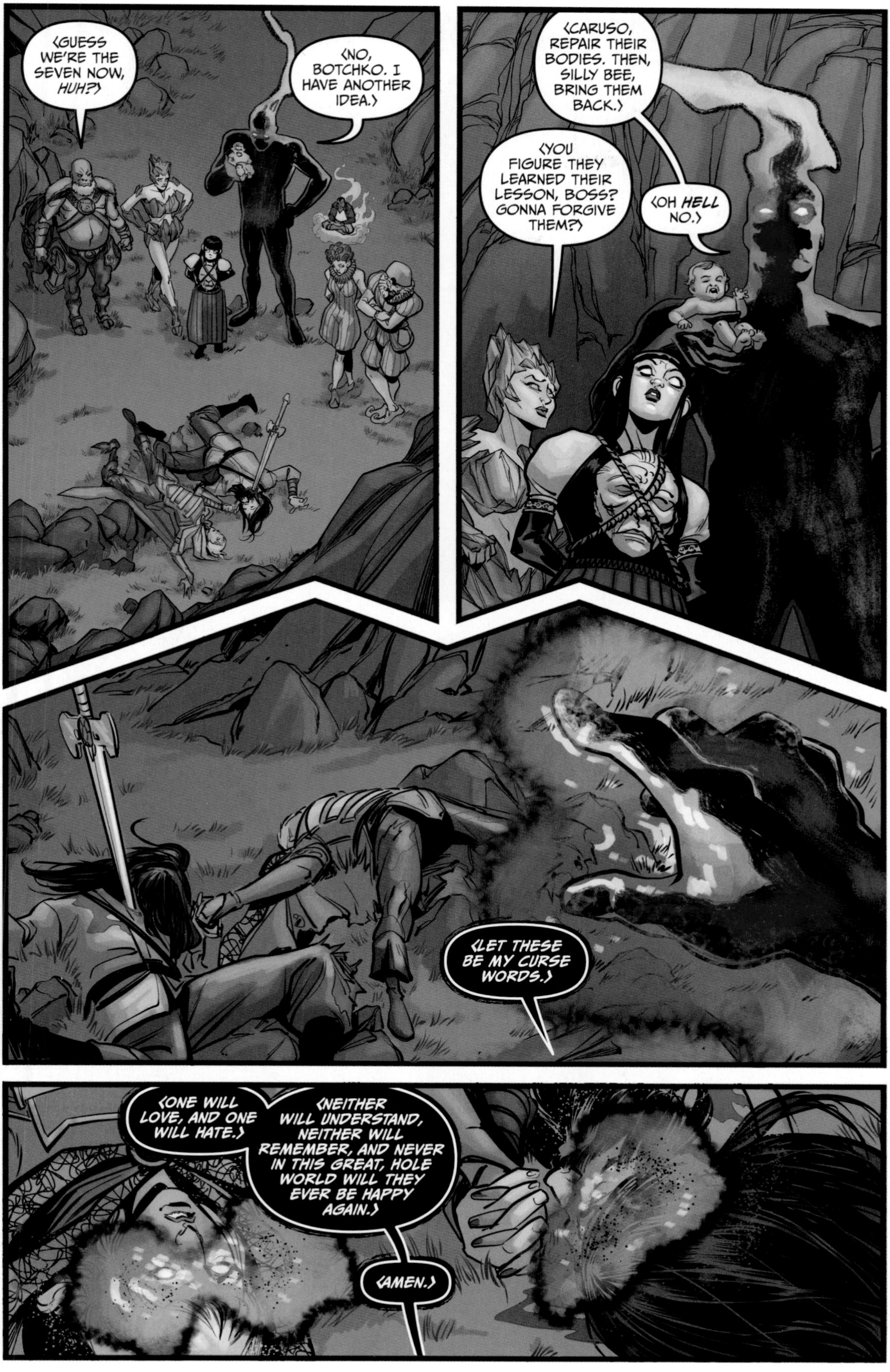
‹GUESS WE'RE THE SEVEN NOW, HUH?›
‹NO, BOTCHKO. I HAVE ANOTHER IDEA.›
‹CARUSO, REPAIR THEIR BODIES. THEN, SILLY BEE, BRING THEM BACK.›
‹YOU FIGURE THEY LEARNED THEIR LESSON, BOSS? GONNA FORGIVE THEM?›
‹OH HELL NO.›
‹LET THESE BE MY CURSE WORDS.›
‹ONE WILL LOVE, AND ONE WILL HATE.›
‹NEITHER WILL UNDERSTAND, NEITHER WILL REMEMBER, AND NEVER IN THIS GREAT, HOLE WORLD WILL THEY EVER BE HAPPY AGAIN.›
‹AMEN.›

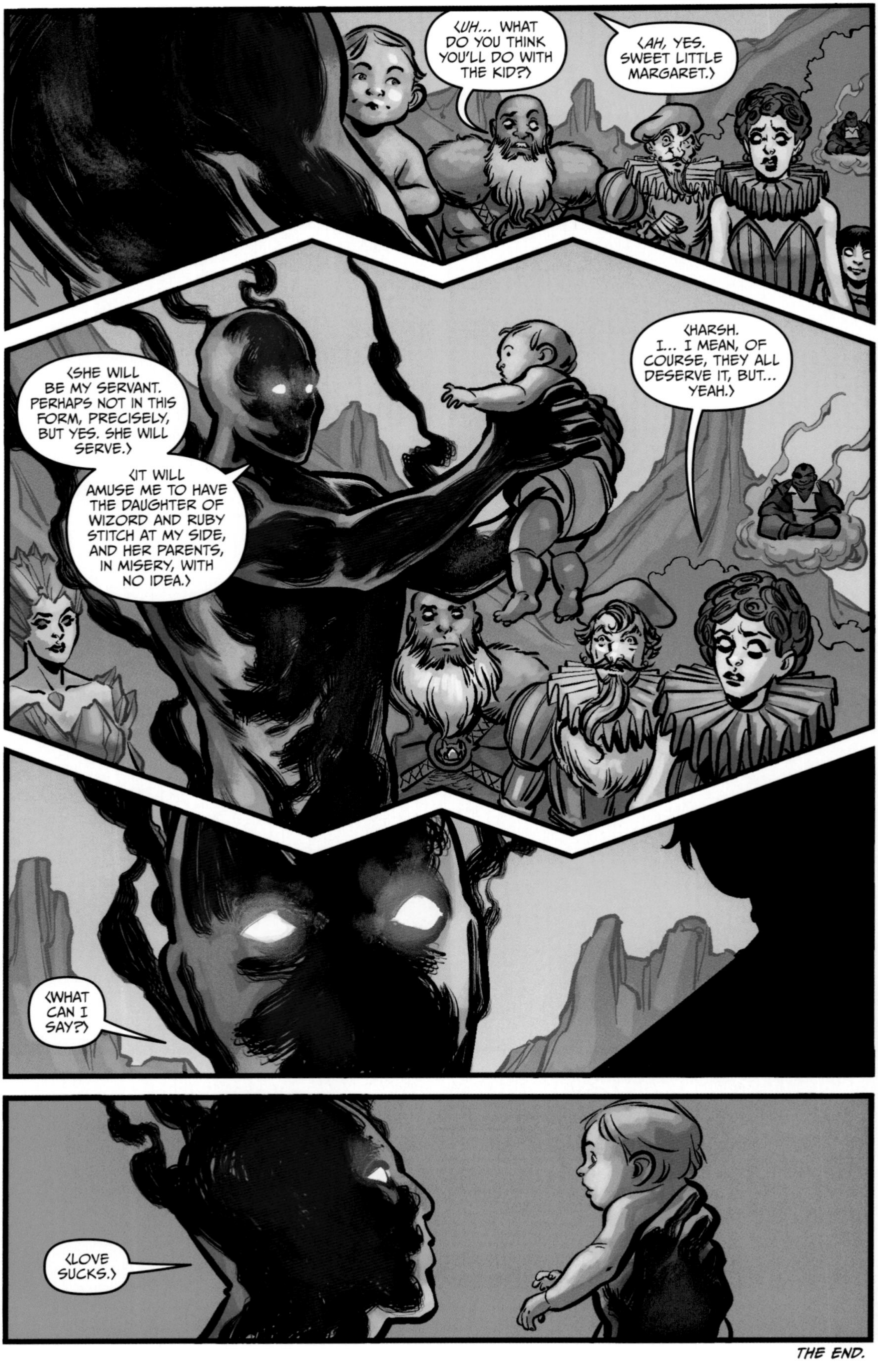
‹*UH*... WHAT DO YOU THINK YOU'LL DO WITH THE KID?›
‹*AH*, YES. SWEET LITTLE MARGARET.›
‹SHE WILL BE MY SERVANT. PERHAPS NOT IN THIS FORM, PRECISELY, BUT YES. SHE WILL SERVE.›
‹IT WILL AMUSE ME TO HAVE THE DAUGHTER OF WIZORD AND RUBY STITCH AT MY SIDE, AND HER PARENTS, IN MISERY, WITH NO IDEA.›
‹HARSH. I... I MEAN, OF COURSE, THEY ALL DESERVE IT, BUT... YEAH.›
‹WHAT CAN I SAY?›
‹LOVE SUCKS.›

THE END.

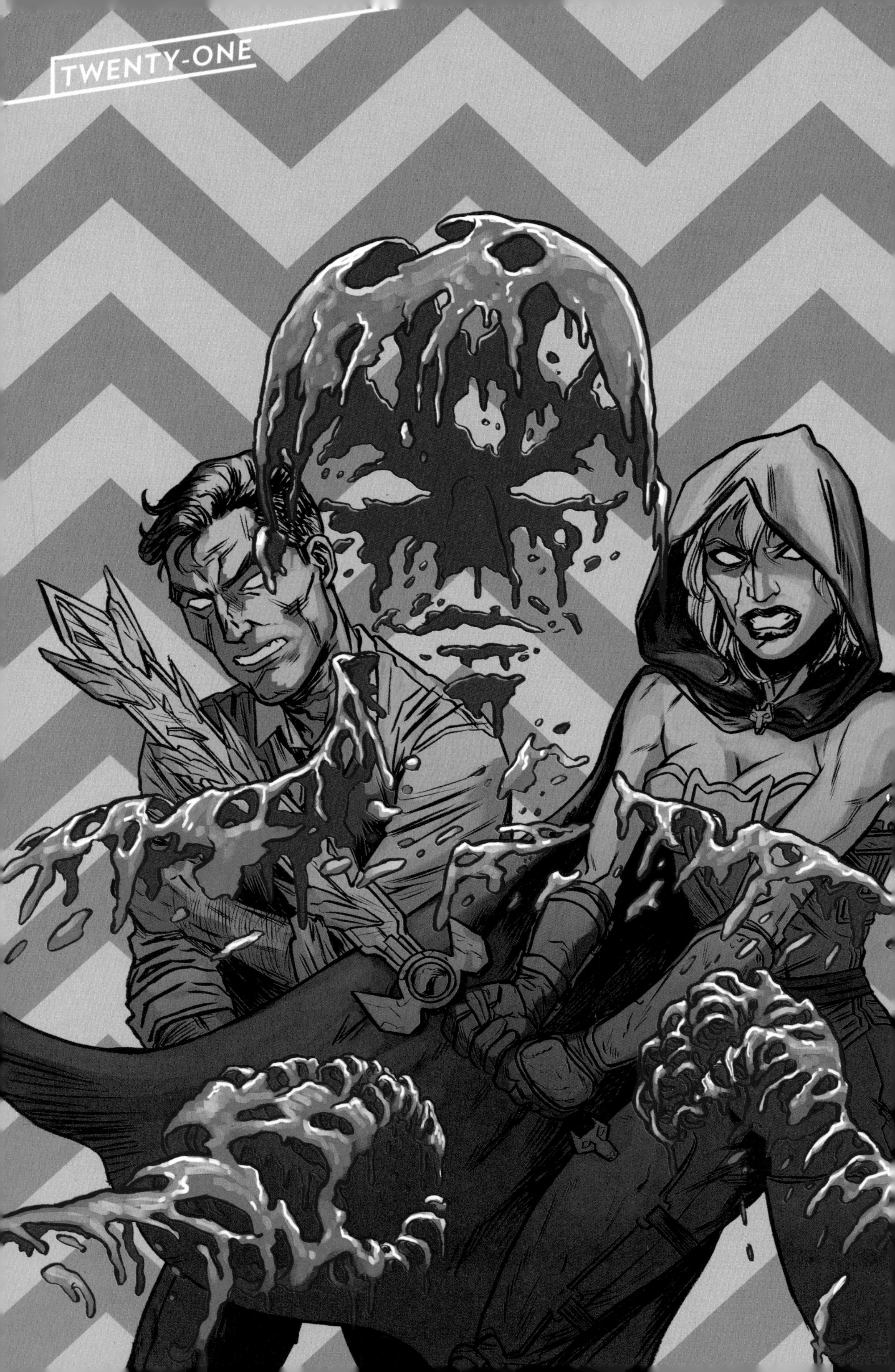
TWENTY-ONE

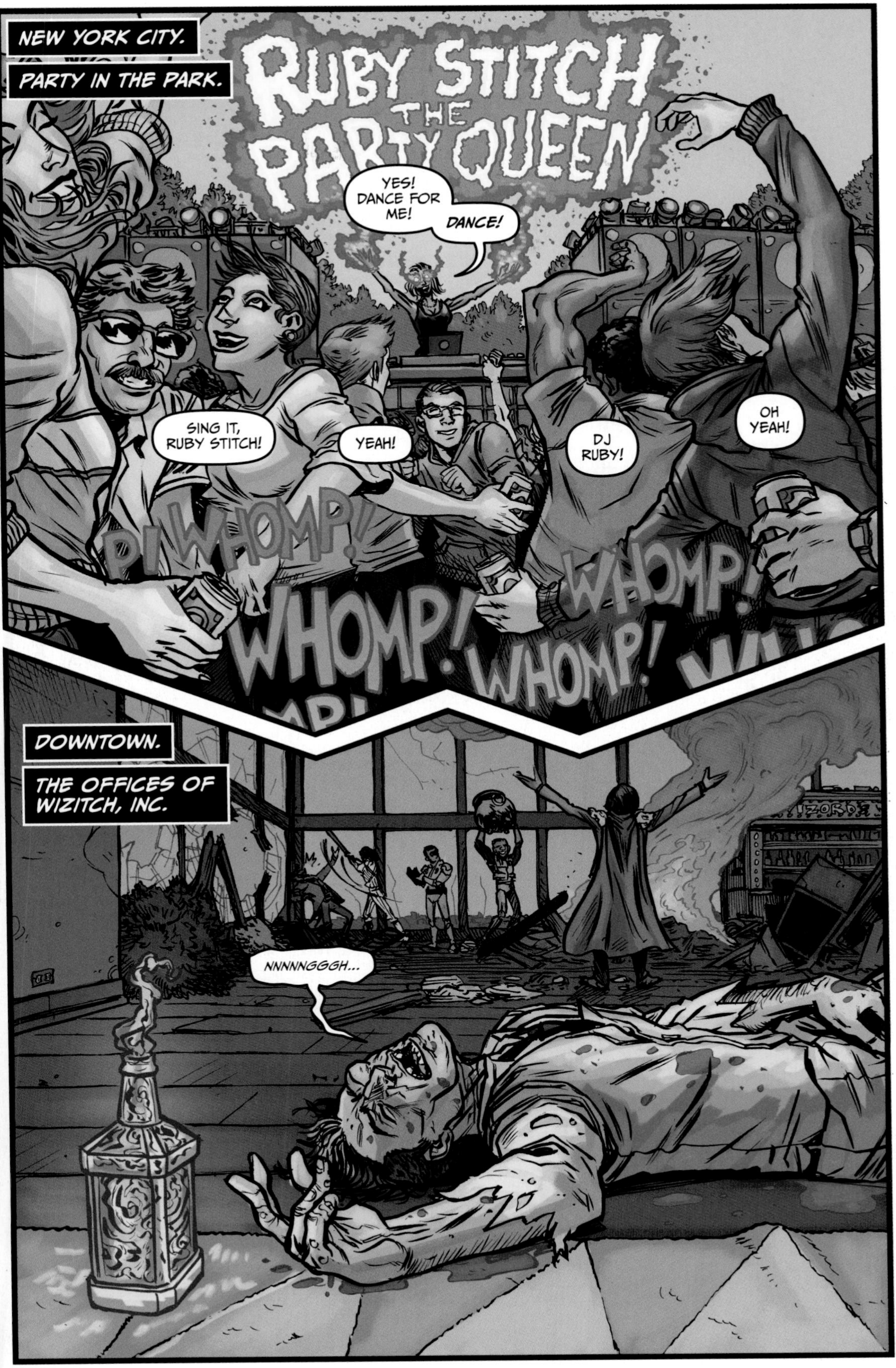
NEW YORK CITY.
PARTY IN THE PARK.
RUBY STITCH THE PARTY QUEEN
YES! DANCE FOR ME!
DANCE!
SING IT, RUBY STITCH!
YEAH!
DJ RUBY!
OH YEAH!
WHOMP!!
WHOMP!
WHOMP!
WHOMP!
DOWNTOWN.
THE OFFICES OF WIZITCH, INC.
NNNNNGGGH...

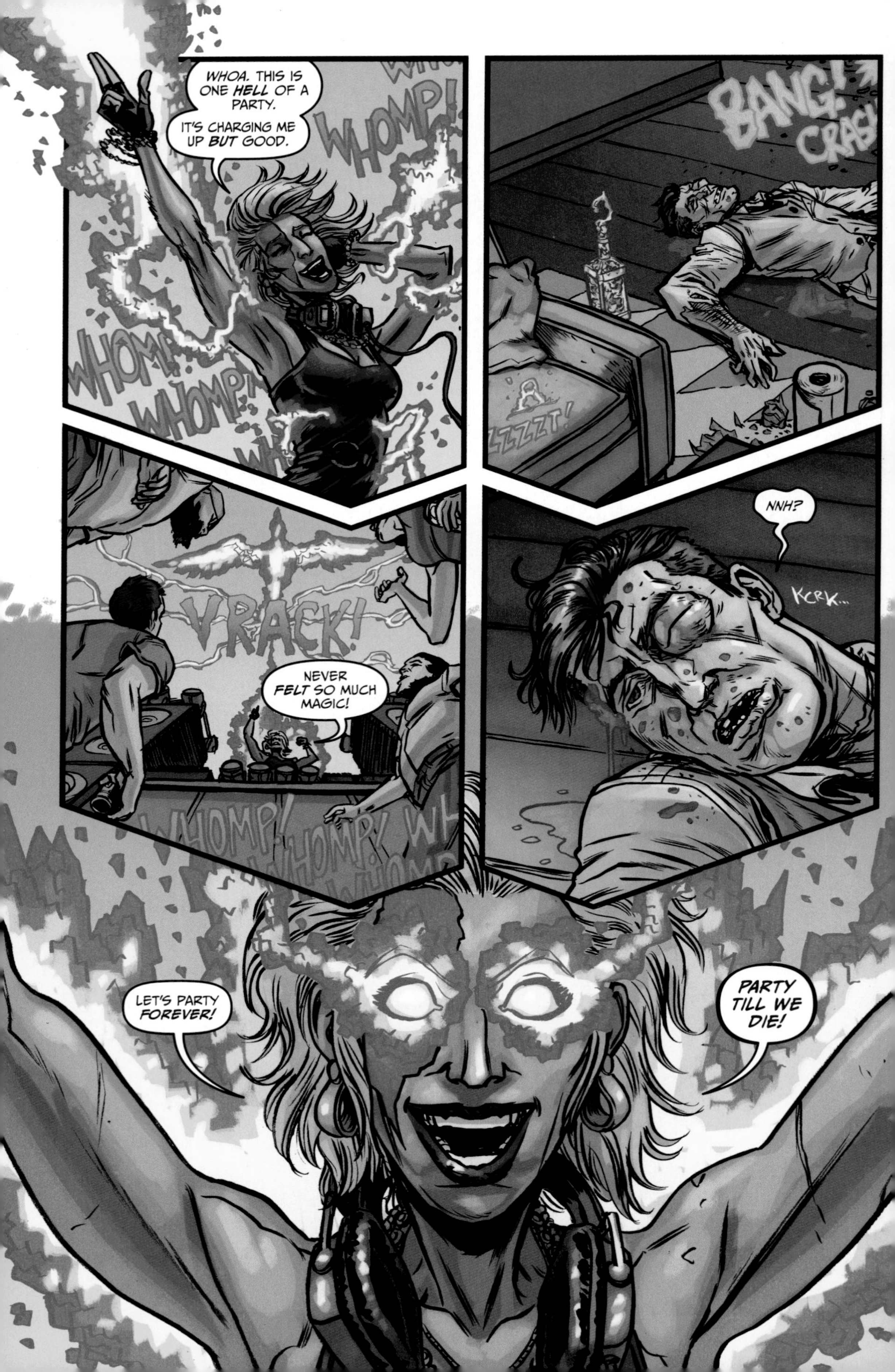
WHOA. THIS IS ONE HELL OF A PARTY.
IT'S CHARGING ME UP BUT GOOD.
WHOMP!
WHOMP!
WHOMP!
BANG!
CRAS
ZZZZZT!
VRACK!
NEVER FELT SO MUCH MAGIC!
WHOMP!
WHOMP!
NNH?
KCRK...
LET'S PARTY FOREVER!
PARTY TILL WE DIE!

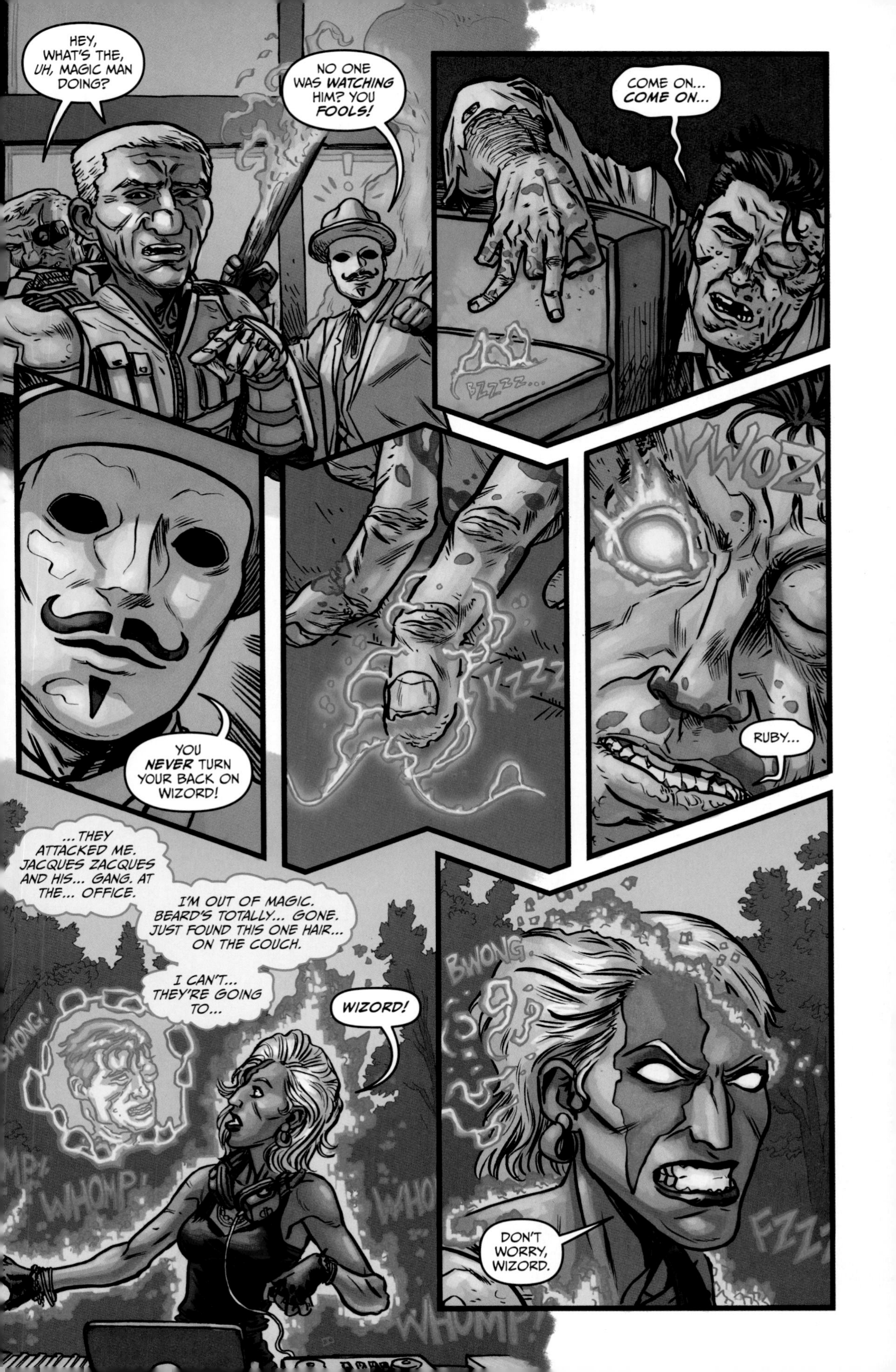
HEY, WHAT'S THE, UH, MAGIC MAN DOING?
NO ONE WAS WATCHING HIM? YOU FOOLS!
COME ON... COME ON...
BZZZZZ...
YOU NEVER TURN YOUR BACK ON WIZORD!
KZZZ
VWOZ!
RUBY...
...THEY ATTACKED ME. JACQUES ZACQUES AND HIS... GANG. AT THE... OFFICE.
I'M OUT OF MAGIC. BEARD'S TOTALLY... GONE. JUST FOUND THIS ONE HAIR... ON THE COUCH.
I CAN'T... THEY'RE GOING TO...
WIZORD!
SWONG!
WHOMP!
WHOMP!
BWONG
FZZ
DON'T WORRY, WIZORD.

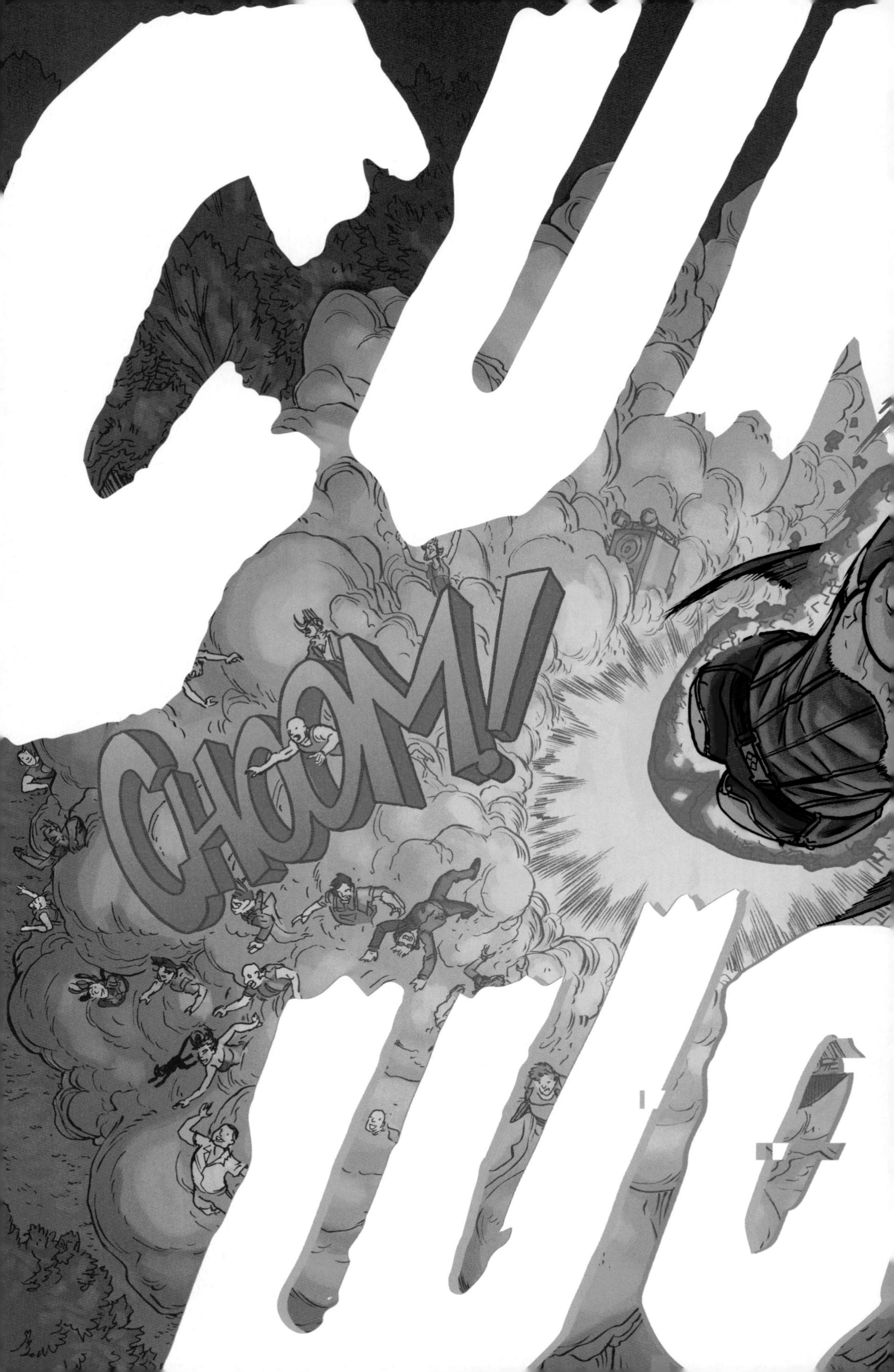
CHOOM!

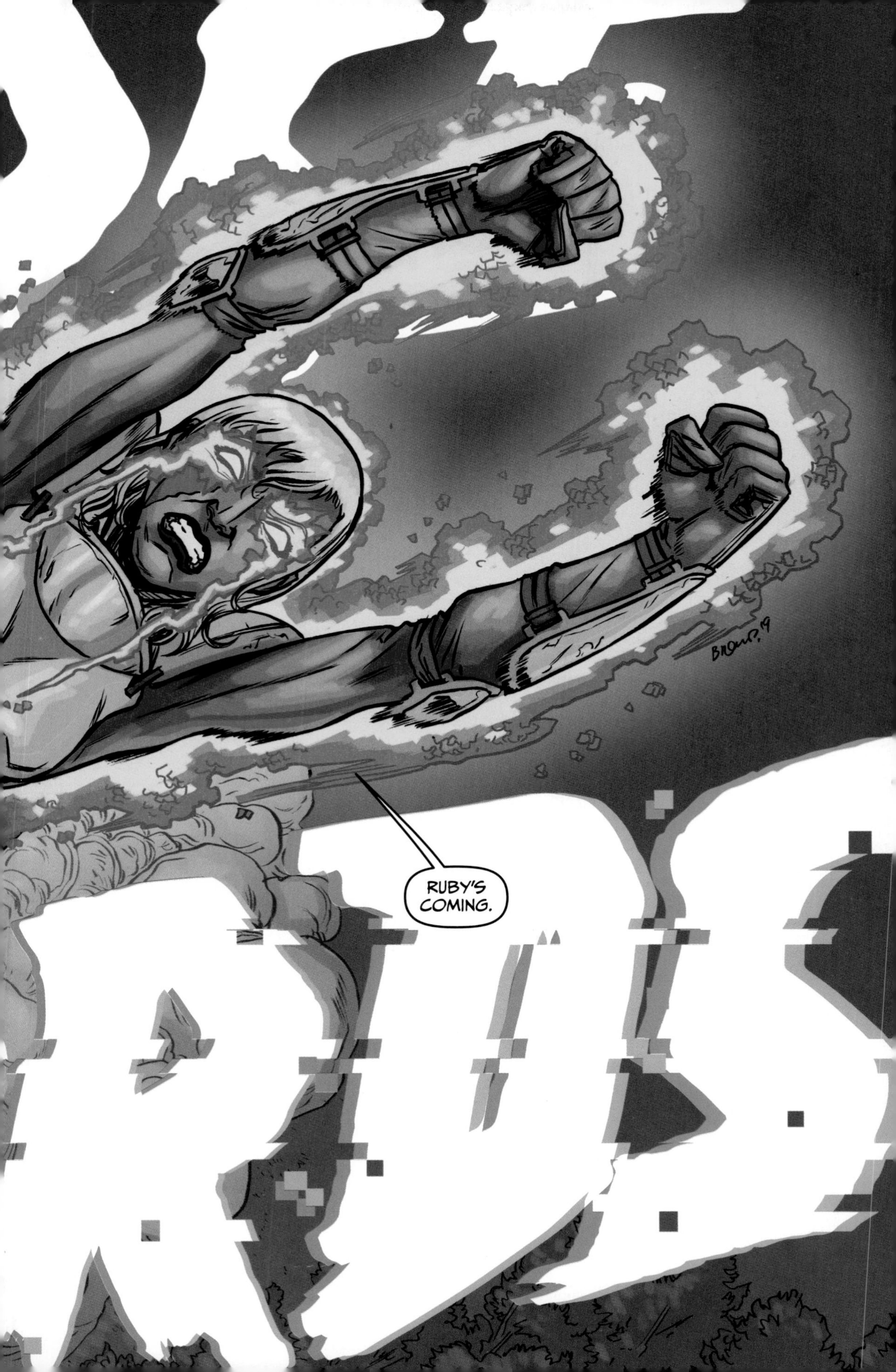
RUBY'S COMING.

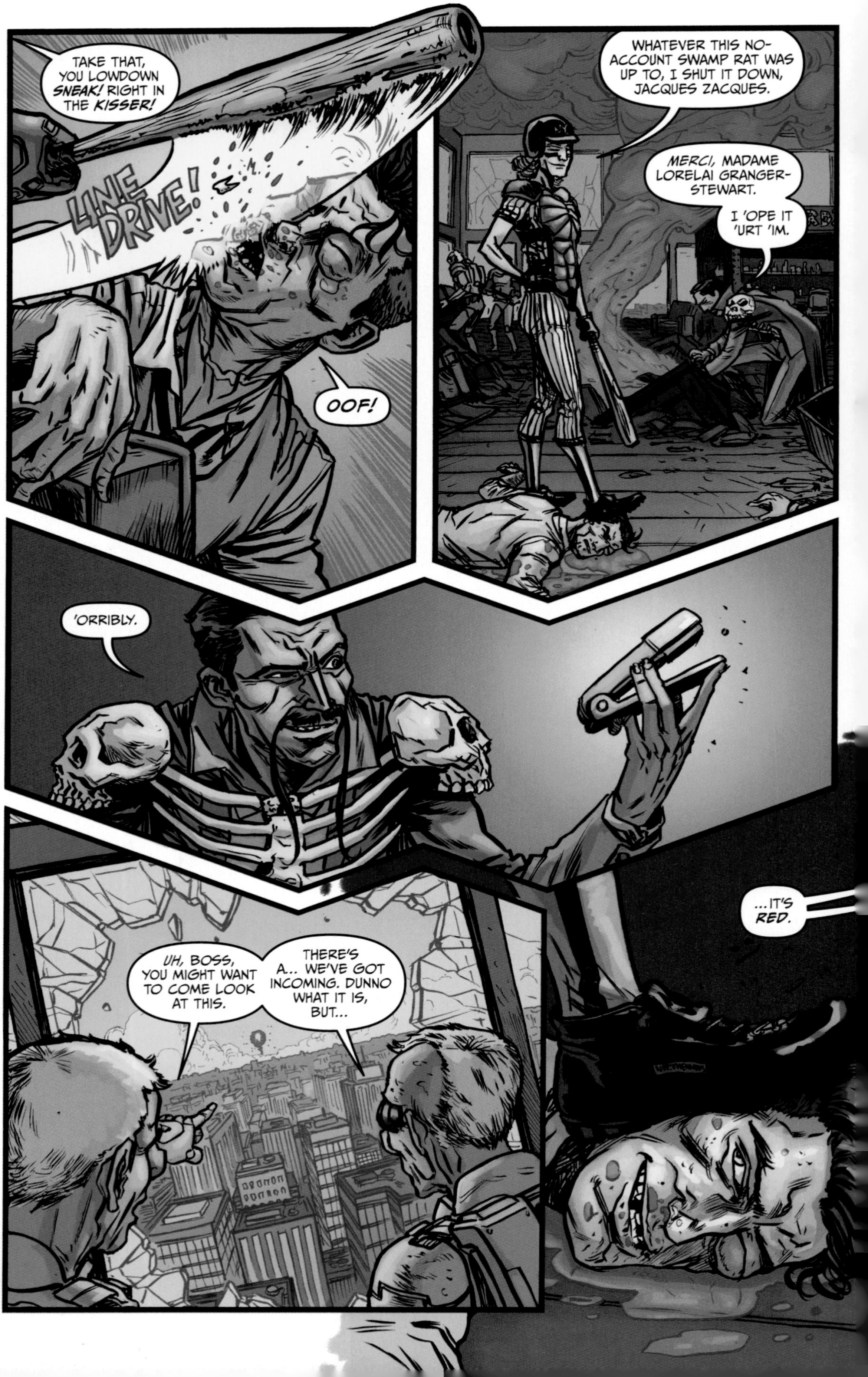
TAKE THAT, YOU LOWDOWN SNEAK! RIGHT IN THE KISSER!
LINE DRIVE!
OOF!
WHATEVER THIS NO-ACCOUNT SWAMP RAT WAS UP TO, I SHUT IT DOWN, JACQUES ZACQUES.
MERCI, MADAME LORELAI GRANGER-STEWART.
I 'OPE IT 'URT 'IM.
'ORRIBLY.
...IT'S RED.
UH, BOSS, YOU MIGHT WANT TO COME LOOK AT THIS.
THERE'S A... WE'VE GOT INCOMING. DUNNO WHAT IT IS, BUT...

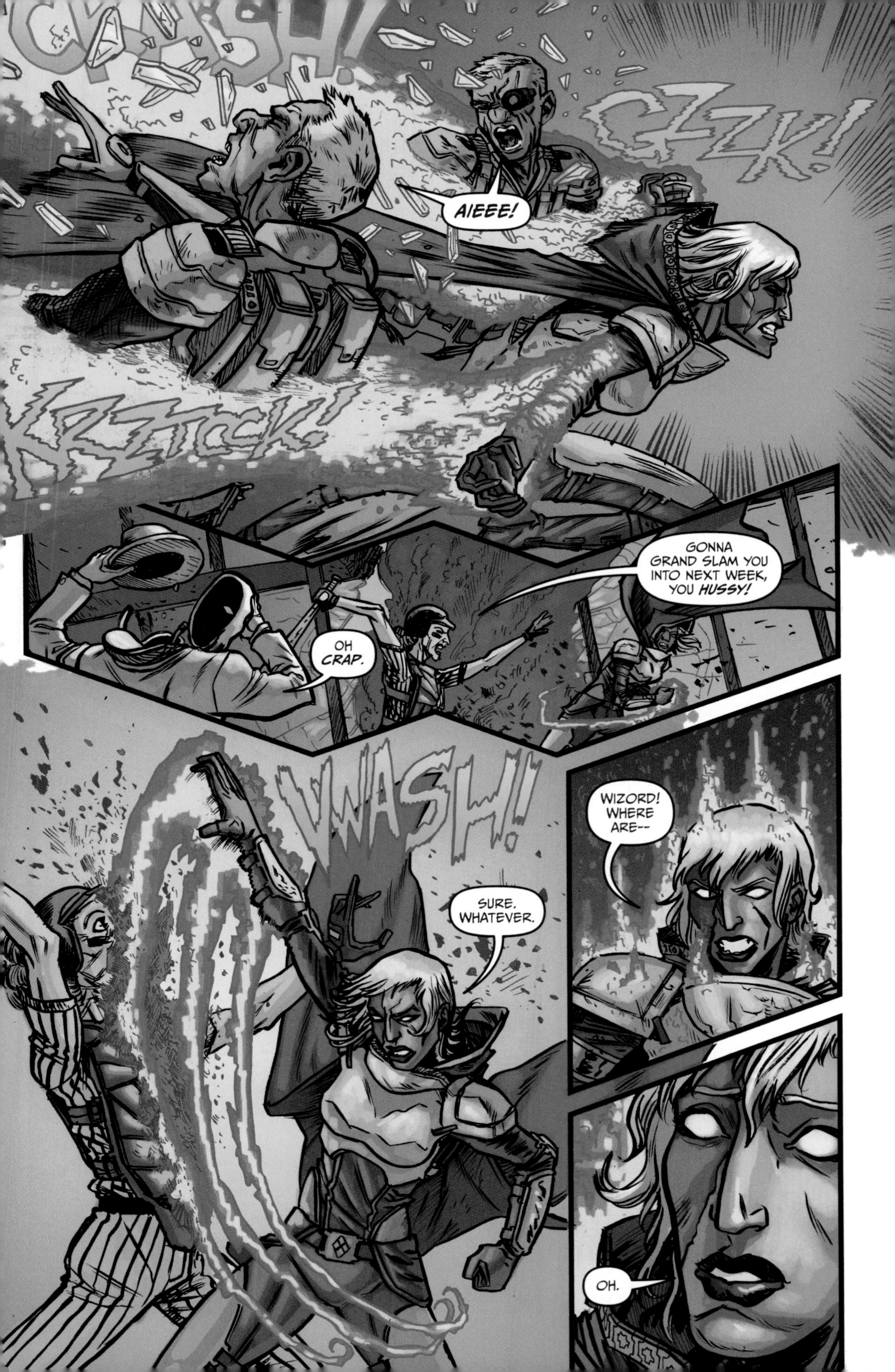

CRASH!
AIEEE!
CZZK!
KRZTACK!
GONNA GRAND SLAM YOU INTO NEXT WEEK, YOU *HUSSY!*
OH *CRAP.*
VWASH!
SURE. WHATEVER.
WIZORD! WHERE ARE--
OH.

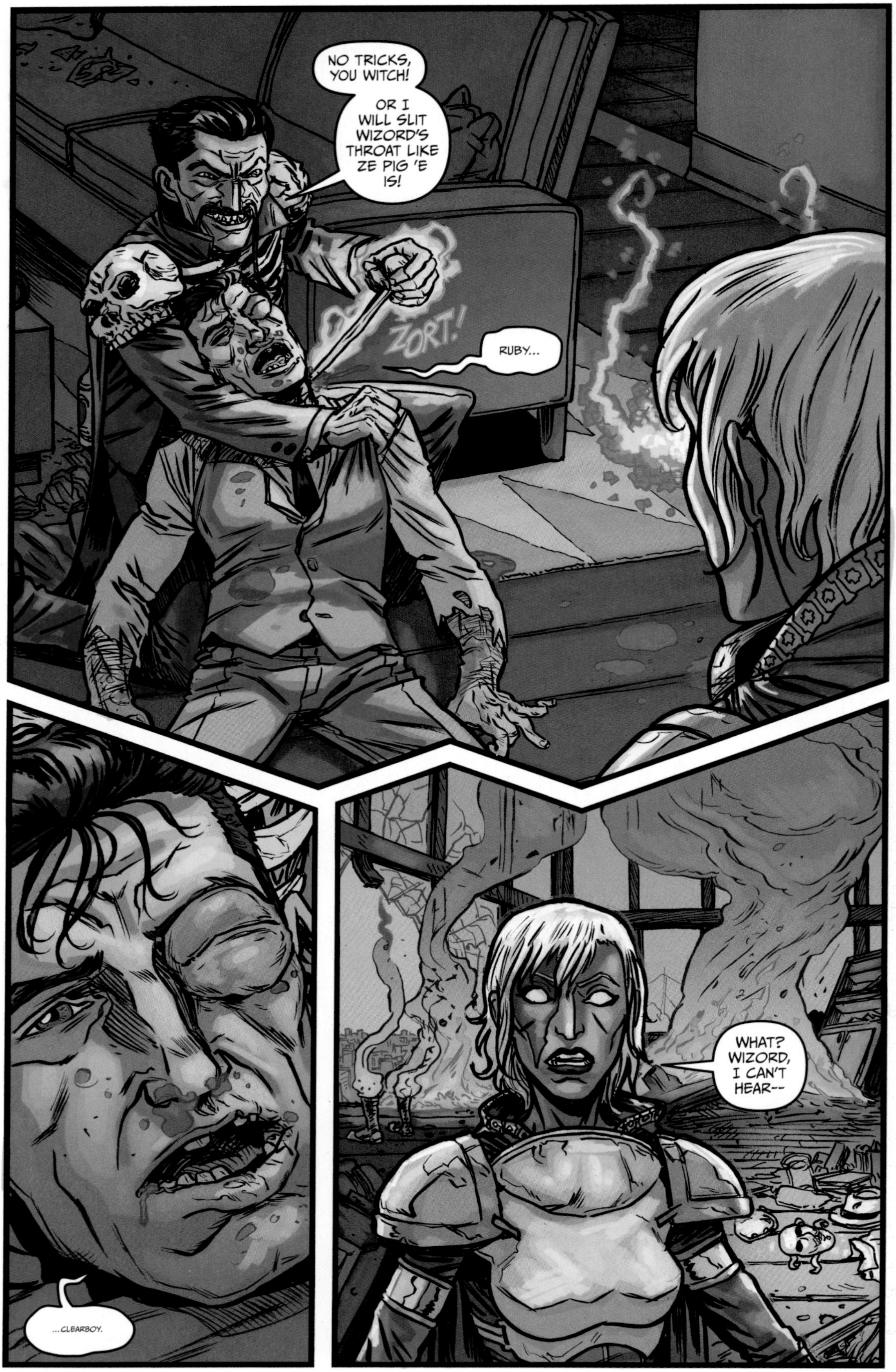
NO TRICKS, YOU WITCH!
OR I WILL SLIT WIZORD'S THROAT LIKE ZE PIG 'E IS!
ZORT!
RUBY...
...CLEARBOY.
WHAT? WIZORD, I CAN'T HEAR--

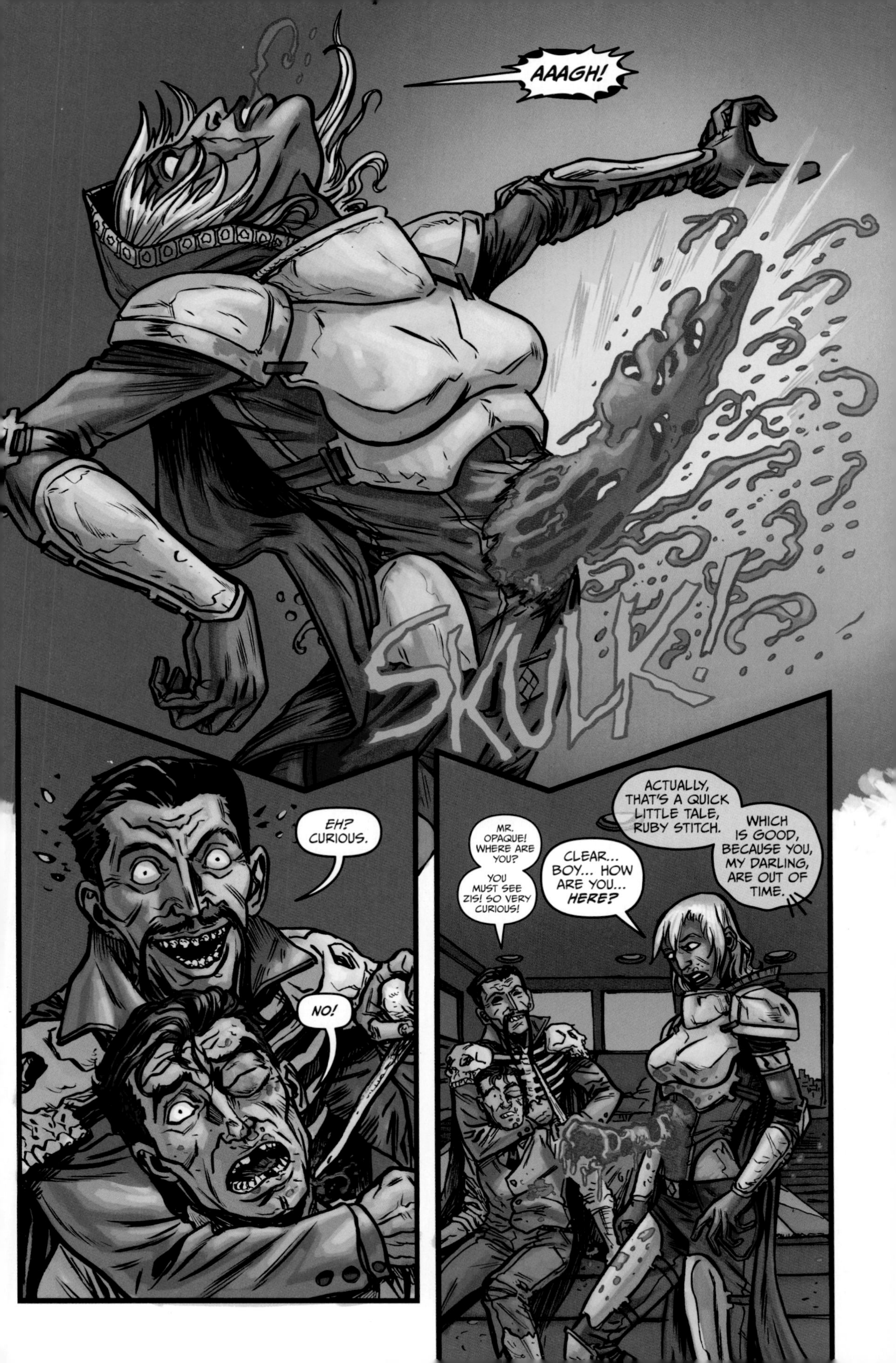
AAAGH!
SKULK!
EH? CURIOUS.
NO!
MR. OPAQUE! WHERE ARE YOU?
YOU MUST SEE ZIS! SO VERY CURIOUS!
CLEAR... BOY... HOW ARE YOU... HERE?
ACTUALLY, THAT'S A QUICK LITTLE TALE, RUBY STITCH.
WHICH IS GOOD, BECAUSE YOU, MY DARLING, ARE OUT OF TIME.

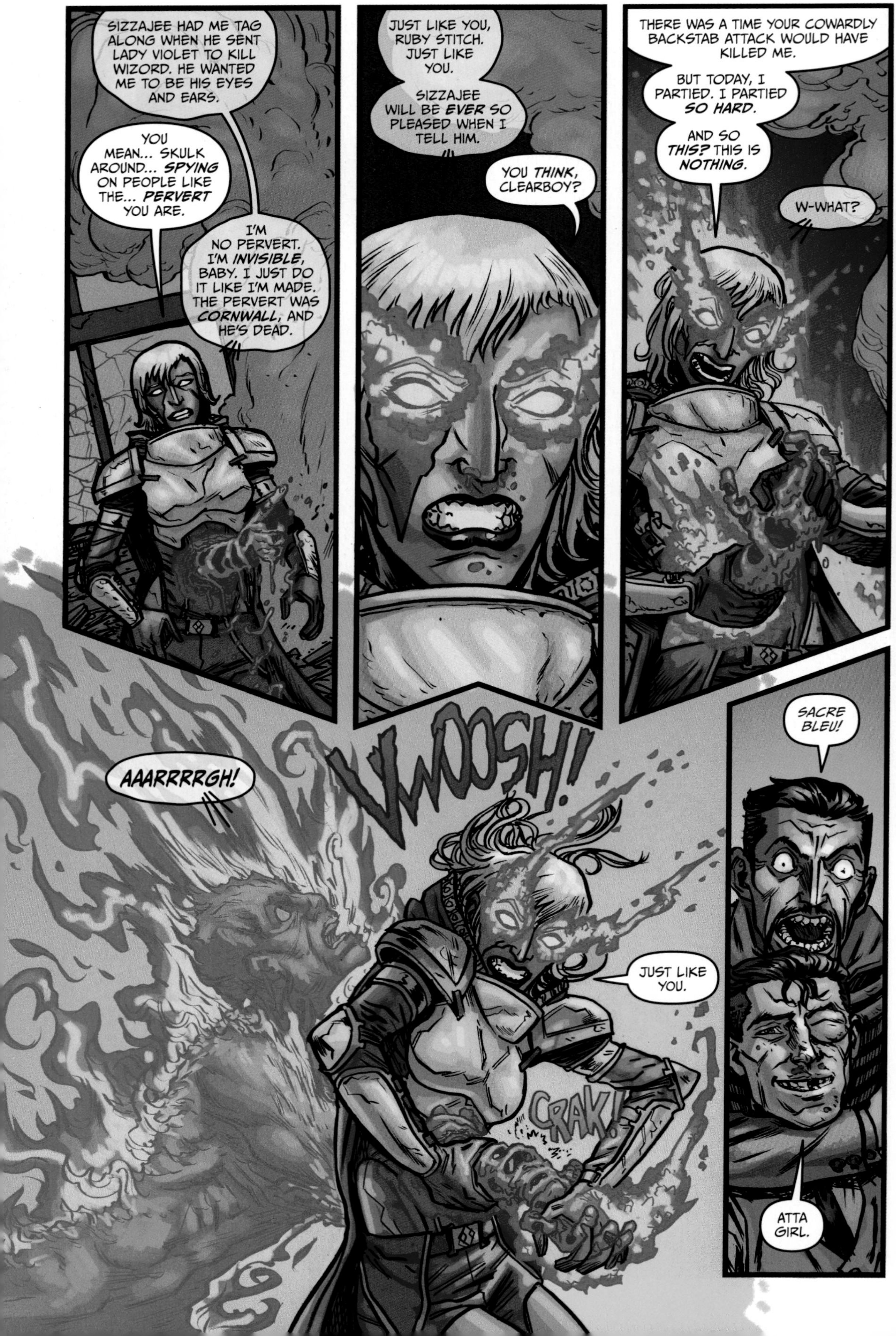
SIZZAJEE HAD ME TAG ALONG WHEN HE SENT LADY VIOLET TO KILL WIZORD. HE WANTED ME TO BE HIS EYES AND EARS.
YOU MEAN... SKULK AROUND... SPYING ON PEOPLE LIKE THE... PERVERT YOU ARE.
I'M NO PERVERT. I'M INVISIBLE, BABY. I JUST DO IT LIKE I'M MADE. THE PERVERT WAS CORNWALL, AND HE'S DEAD.
JUST LIKE YOU, RUBY STITCH. JUST LIKE YOU.
SIZZAJEE WILL BE EVER SO PLEASED WHEN I TELL HIM.
YOU THINK, CLEARBOY?
THERE WAS A TIME YOUR COWARDLY BACKSTAB ATTACK WOULD HAVE KILLED ME.
BUT TODAY, I PARTIED. I PARTIED SO HARD.
AND SO THIS? THIS IS NOTHING.
W-WHAT?
AAARRRRGH!
WOOSH!
JUST LIKE YOU.
CRAK!
SACRE BLEU!
ATTA GIRL.

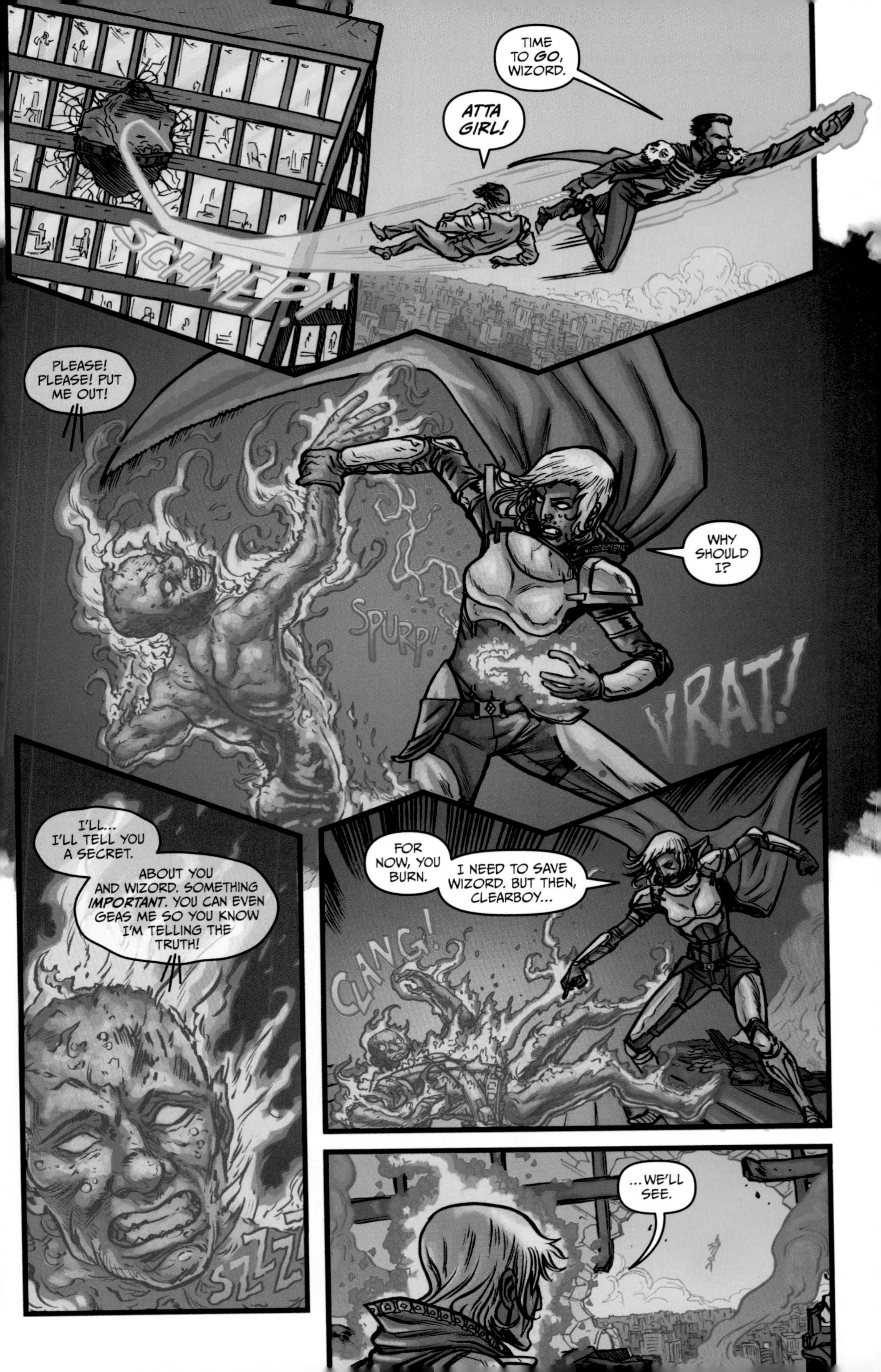
TIME TO GO, WIZORD.
ATTA GIRL!
SCHWEP!
PLEASE! PLEASE! PUT ME OUT!
WHY SHOULD I?
SPURP!
VRAT!
I'LL... I'LL TELL YOU A SECRET.
ABOUT YOU AND WIZORD. SOMETHING IMPORTANT. YOU CAN EVEN GEAS ME SO YOU KNOW I'M TELLING THE TRUTH!
SZZZ
FOR NOW, YOU BURN.
I NEED TO SAVE WIZORD. BUT THEN, CLEARBOY...
CLANG!
...WE'LL SEE.

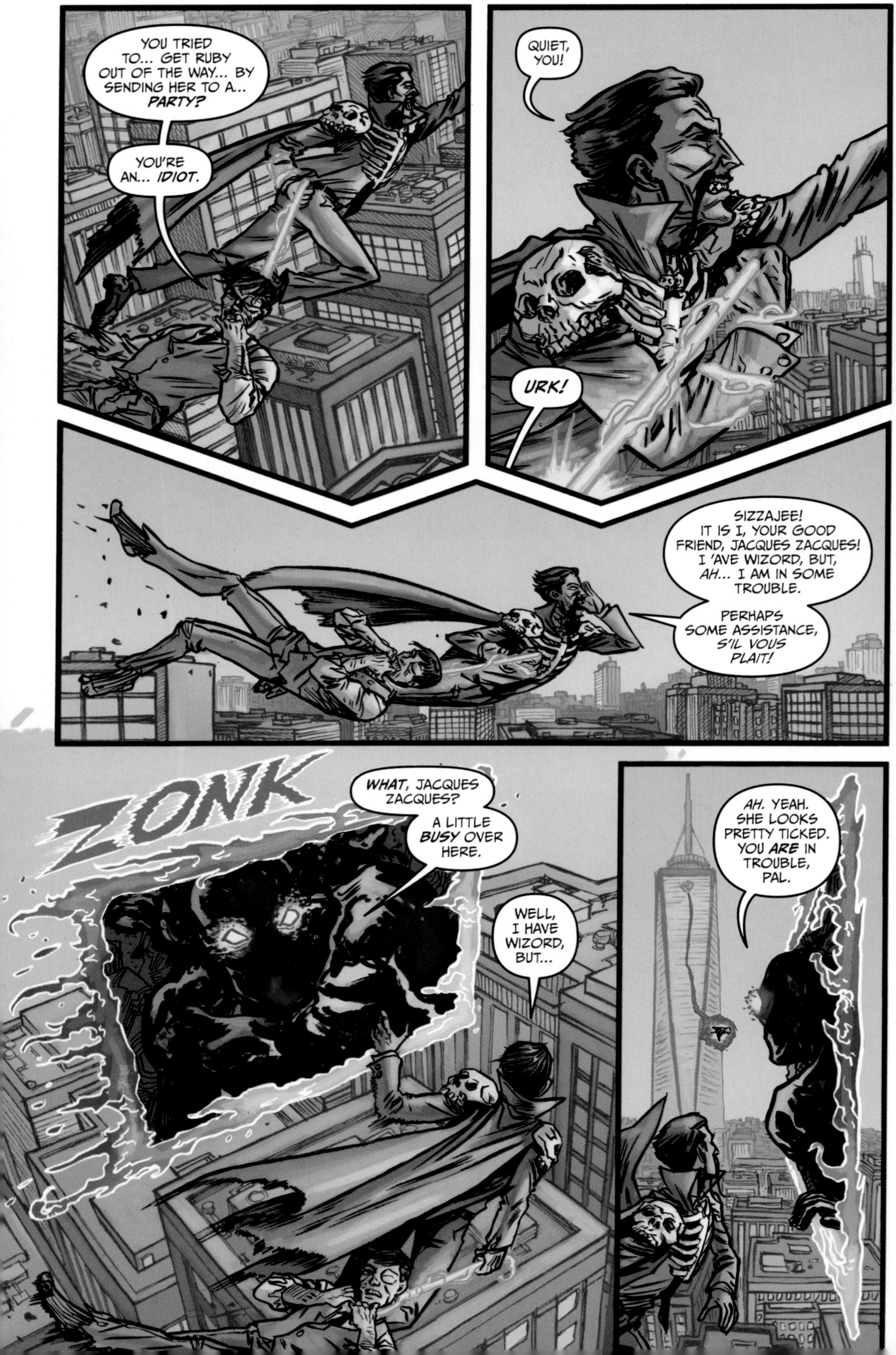

YOU TRIED TO... GET RUBY OUT OF THE WAY... BY SENDING HER TO A... *PARTY?*
YOU'RE AN... *IDIOT*.
QUIET, YOU!
URK!
SIZZAJEE! IT IS I, YOUR GOOD FRIEND, JACQUES ZACQUES! I 'AVE WIZORD, BUT, *AH*... I AM IN SOME TROUBLE.
PERHAPS SOME ASSISTANCE, *S'IL VOUS PLAIT!*
ZONK
WHAT, JACQUES ZACQUES?
A LITTLE *BUSY* OVER HERE.
WELL, I HAVE WIZORD, BUT...
AH. YEAH. SHE LOOKS PRETTY TICKED. YOU *ARE* IN TROUBLE, PAL.

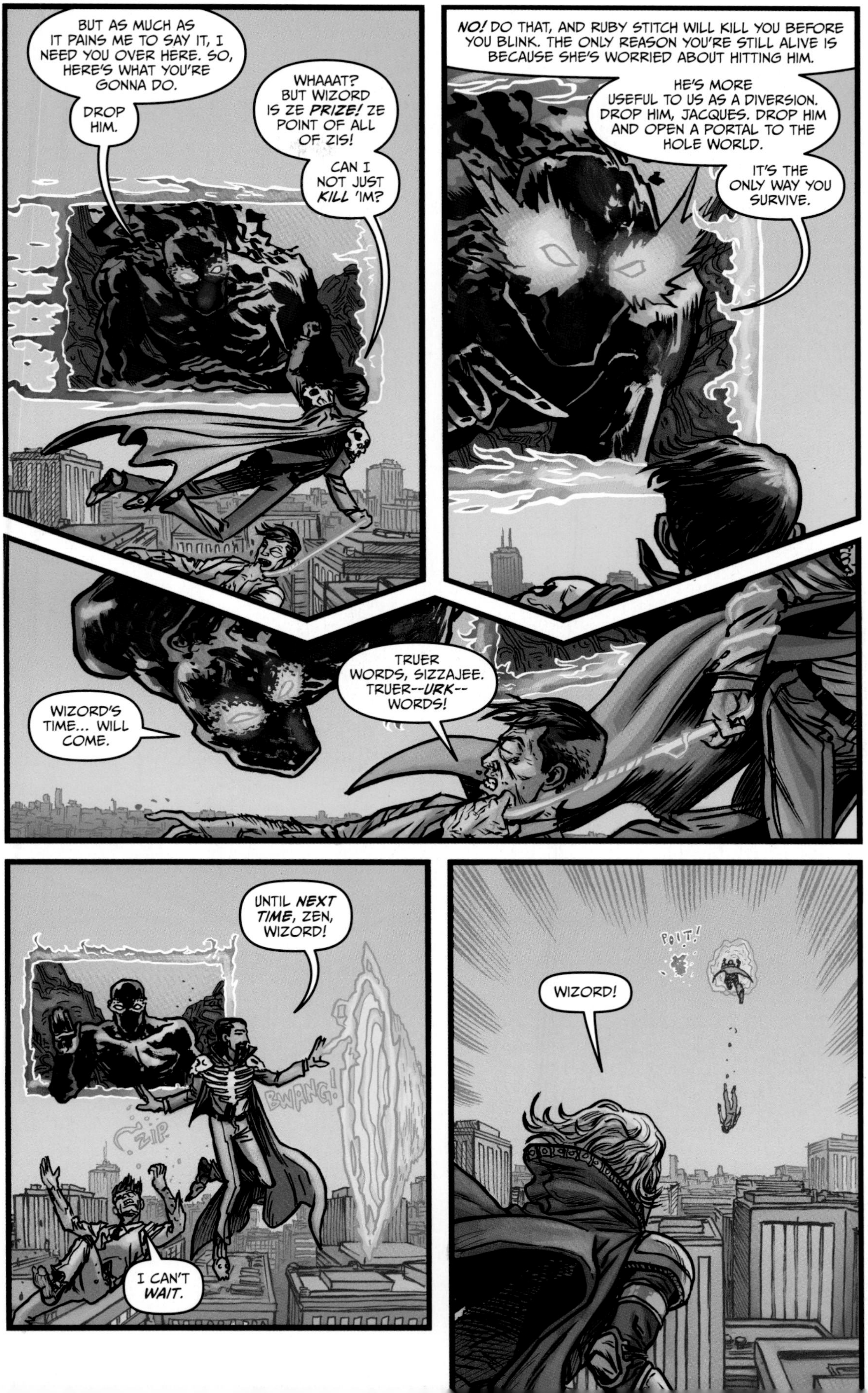
BUT AS MUCH AS IT PAINS ME TO SAY IT, I NEED YOU OVER HERE. SO, HERE'S WHAT YOU'RE GONNA DO.
DROP HIM.
WHAAAT? BUT WIZORD IS ZE PRIZE! ZE POINT OF ALL OF ZIS!
CAN I NOT JUST KILL 'IM?
NO! DO THAT, AND RUBY STITCH WILL KILL YOU BEFORE YOU BLINK. THE ONLY REASON YOU'RE STILL ALIVE IS BECAUSE SHE'S WORRIED ABOUT HITTING HIM.
HE'S MORE USEFUL TO US AS A DIVERSION. DROP HIM, JACQUES. DROP HIM AND OPEN A PORTAL TO THE HOLE WORLD.
IT'S THE ONLY WAY YOU SURVIVE.
WIZORD'S TIME... WILL COME.
TRUER WORDS, SIZZAJEE. TRUER--URK--WORDS!
UNTIL NEXT TIME, ZEN, WIZORD!
BWANG!
ZIP
I CAN'T WAIT.
POIT!
WIZORD!

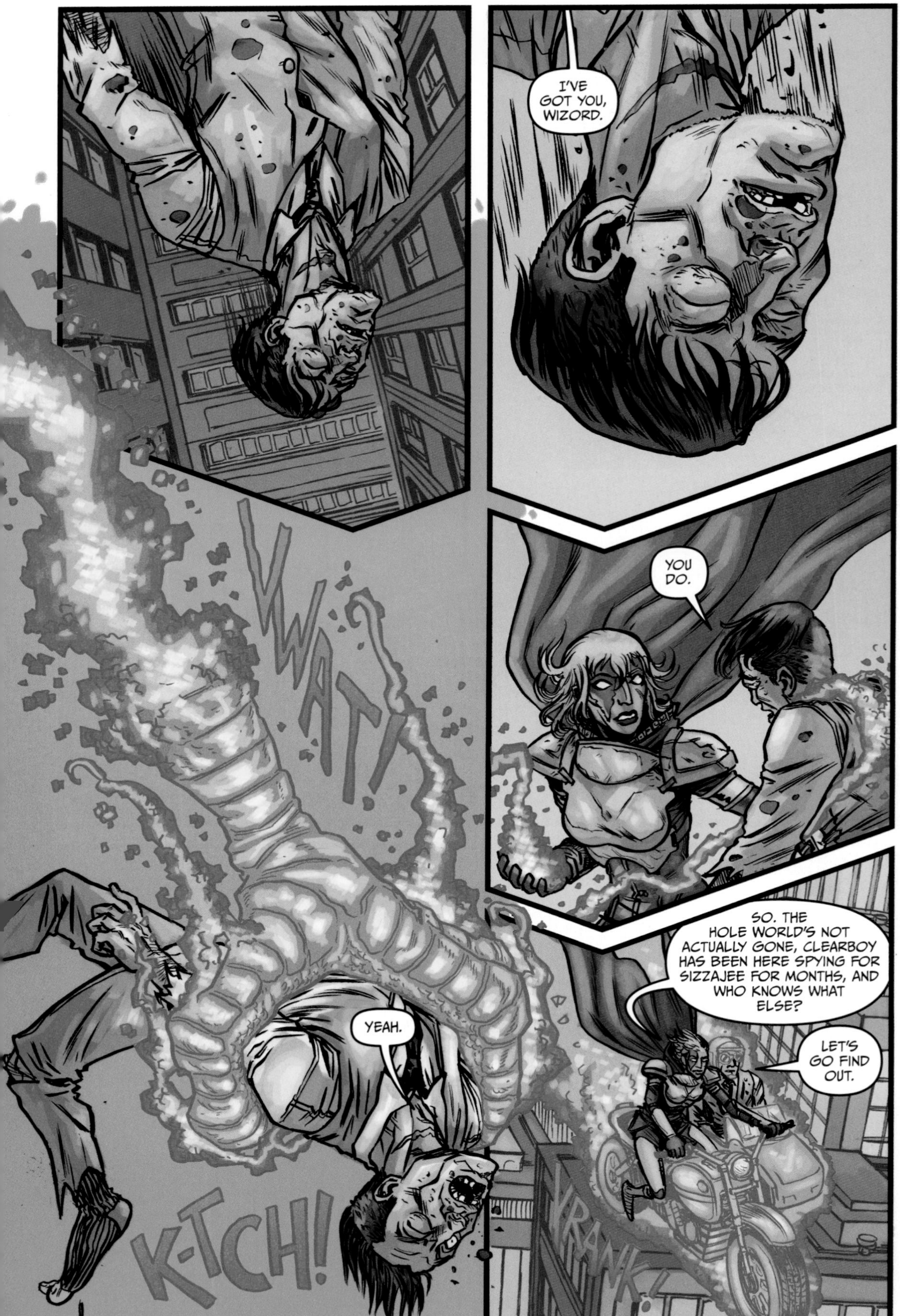
I'VE GOT YOU, WIZORD.
YOU DO.
VWAT!
YEAH.
K-TCH!
SO. THE HOLE WORLD'S NOT ACTUALLY GONE, CLEARBOY HAS BEEN HERE SPYING FOR SIZZAJEE FOR MONTHS, AND WHO KNOWS WHAT ELSE?
LET'S GO FIND OUT.
VRANK!

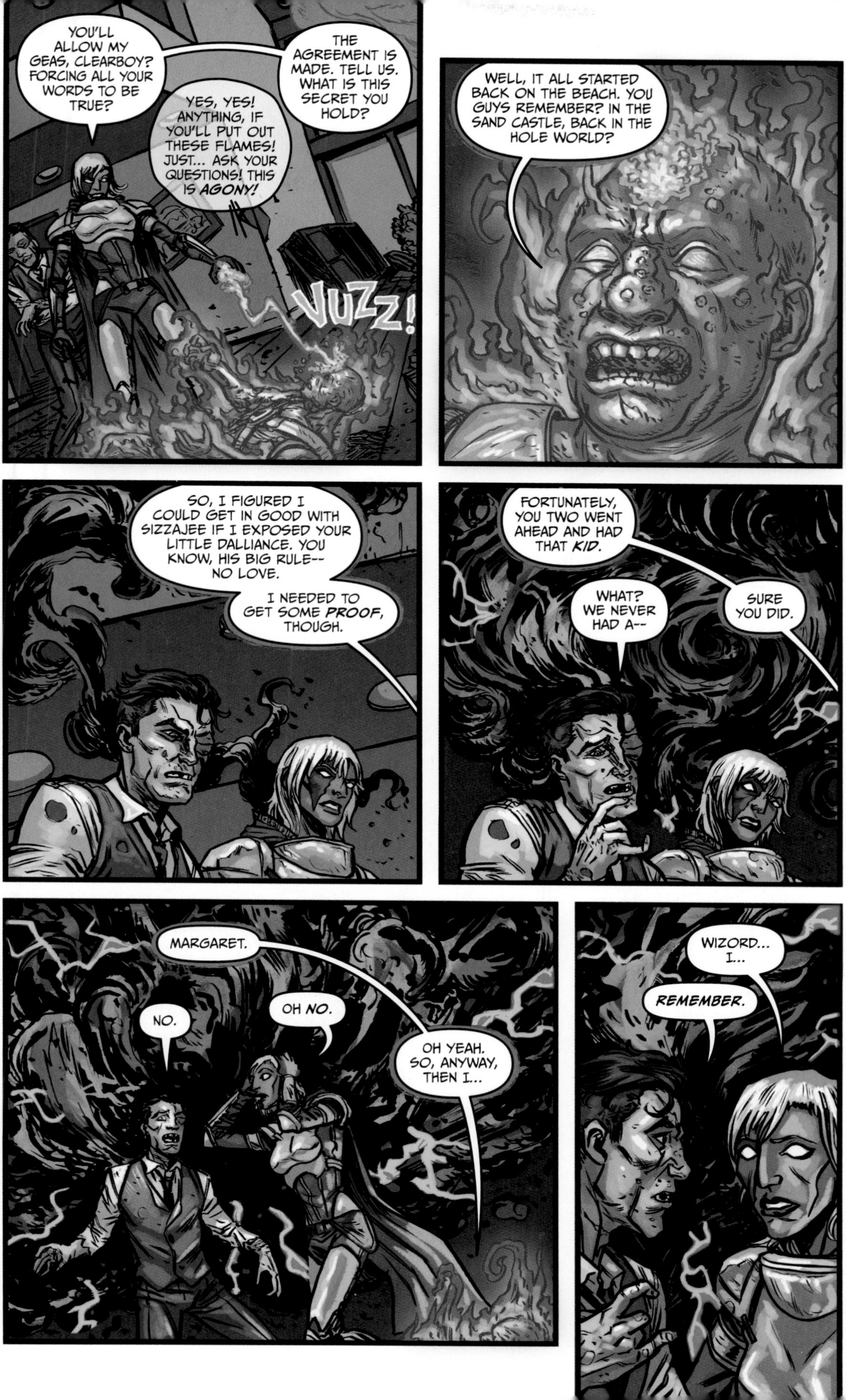
YOU'LL ALLOW MY GEAS, CLEARBOY? FORCING ALL YOUR WORDS TO BE TRUE?
YES, YES! ANYTHING, IF YOU'LL PUT OUT THESE FLAMES! JUST... ASK YOUR QUESTIONS! THIS IS AGONY!
THE AGREEMENT IS MADE. TELL US. WHAT IS THIS SECRET YOU HOLD?
VUZZ!
WELL, IT ALL STARTED BACK ON THE BEACH. YOU GUYS REMEMBER? IN THE SAND CASTLE, BACK IN THE HOLE WORLD?
SO, I FIGURED I COULD GET IN GOOD WITH SIZZAJEE IF I EXPOSED YOUR LITTLE DALLIANCE. YOU KNOW, HIS BIG RULE-- NO LOVE.
I NEEDED TO GET SOME PROOF, THOUGH.
FORTUNATELY, YOU TWO WENT AHEAD AND HAD THAT KID.
WHAT? WE NEVER HAD A--
SURE YOU DID.
MARGARET.
NO.
OH NO.
OH YEAH. SO, ANYWAY, THEN I...
WIZORD... I...
REMEMBER.

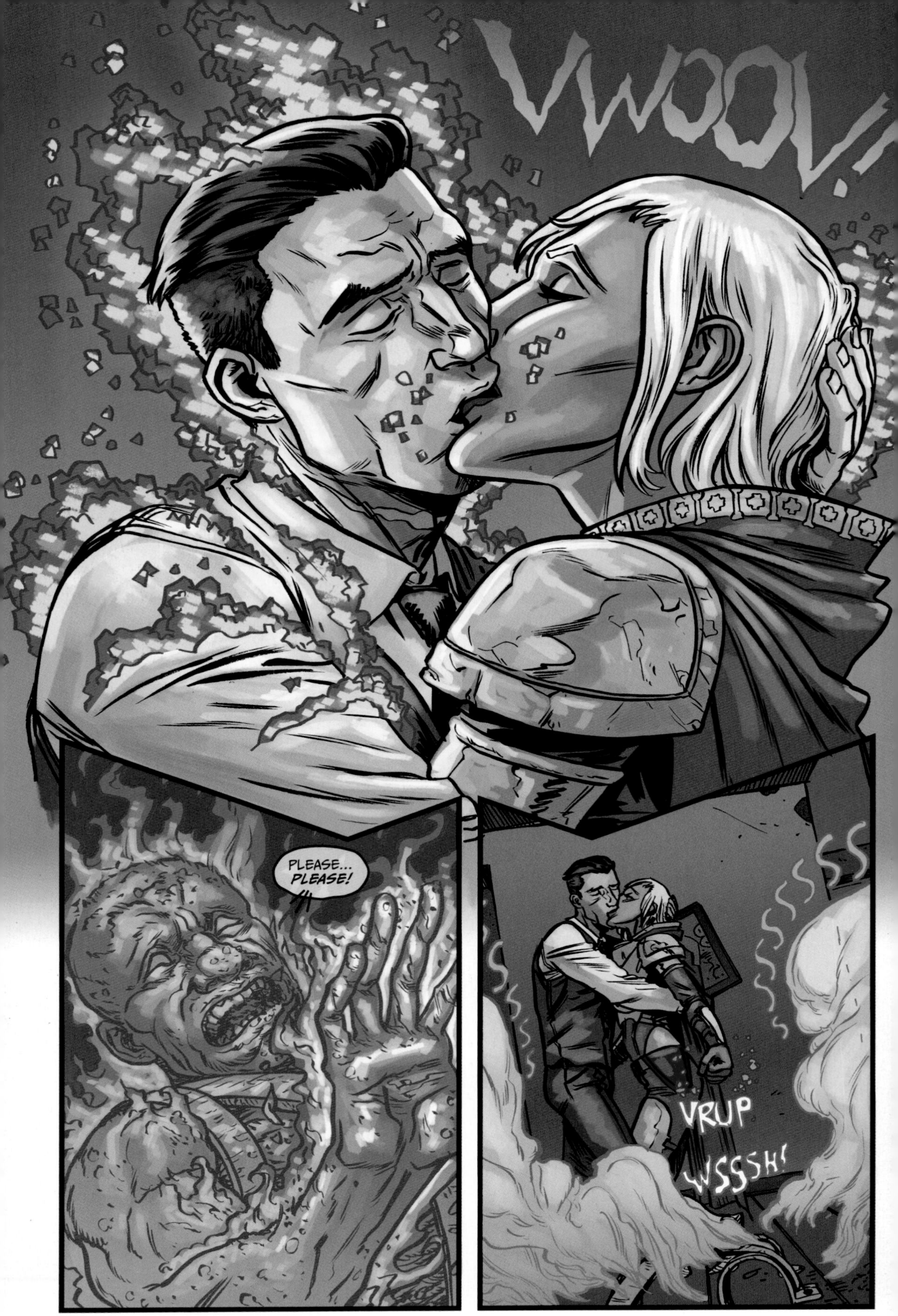
VWOOV!
PLEASE... PLEASE!
VRUP
WSSSH!

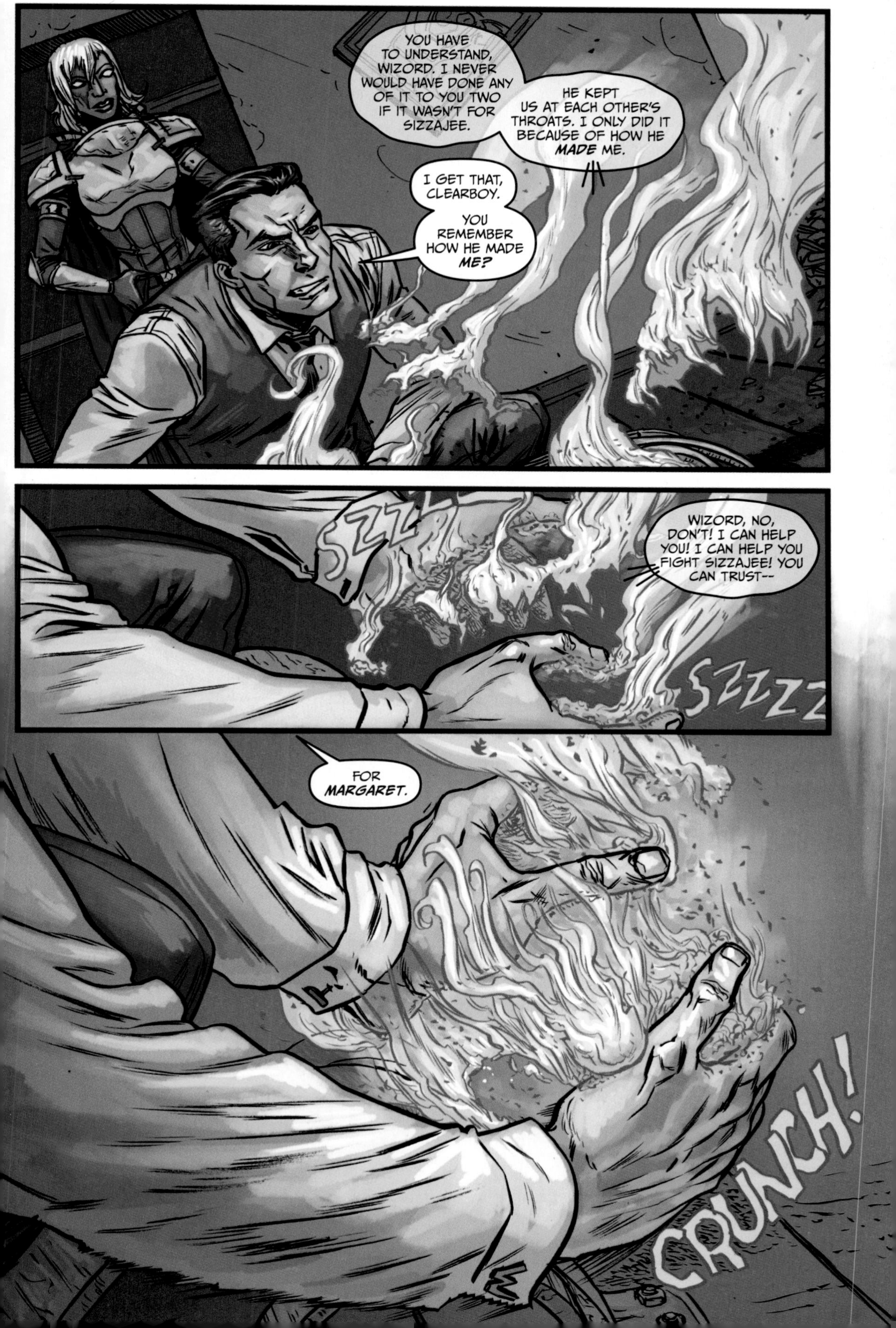
YOU HAVE TO UNDERSTAND, WIZORD. I NEVER WOULD HAVE DONE ANY OF IT TO YOU TWO IF IT WASN'T FOR SIZZAJEE.
HE KEPT US AT EACH OTHER'S THROATS. I ONLY DID IT BECAUSE OF HOW HE MADE ME.
I GET THAT, CLEARBOY.
YOU REMEMBER HOW HE MADE ME?
SZZZ
WIZORD, NO, DON'T! I CAN HELP YOU! I CAN HELP YOU FIGHT SIZZAJEE! YOU CAN TRUST--
SZZZZ
FOR MARGARET.
CRUNCH!

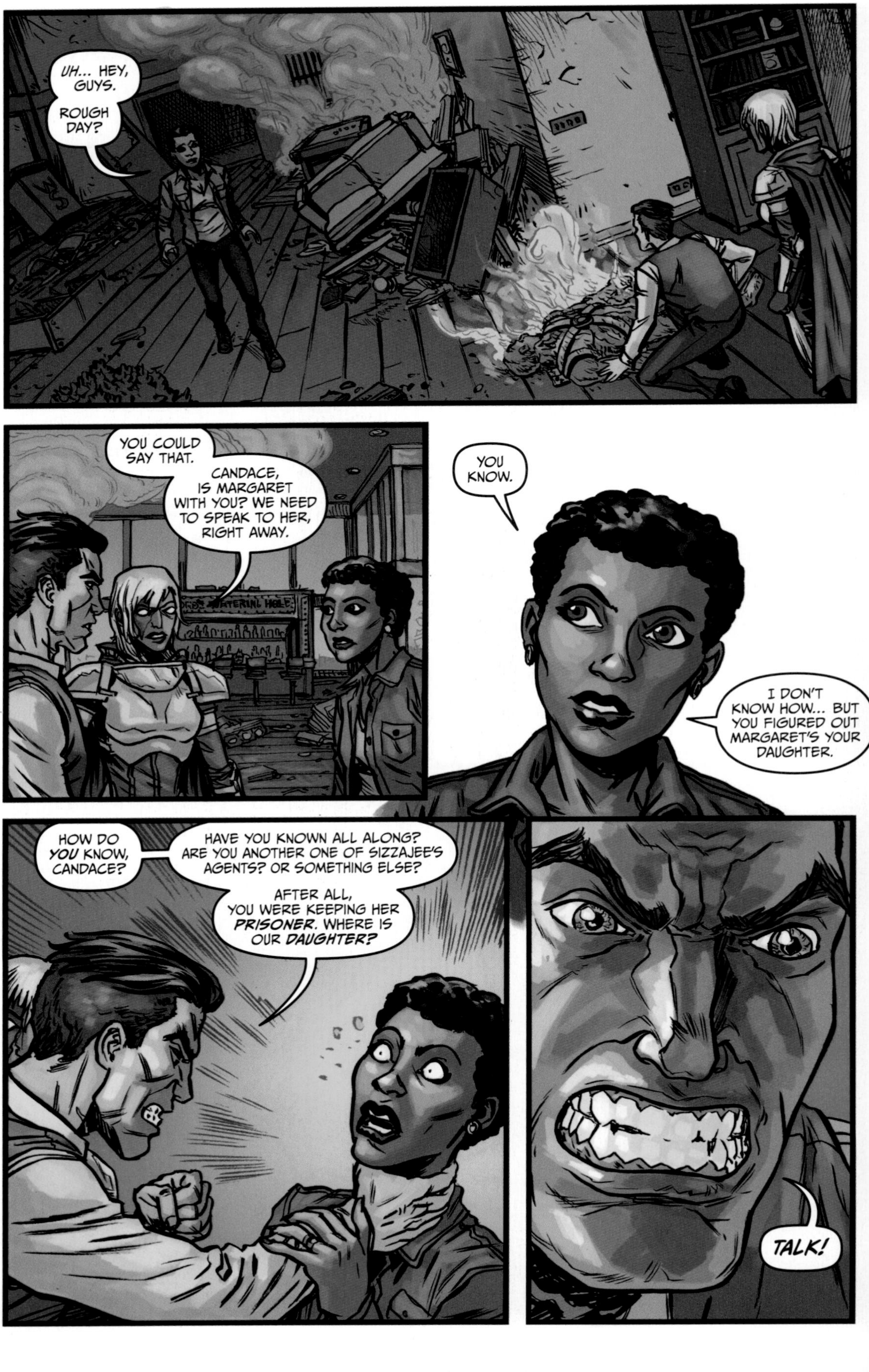
UH... HEY, GUYS.
ROUGH DAY?
YOU COULD SAY THAT.
CANDACE, IS MARGARET WITH YOU? WE NEED TO SPEAK TO HER, RIGHT AWAY.
YOU KNOW.
I DON'T KNOW HOW... BUT YOU FIGURED OUT MARGARET'S YOUR DAUGHTER.
HOW DO *YOU* KNOW, CANDACE?
HAVE YOU KNOWN ALL ALONG? ARE YOU ANOTHER ONE OF SIZZAJEE'S AGENTS? OR SOMETHING ELSE?
AFTER ALL, YOU WERE KEEPING HER *PRISONER*. WHERE IS OUR *DAUGHTER?*
TALK!

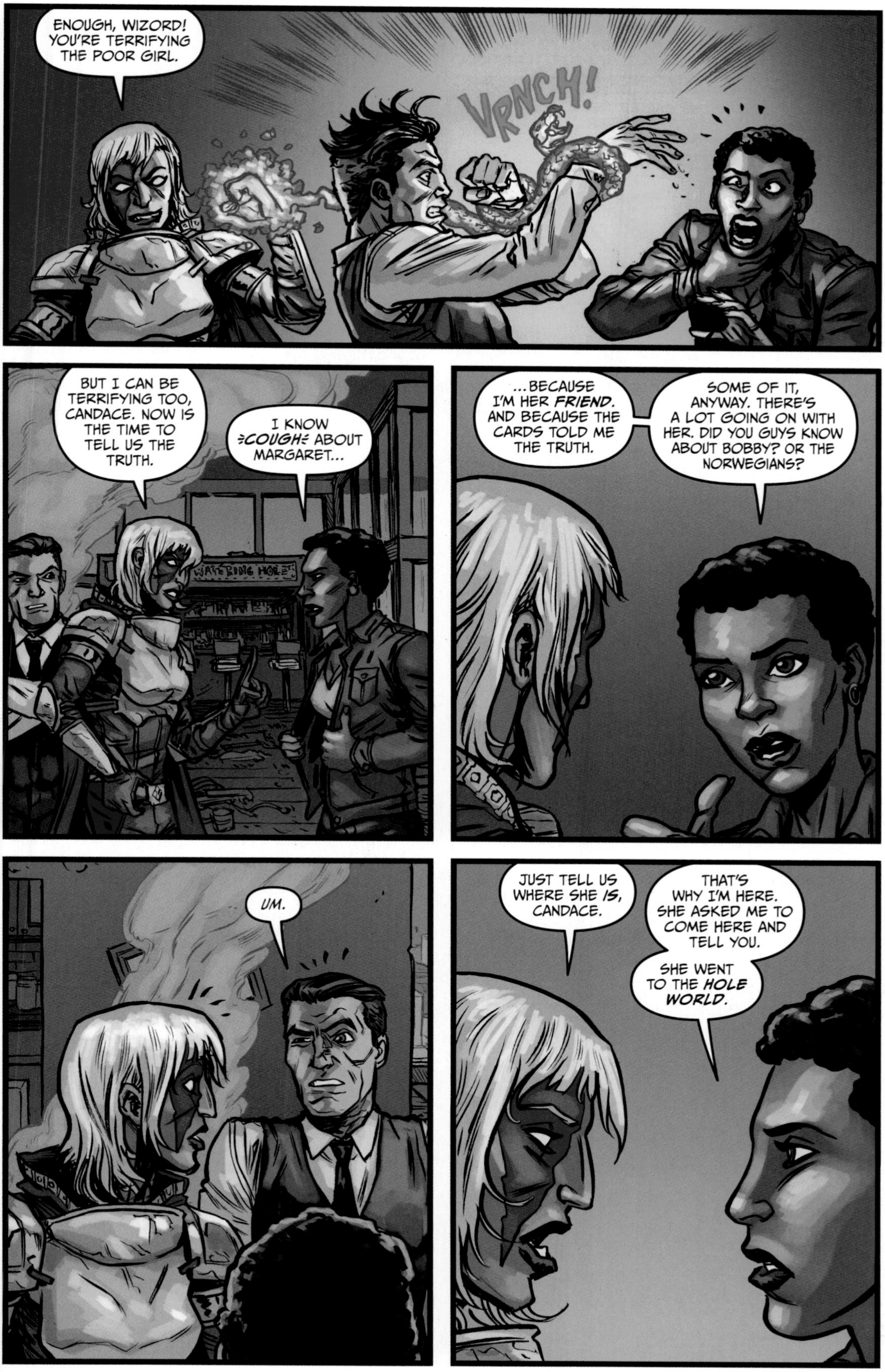
ENOUGH, WIZORD! YOU'RE TERRIFYING THE POOR GIRL.
VRNCH!
BUT I CAN BE TERRIFYING TOO, CANDACE. NOW IS THE TIME TO TELL US THE TRUTH.
I KNOW *COUGH* ABOUT MARGARET...
WATERING HOLE
...BECAUSE I'M HER FRIEND. AND BECAUSE THE CARDS TOLD ME THE TRUTH.
SOME OF IT, ANYWAY. THERE'S A LOT GOING ON WITH HER. DID YOU GUYS KNOW ABOUT BOBBY? OR THE NORWEGIANS?
UM.
JUST TELL US WHERE SHE IS, CANDACE.
THAT'S WHY I'M HERE. SHE ASKED ME TO COME HERE AND TELL YOU.
SHE WENT TO THE HOLE WORLD.

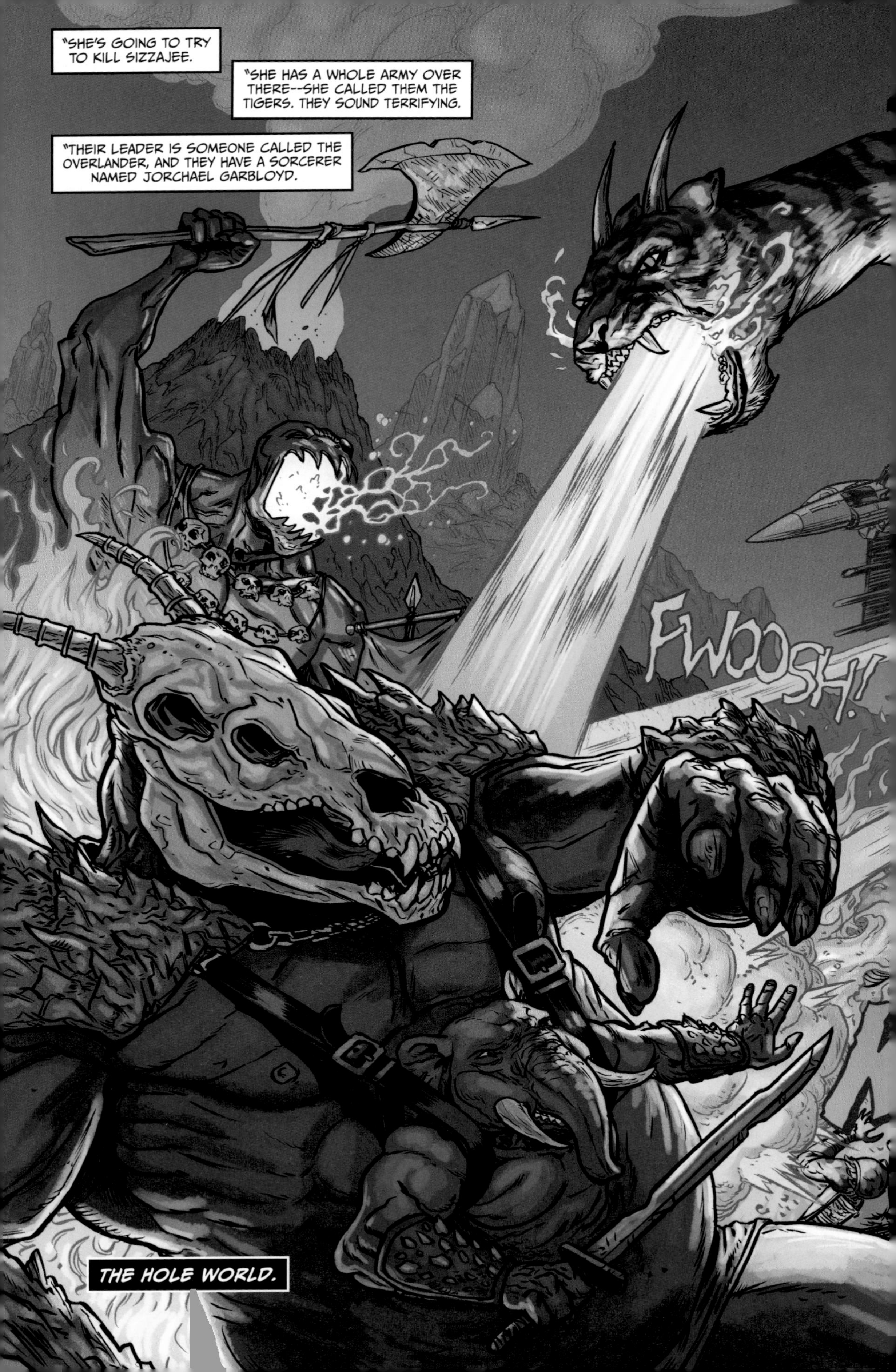
"SHE'S GOING TO TRY TO KILL SIZZAJEE.
"SHE HAS A WHOLE ARMY OVER THERE--SHE CALLED THEM THE TIGERS. THEY SOUND TERRIFYING.
"THEIR LEADER IS SOMEONE CALLED THE OVERLANDER, AND THEY HAVE A SORCERER NAMED JORCHAEL GARBLOYD.
FWOOSH!
THE HOLE WORLD.

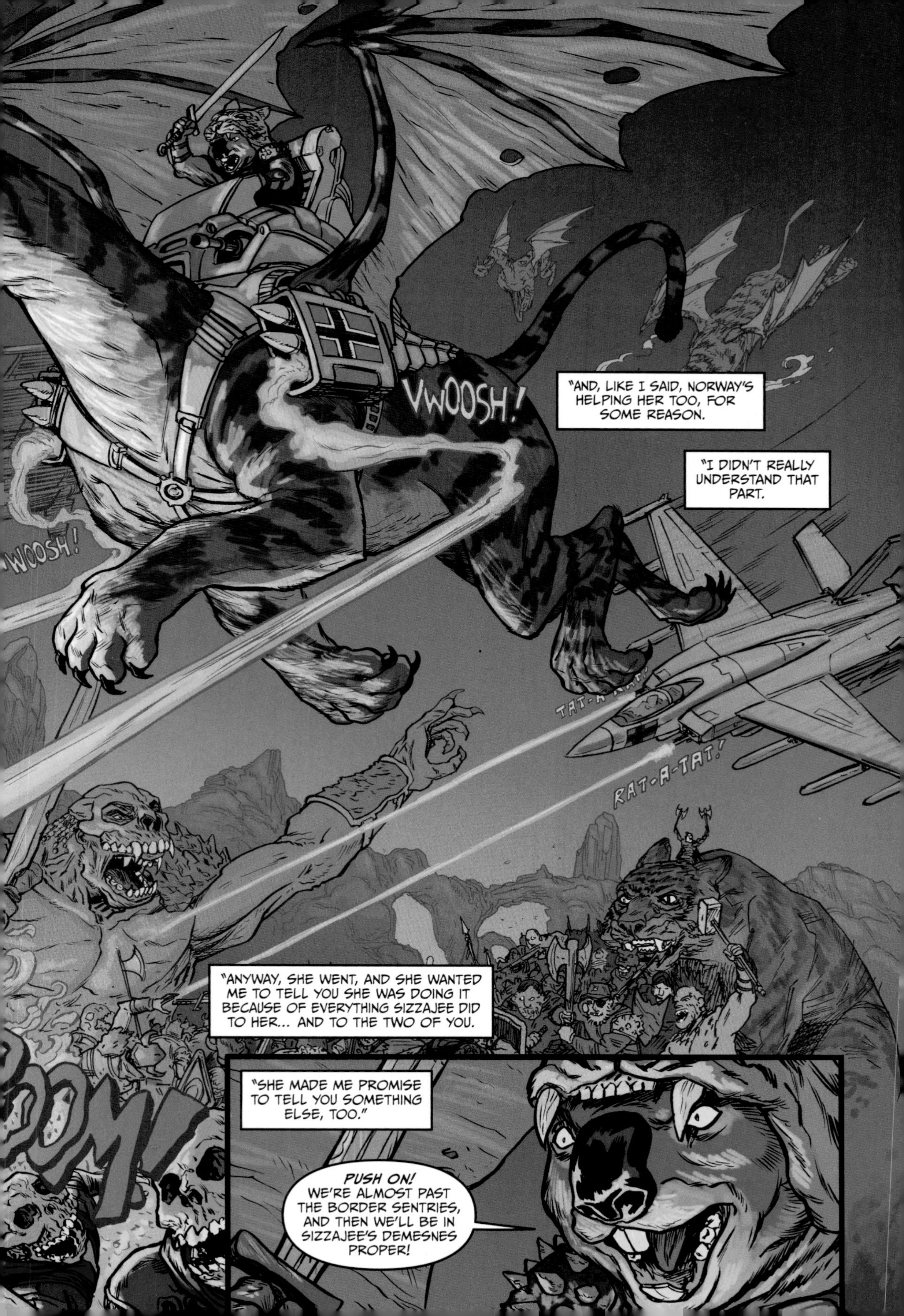
VWOOSH!
"AND, LIKE I SAID, NORWAY'S HELPING HER TOO, FOR SOME REASON.
"I DIDN'T REALLY UNDERSTAND THAT PART.
WOOSH!
RAT-A-TAT!
"ANYWAY, SHE WENT, AND SHE WANTED ME TO TELL YOU SHE WAS DOING IT BECAUSE OF EVERYTHING SIZZAJEE DID TO HER... AND TO THE TWO OF YOU.
"SHE MADE ME PROMISE TO TELL YOU SOMETHING ELSE, TOO."
PUSH ON! WE'RE ALMOST PAST THE BORDER SENTRIES, AND THEN WE'LL BE IN SIZZAJEE'S DEMESNES PROPER!

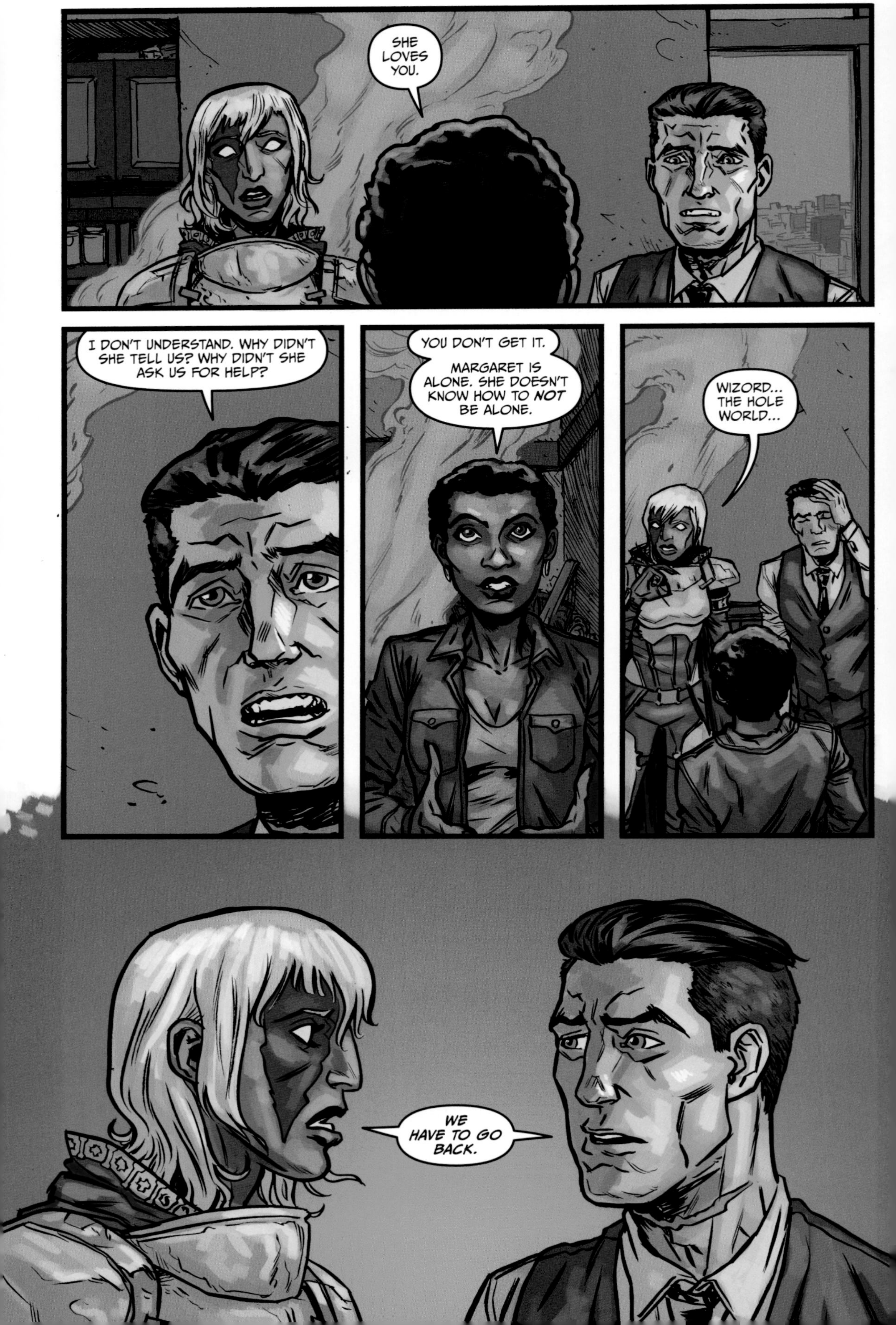
SHE LOVES YOU.
I DON'T UNDERSTAND. WHY DIDN'T SHE TELL US? WHY DIDN'T SHE ASK US FOR HELP?
YOU DON'T GET IT.
MARGARET IS ALONE. SHE DOESN'T KNOW HOW TO *NOT* BE ALONE.
WIZORD... THE HOLE WORLD...
WE HAVE TO GO BACK.

TWENTY-TWO

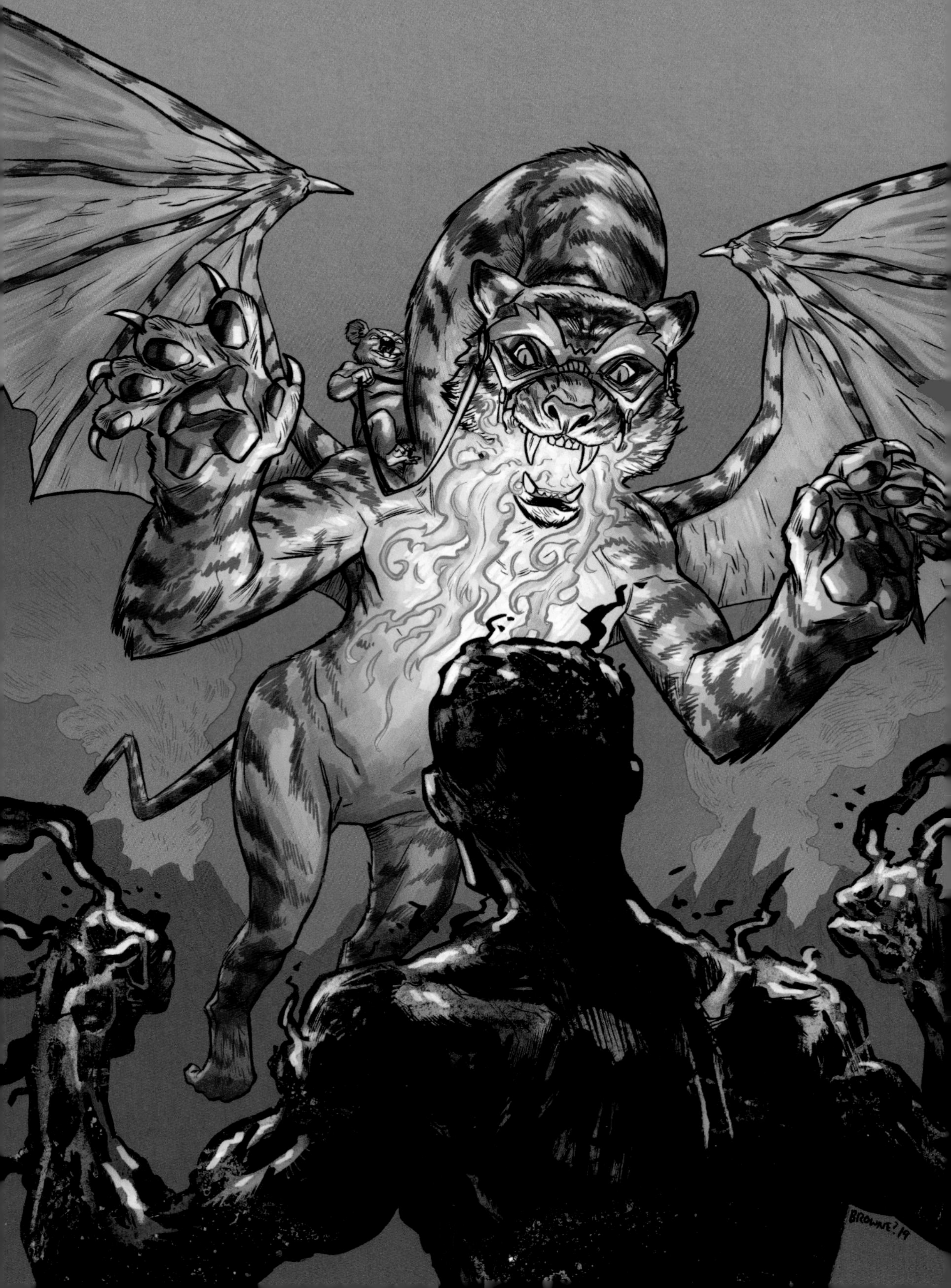
BROWNE '19

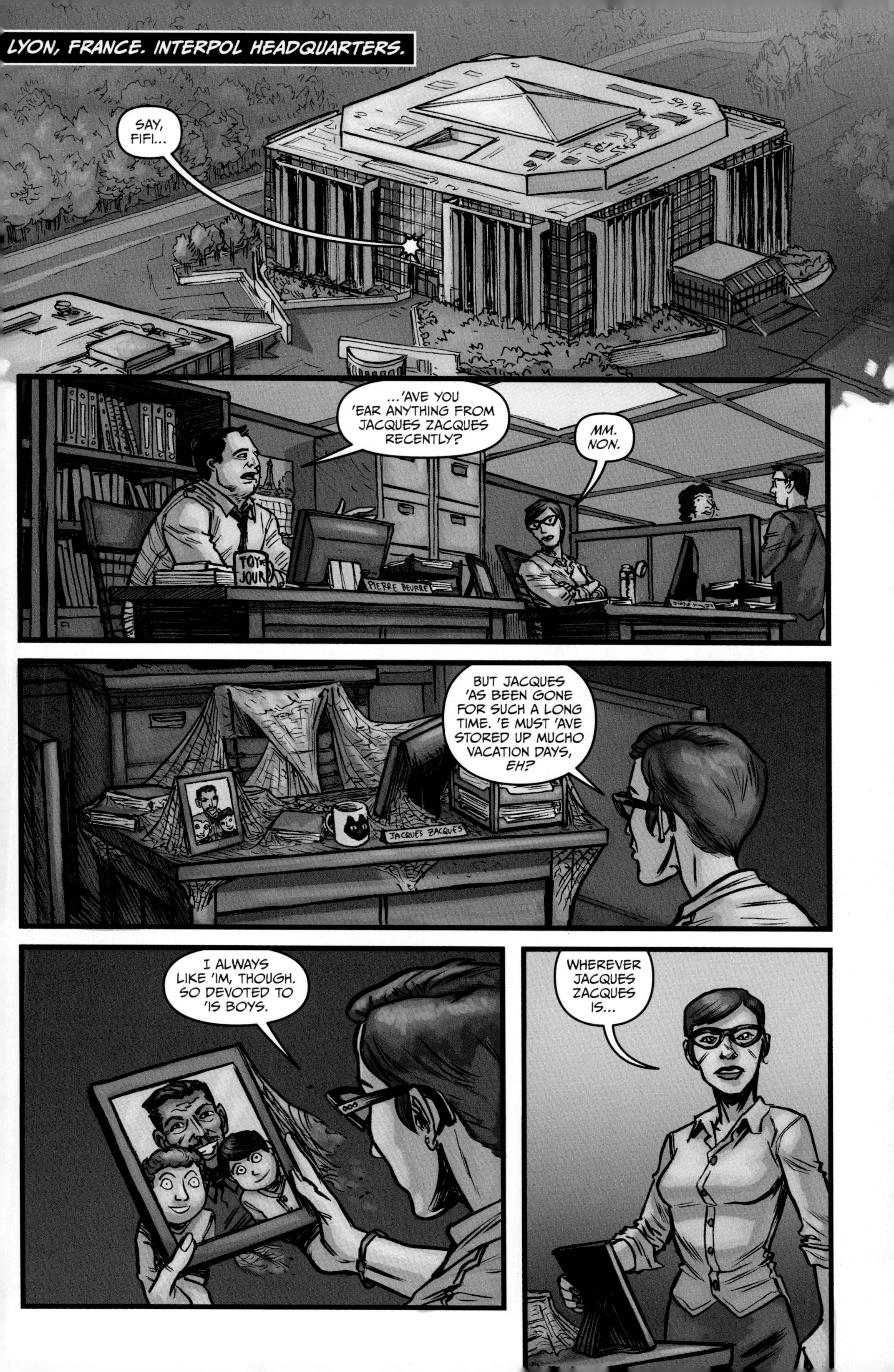
LYON, FRANCE. INTERPOL HEADQUARTERS.
SAY, FIFI...
...'AVE YOU 'EAR ANYTHING FROM JACQUES ZACQUES RECENTLY?
MM. NON.
PIERRE BEURRE
BUT JACQUES 'AS BEEN GONE FOR SUCH A LONG TIME. 'E MUST 'AVE STORED UP MUCHO VACATION DAYS, EH?
JACQUES ZACQUES
I ALWAYS LIKE 'IM, THOUGH. SO DEVOTED TO 'IS BOYS.
WHEREVER JACQUES ZACQUES IS...

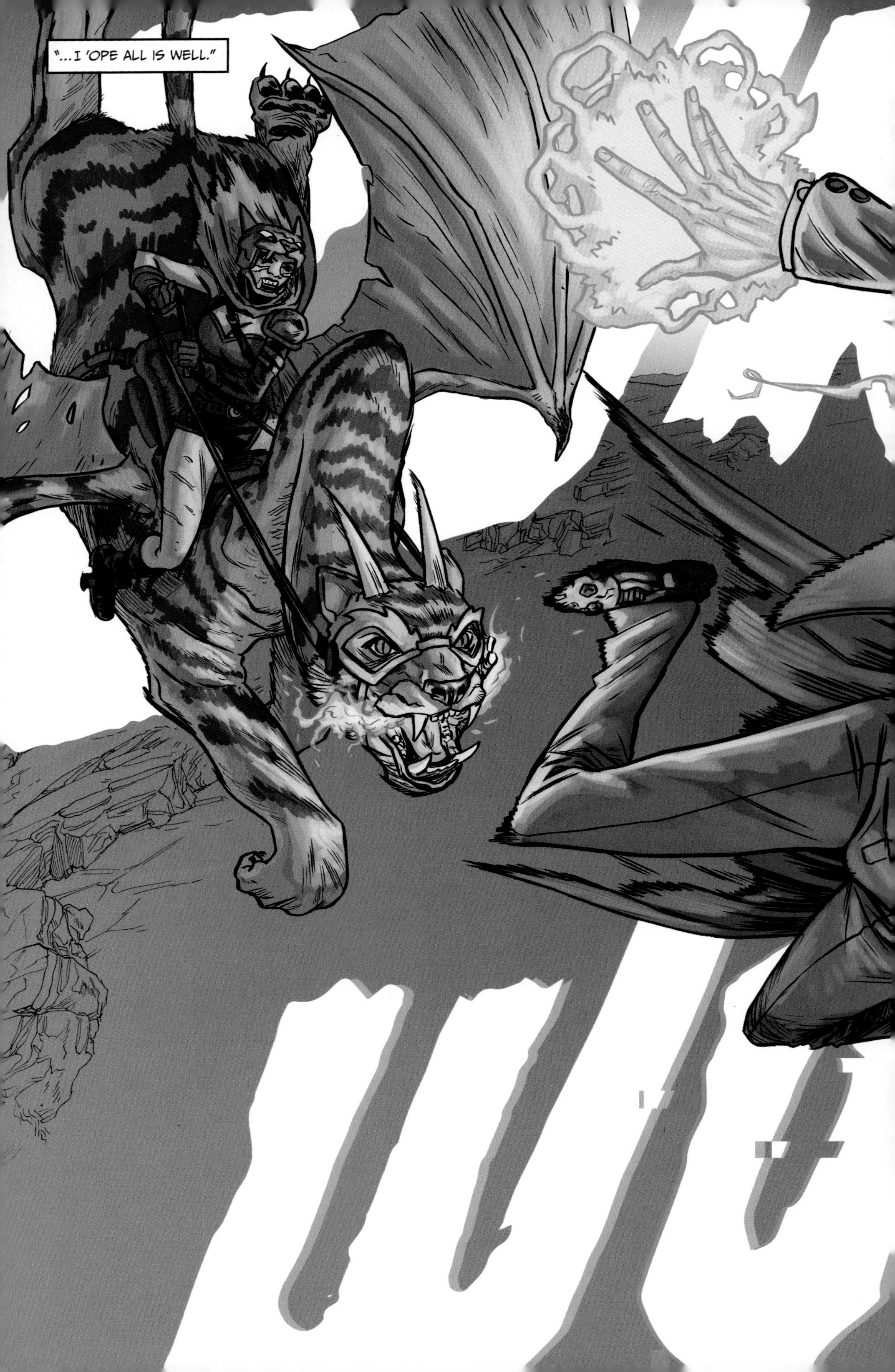
"...I 'OPE ALL IS WELL."

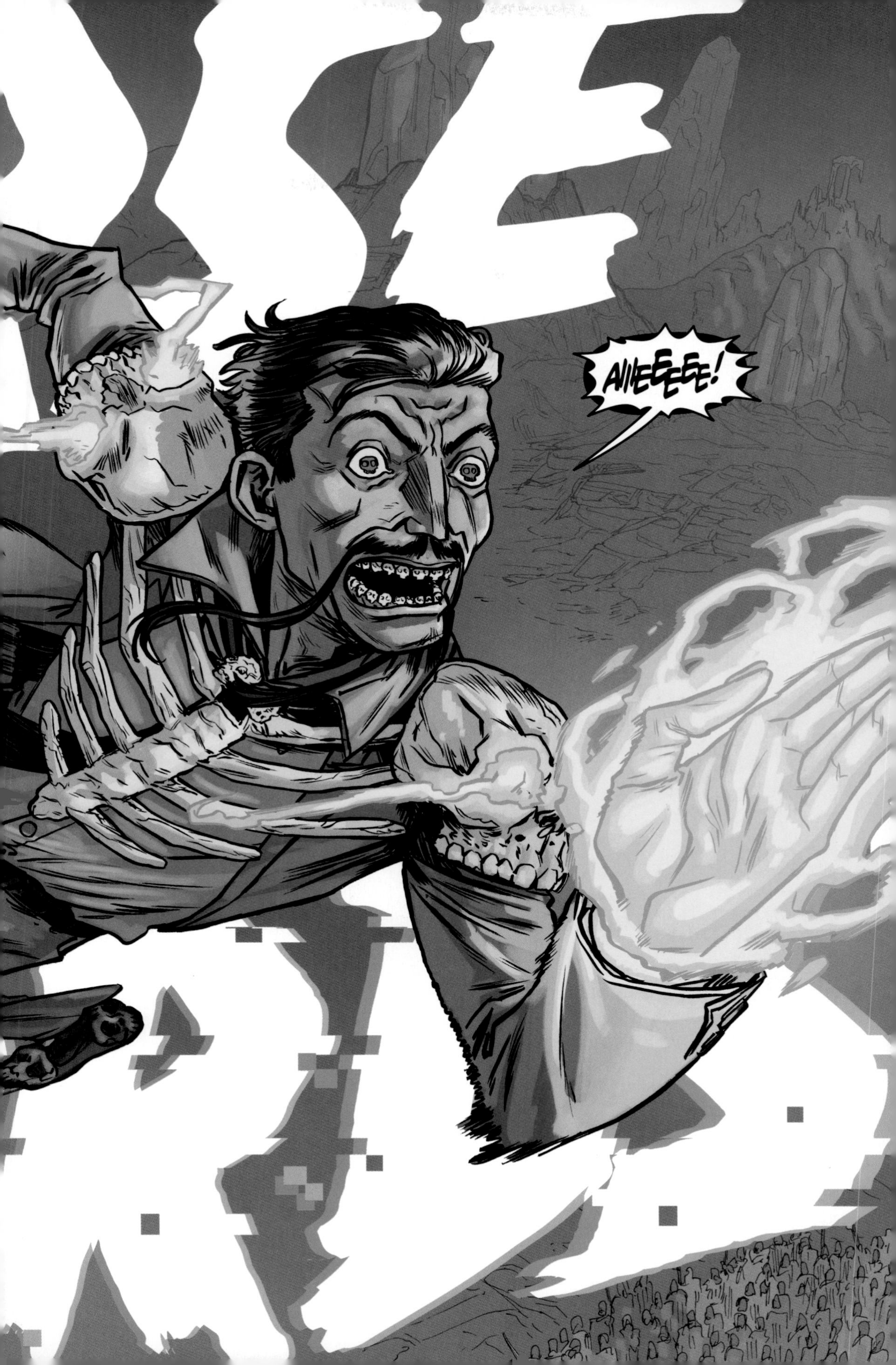
AIIIEEEEEE!

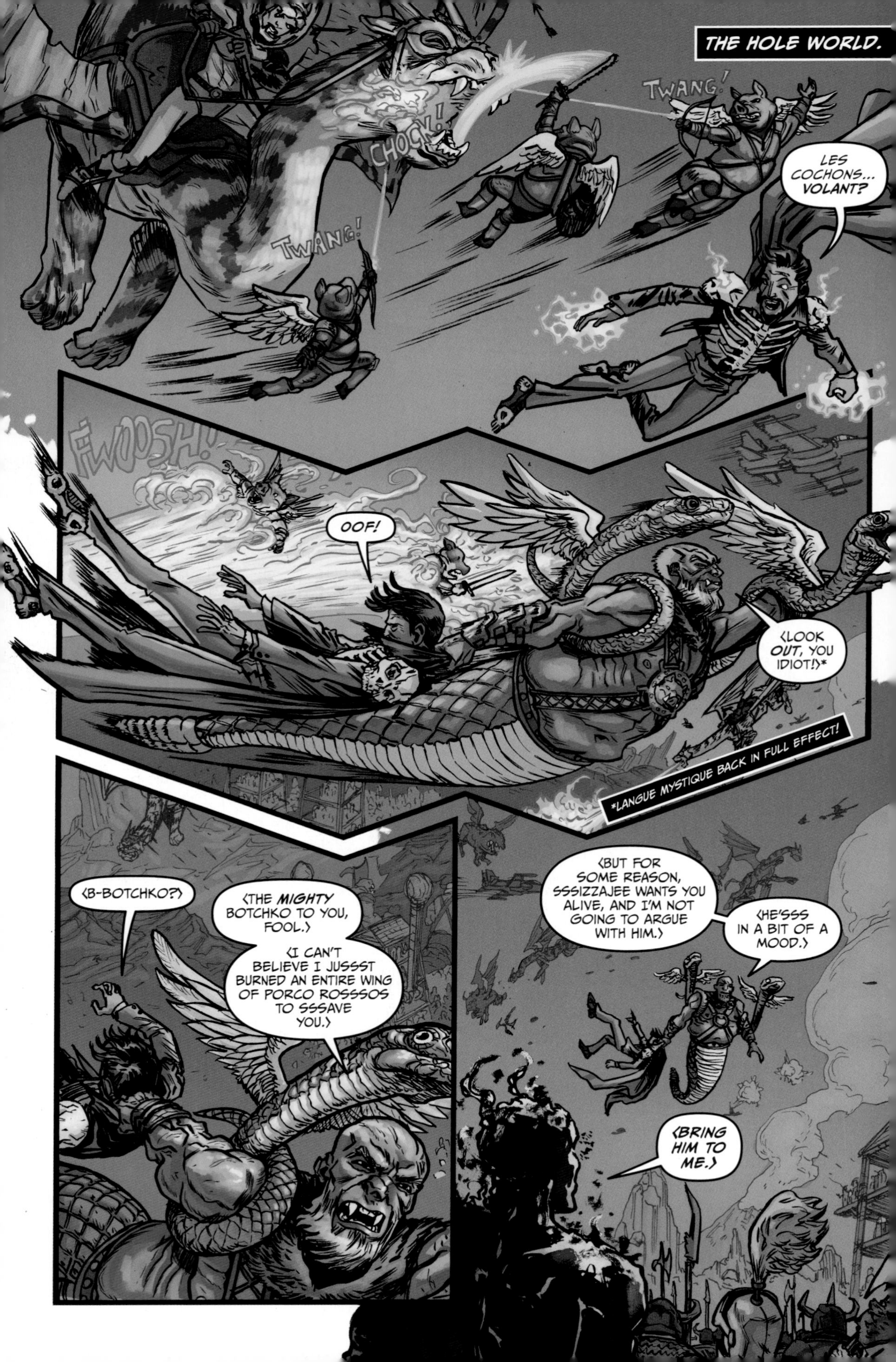
THE HOLE WORLD.
CHOCK!
TWANG!
TWANG!
LES COCHONS... VOLANT?
FWOOSH!
OOF!
‹LOOK OUT, YOU IDIOT!›*
*LANGUE MYSTIQUE BACK IN FULL EFFECT!
‹B-BOTCHKO?›
‹THE *MIGHTY* BOTCHKO TO YOU, FOOL.›
‹I CAN'T BELIEVE I JUSSST BURNED AN ENTIRE WING OF PORCO ROSSSOS TO SSSAVE YOU.›
‹BUT FOR SOME REASON, SSSIZZAJEE WANTS YOU ALIVE, AND I'M NOT GOING TO ARGUE WITH HIM.›
‹HE'SSS IN A BIT OF A MOOD.›
‹*BRING HIM TO ME.*›

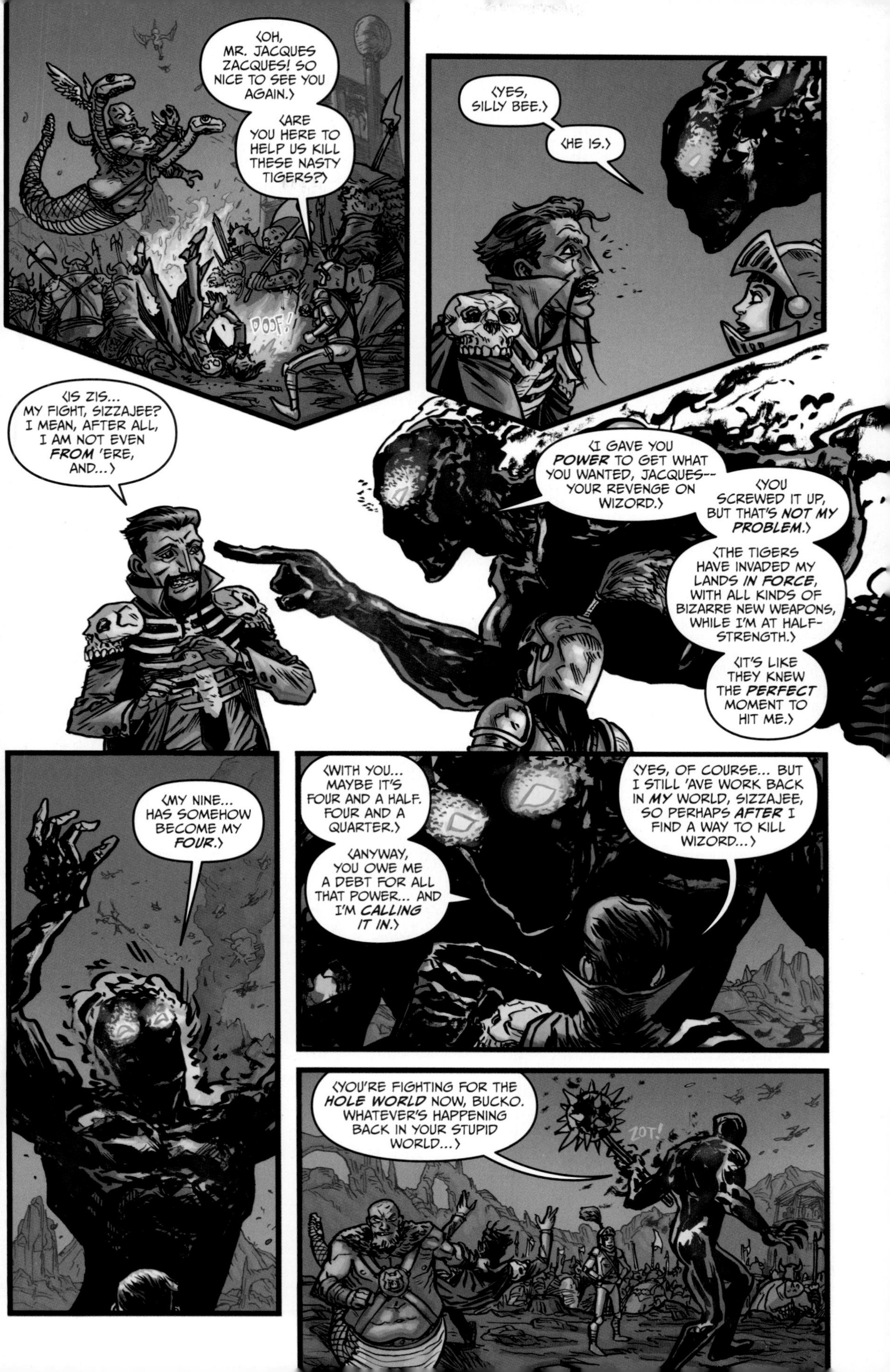

‹OH, MR. JACQUES ZACQUES! SO NICE TO SEE YOU AGAIN.›
‹ARE YOU HERE TO HELP US KILL THESE NASTY TIGERS?›
DOOF!
‹YES, SILLY BEE.›
‹HE IS.›
‹IS ZIS... MY FIGHT, SIZZAJEE? I MEAN, AFTER ALL, I AM NOT EVEN FROM 'ERE, AND...›
‹I GAVE YOU POWER TO GET WHAT YOU WANTED, JACQUES-- YOUR REVENGE ON WIZORD.›
‹YOU SCREWED IT UP, BUT THAT'S NOT MY PROBLEM.›
‹THE TIGERS HAVE INVADED MY LANDS IN FORCE, WITH ALL KINDS OF BIZARRE NEW WEAPONS, WHILE I'M AT HALF-STRENGTH.›
‹IT'S LIKE THEY KNEW THE PERFECT MOMENT TO HIT ME.›
‹MY NINE... HAS SOMEHOW BECOME MY FOUR.›
‹WITH YOU... MAYBE IT'S FOUR AND A HALF. FOUR AND A QUARTER.›
‹ANYWAY, YOU OWE ME A DEBT FOR ALL THAT POWER... AND I'M CALLING IT IN.›
‹YES, OF COURSE... BUT I STILL 'AVE WORK BACK IN MY WORLD, SIZZAJEE, SO PERHAPS AFTER I FIND A WAY TO KILL WIZORD...›
‹YOU'RE FIGHTING FOR THE HOLE WORLD NOW, BUCKO. WHATEVER'S HAPPENING BACK IN YOUR STUPID WORLD...›
ZOT!

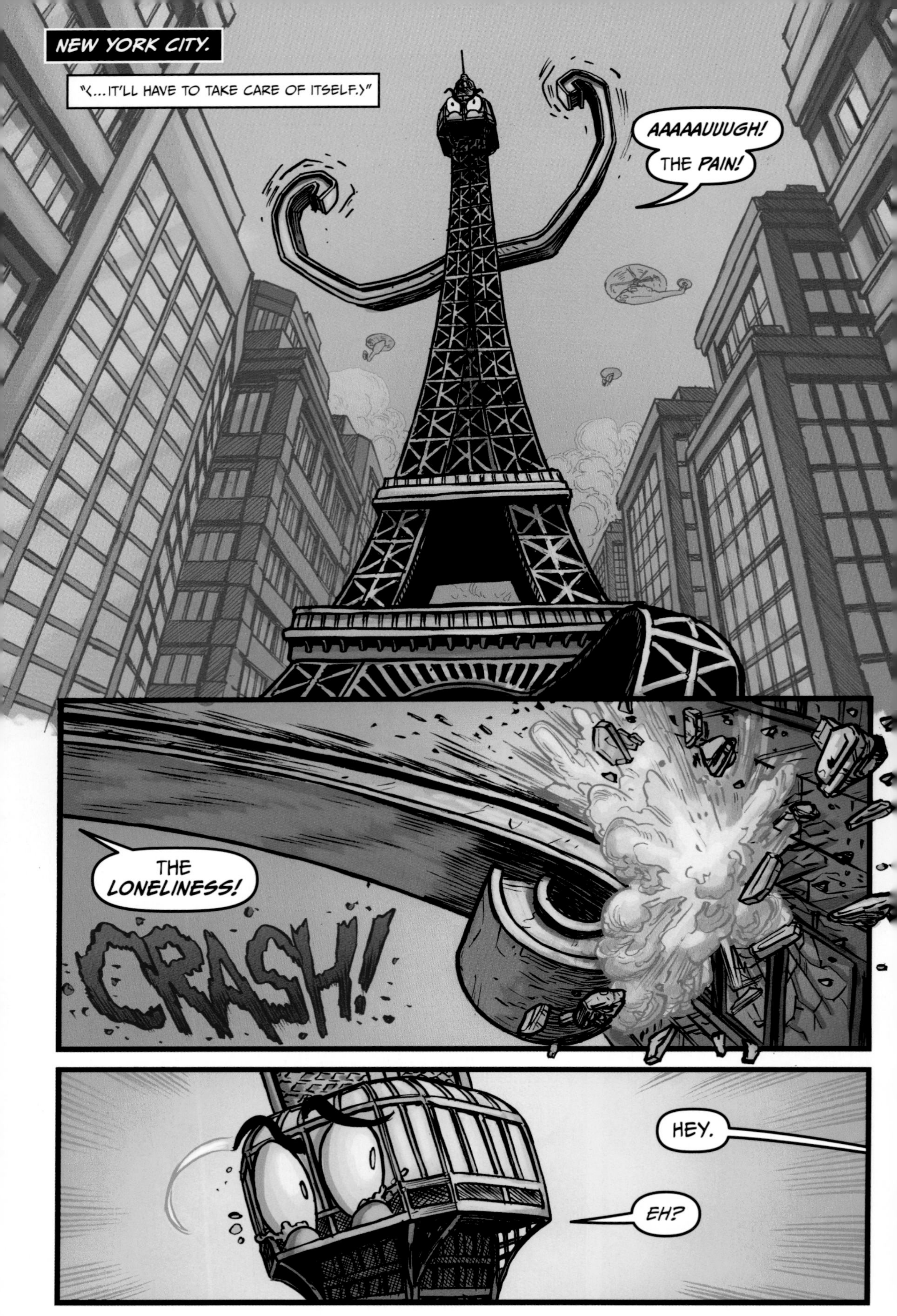
NEW YORK CITY.
"‹...IT'LL HAVE TO TAKE CARE OF ITSELF.›"
AAAAAUUUGH!
THE PAIN!
THE LONELINESS!
CRASH!
HEY.
EH?

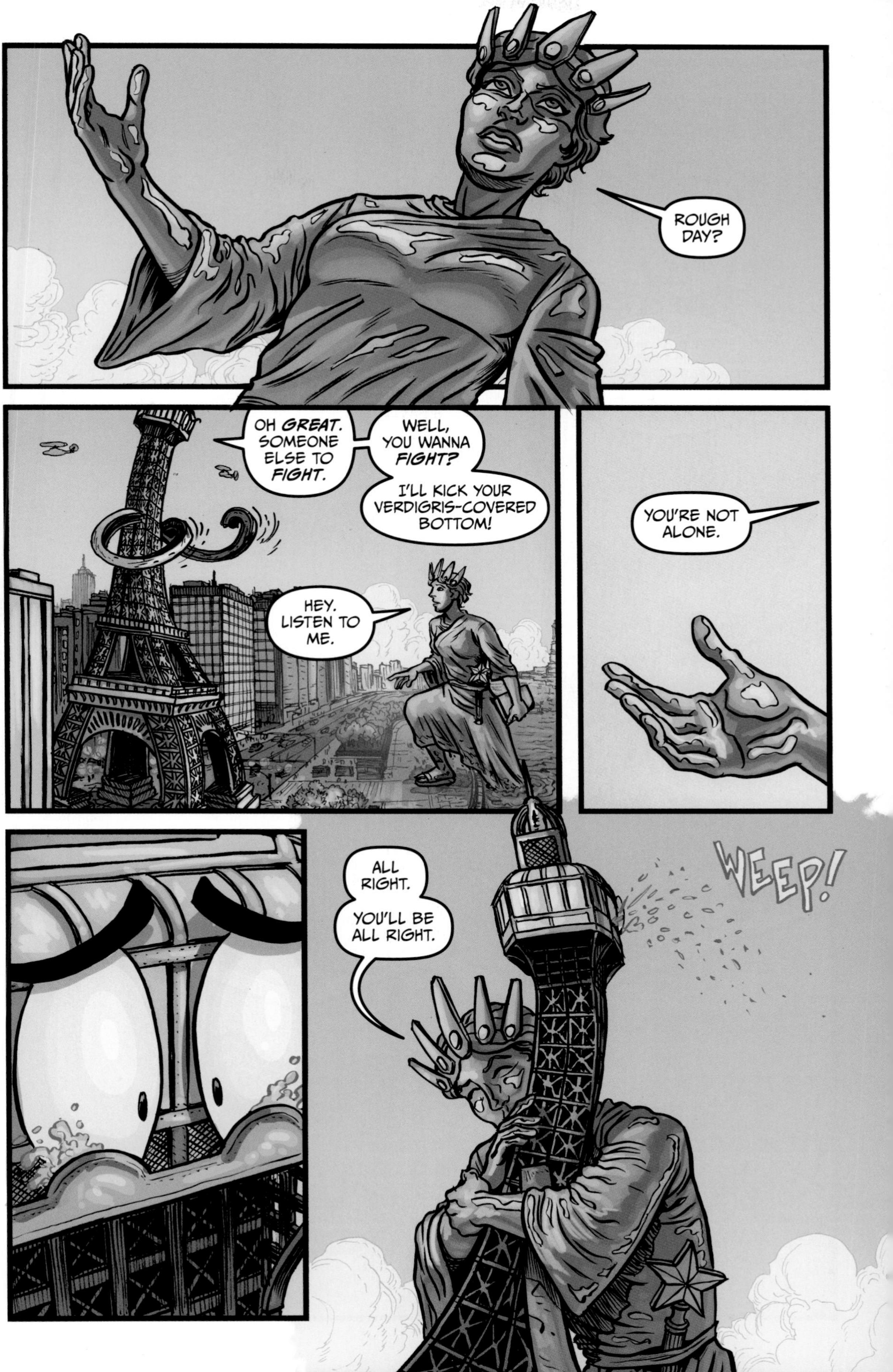
ROUGH DAY?
OH GREAT. SOMEONE ELSE TO FIGHT.
WELL, YOU WANNA FIGHT?
I'LL KICK YOUR VERDIGRIS-COVERED BOTTOM!
HEY. LISTEN TO ME.
YOU'RE NOT ALONE.
ALL RIGHT.
YOU'LL BE ALL RIGHT.
WEEP!

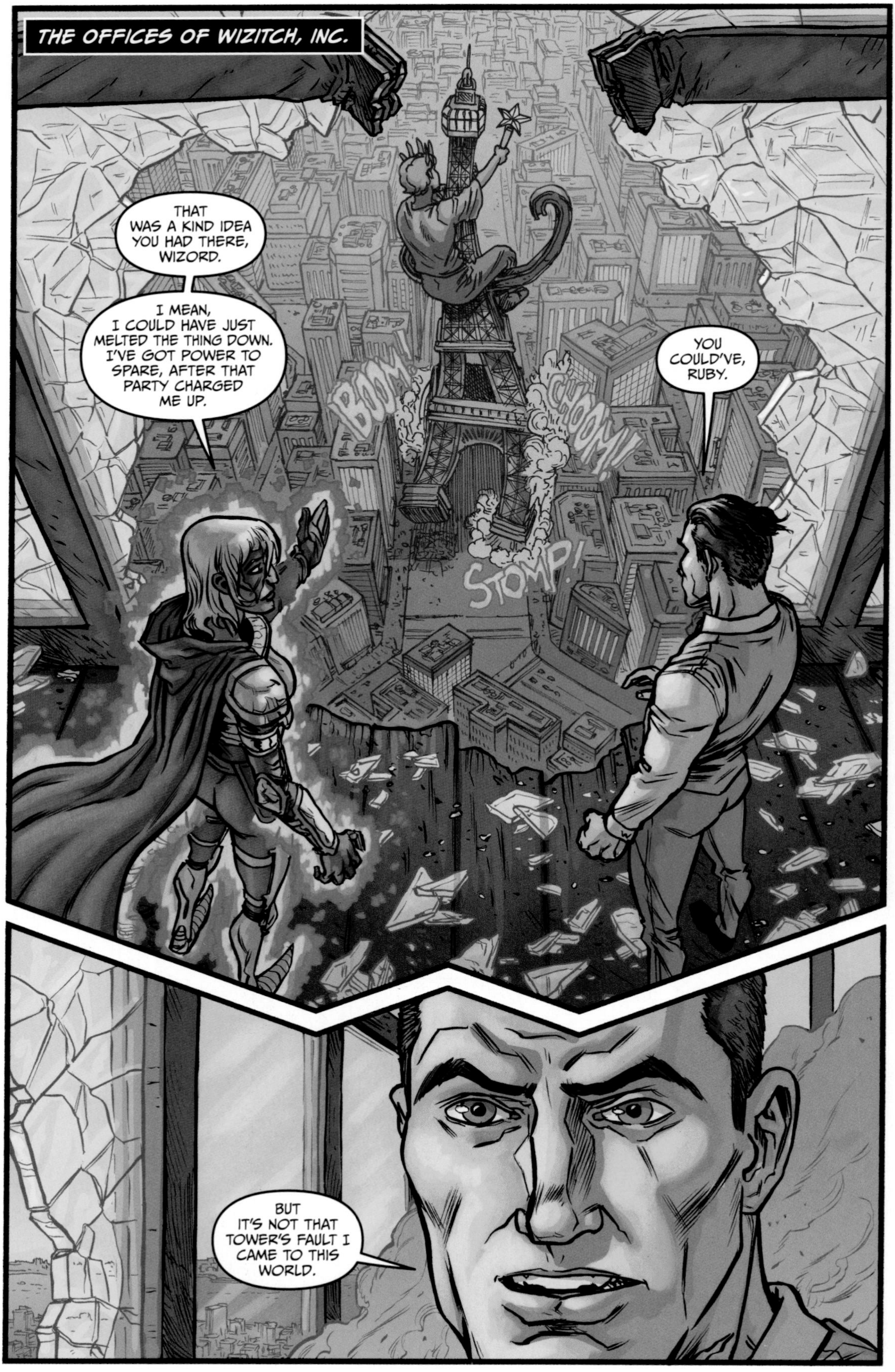
THE OFFICES OF WIZITCH, INC.
THAT WAS A KIND IDEA YOU HAD THERE, WIZORD.
I MEAN, I COULD HAVE JUST MELTED THE THING DOWN. I'VE GOT POWER TO SPARE, AFTER THAT PARTY CHARGED ME UP.
YOU COULD'VE, RUBY.
BOOM!
CHOOM!
STOMP!
BUT IT'S NOT THAT TOWER'S FAULT I CAME TO THIS WORLD.

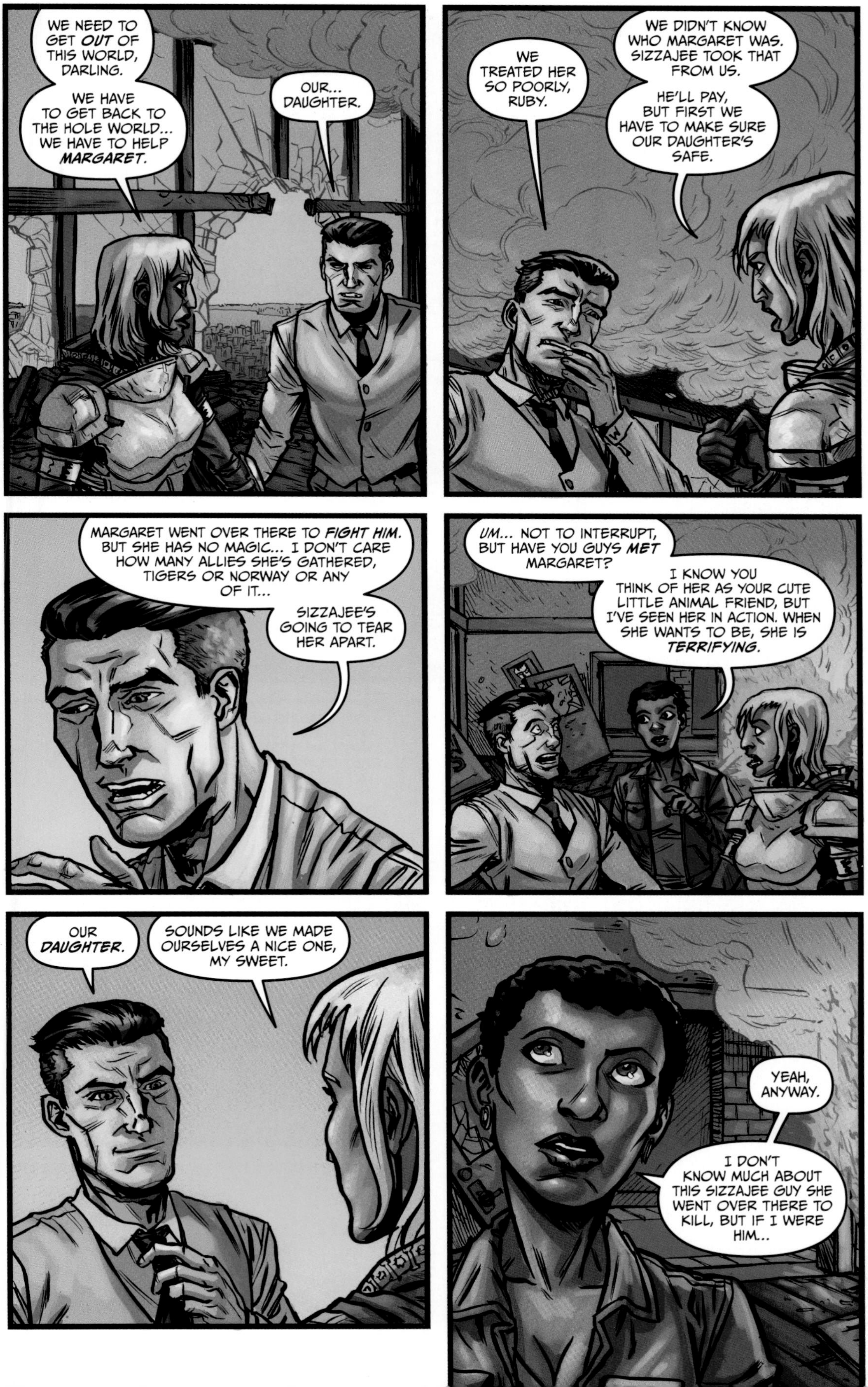
WE NEED TO GET OUT OF THIS WORLD, DARLING.
WE HAVE TO GET BACK TO THE HOLE WORLD... WE HAVE TO HELP MARGARET.
OUR... DAUGHTER.
WE TREATED HER SO POORLY, RUBY.
WE DIDN'T KNOW WHO MARGARET WAS. SIZZAJEE TOOK THAT FROM US.
HE'LL PAY, BUT FIRST WE HAVE TO MAKE SURE OUR DAUGHTER'S SAFE.
MARGARET WENT OVER THERE TO FIGHT HIM. BUT SHE HAS NO MAGIC... I DON'T CARE HOW MANY ALLIES SHE'S GATHERED, TIGERS OR NORWAY OR ANY OF IT...
SIZZAJEE'S GOING TO TEAR HER APART.
UM... NOT TO INTERRUPT, BUT HAVE YOU GUYS MET MARGARET?
I KNOW YOU THINK OF HER AS YOUR CUTE LITTLE ANIMAL FRIEND, BUT I'VE SEEN HER IN ACTION. WHEN SHE WANTS TO BE, SHE IS TERRIFYING.
OUR DAUGHTER.
SOUNDS LIKE WE MADE OURSELVES A NICE ONE, MY SWEET.
YEAH, ANYWAY.
I DON'T KNOW MUCH ABOUT THIS SIZZAJEE GUY SHE WENT OVER THERE TO KILL, BUT IF I WERE HIM...

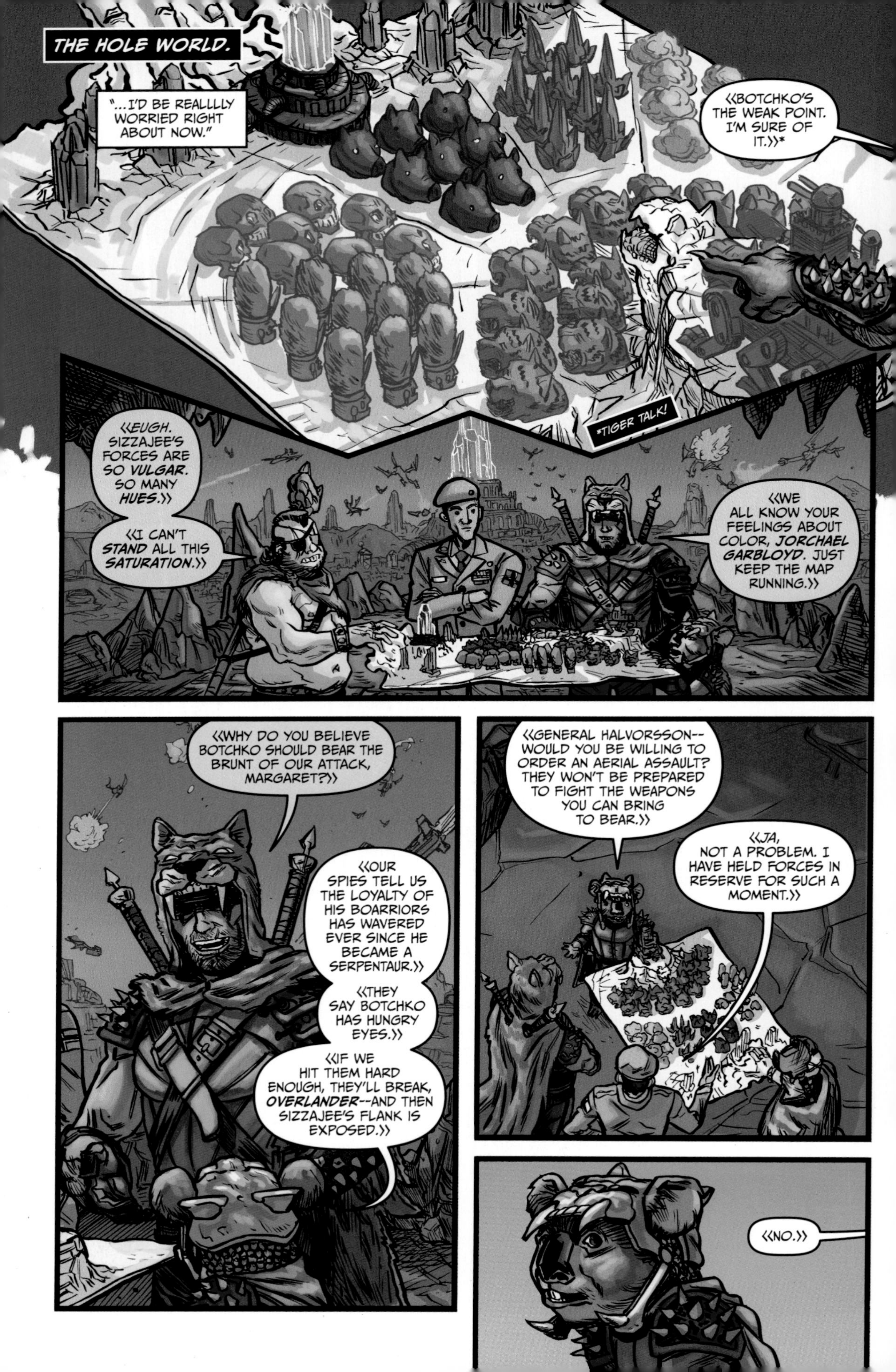
THE HOLE WORLD.
"...I'D BE REALLLLY WORRIED RIGHT ABOUT NOW."
<<BOTCHKO'S THE WEAK POINT. I'M SURE OF IT.>>*
*TIGER TALK!
<<EUGH. SIZZAJEE'S FORCES ARE SO VULGAR. SO MANY HUES.>>
<<I CAN'T STAND ALL THIS SATURATION.>>
<<WE ALL KNOW YOUR FEELINGS ABOUT COLOR, JORCHAEL GARBLOYD. JUST KEEP THE MAP RUNNING.>>
<<WHY DO YOU BELIEVE BOTCHKO SHOULD BEAR THE BRUNT OF OUR ATTACK, MARGARET?>>
<<OUR SPIES TELL US THE LOYALTY OF HIS BOARRIORS HAS WAVERED EVER SINCE HE BECAME A SERPENTAUR.>>
<<THEY SAY BOTCHKO HAS HUNGRY EYES.>>
<<IF WE HIT THEM HARD ENOUGH, THEY'LL BREAK, OVERLANDER--AND THEN SIZZAJEE'S FLANK IS EXPOSED.>>
<<GENERAL HALVORSSON--WOULD YOU BE WILLING TO ORDER AN AERIAL ASSAULT? THEY WON'T BE PREPARED TO FIGHT THE WEAPONS YOU CAN BRING TO BEAR.>>
<<JA, NOT A PROBLEM. I HAVE HELD FORCES IN RESERVE FOR SUCH A MOMENT.>>
<<NO.>>

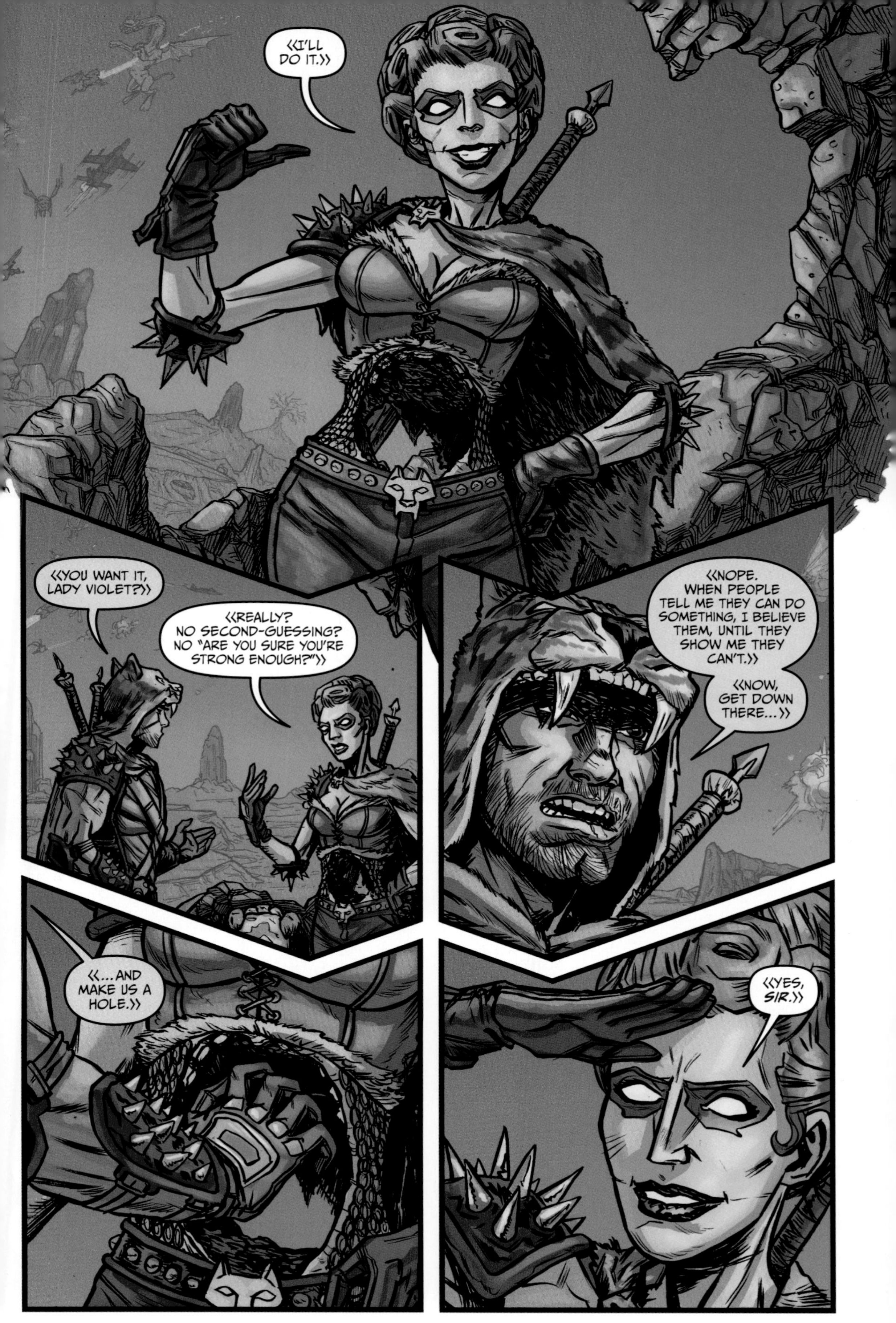

<<I'LL DO IT.>>
<<YOU WANT IT, LADY VIOLET?>>
<<REALLY? NO SECOND-GUESSING? NO "ARE YOU SURE YOU'RE STRONG ENOUGH?">>
<<NOPE. WHEN PEOPLE TELL ME THEY CAN DO SOMETHING, I BELIEVE THEM, UNTIL THEY SHOW ME THEY CAN'T.>>
<<NOW, GET DOWN THERE...>>
<<...AND MAKE US A HOLE.>>
<<YES, SIR.>>

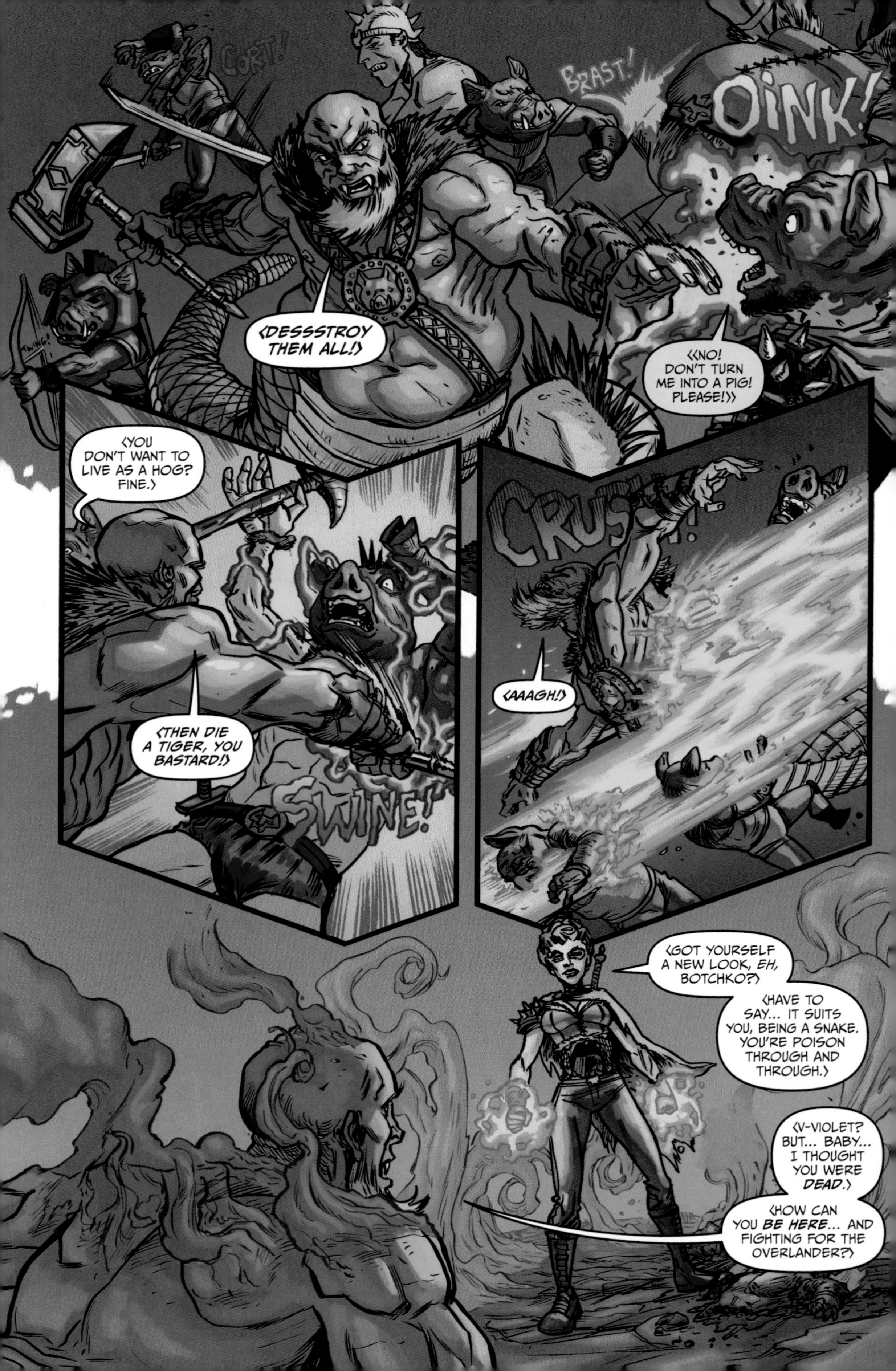
CORT!
BRAST!
OINK!
<DESSSTROY THEM ALL!>
<<NO! DON'T TURN ME INTO A PIG! PLEASE!>>
TWING!
<YOU DON'T WANT TO LIVE AS A HOG? FINE.>
<THEN DIE A TIGER, YOU BASTARD!>
SWINE!
CRUSH!
<AAAGH!>
<GOT YOURSELF A NEW LOOK, EH, BOTCHKO?>
<HAVE TO SAY... IT SUITS YOU, BEING A SNAKE. YOU'RE POISON THROUGH AND THROUGH.>
<V-VIOLET? BUT... BABY... I THOUGHT YOU WERE *DEAD*.>
<HOW CAN YOU ***BE HERE***... AND FIGHTING FOR THE OVERLANDER?>

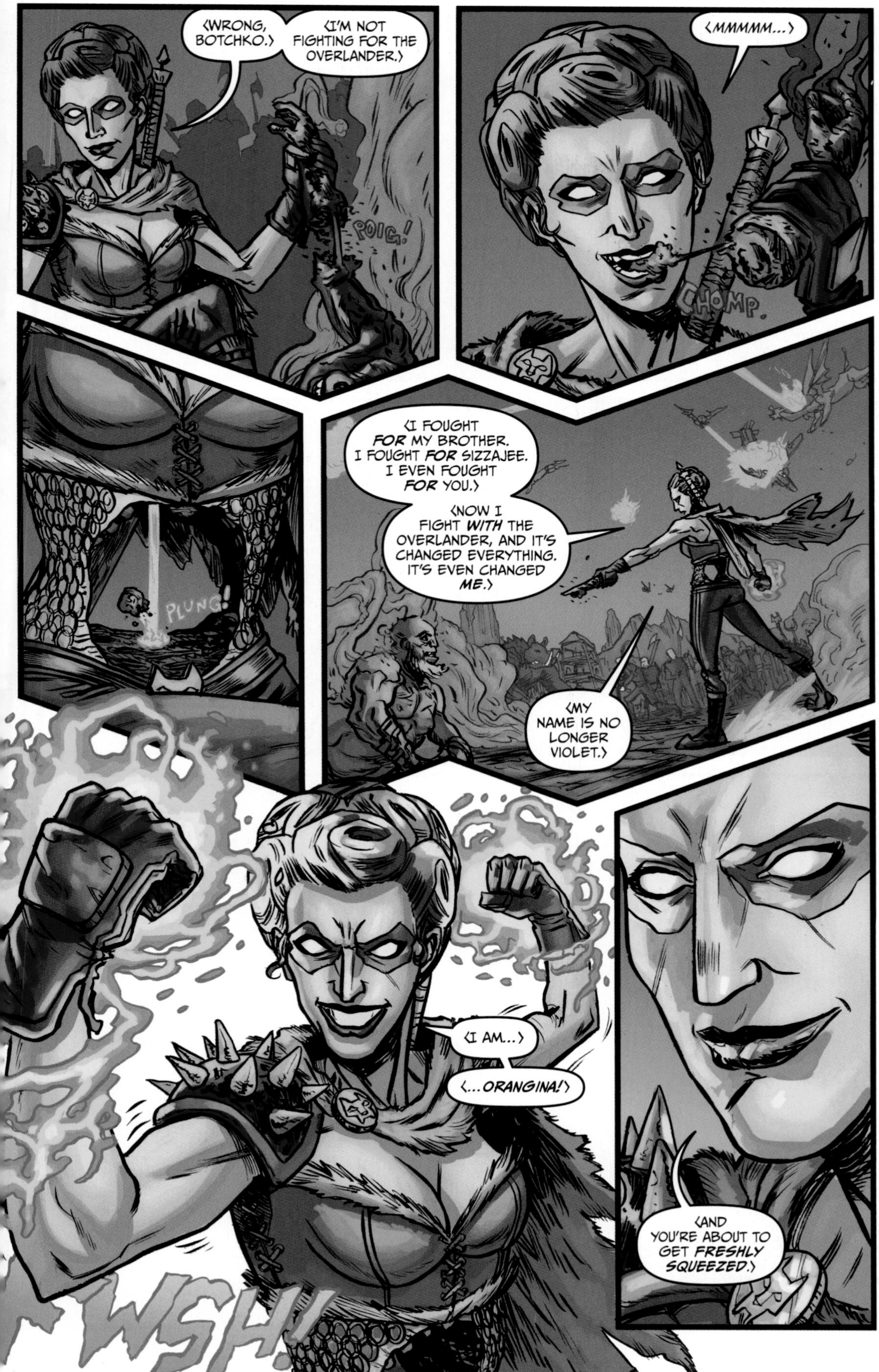
‹WRONG, BOTCHKO.›
‹I'M NOT FIGHTING FOR THE OVERLANDER.›
POIG!
‹MMMMM...›
CHOMP.
PLUNG!
‹I FOUGHT FOR MY BROTHER. I FOUGHT FOR SIZZAJEE. I EVEN FOUGHT FOR YOU.›
‹NOW I FIGHT WITH THE OVERLANDER, AND IT'S CHANGED EVERYTHING. IT'S EVEN CHANGED ME.›
‹MY NAME IS NO LONGER VIOLET.›
‹I AM...›
‹...ORANGINA!›
WSH!
‹AND YOU'RE ABOUT TO GET FRESHLY SQUEEZED.›

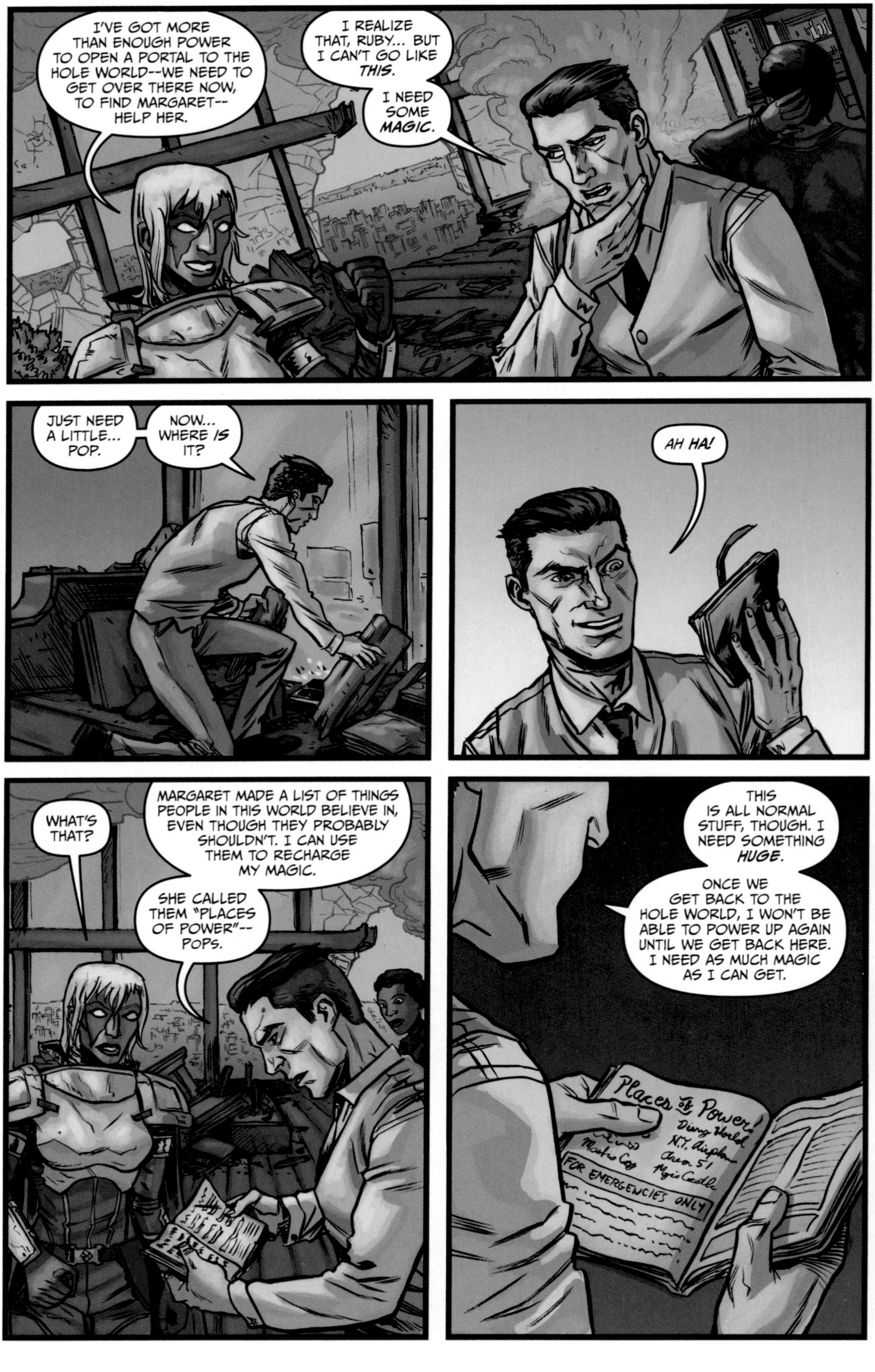
I'VE GOT MORE THAN ENOUGH POWER TO OPEN A PORTAL TO THE HOLE WORLD--WE NEED TO GET OVER THERE NOW, TO FIND MARGARET--HELP HER.
I REALIZE THAT, RUBY... BUT I CAN'T GO LIKE *THIS.*
I NEED SOME *MAGIC.*
JUST NEED A LITTLE... POP.
NOW... WHERE *IS* IT?
AH *HA!*
WHAT'S THAT?
MARGARET MADE A LIST OF THINGS PEOPLE IN THIS WORLD BELIEVE IN, EVEN THOUGH THEY PROBABLY SHOULDN'T. I CAN USE THEM TO RECHARGE MY MAGIC.
SHE CALLED THEM "PLACES OF POWER"--POPS.
THIS IS ALL NORMAL STUFF, THOUGH. I NEED SOMETHING *HUGE.*
ONCE WE GET BACK TO THE HOLE WORLD, I WON'T BE ABLE TO POWER UP AGAIN UNTIL WE GET BACK HERE. I NEED AS MUCH MAGIC AS I CAN GET.
Places of Power!
Disney World
Area 51
Magic Castle
FOR EMERGENCIES ONLY

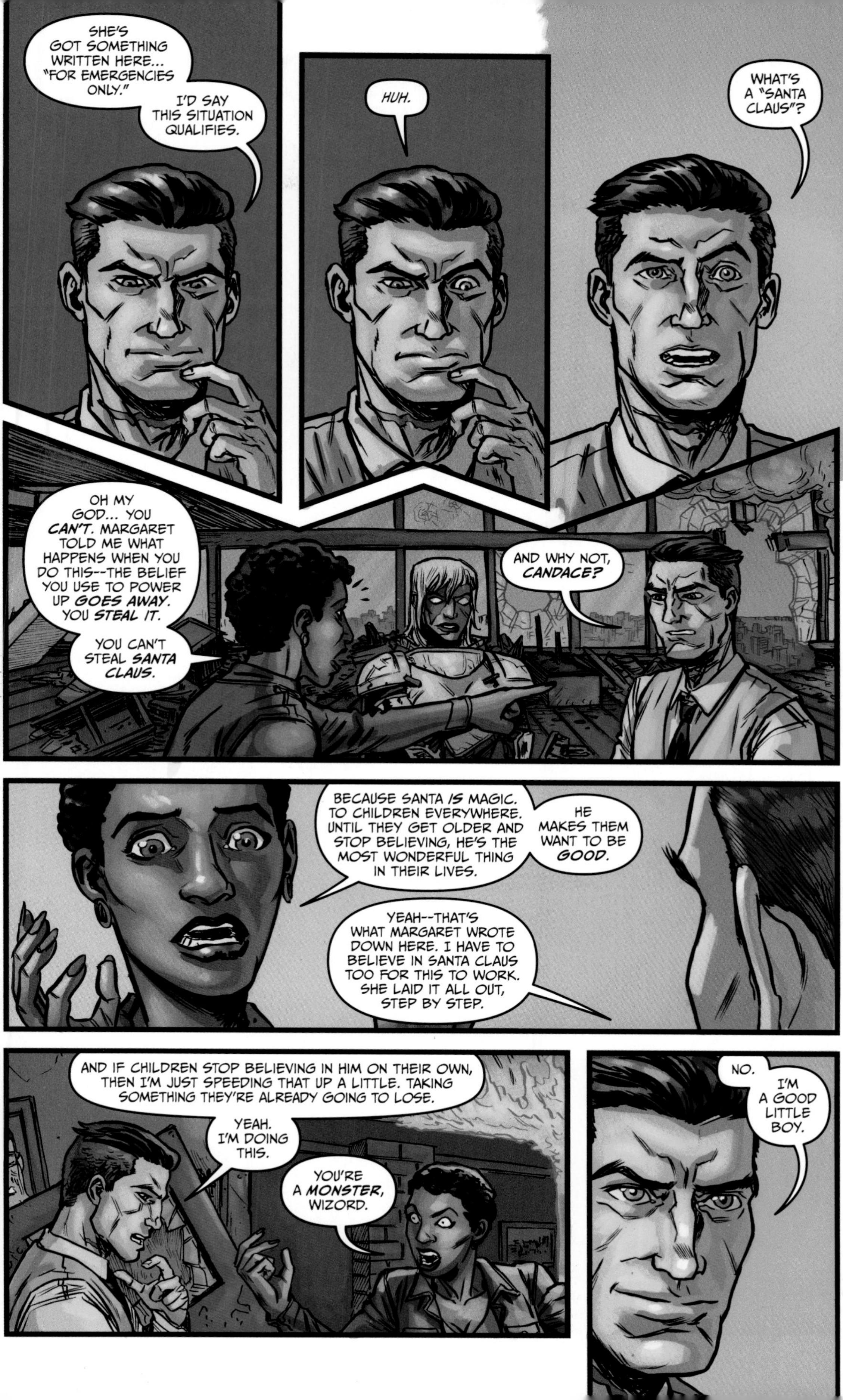
SHE'S GOT SOMETHING WRITTEN HERE... "FOR EMERGENCIES ONLY."
I'D SAY THIS SITUATION QUALIFIES.
HUH.
WHAT'S A "SANTA CLAUS"?
OH MY GOD... YOU CAN'T. MARGARET TOLD ME WHAT HAPPENS WHEN YOU DO THIS--THE BELIEF YOU USE TO POWER UP GOES AWAY. YOU STEAL IT.
YOU CAN'T STEAL SANTA CLAUS.
AND WHY NOT, CANDACE?
BECAUSE SANTA IS MAGIC. TO CHILDREN EVERYWHERE. UNTIL THEY GET OLDER AND STOP BELIEVING, HE'S THE MOST WONDERFUL THING IN THEIR LIVES.
HE MAKES THEM WANT TO BE GOOD.
YEAH--THAT'S WHAT MARGARET WROTE DOWN HERE. I HAVE TO BELIEVE IN SANTA CLAUS TOO FOR THIS TO WORK. SHE LAID IT ALL OUT, STEP BY STEP.
AND IF CHILDREN STOP BELIEVING IN HIM ON THEIR OWN, THEN I'M JUST SPEEDING THAT UP A LITTLE. TAKING SOMETHING THEY'RE ALREADY GOING TO LOSE.
YEAH. I'M DOING THIS.
YOU'RE A MONSTER, WIZORD.
NO.
I'M A GOOD LITTLE BOY.

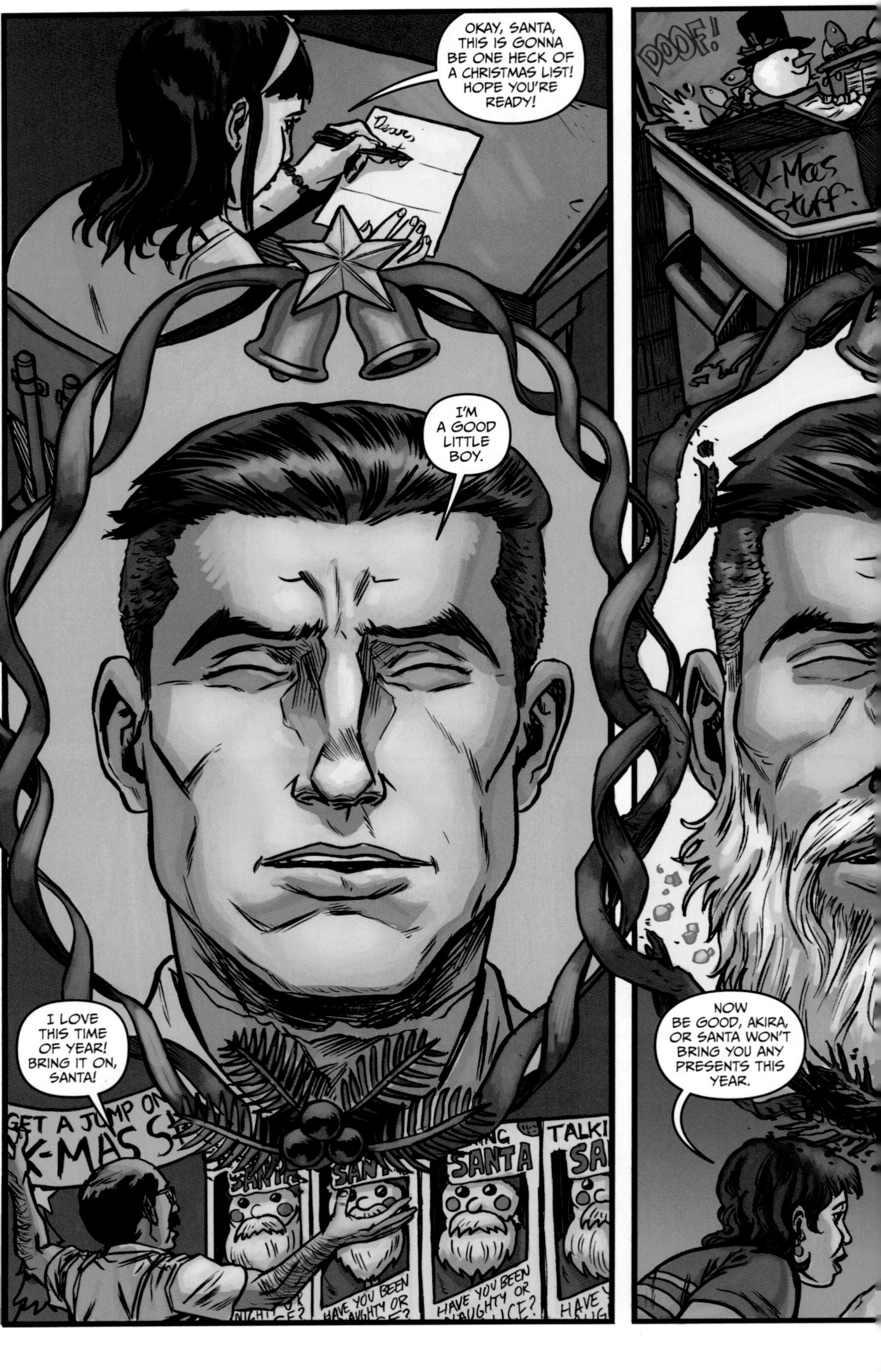
OKAY, SANTA, THIS IS GONNA BE ONE HECK OF A CHRISTMAS LIST! HOPE YOU'RE READY!
Dear,
I'M A GOOD LITTLE BOY.
I LOVE THIS TIME OF YEAR! BRING IT ON, SANTA!
GET A JUMP ON
SANTA
HAVE YOU BEEN
DOOF!
X-Mas Stuff
NOW BE GOOD, AKIRA, OR SANTA WON'T BRING YOU ANY PRESENTS THIS YEAR.

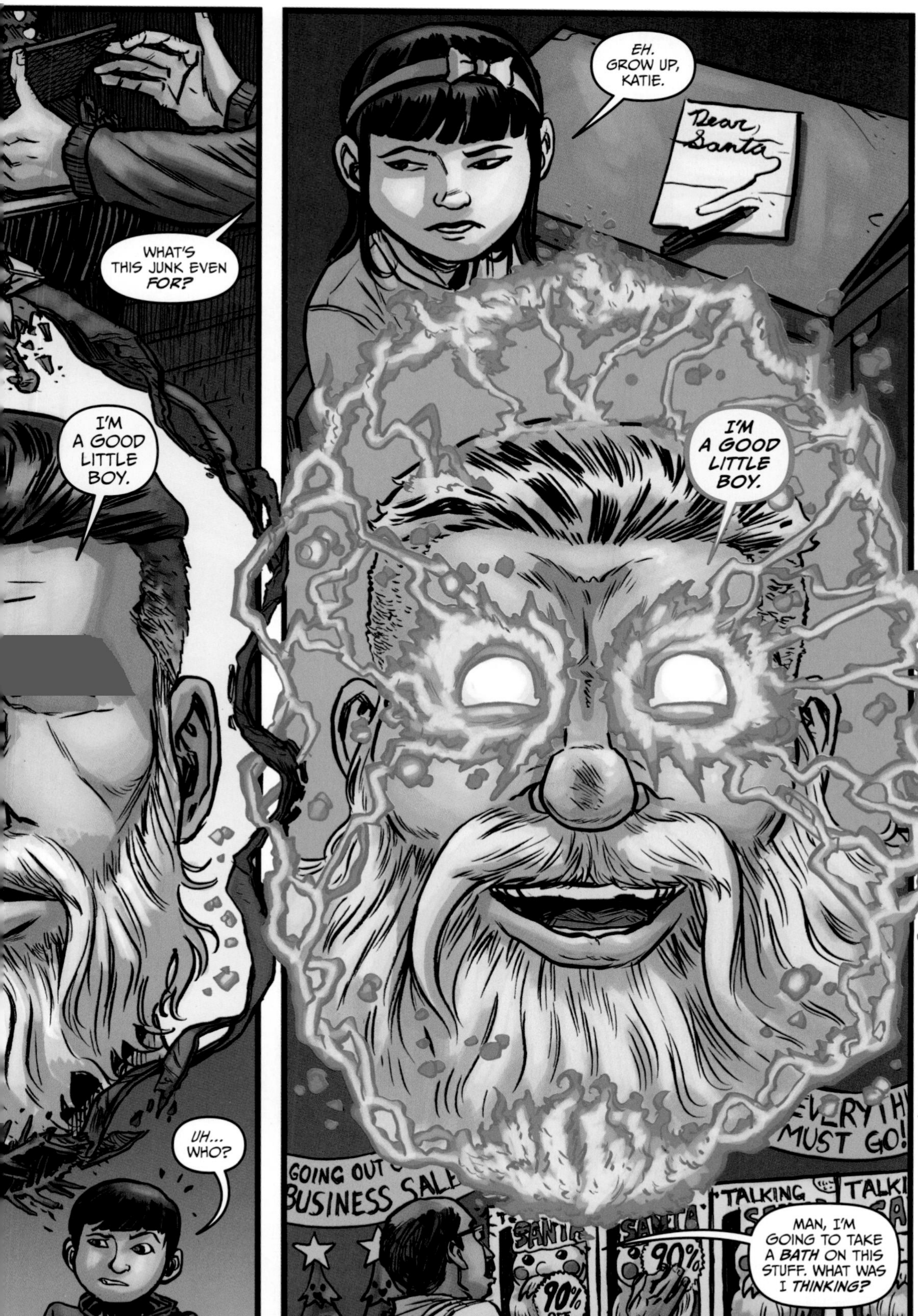
WHAT'S THIS JUNK EVEN *FOR?*
I'M A GOOD LITTLE BOY.
UH... WHO?
EH. GROW UP, KATIE.
Dear Santa
I'M A GOOD LITTLE BOY.
MUST GO!
BUSINESS SALE
TALKING
90% OFF
HAVE YOU BEEN
MAN, I'M GOING TO TAKE A *BATH* ON THIS STUFF. WHAT WAS I *THINKING?*

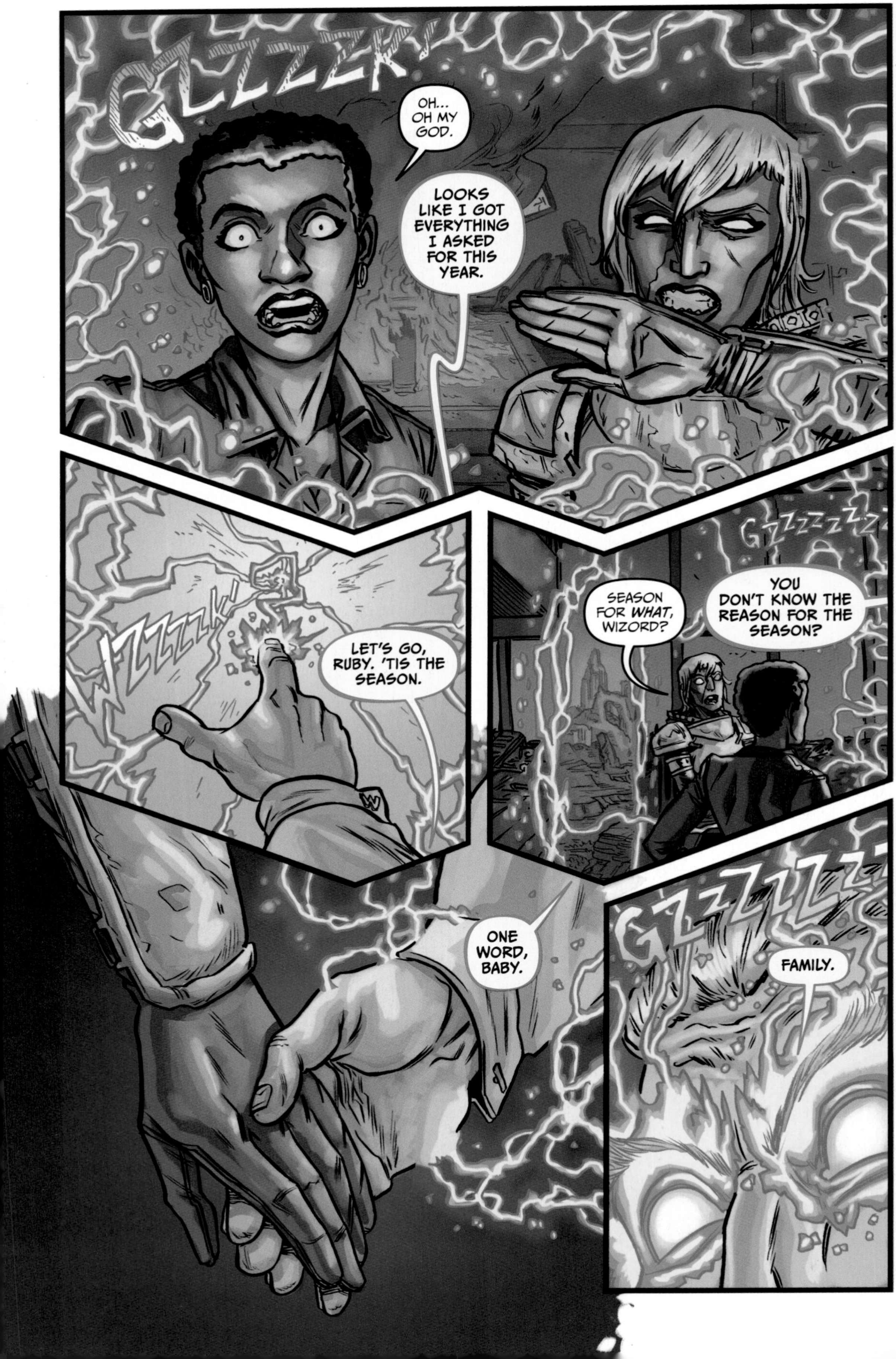
GZZZZK!
OH... OH MY GOD.
LOOKS LIKE I GOT EVERYTHING I ASKED FOR THIS YEAR.
WZZZZZK!
LET'S GO, RUBY. 'TIS THE SEASON.
GZZZZZZZZ
SEASON FOR WHAT, WIZORD?
YOU DON'T KNOW THE REASON FOR THE SEASON?
ONE WORD, BABY.
GZZZZZZZ
FAMILY.

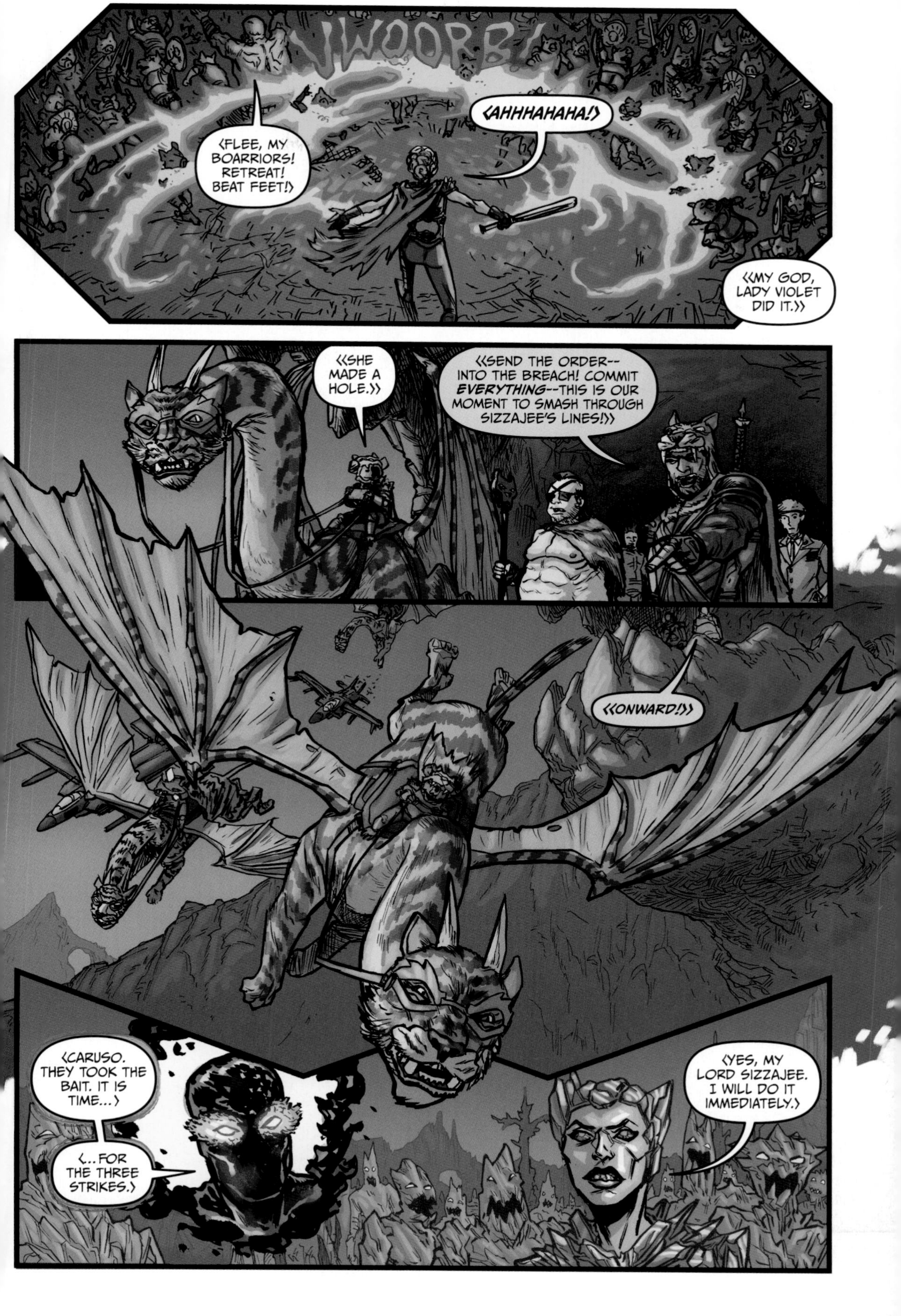
VWOORB!
‹FLEE, MY BOARRIORS! RETREAT! BEAT FEET!›
‹AHHHAHAHA!›
‹‹MY GOD, LADY VIOLET DID IT.››
‹‹SHE MADE A HOLE.››
‹‹SEND THE ORDER-- INTO THE BREACH! COMMIT *EVERYTHING*--THIS IS OUR MOMENT TO SMASH THROUGH SIZZAJEE'S LINES!››
‹‹ONWARD!››
‹CARUSO. THEY TOOK THE BAIT. IT IS TIME...›
‹...FOR THE THREE STRIKES.›
‹YES, MY LORD SIZZAJEE. I WILL DO IT IMMEDIATELY.›

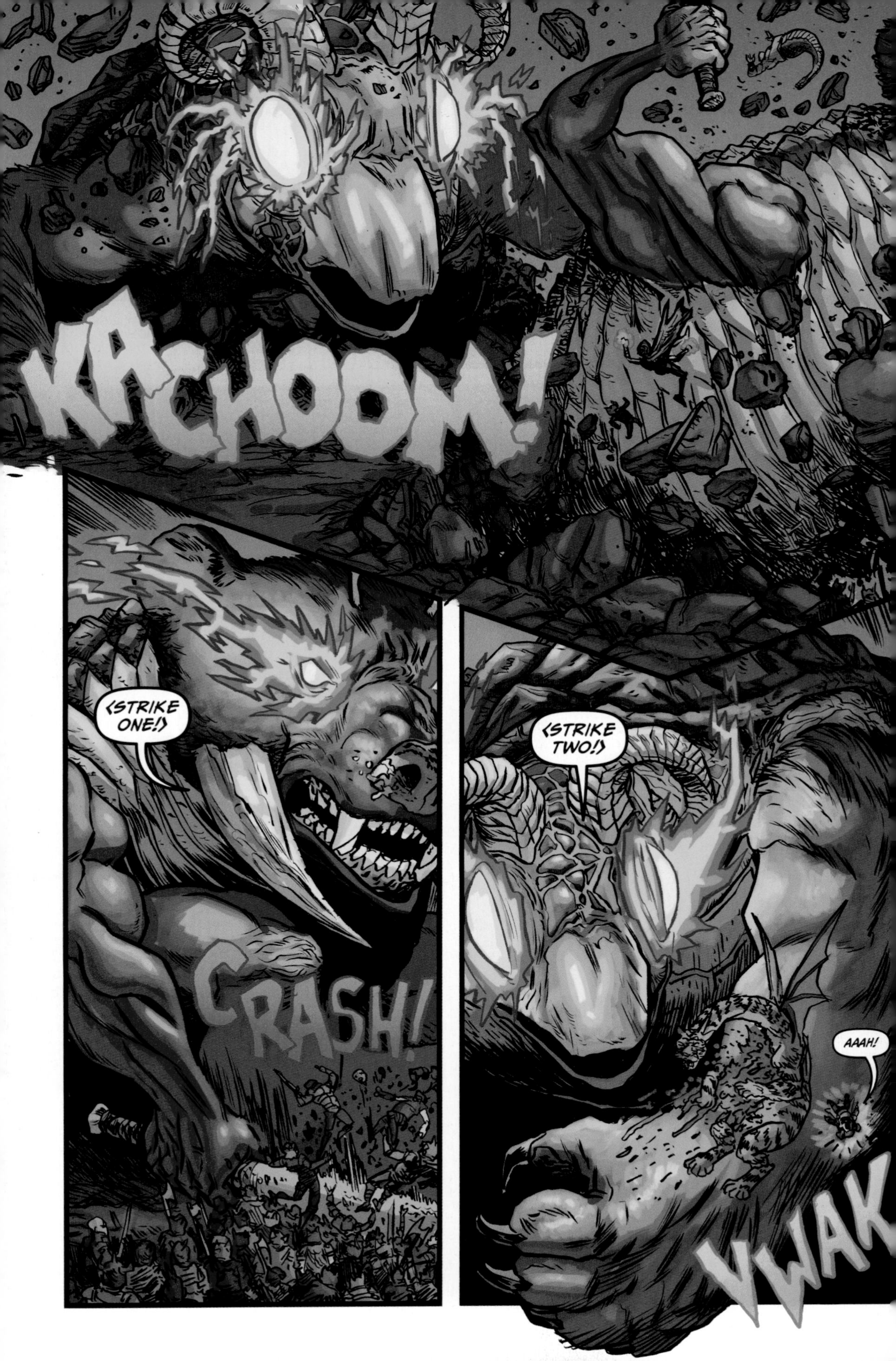

KA-CHOOM!
<STRIKE ONE!>
CRASH!
<STRIKE TWO!>
AAAH!
VWAK

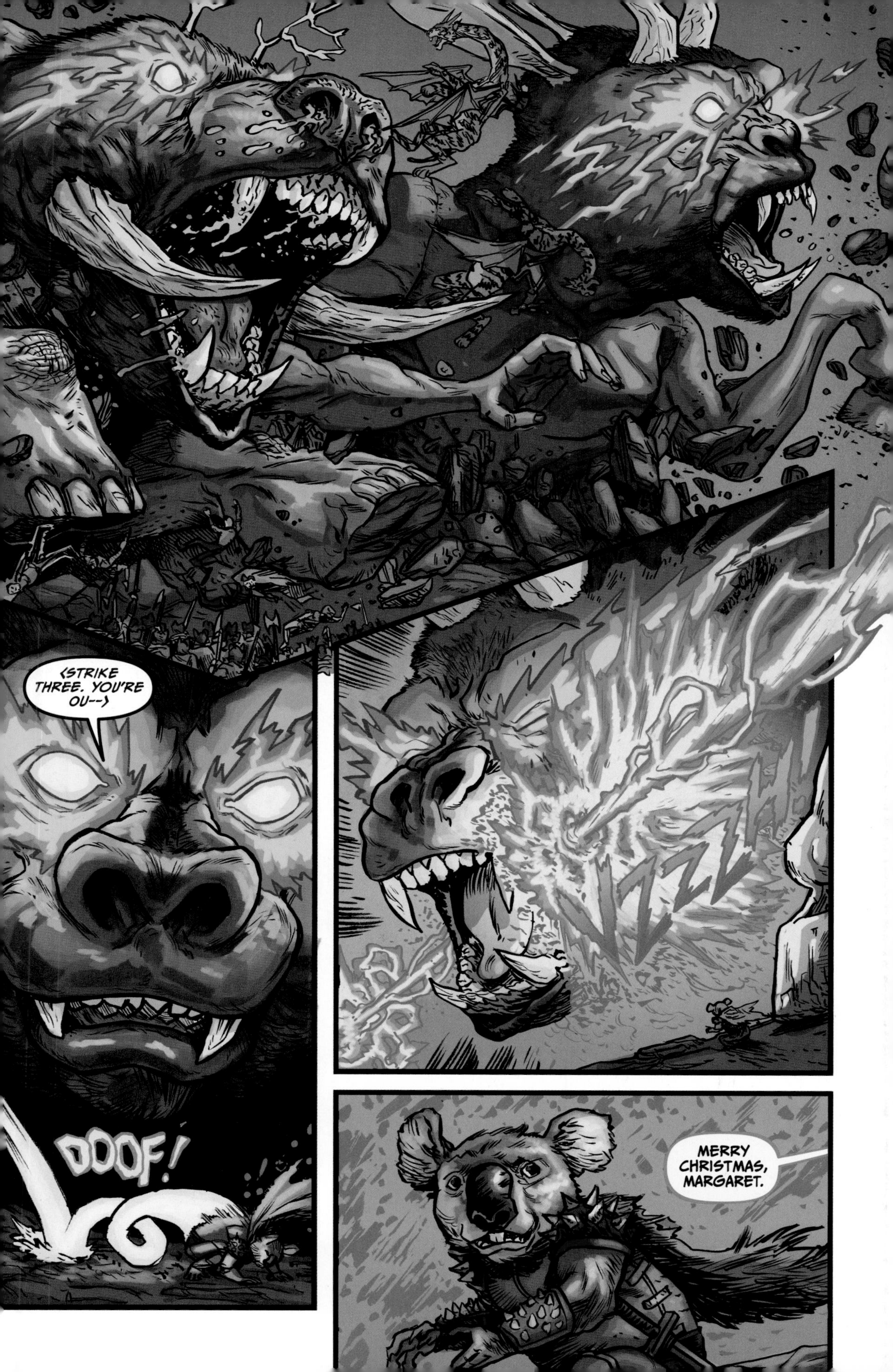
<STRIKE THREE. YOU'RE OU-->
DOOF!
MERRY CHRISTMAS, MARGARET.

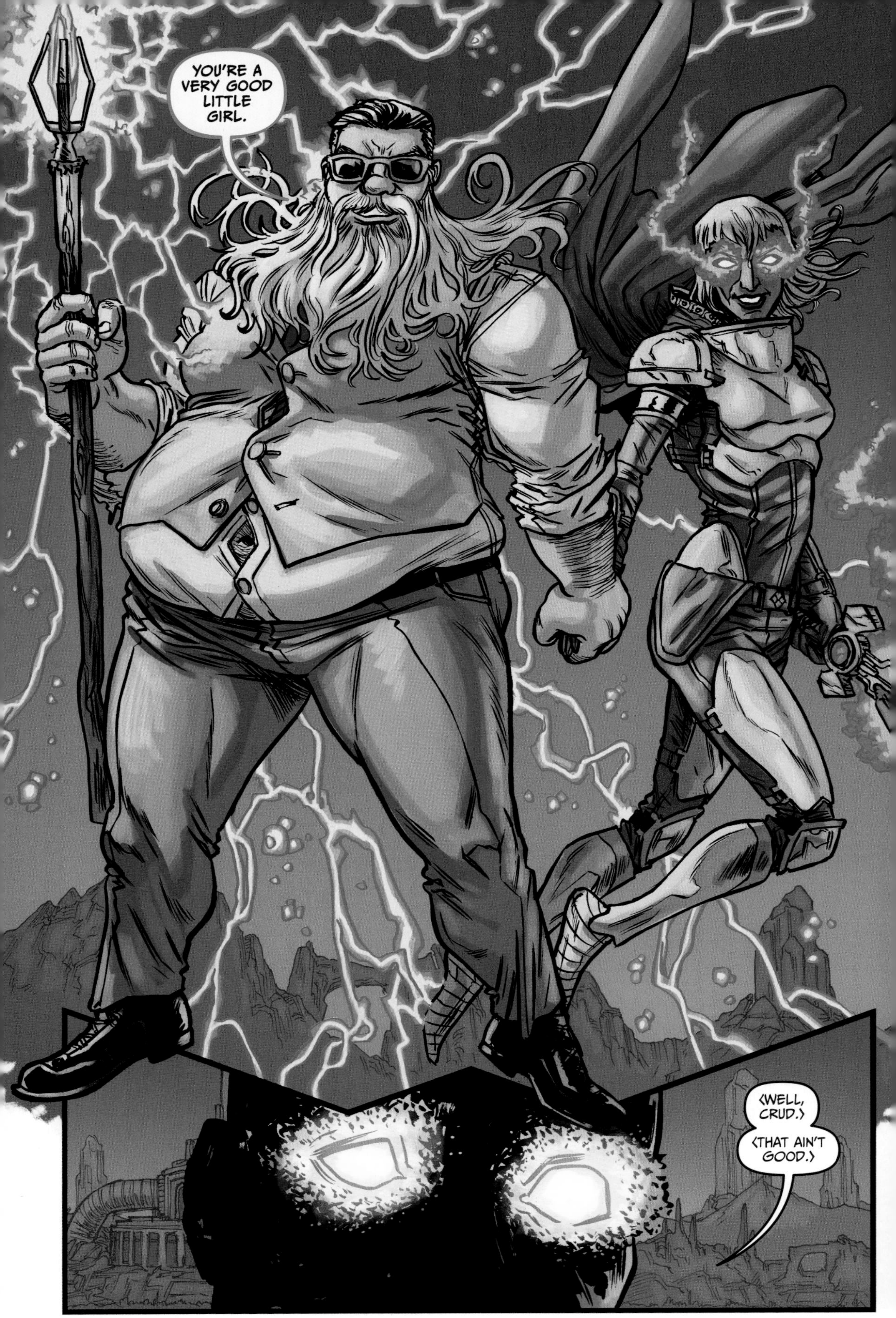
YOU'RE A VERY GOOD LITTLE GIRL.
‹WELL, CRUD.›
‹THAT AIN'T GOOD.›

TWENTY-THREE

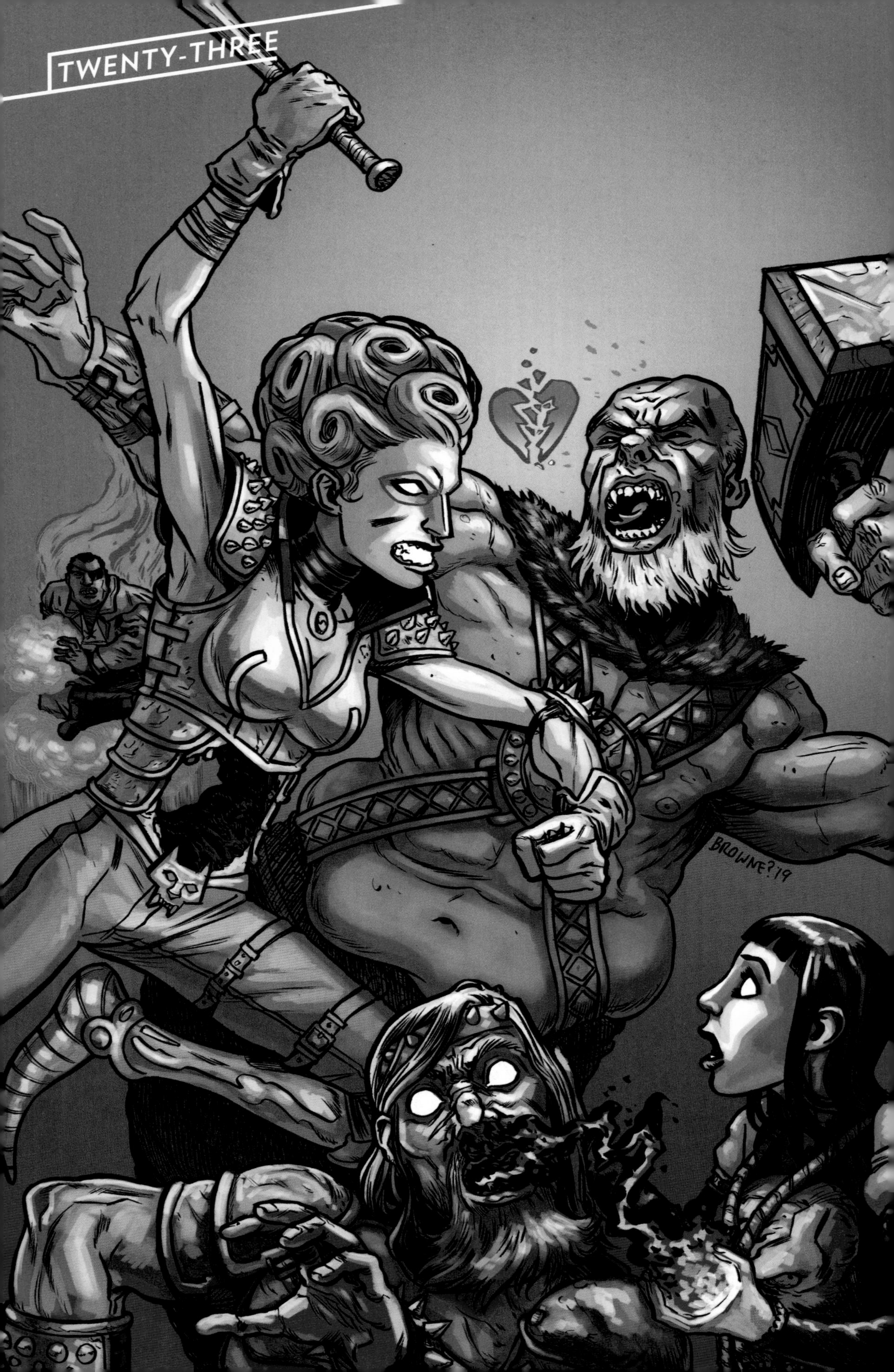
BROWNE?'19

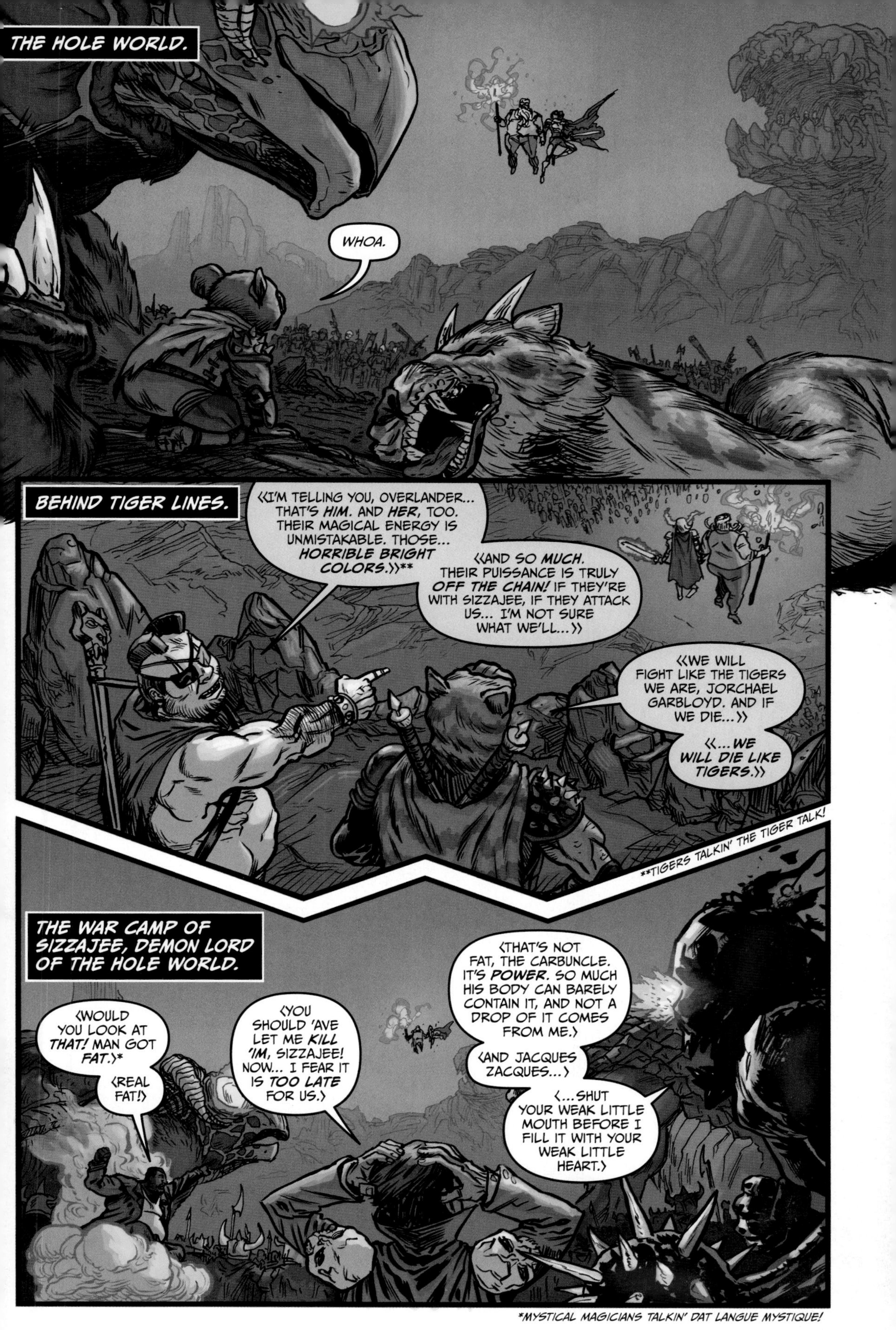
THE HOLE WORLD.
WHOA.
BEHIND TIGER LINES.
<<I'M TELLING YOU, OVERLANDER... THAT'S HIM. AND HER, TOO. THEIR MAGICAL ENERGY IS UNMISTAKABLE. THOSE... HORRIBLE BRIGHT COLORS.>>**
<<AND SO MUCH. THEIR PUISSANCE IS TRULY OFF THE CHAIN! IF THEY'RE WITH SIZZAJEE, IF THEY ATTACK US... I'M NOT SURE WHAT WE'LL...>>
<<WE WILL FIGHT LIKE THE TIGERS WE ARE, JORCHAEL GARBLOYD. AND IF WE DIE...>>
<<...WE WILL DIE LIKE TIGERS.>>
**TIGERS TALKIN' THE TIGER TALK!
THE WAR CAMP OF SIZZAJEE, DEMON LORD OF THE HOLE WORLD.
<WOULD YOU LOOK AT THAT! MAN GOT FAT.>*
<REAL FAT!>
<YOU SHOULD 'AVE LET ME KILL 'IM, SIZZAJEE! NOW... I FEAR IT IS TOO LATE FOR US.>
<THAT'S NOT FAT, THE CARBUNCLE. IT'S POWER. SO MUCH HIS BODY CAN BARELY CONTAIN IT, AND NOT A DROP OF IT COMES FROM ME.>
<AND JACQUES ZACQUES...>
<...SHUT YOUR WEAK LITTLE MOUTH BEFORE I FILL IT WITH YOUR WEAK LITTLE HEART.>

*MYSTICAL MAGICIANS TALKIN' DAT LANGUE MYSTIQUE!

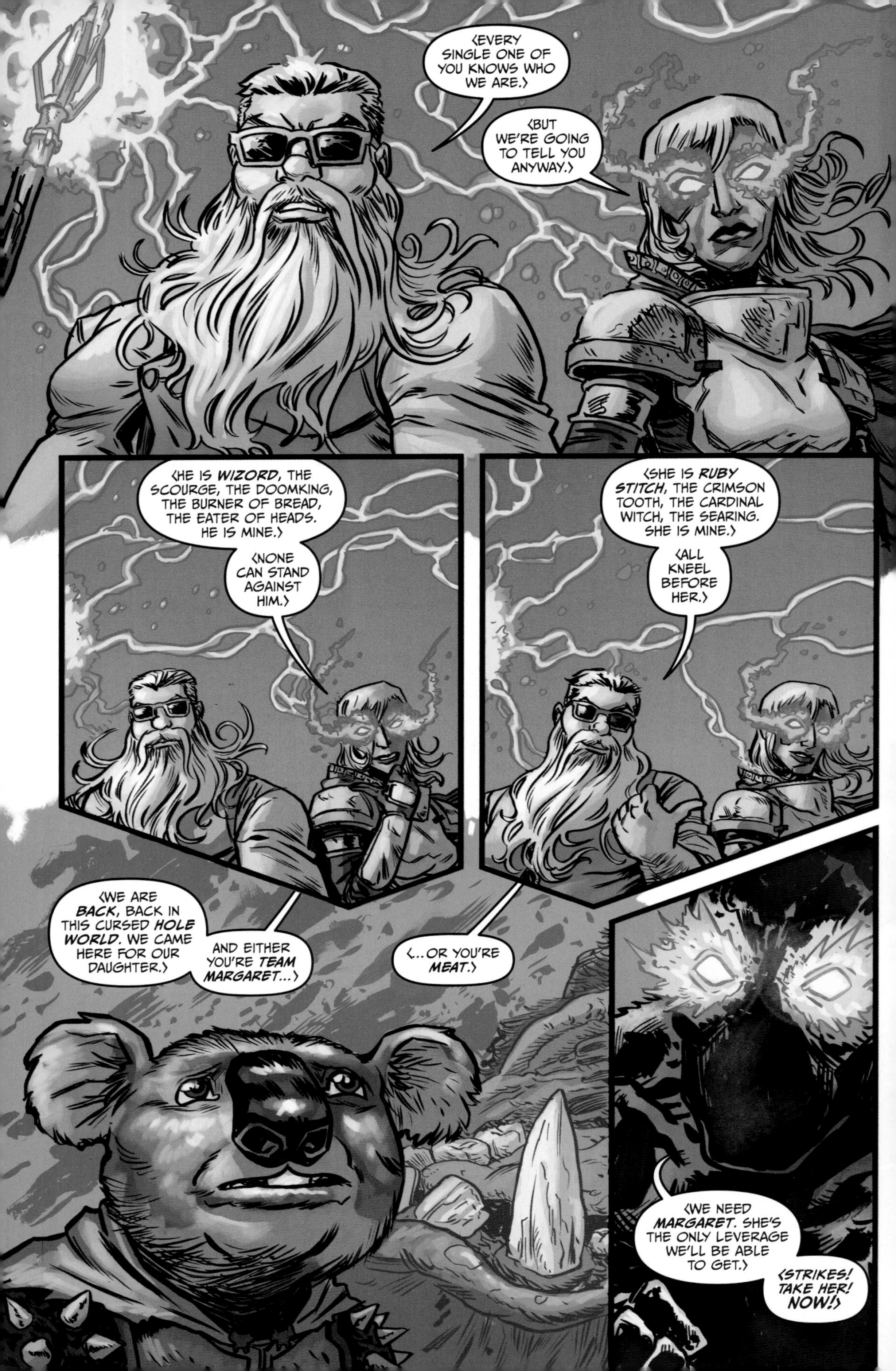

‹EVERY SINGLE ONE OF YOU KNOWS WHO WE ARE.›
‹BUT WE'RE GOING TO TELL YOU ANYWAY.›
‹HE IS ***WIZORD***, THE SCOURGE, THE DOOMKING, THE BURNER OF BREAD, THE EATER OF HEADS. HE IS MINE.›
‹NONE CAN STAND AGAINST HIM.›
‹SHE IS ***RUBY STITCH***, THE CRIMSON TOOTH, THE CARDINAL WITCH, THE SEARING. SHE IS MINE.›
‹ALL KNEEL BEFORE HER.›
‹WE ARE ***BACK***, BACK IN THIS CURSED ***HOLE WORLD***. WE CAME HERE FOR OUR DAUGHTER.›
AND EITHER YOU'RE ***TEAM MARGARET***...›
‹...OR YOU'RE ***MEAT***.›
‹WE NEED ***MARGARET***. SHE'S THE ONLY LEVERAGE WE'LL BE ABLE TO GET.›
‹STRIKES! TAKE HER! NOW!›

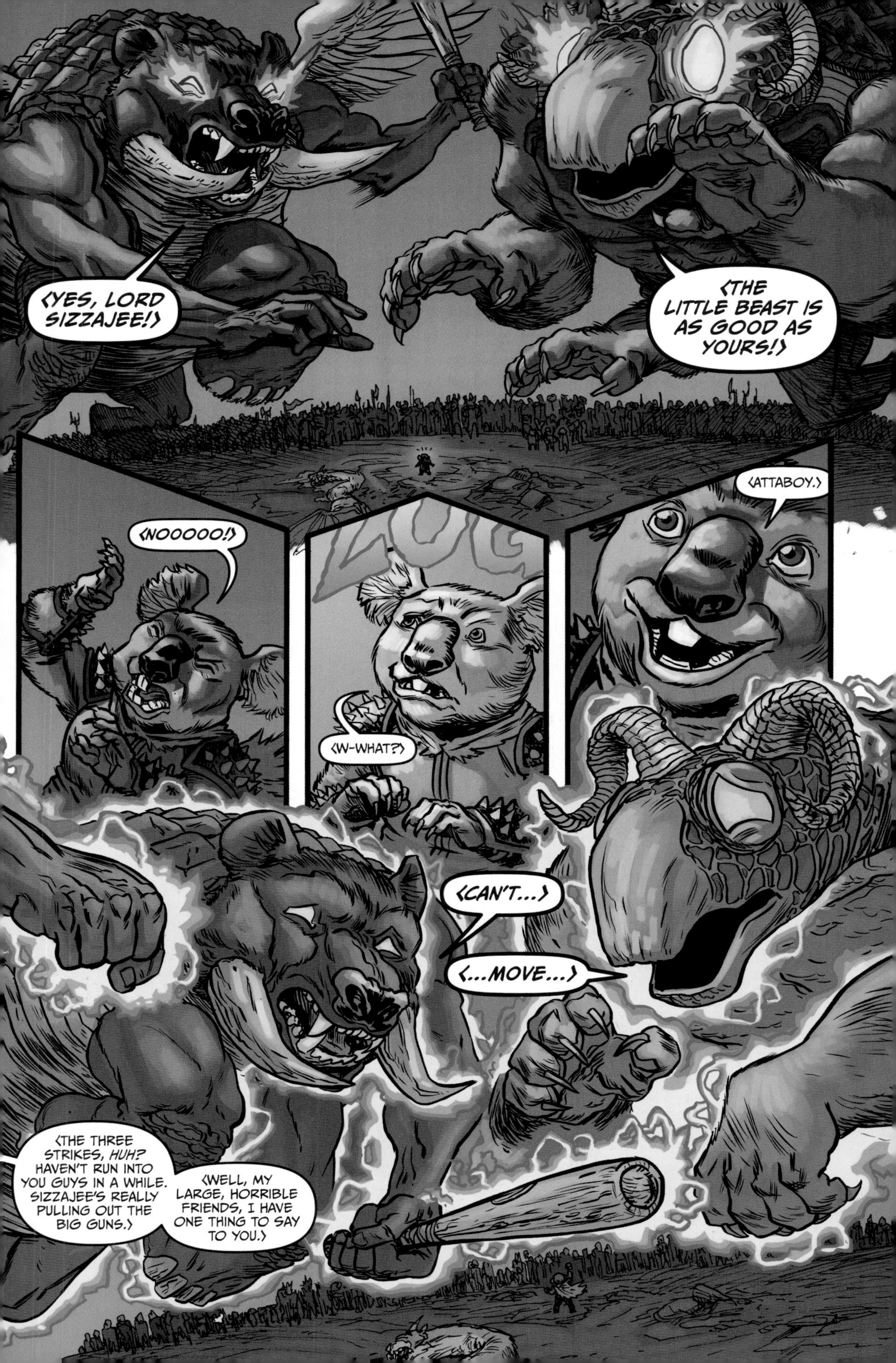

‹YES, LORD SIZZAJEE!›
‹THE LITTLE BEAST IS AS GOOD AS YOURS!›
‹NOOOOO!›
ZOG
‹W-WHAT?›
‹ATTABOY.›
‹CAN'T...›
‹...MOVE...›
‹THE THREE STRIKES, *HUH?* HAVEN'T RUN INTO YOU GUYS IN A WHILE. SIZZAJEE'S REALLY PULLING OUT THE BIG GUNS.›
‹WELL, MY LARGE, HORRIBLE FRIENDS, I HAVE ONE THING TO SAY TO YOU.›

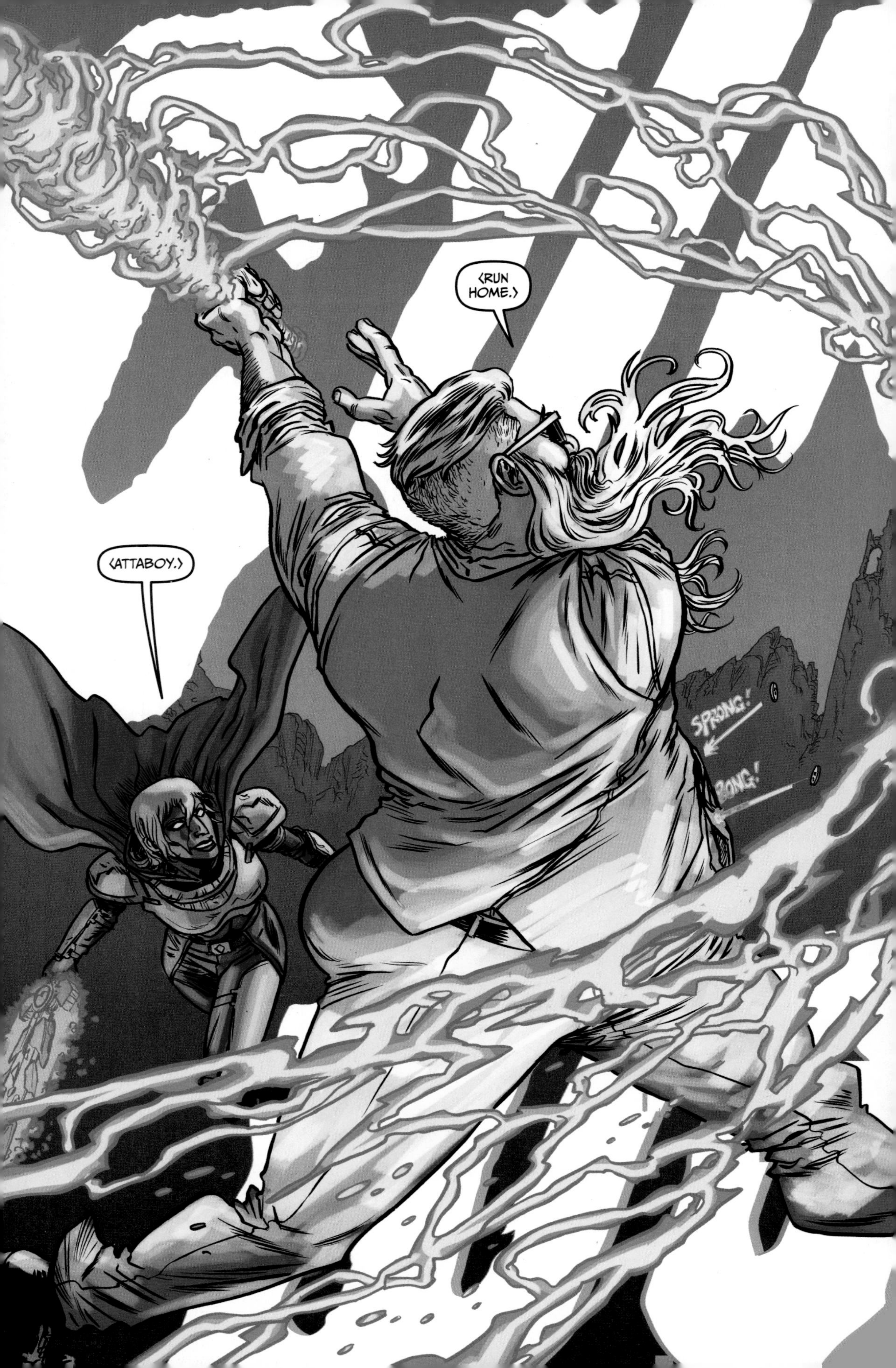
<RUN HOME.>
<ATTABOY.>
SPRONG!
BONG!

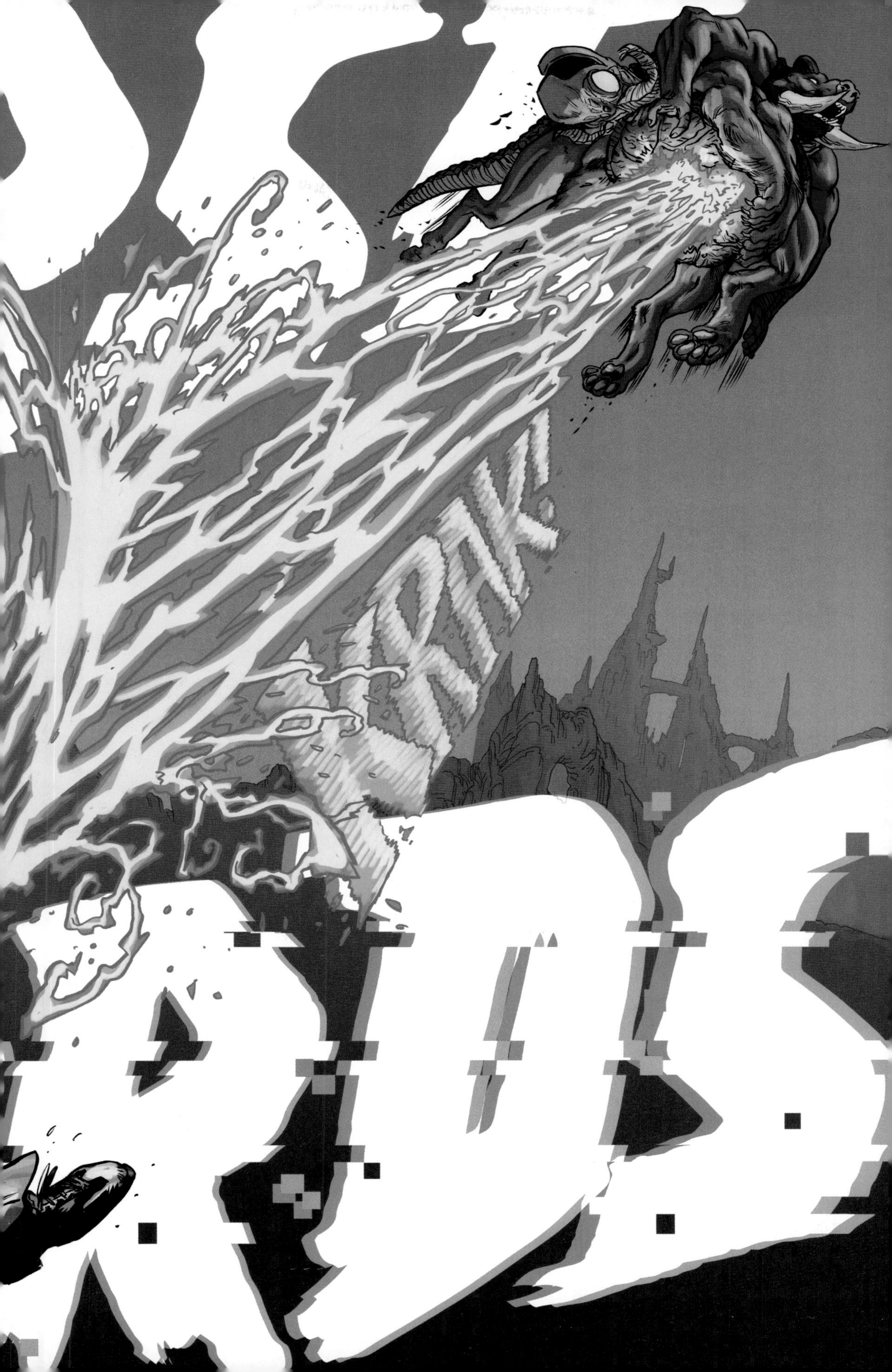

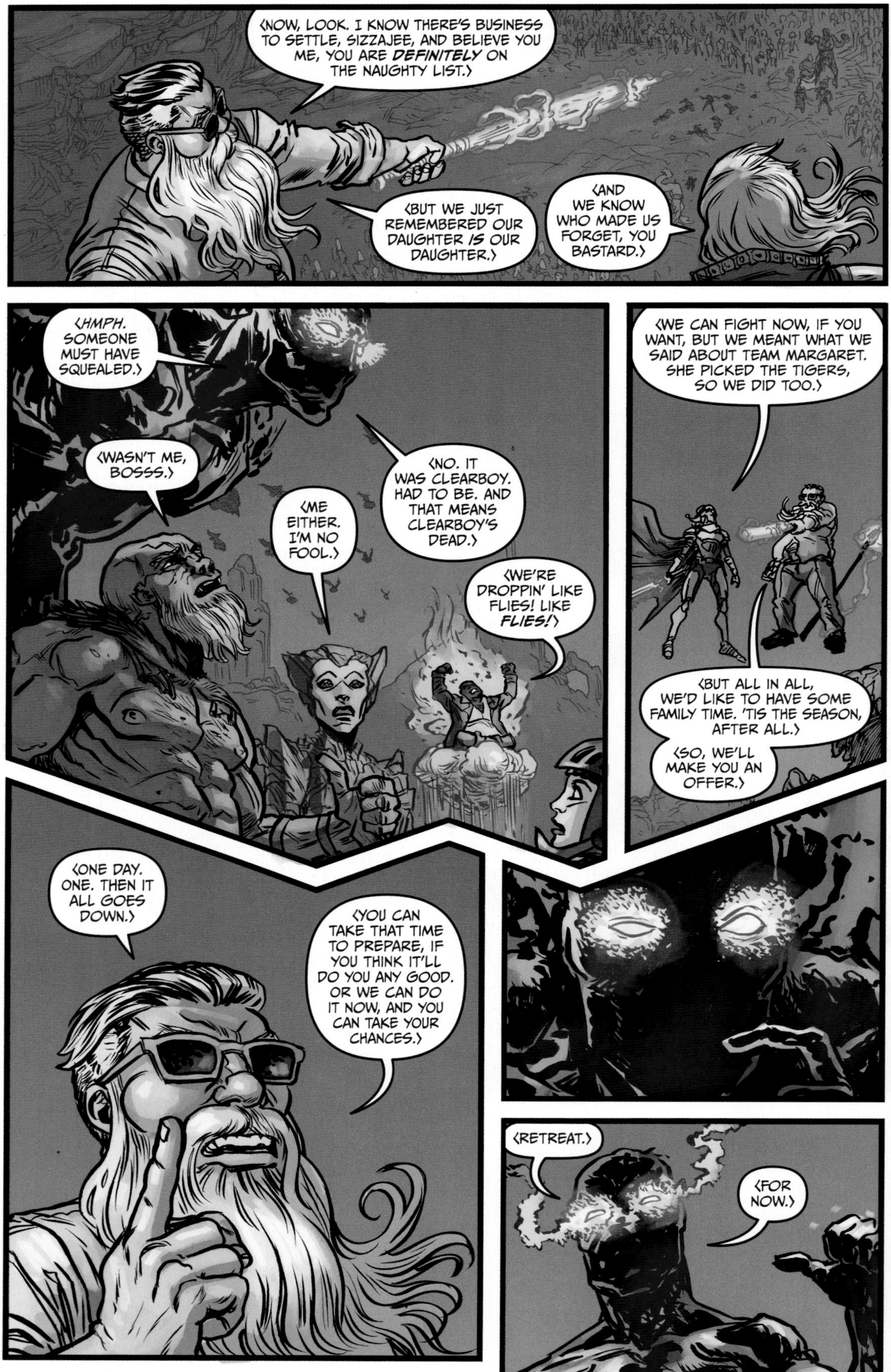
‹NOW, LOOK. I KNOW THERE'S BUSINESS TO SETTLE, SIZZAJEE, AND BELIEVE YOU ME, YOU ARE *DEFINITELY* ON THE NAUGHTY LIST.›
‹BUT WE JUST REMEMBERED OUR DAUGHTER *IS* OUR DAUGHTER.›
‹AND WE KNOW WHO MADE US FORGET, YOU BASTARD.›
‹HMPH. SOMEONE MUST HAVE SQUEALED.›
‹WASN'T ME, BOSSS.›
‹ME EITHER. I'M NO FOOL.›
‹NO. IT WAS CLEARBOY. HAD TO BE. AND THAT MEANS CLEARBOY'S DEAD.›
‹WE'RE DROPPIN' LIKE FLIES! LIKE *FLIES!*›
‹WE CAN FIGHT NOW, IF YOU WANT, BUT WE MEANT WHAT WE SAID ABOUT TEAM MARGARET. SHE PICKED THE TIGERS, SO WE DID TOO.›
‹BUT ALL IN ALL, WE'D LIKE TO HAVE SOME FAMILY TIME. 'TIS THE SEASON, AFTER ALL.›
‹SO, WE'LL MAKE YOU AN OFFER.›
‹ONE DAY. ONE. THEN IT ALL GOES DOWN.›
‹YOU CAN TAKE THAT TIME TO PREPARE, IF YOU THINK IT'LL DO YOU ANY GOOD. OR WE CAN DO IT NOW, AND YOU CAN TAKE YOUR CHANCES.›
‹RETREAT.›
‹FOR NOW.›

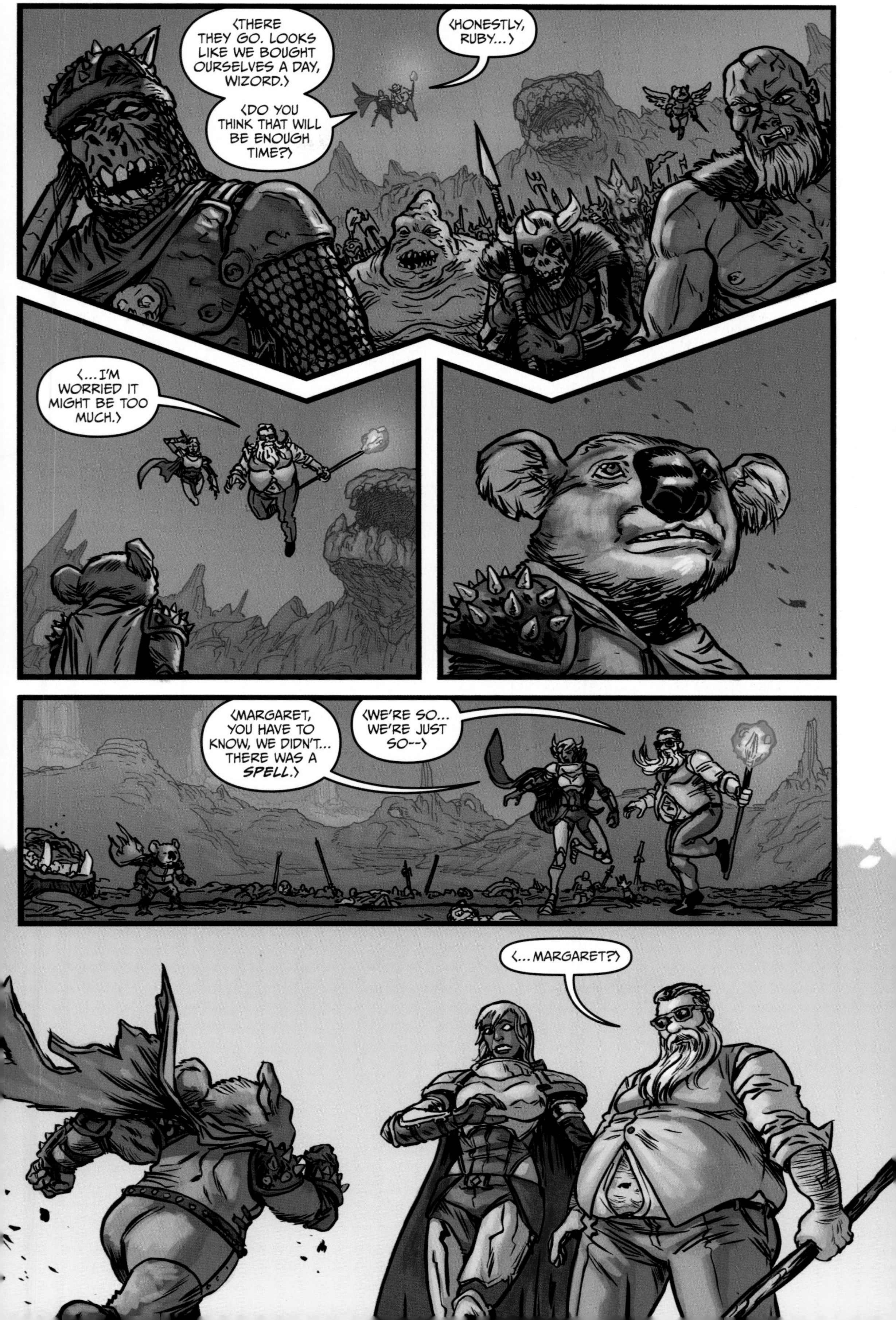

<THERE THEY GO. LOOKS LIKE WE BOUGHT OURSELVES A DAY, WIZORD.>
<DO YOU THINK THAT WILL BE ENOUGH TIME?>
<HONESTLY, RUBY...>
<...I'M WORRIED IT MIGHT BE TOO MUCH.>
<MARGARET, YOU HAVE TO KNOW, WE DIDN'T... THERE WAS A *SPELL*.>
<WE'RE SO... WE'RE JUST SO-->
<...MARGARET?>

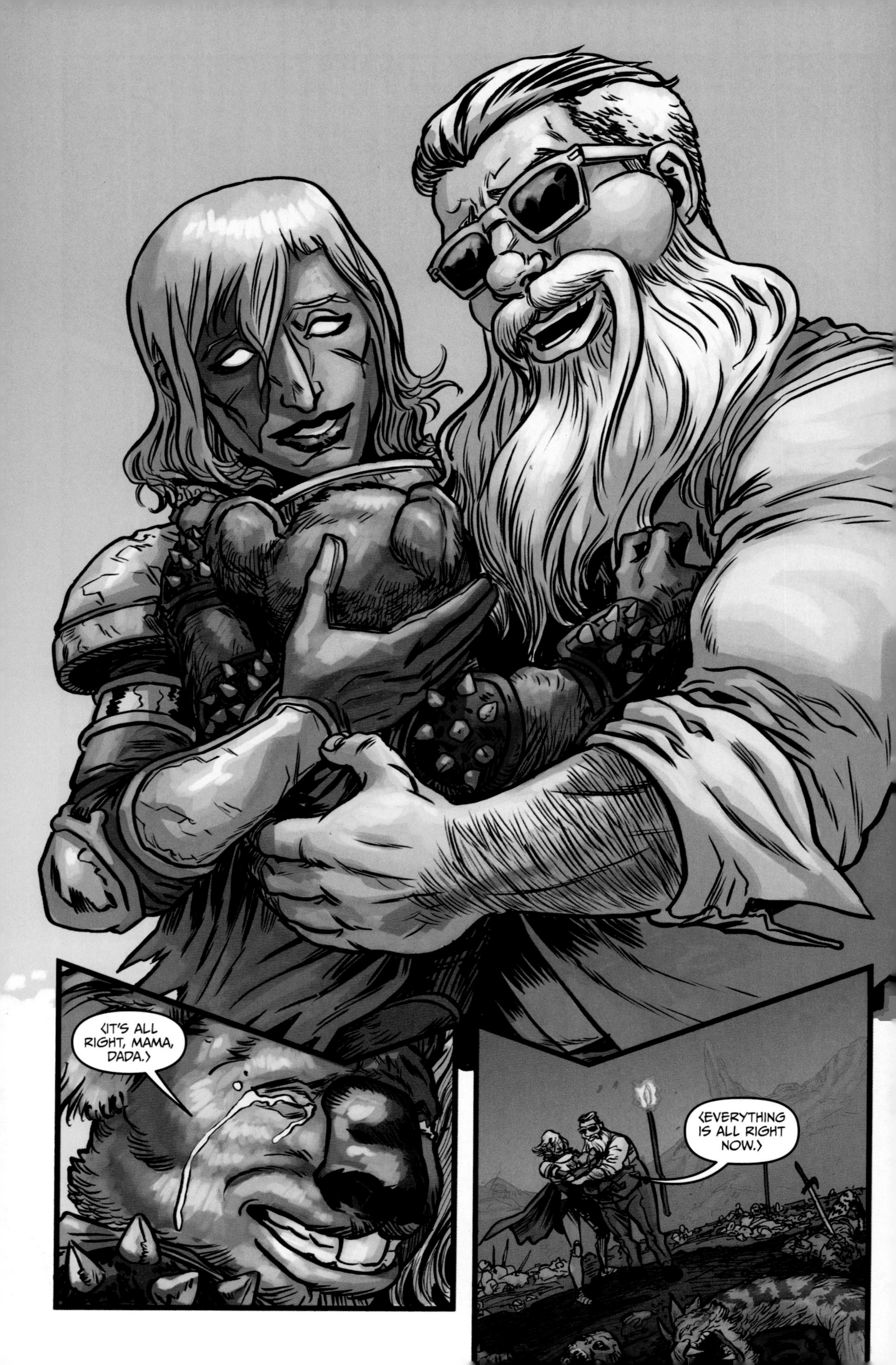

‹IT'S ALL RIGHT, MAMA, DADA.›
‹EVERYTHING IS ALL RIGHT NOW.›

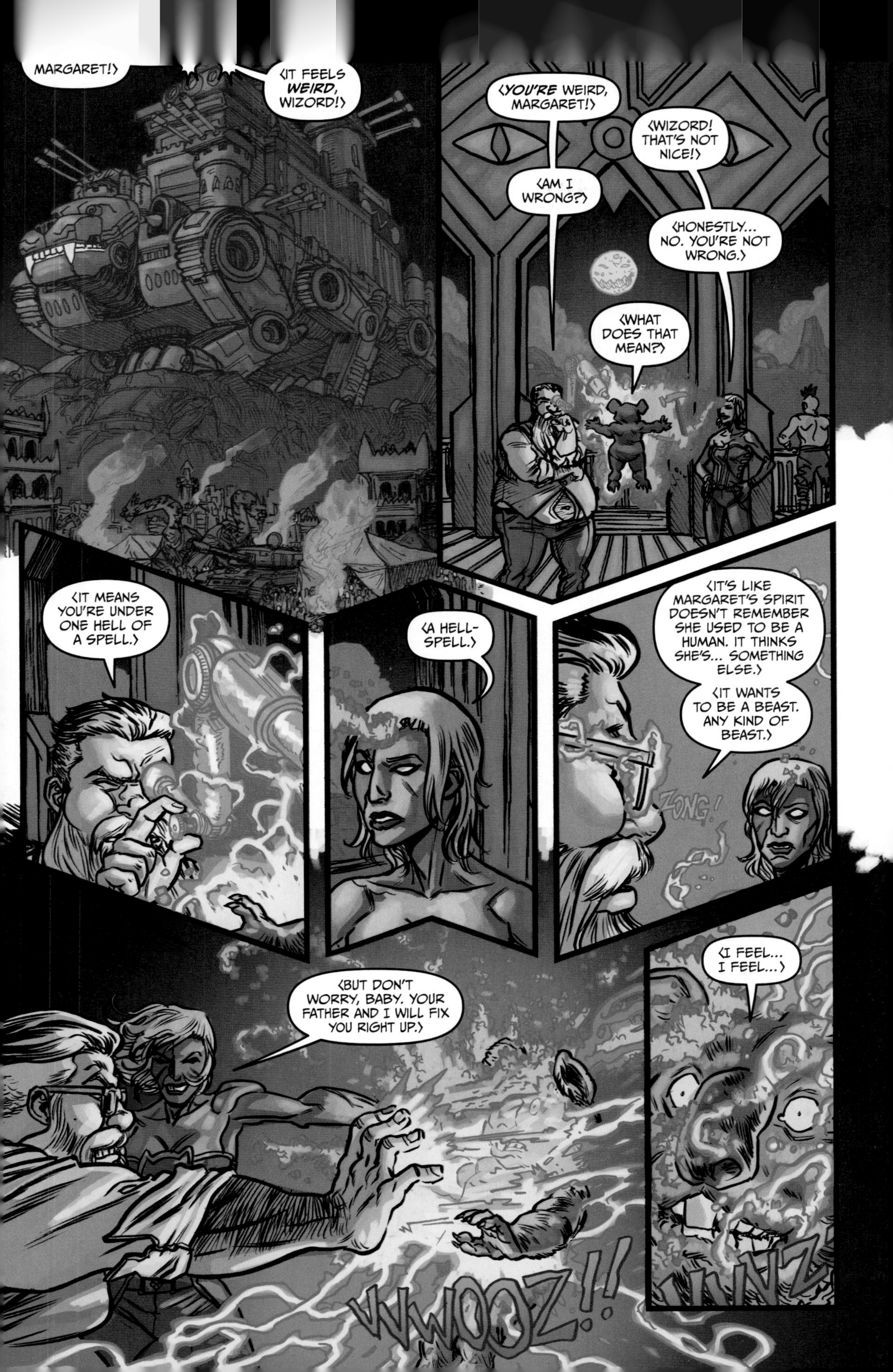

MARGARET!〉
〈IT FEELS *WEIRD*, WIZORD!〉
〈*YOU'RE* WEIRD, MARGARET!〉
〈WIZORD! THAT'S NOT NICE!〉
〈AM I WRONG?〉
〈HONESTLY... NO. YOU'RE NOT WRONG.〉
〈WHAT DOES THAT MEAN?〉
〈IT MEANS YOU'RE UNDER ONE HELL OF A SPELL.〉
〈A HELL-SPELL.〉
〈IT'S LIKE MARGARET'S SPIRIT DOESN'T REMEMBER SHE USED TO BE A HUMAN. IT THINKS SHE'S... SOMETHING ELSE.〉
〈IT WANTS TO BE A BEAST. ANY KIND OF BEAST.〉
ZONG!
〈BUT DON'T WORRY, BABY. YOUR FATHER AND I WILL FIX YOU RIGHT UP.〉
〈I FEEL... I FEEL...〉
WWOOZ!!

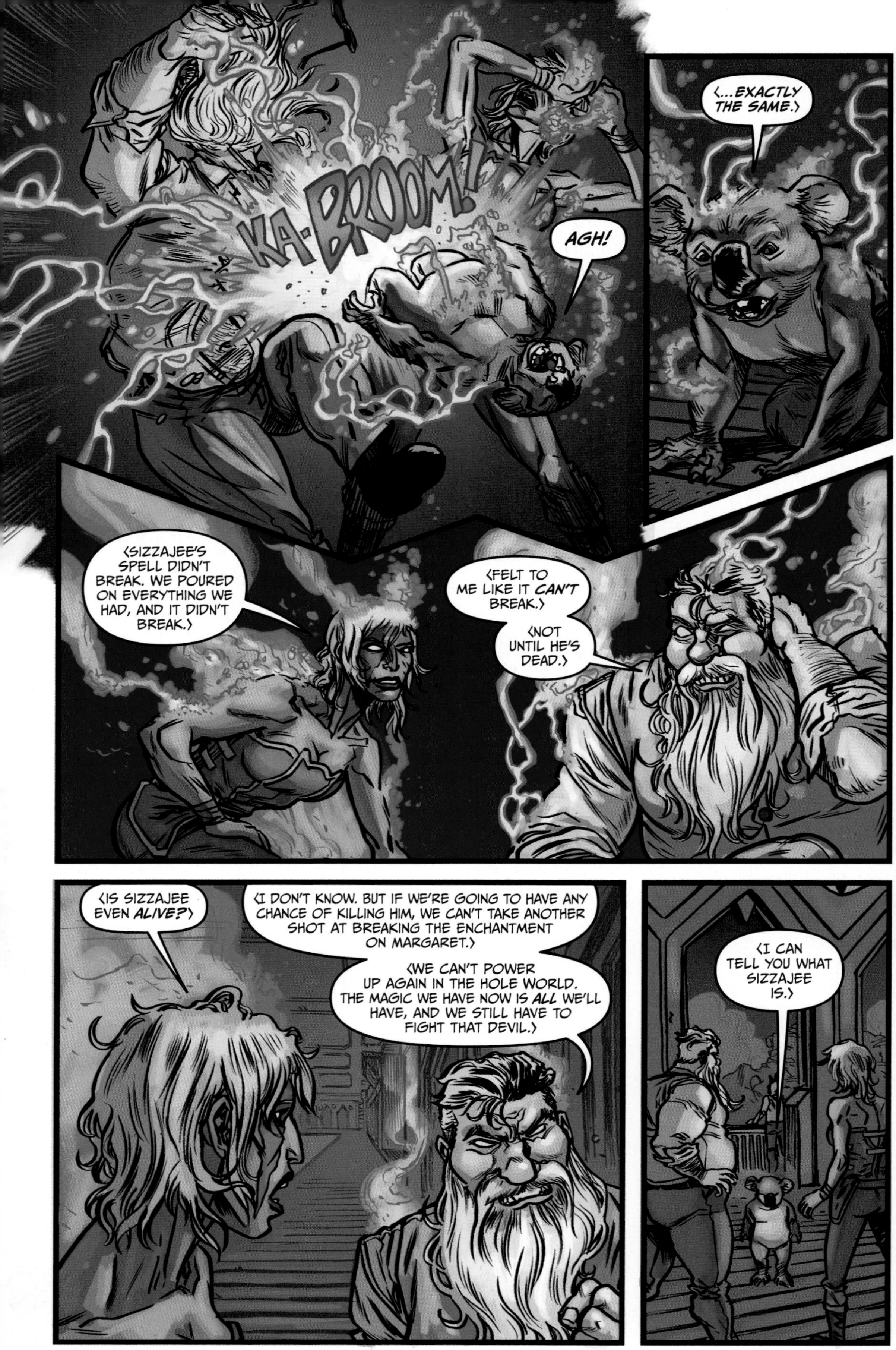
KA-BROOM!!
AGH!
<...EXACTLY THE SAME.>
<SIZZAJEE'S SPELL DIDN'T BREAK. WE POURED ON EVERYTHING WE HAD, AND IT DIDN'T BREAK.>
<FELT TO ME LIKE IT *CAN'T* BREAK.>
<NOT UNTIL HE'S DEAD.>
<IS SIZZAJEE EVEN *ALIVE?*>
<I DON'T KNOW. BUT IF WE'RE GOING TO HAVE ANY CHANCE OF KILLING HIM, WE CAN'T TAKE ANOTHER SHOT AT BREAKING THE ENCHANTMENT ON MARGARET.>
<WE CAN'T POWER UP AGAIN IN THE HOLE WORLD. THE MAGIC WE HAVE NOW IS *ALL* WE'LL HAVE, AND WE STILL HAVE TO FIGHT THAT DEVIL.>
<I CAN TELL YOU WHAT SIZZAJEE IS.>

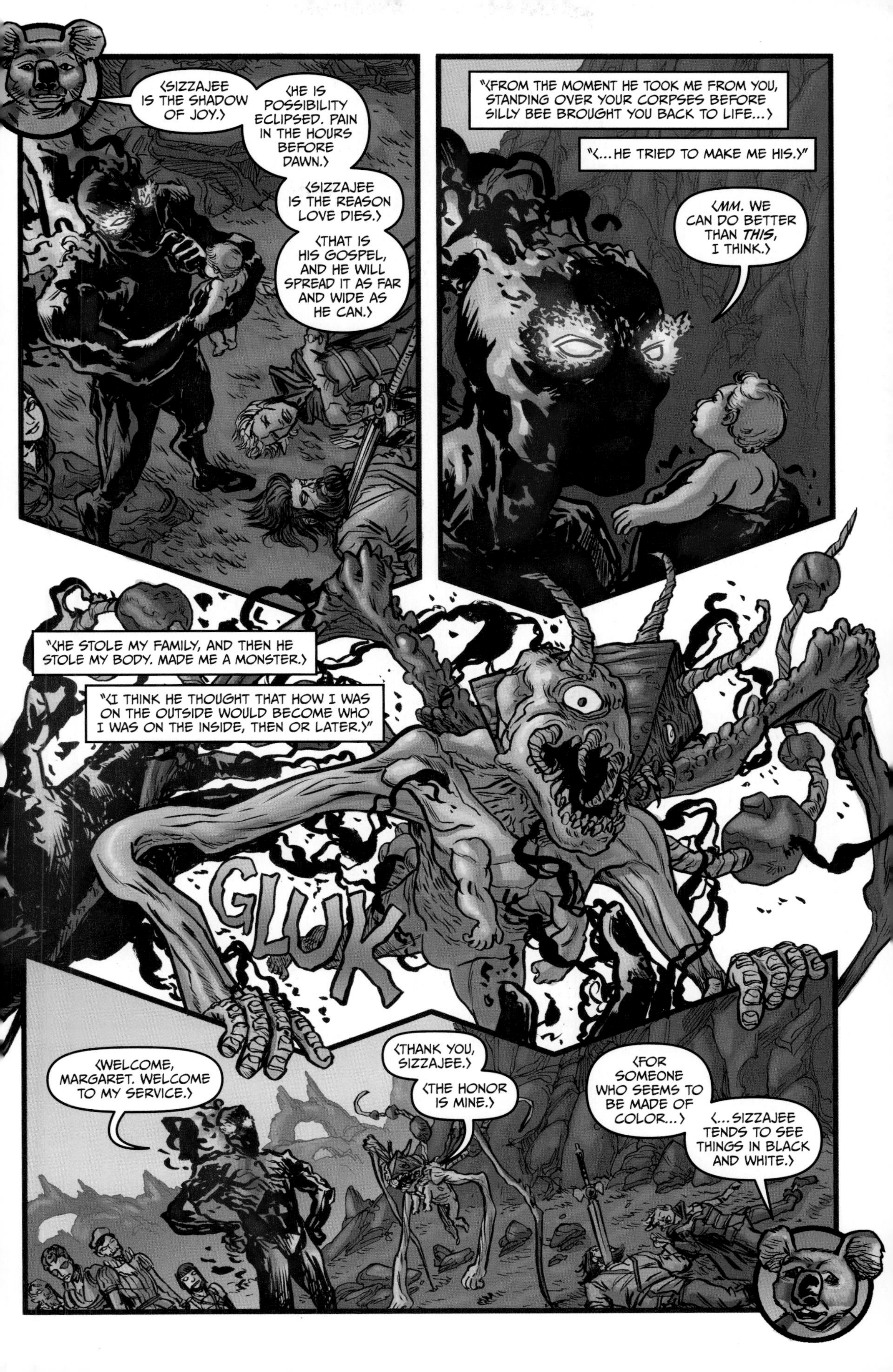
‹SIZZAJEE IS THE SHADOW OF JOY.›
‹HE IS POSSIBILITY ECLIPSED. PAIN IN THE HOURS BEFORE DAWN.›
‹SIZZAJEE IS THE REASON LOVE DIES.›
‹THAT IS HIS GOSPEL, AND HE WILL SPREAD IT AS FAR AND WIDE AS HE CAN.›
"‹FROM THE MOMENT HE TOOK ME FROM YOU, STANDING OVER YOUR CORPSES BEFORE SILLY BEE BROUGHT YOU BACK TO LIFE...›
"‹...HE TRIED TO MAKE ME HIS.›"
‹MM. WE CAN DO BETTER THAN THIS, I THINK.›
"‹HE STOLE MY FAMILY, AND THEN HE STOLE MY BODY. MADE ME A MONSTER.›
"‹I THINK HE THOUGHT THAT HOW I WAS ON THE OUTSIDE WOULD BECOME WHO I WAS ON THE INSIDE, THEN OR LATER.›"
GLUK
‹WELCOME, MARGARET. WELCOME TO MY SERVICE.›
‹THANK YOU, SIZZAJEE.›
‹THE HONOR IS MINE.›
‹FOR SOMEONE WHO SEEMS TO BE MADE OF COLOR...›
‹...SIZZAJEE TENDS TO SEE THINGS IN BLACK AND WHITE.›

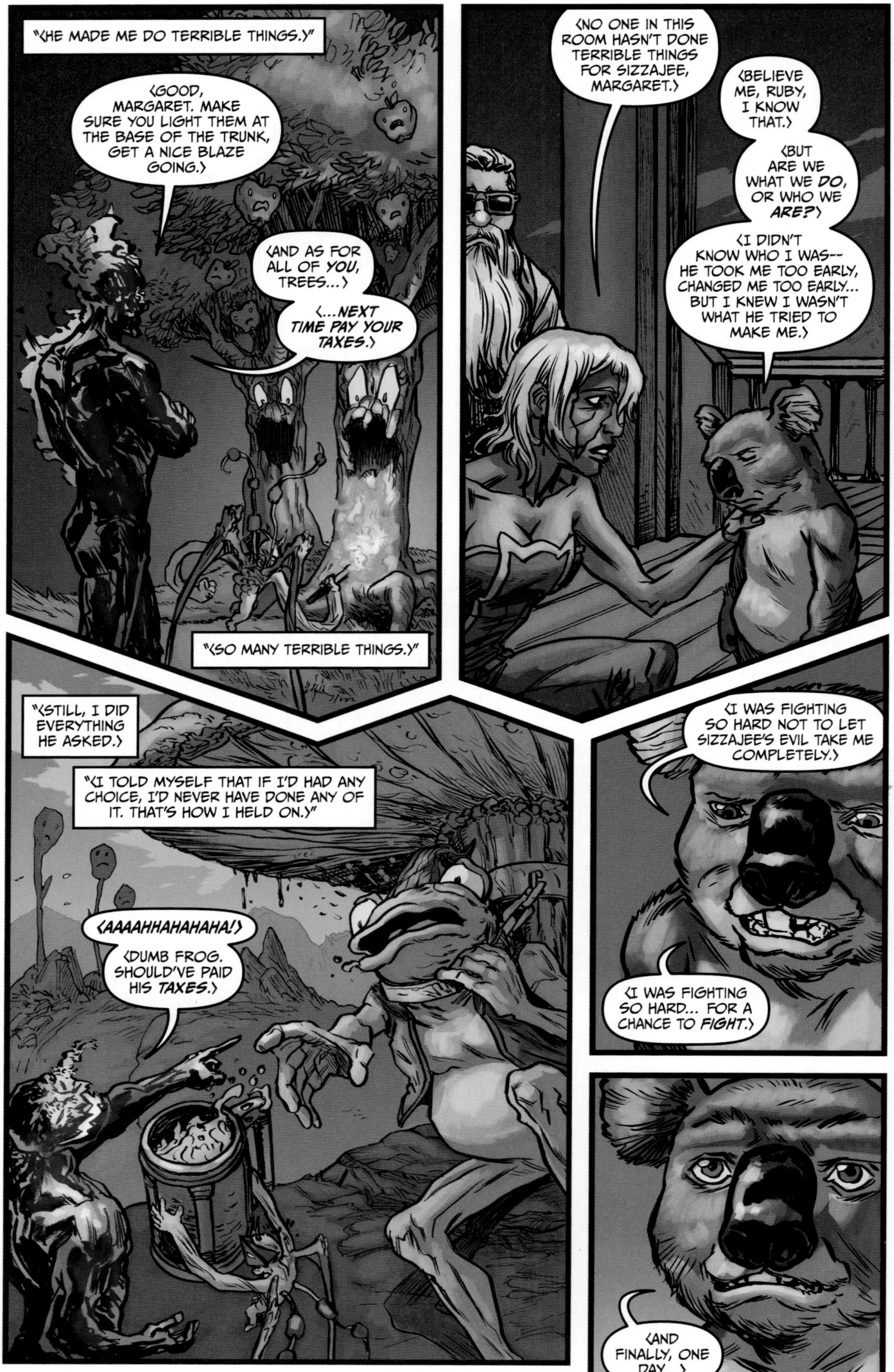
"‹HE MADE ME DO TERRIBLE THINGS.›"
‹GOOD, MARGARET. MAKE SURE YOU LIGHT THEM AT THE BASE OF THE TRUNK, GET A NICE BLAZE GOING.›
‹AND AS FOR ALL OF *YOU*, TREES...›
‹...*NEXT TIME PAY YOUR TAXES*.›
"‹SO MANY TERRIBLE THINGS.›"
‹NO ONE IN THIS ROOM HASN'T DONE TERRIBLE THINGS FOR SIZZAJEE, MARGARET.›
‹BELIEVE ME, RUBY, I KNOW THAT.›
‹BUT ARE WE WHAT WE *DO*, OR WHO WE *ARE?*›
‹I DIDN'T KNOW WHO I WAS-- HE TOOK ME TOO EARLY, CHANGED ME TOO EARLY... BUT I KNEW I WASN'T WHAT HE TRIED TO MAKE ME.›
"‹STILL, I DID EVERYTHING HE ASKED.›
"‹I TOLD MYSELF THAT IF I'D HAD ANY CHOICE, I'D NEVER HAVE DONE ANY OF IT. THAT'S HOW I HELD ON.›"
‹AAAAHHAHAHAHA!›
‹DUMB FROG. SHOULD'VE PAID HIS *TAXES*.›
‹I WAS FIGHTING SO HARD NOT TO LET SIZZAJEE'S EVIL TAKE ME COMPLETELY.›
‹I WAS FIGHTING SO HARD... FOR A CHANCE TO *FIGHT*.›
‹AND FINALLY, ONE DAY...›

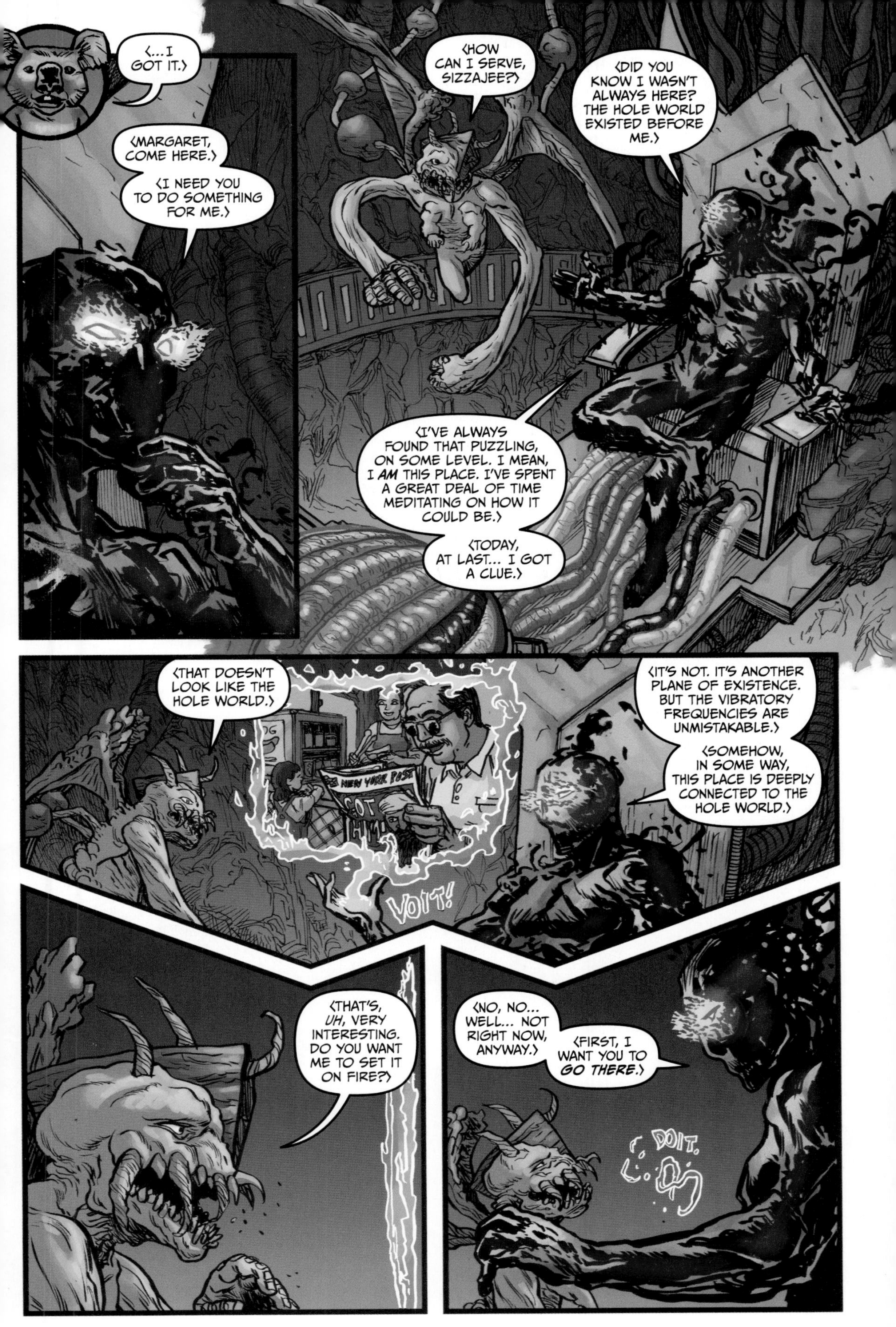
‹...I GOT IT.›
‹HOW CAN I SERVE, SIZZAJEE?›
‹DID YOU KNOW I WASN'T ALWAYS HERE? THE HOLE WORLD EXISTED BEFORE ME.›
‹MARGARET, COME HERE.›
‹I NEED YOU TO DO SOMETHING FOR ME.›
‹I'VE ALWAYS FOUND THAT PUZZLING, ON SOME LEVEL. I MEAN, I **AM** THIS PLACE. I'VE SPENT A GREAT DEAL OF TIME MEDITATING ON HOW IT COULD BE.›
‹TODAY, AT LAST... I GOT A CLUE.›
‹THAT DOESN'T LOOK LIKE THE HOLE WORLD.›
NEW YORK POST
‹IT'S NOT. IT'S ANOTHER PLANE OF EXISTENCE. BUT THE VIBRATORY FREQUENCIES ARE UNMISTAKABLE.›
‹SOMEHOW, IN SOME WAY, THIS PLACE IS DEEPLY CONNECTED TO THE HOLE WORLD.›
VOIT!
‹THAT'S, *UH*, VERY INTERESTING. DO YOU WANT ME TO SET IT ON FIRE?›
‹NO, NO... WELL... NOT RIGHT NOW, ANYWAY.›
‹FIRST, I WANT YOU TO ***GO THERE.***›
DOIT.

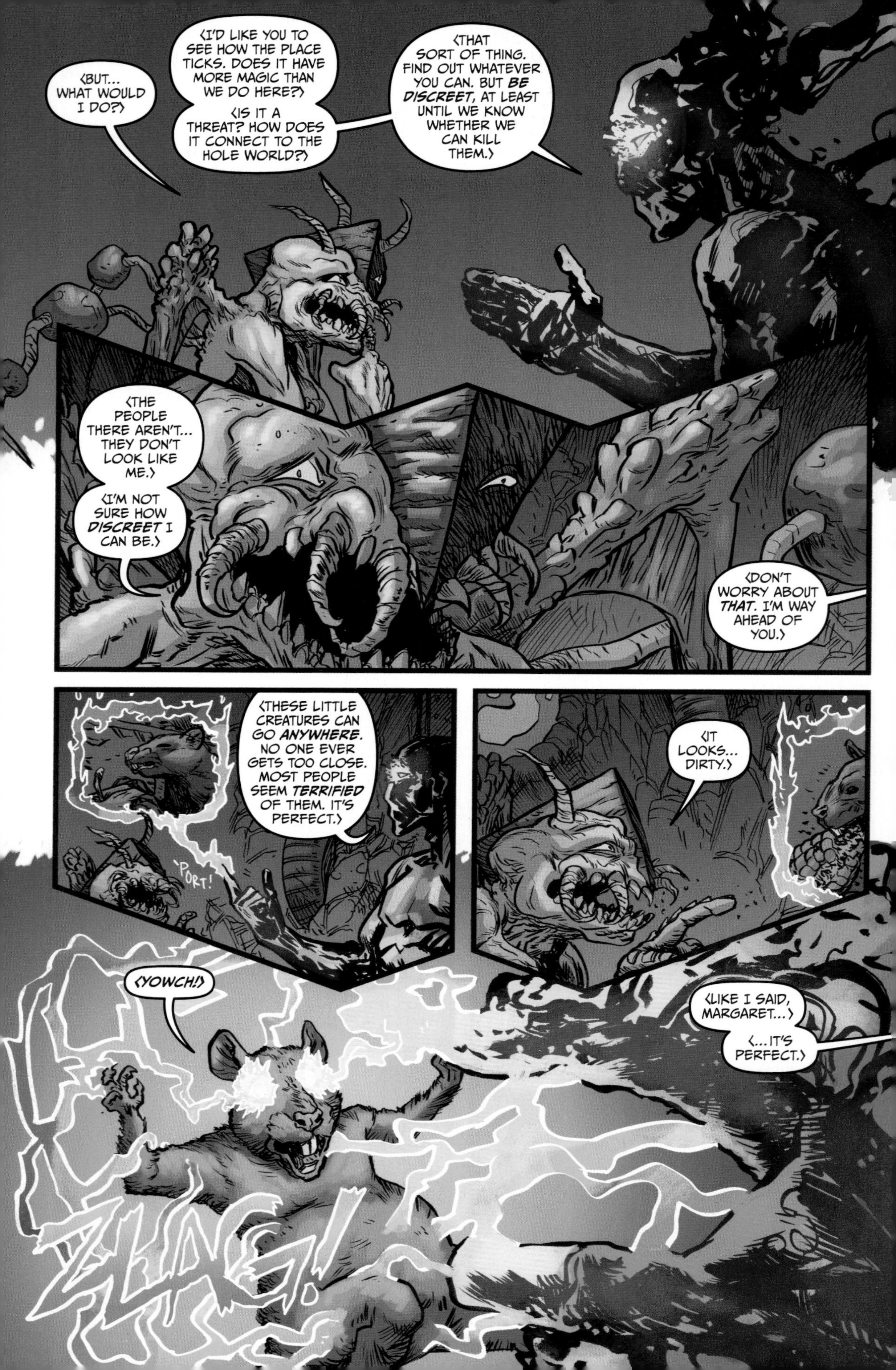

‹BUT... WHAT WOULD I DO?›
‹I'D LIKE YOU TO SEE HOW THE PLACE TICKS. DOES IT HAVE MORE MAGIC THAN WE DO HERE?›
‹IS IT A THREAT? HOW DOES IT CONNECT TO THE HOLE WORLD?›
‹THAT SORT OF THING. FIND OUT WHATEVER YOU CAN. BUT **BE DISCREET**, AT LEAST UNTIL WE KNOW WHETHER WE CAN KILL THEM.›
‹THE PEOPLE THERE AREN'T... THEY DON'T LOOK LIKE ME.›
‹I'M NOT SURE HOW **DISCREET** I CAN BE.›
‹DON'T WORRY ABOUT **THAT**. I'M WAY AHEAD OF YOU.›
‹THESE LITTLE CREATURES CAN GO **ANYWHERE**. NO ONE EVER GETS TOO CLOSE. MOST PEOPLE SEEM **TERRIFIED** OF THEM. IT'S PERFECT.›
'PORT!
‹IT LOOKS... DIRTY.›
‹YOWCH!›
‹LIKE I SAID, MARGARET...›
‹...IT'S PERFECT.›
ZZAG!

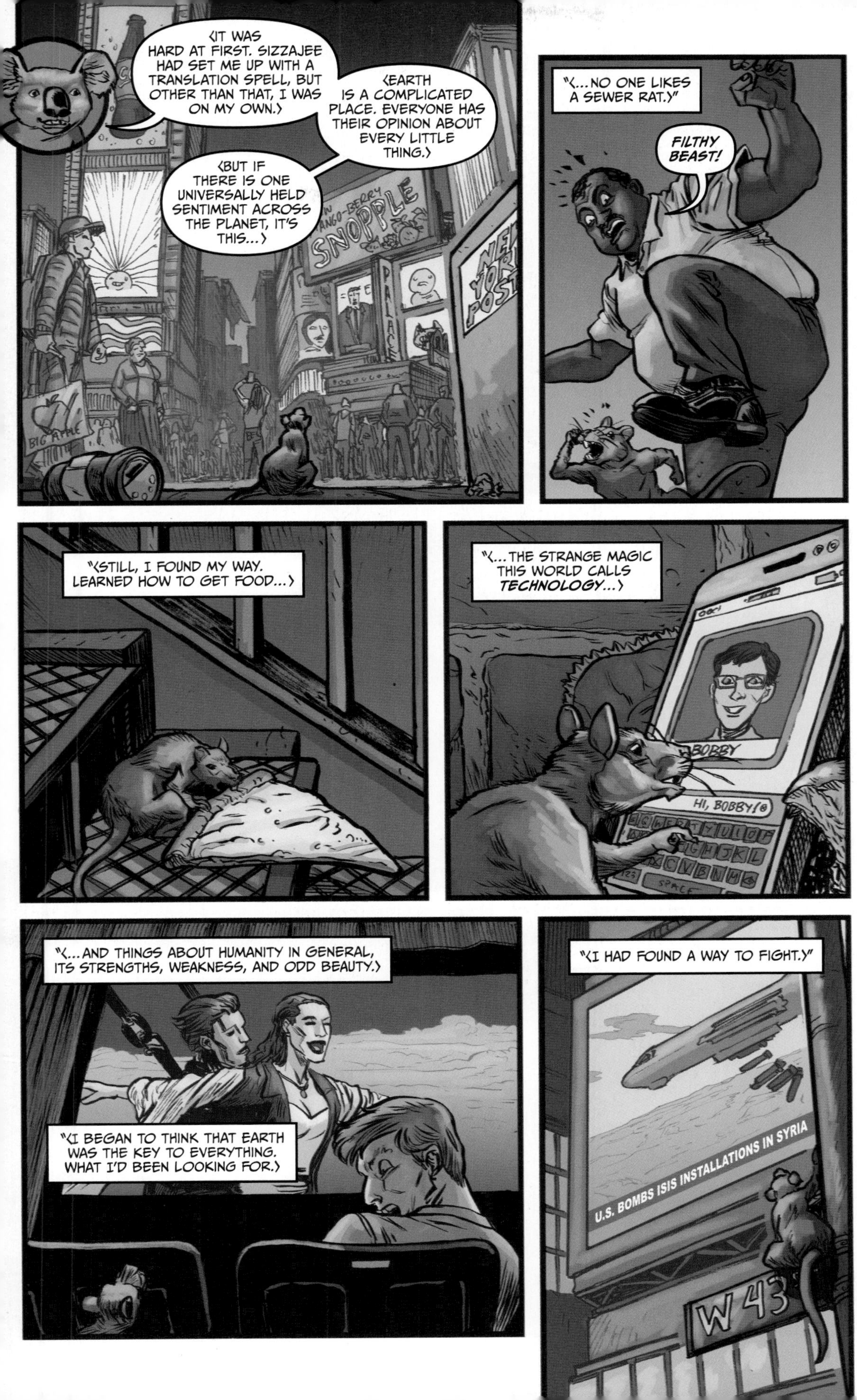
‹IT WAS HARD AT FIRST. SIZZAJEE HAD SET ME UP WITH A TRANSLATION SPELL, BUT OTHER THAN THAT, I WAS ON MY OWN.›
‹EARTH IS A COMPLICATED PLACE. EVERYONE HAS THEIR OPINION ABOUT EVERY LITTLE THING.›
‹BUT IF THERE IS ONE UNIVERSALLY HELD SENTIMENT ACROSS THE PLANET, IT'S THIS...›
SNOPPLE
PALACE
BIG APPLE
"‹...NO ONE LIKES A SEWER RAT.›"
FILTHY BEAST!
"‹STILL, I FOUND MY WAY. LEARNED HOW TO GET FOOD...›
"‹...THE STRANGE MAGIC THIS WORLD CALLS *TECHNOLOGY*...›
BOBBY
HI, BOBBY!
"‹...AND THINGS ABOUT HUMANITY IN GENERAL, ITS STRENGTHS, WEAKNESS, AND ODD BEAUTY.›
"‹I BEGAN TO THINK THAT EARTH WAS THE KEY TO EVERYTHING. WHAT I'D BEEN LOOKING FOR.›
"‹I HAD FOUND A WAY TO FIGHT.›"
U.S. BOMBS ISIS INSTALLATIONS IN SYRIA
W 43

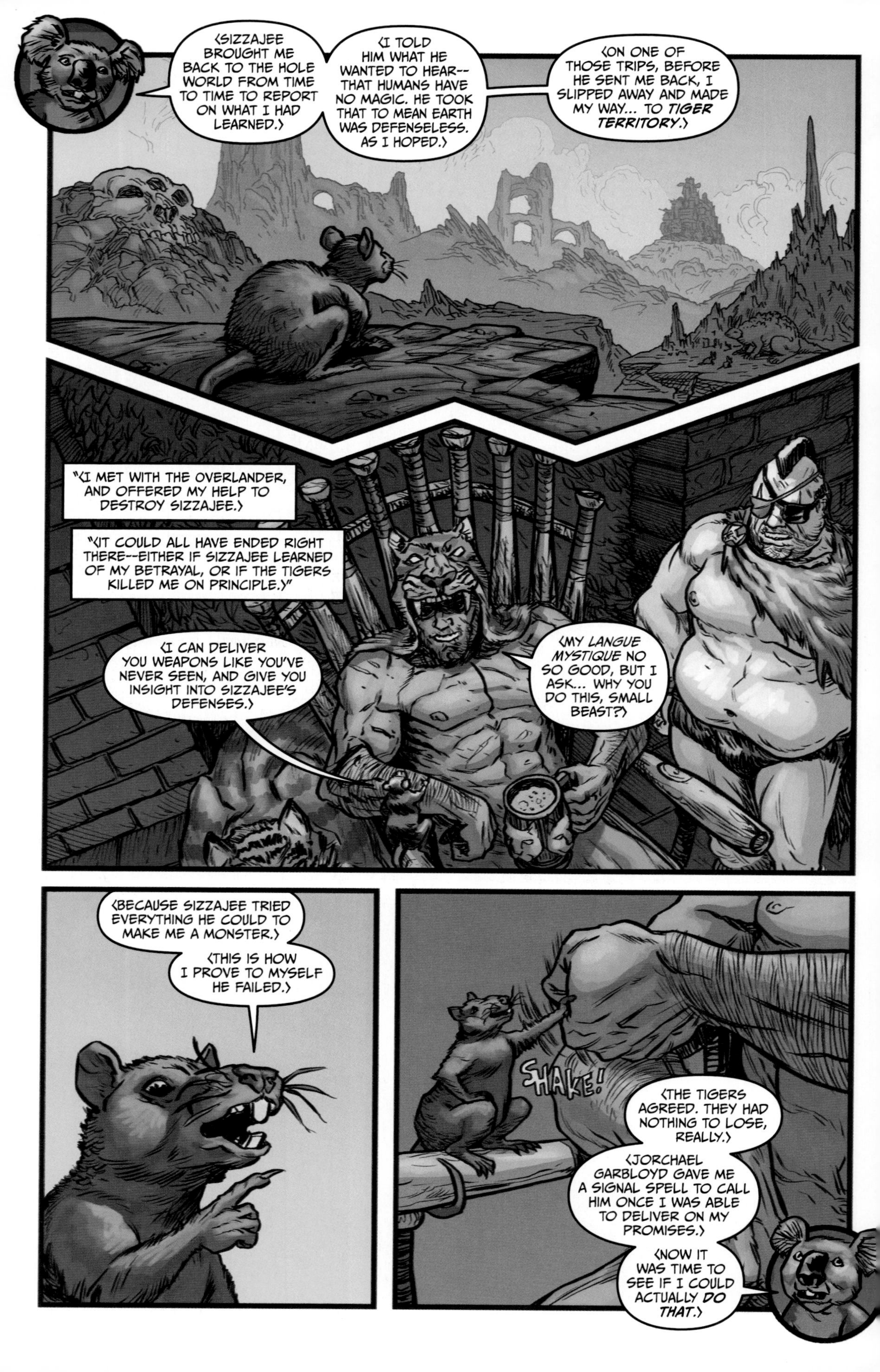
‹SIZZAJEE BROUGHT ME BACK TO THE HOLE WORLD FROM TIME TO TIME TO REPORT ON WHAT I HAD LEARNED.›
‹I TOLD HIM WHAT HE WANTED TO HEAR-- THAT HUMANS HAVE NO MAGIC. HE TOOK THAT TO MEAN EARTH WAS DEFENSELESS. AS I HOPED.›
‹ON ONE OF THOSE TRIPS, BEFORE HE SENT ME BACK, I SLIPPED AWAY AND MADE MY WAY... TO *TIGER TERRITORY*.›
"‹I MET WITH THE OVERLANDER, AND OFFERED MY HELP TO DESTROY SIZZAJEE.›
"‹IT COULD ALL HAVE ENDED RIGHT THERE--EITHER IF SIZZAJEE LEARNED OF MY BETRAYAL, OR IF THE TIGERS KILLED ME ON PRINCIPLE.›"
‹I CAN DELIVER YOU WEAPONS LIKE YOU'VE NEVER SEEN, AND GIVE YOU INSIGHT INTO SIZZAJEE'S DEFENSES.›
‹MY *LANGUE MYSTIQUE* NO SO GOOD, BUT I ASK... WHY YOU DO THIS, SMALL BEAST?›
‹BECAUSE SIZZAJEE TRIED EVERYTHING HE COULD TO MAKE ME A MONSTER.›
‹THIS IS HOW I PROVE TO MYSELF HE FAILED.›
SHAKE!
‹THE TIGERS AGREED. THEY HAD NOTHING TO LOSE, REALLY.›
‹JORCHAEL GARBLOYD GAVE ME A SIGNAL SPELL TO CALL HIM ONCE I WAS ABLE TO DELIVER ON MY PROMISES.›
‹NOW IT WAS TIME TO SEE IF I COULD ACTUALLY *DO THAT*.›

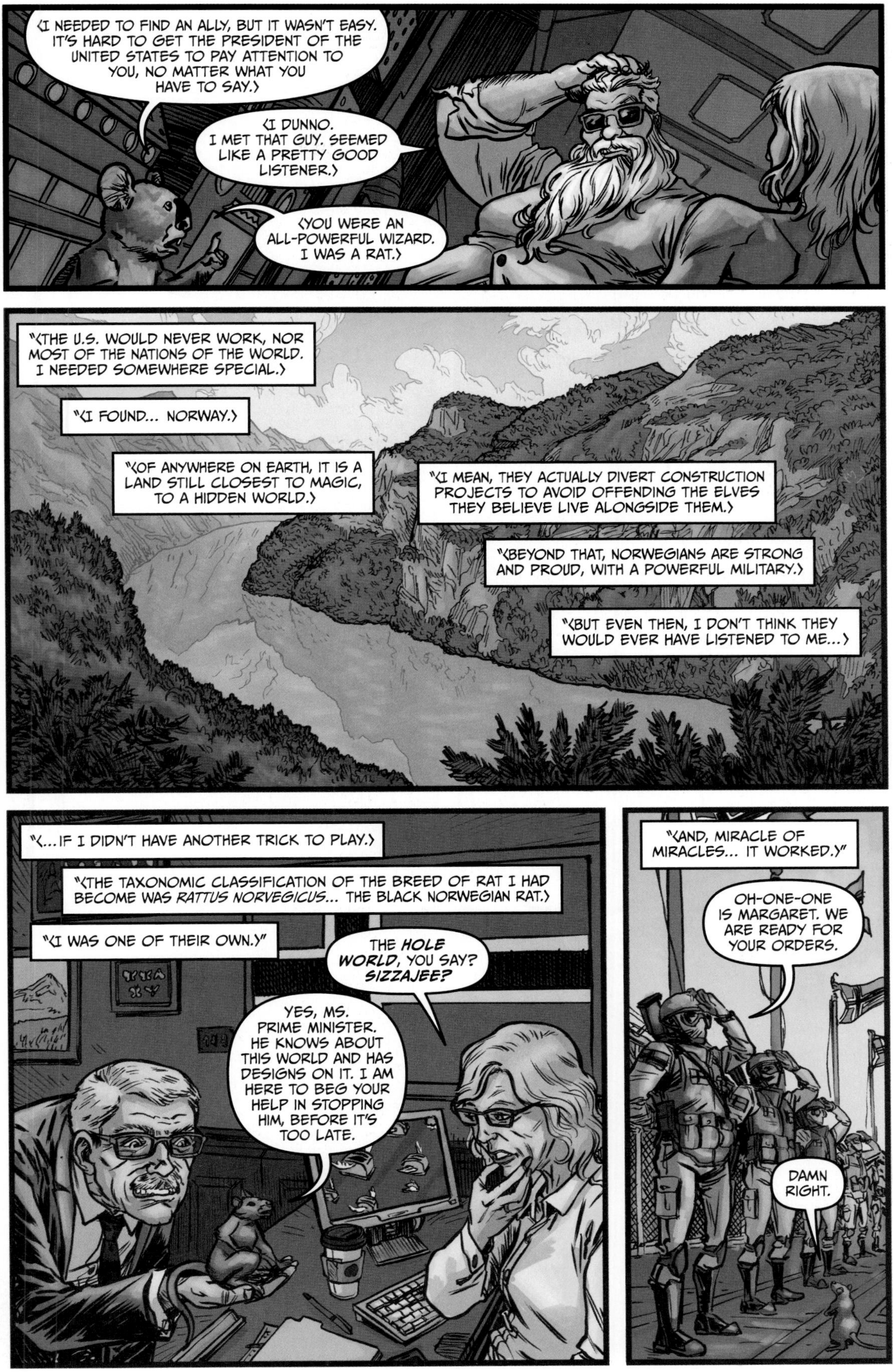
‹I NEEDED TO FIND AN ALLY, BUT IT WASN'T EASY. IT'S HARD TO GET THE PRESIDENT OF THE UNITED STATES TO PAY ATTENTION TO YOU, NO MATTER WHAT YOU HAVE TO SAY.›
‹I DUNNO. I MET THAT GUY. SEEMED LIKE A PRETTY GOOD LISTENER.›
‹YOU WERE AN ALL-POWERFUL WIZARD. I WAS A RAT.›
"‹THE U.S. WOULD NEVER WORK, NOR MOST OF THE NATIONS OF THE WORLD. I NEEDED SOMEWHERE SPECIAL.›
"‹I FOUND... NORWAY.›
"‹OF ANYWHERE ON EARTH, IT IS A LAND STILL CLOSEST TO MAGIC, TO A HIDDEN WORLD.›
"‹I MEAN, THEY ACTUALLY DIVERT CONSTRUCTION PROJECTS TO AVOID OFFENDING THE ELVES THEY BELIEVE LIVE ALONGSIDE THEM.›
"‹BEYOND THAT, NORWEGIANS ARE STRONG AND PROUD, WITH A POWERFUL MILITARY.›
"‹BUT EVEN THEN, I DON'T THINK THEY WOULD EVER HAVE LISTENED TO ME...›
"‹...IF I DIDN'T HAVE ANOTHER TRICK TO PLAY.›
"‹THE TAXONOMIC CLASSIFICATION OF THE BREED OF RAT I HAD BECOME WAS *RATTUS NORVEGICUS*... THE BLACK NORWEGIAN RAT.›
"‹I WAS ONE OF THEIR OWN.›"
THE ***HOLE WORLD***, YOU SAY? ***SIZZAJEE?***
YES, MS. PRIME MINISTER. HE KNOWS ABOUT THIS WORLD AND HAS DESIGNS ON IT. I AM HERE TO BEG YOUR HELP IN STOPPING HIM, BEFORE IT'S TOO LATE.
"‹AND, MIRACLE OF MIRACLES... IT WORKED.›"
OH-ONE-ONE IS MARGARET. WE ARE READY FOR YOUR ORDERS.
DAMN RIGHT.

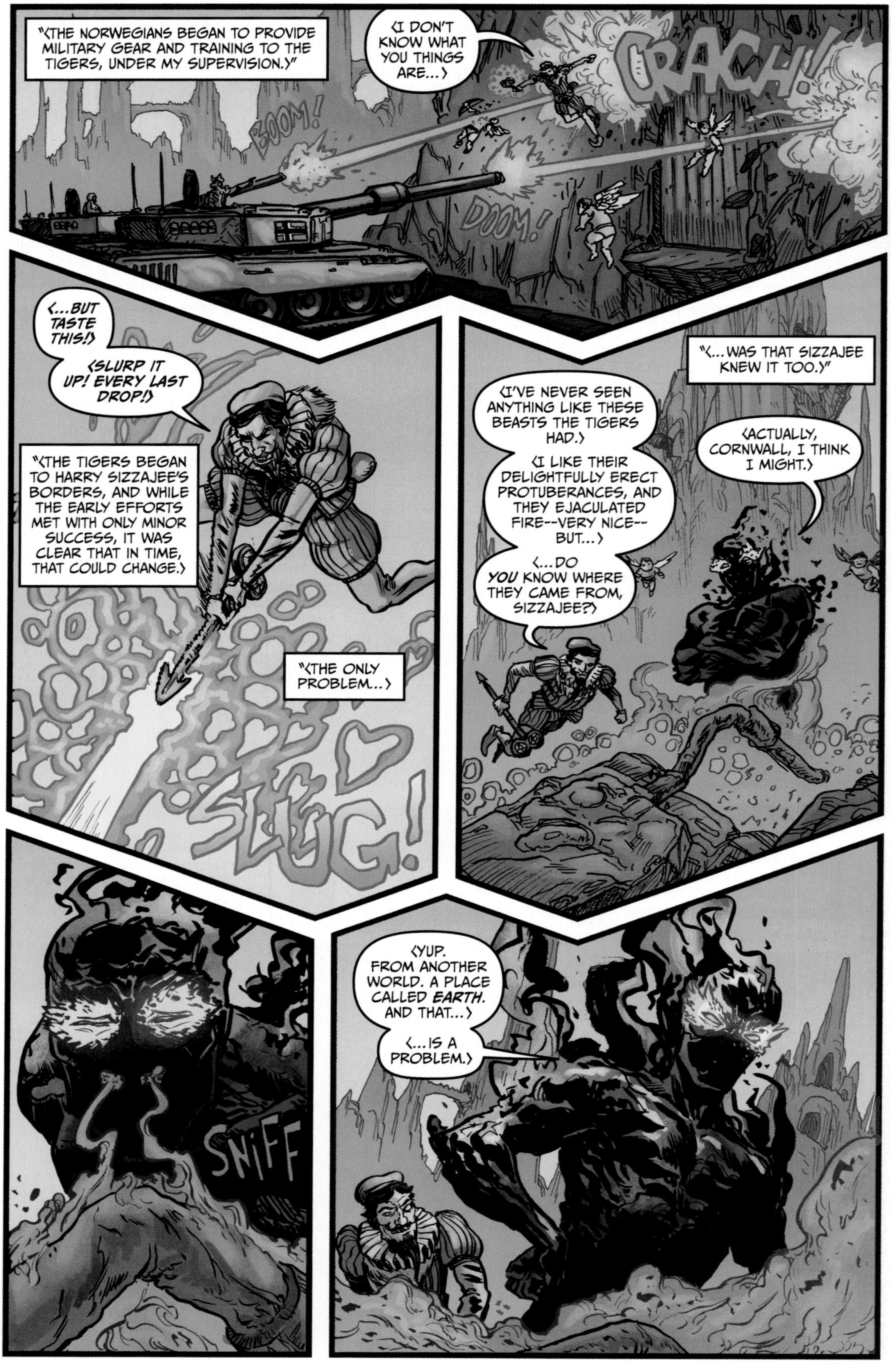
"‹THE NORWEGIANS BEGAN TO PROVIDE MILITARY GEAR AND TRAINING TO THE TIGERS, UNDER MY SUPERVISION.›"
‹I DON'T KNOW WHAT YOU THINGS ARE...›
CRACH!!
BOOM!
DOOM!
‹...BUT TASTE THIS!›
‹SLURP IT UP! EVERY LAST DROP!›
"‹THE TIGERS BEGAN TO HARRY SIZZAJEE'S BORDERS, AND WHILE THE EARLY EFFORTS MET WITH ONLY MINOR SUCCESS, IT WAS CLEAR THAT IN TIME, THAT COULD CHANGE.›
"‹THE ONLY PROBLEM...›
SLUG!
"‹...WAS THAT SIZZAJEE KNEW IT TOO.›"
‹I'VE NEVER SEEN ANYTHING LIKE THESE BEASTS THE TIGERS HAD.›
‹I LIKE THEIR DELIGHTFULLY ERECT PROTUBERANCES, AND THEY EJACULATED FIRE--VERY NICE--BUT...›
‹...DO YOU KNOW WHERE THEY CAME FROM, SIZZAJEE?›
‹ACTUALLY, CORNWALL, I THINK I MIGHT.›
SNIFF
‹YUP. FROM ANOTHER WORLD. A PLACE CALLED EARTH. AND THAT...›
‹...IS A PROBLEM.›

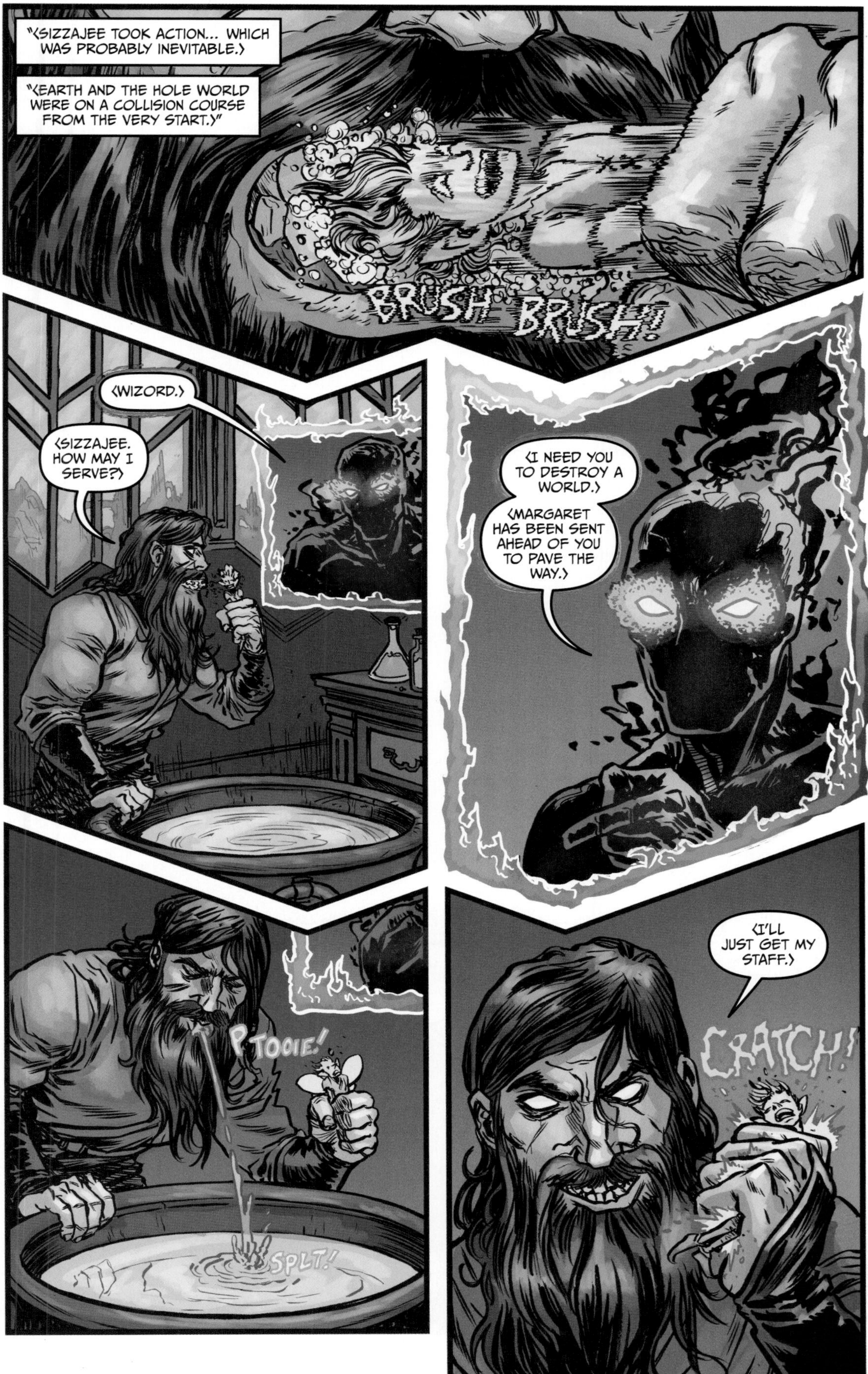
"<SIZZAJEE TOOK ACTION... WHICH WAS PROBABLY INEVITABLE.>
"<EARTH AND THE HOLE WORLD WERE ON A COLLISION COURSE FROM THE VERY START.>"
BRUSH BRUSH!
<WIZORD.>
<SIZZAJEE. HOW MAY I SERVE?>
<I NEED YOU TO DESTROY A WORLD.>
<MARGARET HAS BEEN SENT AHEAD OF YOU TO PAVE THE WAY.>
PTOOIE!
SPLT!
<I'LL JUST GET MY STAFF.>
CRATCH!

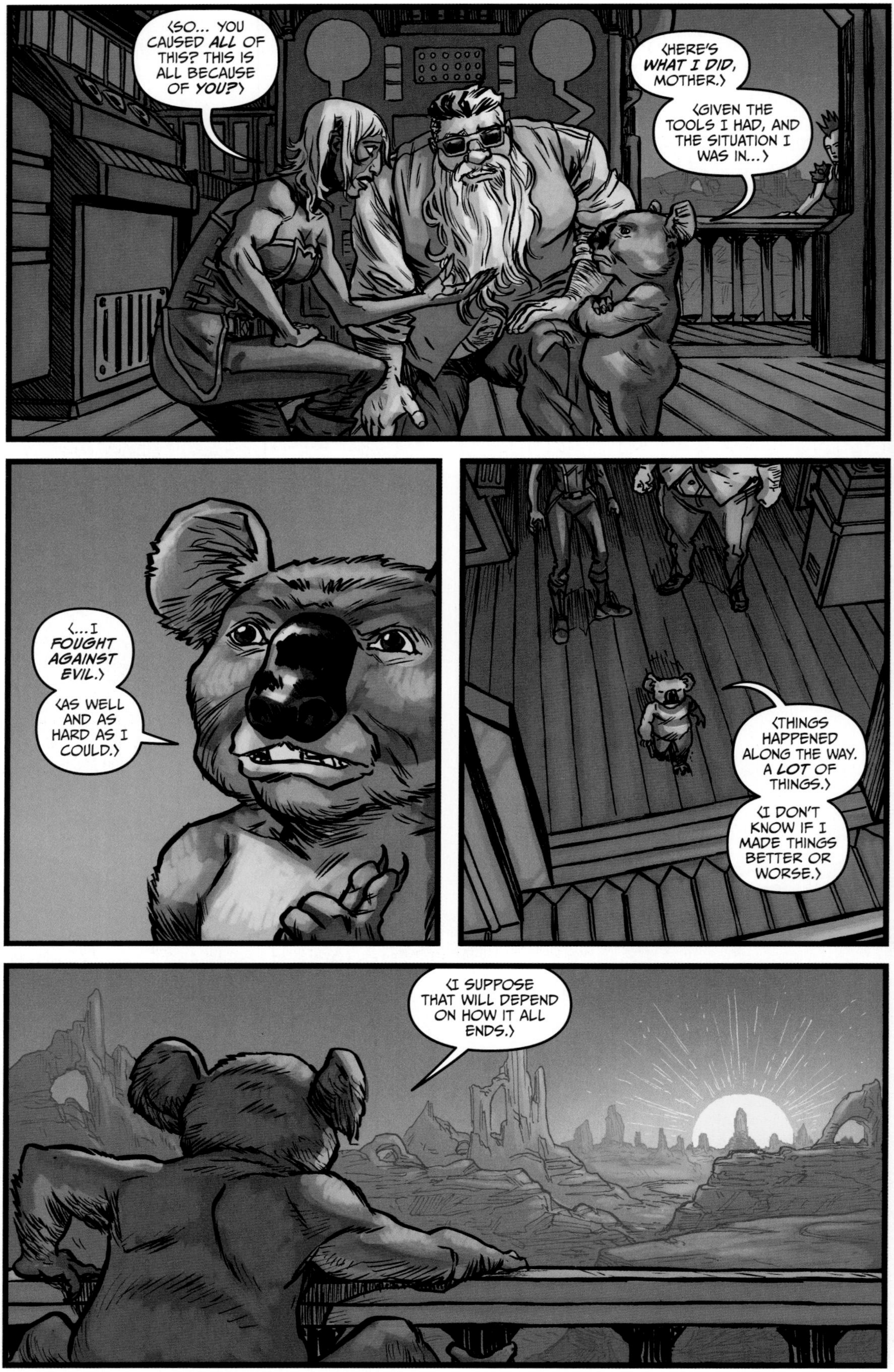
<SO... YOU CAUSED **ALL** OF THIS? THIS IS ALL BECAUSE OF **YOU?**>
<HERE'S **WHAT I DID**, MOTHER.>
<GIVEN THE TOOLS I HAD, AND THE SITUATION I WAS IN...>
<...I **FOUGHT AGAINST EVIL.**>
<AS WELL AND AS HARD AS I COULD.>
<THINGS HAPPENED ALONG THE WAY. A **LOT** OF THINGS.>
<I DON'T KNOW IF I MADE THINGS BETTER OR WORSE.>
<I SUPPOSE THAT WILL DEPEND ON HOW IT ALL ENDS.>

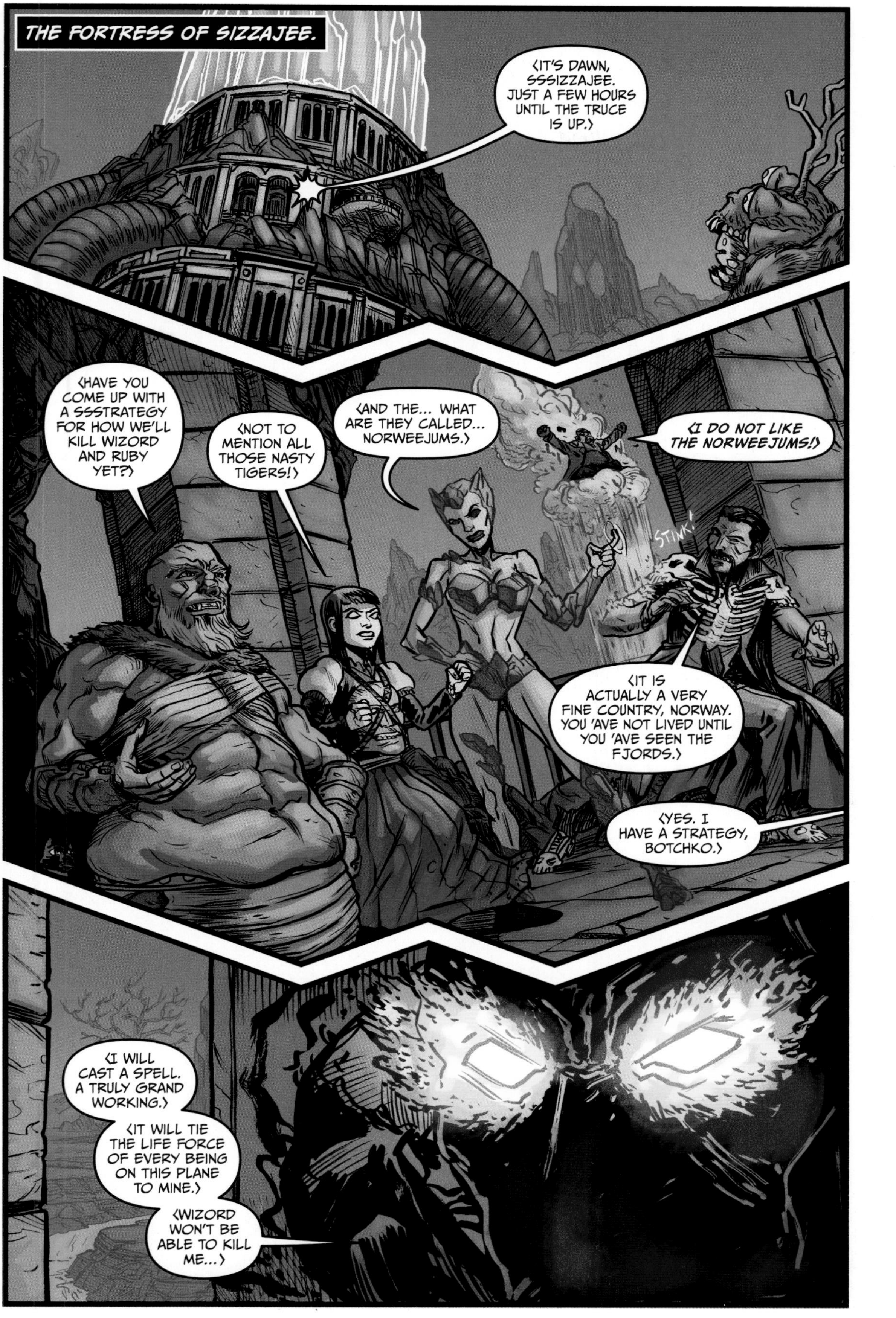
THE FORTRESS OF SIZZAJEE.
⟨IT'S DAWN, SSSIZZAJEE. JUST A FEW HOURS UNTIL THE TRUCE IS UP.⟩
⟨HAVE YOU COME UP WITH A SSSTRATEGY FOR HOW WE'LL KILL WIZORD AND RUBY YET?⟩
⟨NOT TO MENTION ALL THOSE NASTY TIGERS!⟩
⟨AND THE... WHAT ARE THEY CALLED... NORWEEJUMS.⟩
⟨I DO NOT LIKE THE NORWEEJUMS!⟩
STINK!
⟨IT IS ACTUALLY A VERY FINE COUNTRY, NORWAY. YOU 'AVE NOT LIVED UNTIL YOU 'AVE SEEN THE FJORDS.⟩
⟨YES. I HAVE A STRATEGY, BOTCHKO.⟩
⟨I WILL CAST A SPELL. A TRULY GRAND WORKING.⟩
⟨IT WILL TIE THE LIFE FORCE OF EVERY BEING ON THIS PLANE TO MINE.⟩
⟨WIZORD WON'T BE ABLE TO KILL ME...⟩

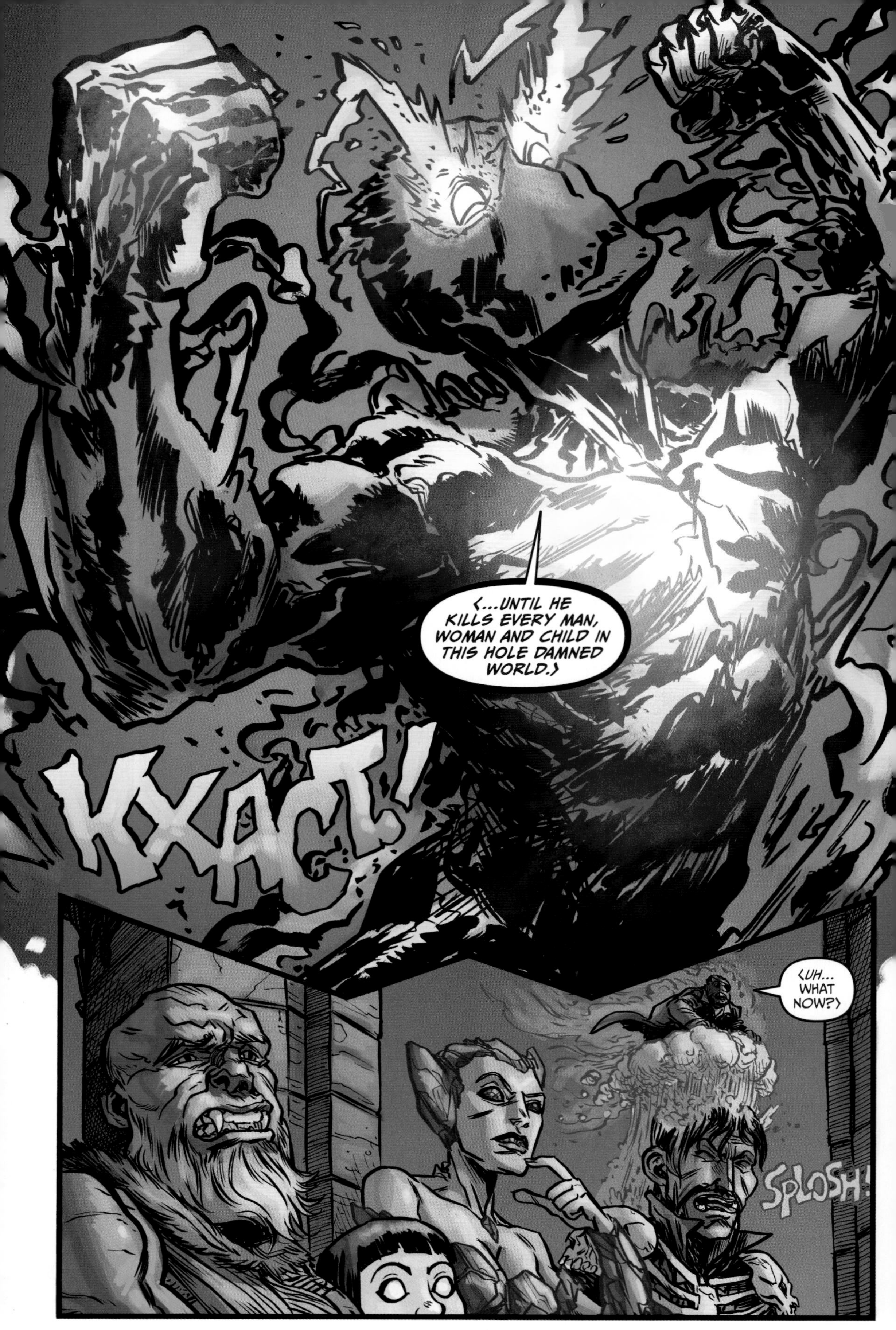
‹...UNTIL HE KILLS EVERY MAN, WOMAN AND CHILD IN THIS HOLE DAMNED WORLD.›
KXACT!
‹UH... WHAT NOW?›
SPLOSH!

TWENTY-FOUR

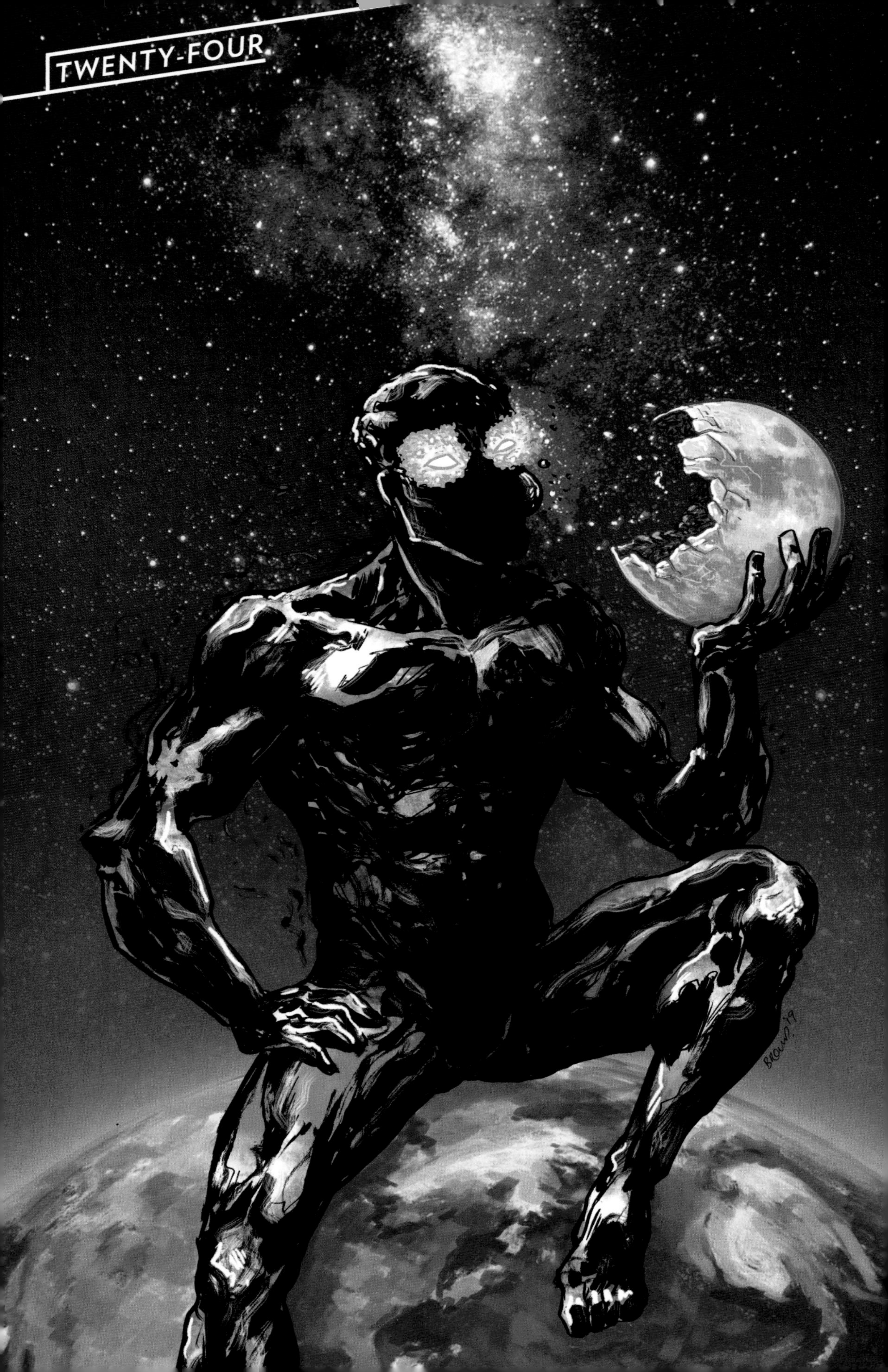
BROWN '19

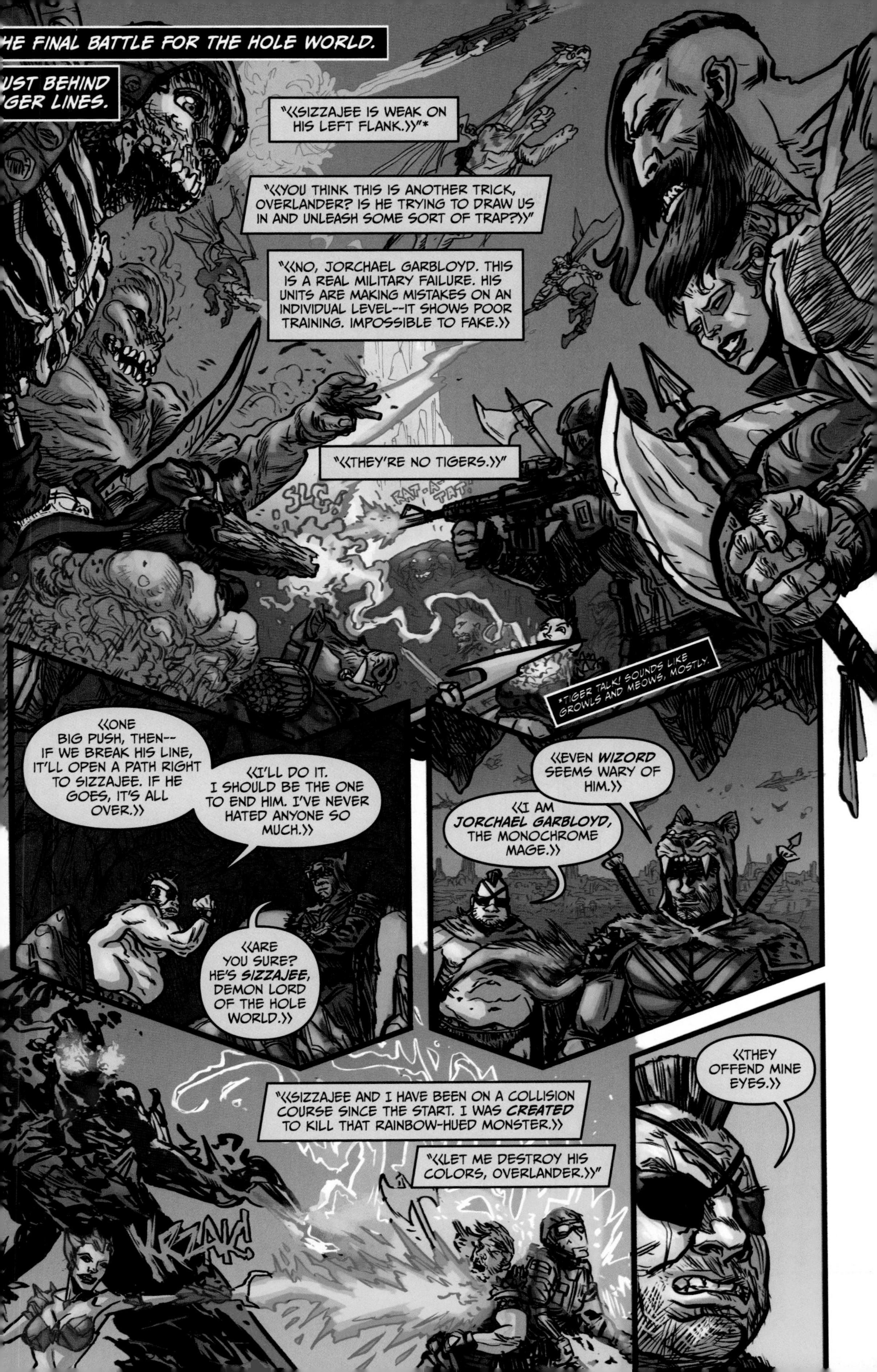
HE FINAL BATTLE FOR THE HOLE WORLD.
UST BEHIND GER LINES.
"<<SIZZAJEE IS WEAK ON HIS LEFT FLANK.>>"*
"<<YOU THINK THIS IS ANOTHER TRICK, OVERLANDER? IS HE TRYING TO DRAW US IN AND UNLEASH SOME SORT OF TRAP?>>"
"<<NO, JORCHAEL GARBLOYD. THIS IS A REAL MILITARY FAILURE. HIS UNITS ARE MAKING MISTAKES ON AN INDIVIDUAL LEVEL--IT SHOWS POOR TRAINING. IMPOSSIBLE TO FAKE.>>
"<<THEY'RE NO TIGERS.>>"
SLC!
RAT-A-TAT!
*TIGER TALK! SOUNDS LIKE GROWLS AND MEOWS, MOSTLY.
<<ONE BIG PUSH, THEN-- IF WE BREAK HIS LINE, IT'LL OPEN A PATH RIGHT TO SIZZAJEE. IF HE GOES, IT'S ALL OVER.>>
<<I'LL DO IT. I SHOULD BE THE ONE TO END HIM. I'VE NEVER HATED ANYONE SO MUCH.>>
<<ARE YOU SURE? HE'S SIZZAJEE, DEMON LORD OF THE HOLE WORLD.>>
<<EVEN WIZORD SEEMS WARY OF HIM.>>
<<I AM JORCHAEL GARBLOYD, THE MONOCHROME MAGE.>>
"<<SIZZAJEE AND I HAVE BEEN ON A COLLISION COURSE SINCE THE START. I WAS CREATED TO KILL THAT RAINBOW-HUED MONSTER.>>
"<<LET ME DESTROY HIS COLORS, OVERLANDER.>>"
<<THEY OFFEND MINE EYES.>>
KRZAK!

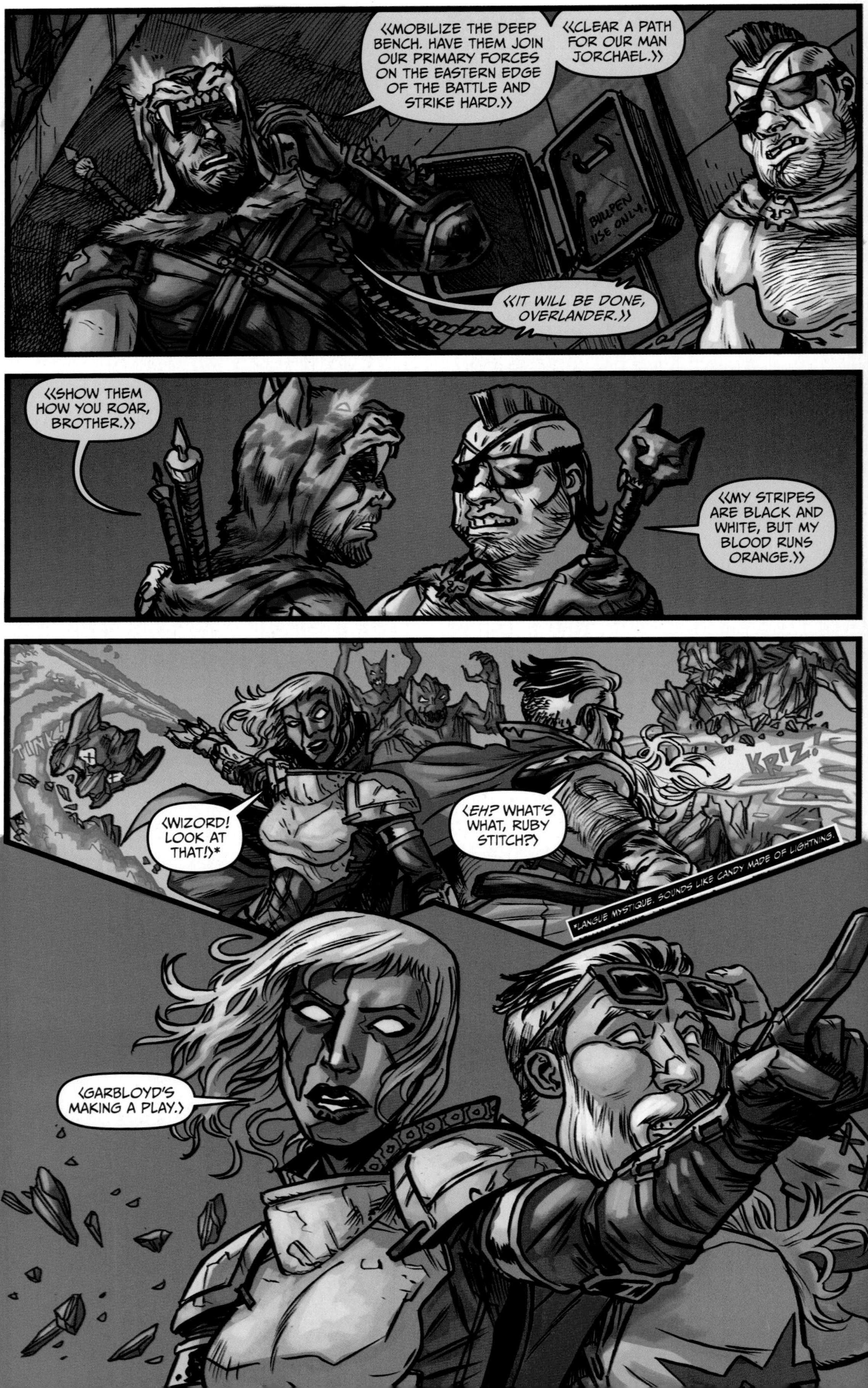

<<MOBILIZE THE DEEP BENCH. HAVE THEM JOIN OUR PRIMARY FORCES ON THE EASTERN EDGE OF THE BATTLE AND STRIKE HARD.>>
<<CLEAR A PATH FOR OUR MAN JORCHAEL.>>
BULLPEN USE ONLY!
<<IT WILL BE DONE, OVERLANDER.>>
<<SHOW THEM HOW YOU ROAR, BROTHER.>>
<<MY STRIPES ARE BLACK AND WHITE, BUT MY BLOOD RUNS ORANGE.>>
TINK!
KRIZ!
<WIZORD! LOOK AT THAT!>*
<EH? WHAT'S WHAT, RUBY STITCH?>
*LANGUE MYSTIQUE. SOUNDS LIKE CANDY MADE OF LIGHTNING.
<GARBLOYD'S MAKING A PLAY.>

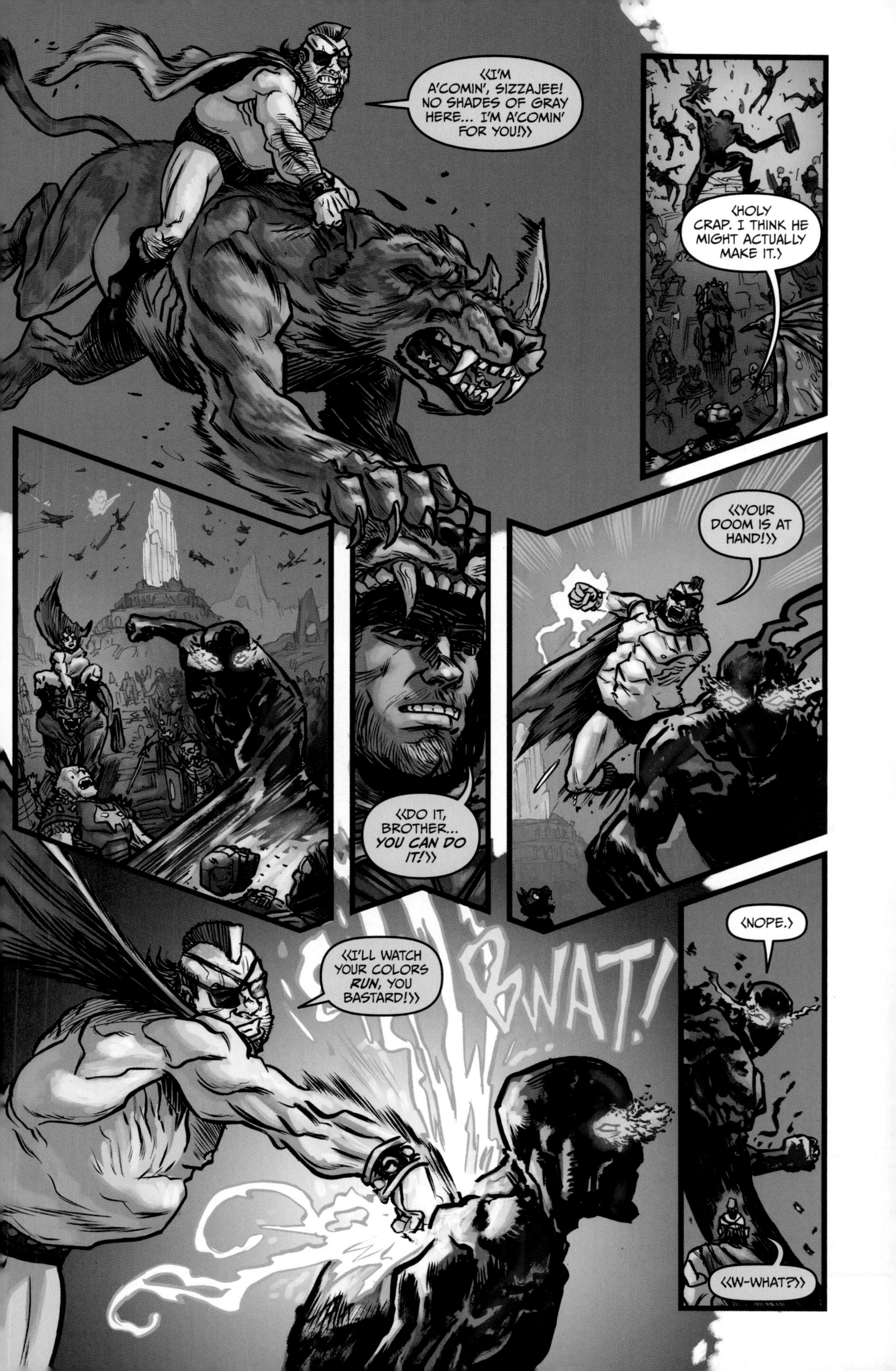

<<I'M A'COMIN', SIZZAJEE! NO SHADES OF GRAY HERE... I'M A'COMIN' FOR YOU!>>
<HOLY CRAP. I THINK HE MIGHT ACTUALLY MAKE IT.>
<<DO IT, BROTHER... *YOU CAN DO IT!*>>
<<YOUR DOOM IS AT HAND!>>
<<I'LL WATCH YOUR COLORS *RUN*, YOU BASTARD!>>
BWAT!
<NOPE.>
<<W-WHAT?>>

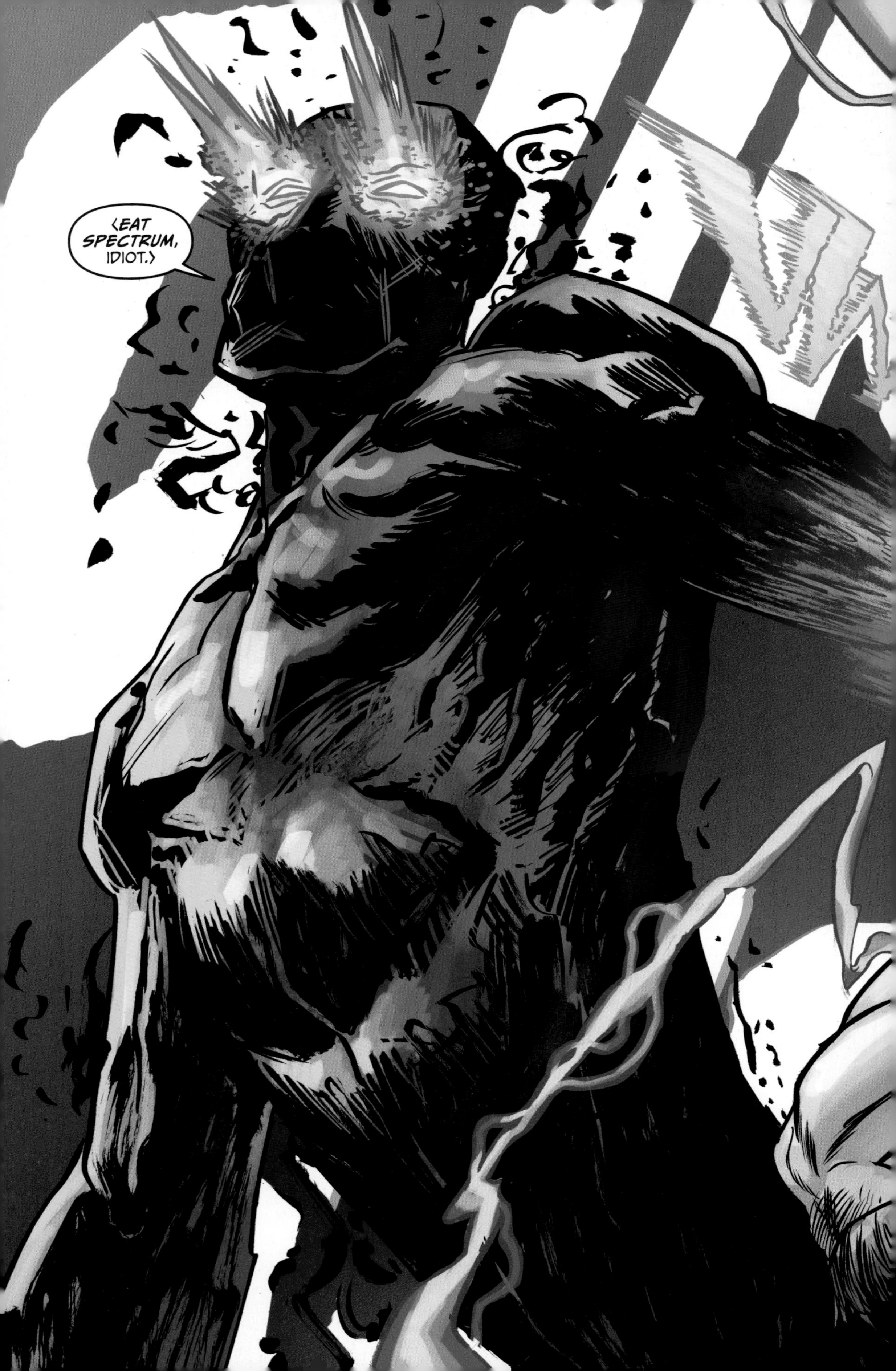
<EAT SPECTRUM, IDIOT.>

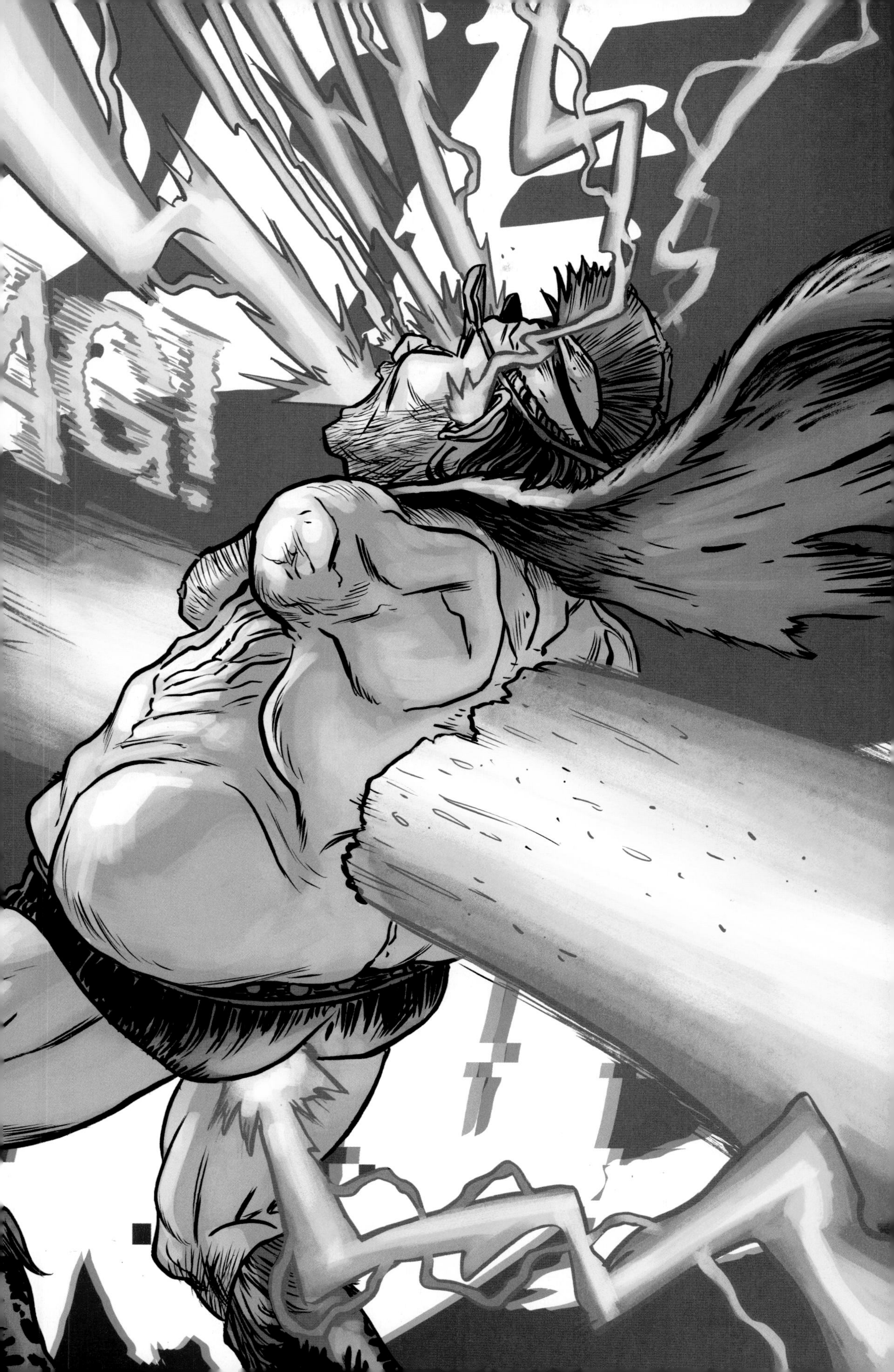

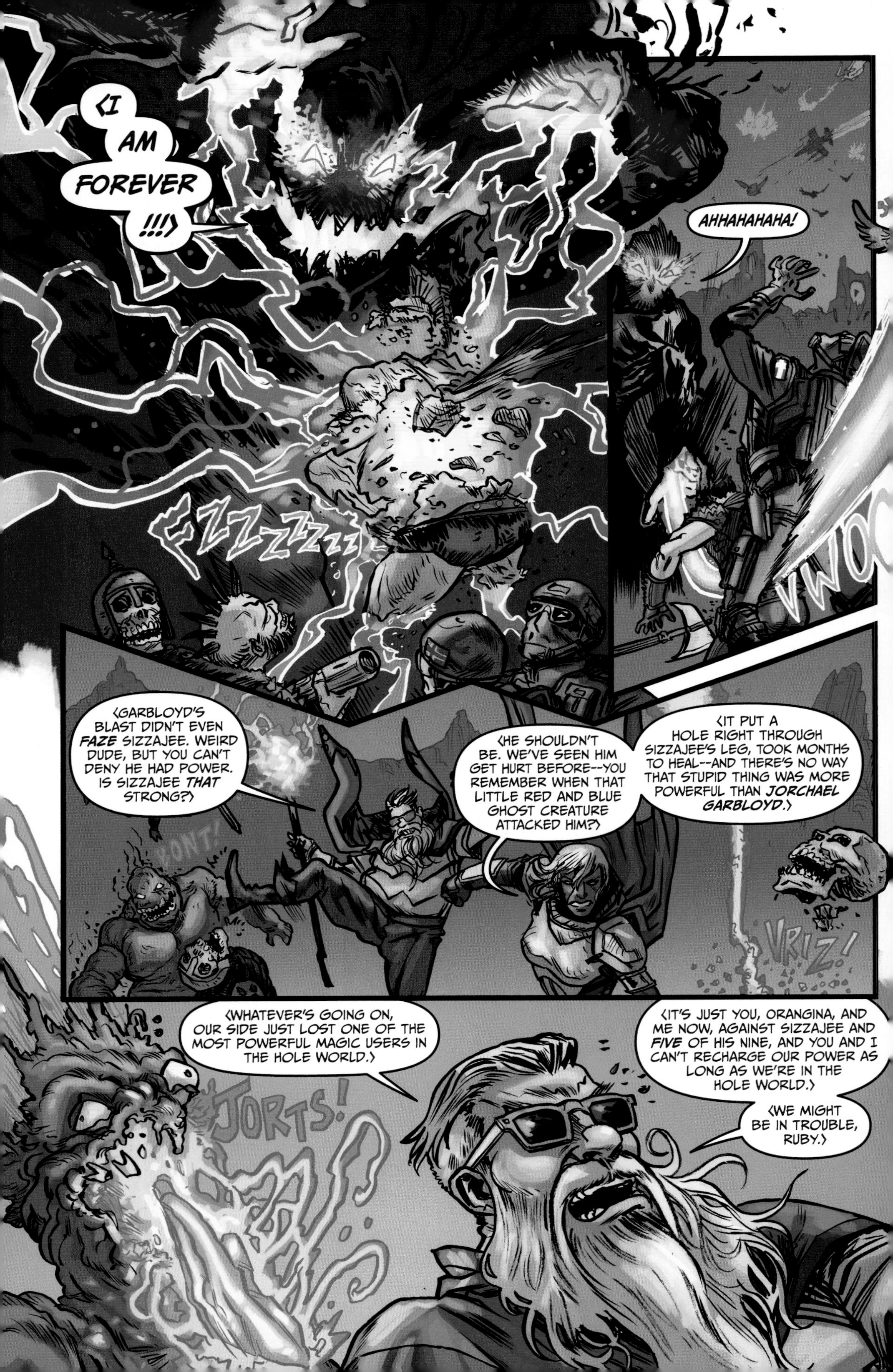
<I AM FOREVER !!!>
FZZZZZZZZ
AHHAHAHAHA!
VWOO
<GARBLOYD'S BLAST DIDN'T EVEN *FAZE* SIZZAJEE. WEIRD DUDE, BUT YOU CAN'T DENY HE HAD POWER. IS SIZZAJEE *THAT* STRONG?>
<HE SHOULDN'T BE. WE'VE SEEN HIM GET HURT BEFORE--YOU REMEMBER WHEN THAT LITTLE RED AND BLUE GHOST CREATURE ATTACKED HIM?>
<IT PUT A HOLE RIGHT THROUGH SIZZAJEE'S LEG, TOOK MONTHS TO HEAL--AND THERE'S NO WAY THAT STUPID THING WAS MORE POWERFUL THAN *JORCHAEL GARBLOYD*.>
BONT!
VRIZ!
<WHATEVER'S GOING ON, OUR SIDE JUST LOST ONE OF THE MOST POWERFUL MAGIC USERS IN THE HOLE WORLD.>
JORTS!
<IT'S JUST YOU, ORANGINA, AND ME NOW, AGAINST SIZZAJEE AND *FIVE* OF HIS NINE, AND YOU AND I CAN'T RECHARGE OUR POWER AS LONG AS WE'RE IN THE HOLE WORLD.>
<WE MIGHT BE IN TROUBLE, RUBY.>

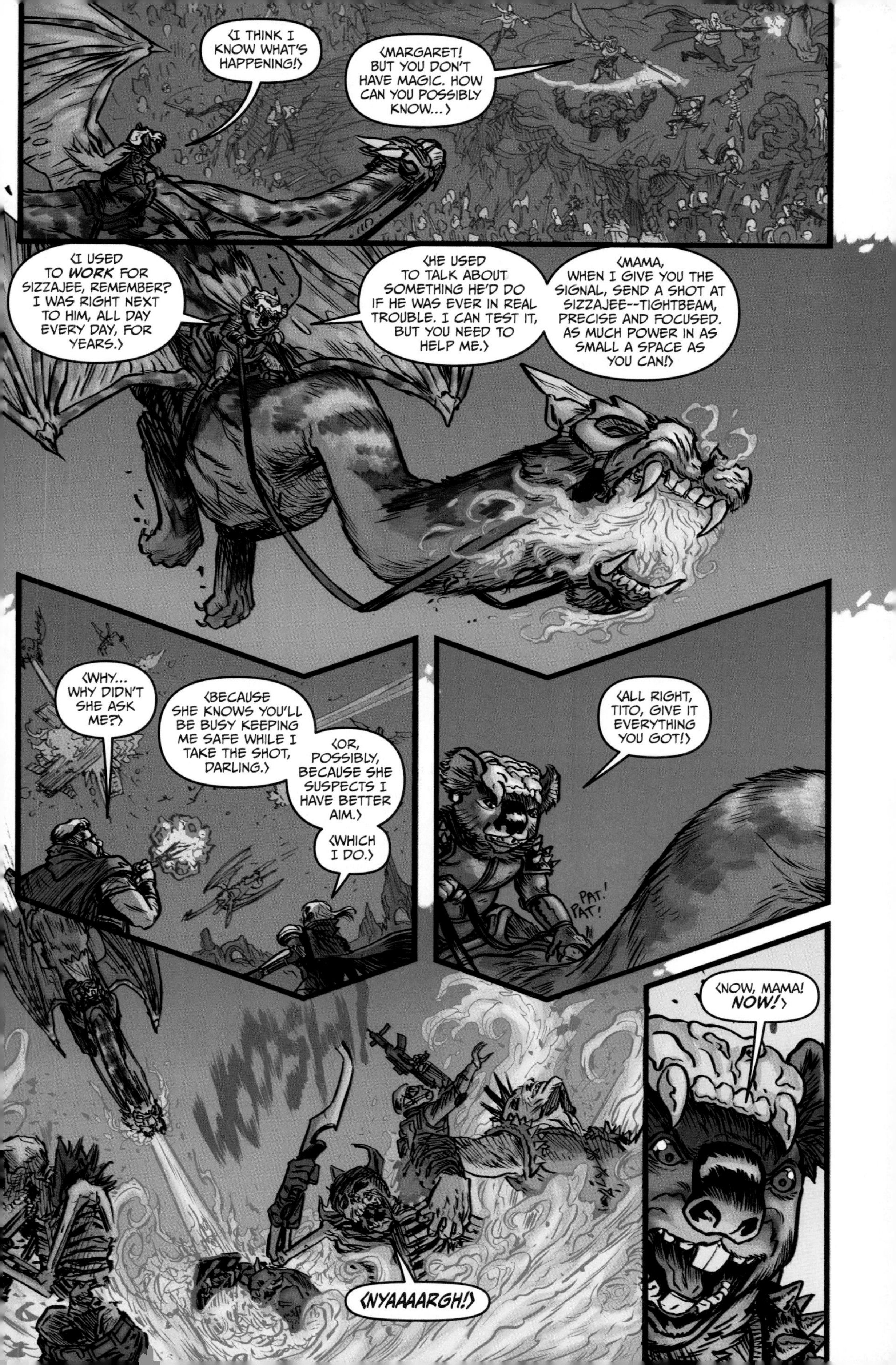

<I THINK I KNOW WHAT'S HAPPENING!>
<MARGARET! BUT YOU DON'T HAVE MAGIC. HOW CAN YOU POSSIBLY KNOW...>
<I USED TO WORK FOR SIZZAJEE, REMEMBER? I WAS RIGHT NEXT TO HIM, ALL DAY EVERY DAY, FOR YEARS.>
<HE USED TO TALK ABOUT SOMETHING HE'D DO IF HE WAS EVER IN REAL TROUBLE. I CAN TEST IT, BUT YOU NEED TO HELP ME.>
<MAMA, WHEN I GIVE YOU THE SIGNAL, SEND A SHOT AT SIZZAJEE--TIGHTBEAM, PRECISE AND FOCUSED. AS MUCH POWER IN AS SMALL A SPACE AS YOU CAN!>
<WHY... WHY DIDN'T SHE ASK ME?>
<BECAUSE SHE KNOWS YOU'LL BE BUSY KEEPING ME SAFE WHILE I TAKE THE SHOT, DARLING.>
<OR, POSSIBLY, BECAUSE SHE SUSPECTS I HAVE BETTER AIM.>
<WHICH I DO.>
<ALL RIGHT, TITO, GIVE IT EVERYTHING YOU GOT!>
PAT! PAT!
<NOW, MAMA! NOW!>
WOOSH!
<NYAAAARGH!>

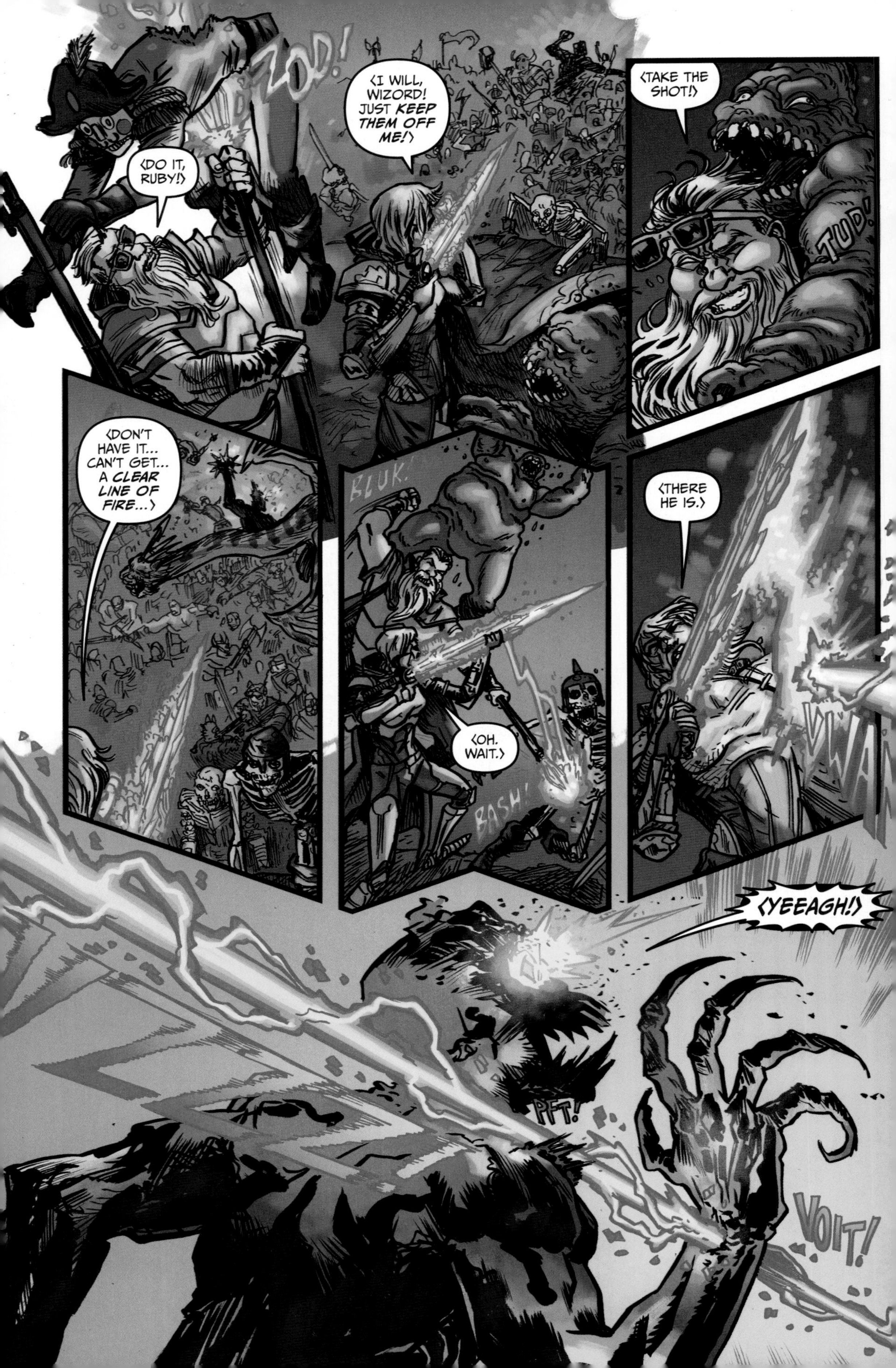
ZZOD!
‹DO IT, RUBY!›
‹I WILL, WIZORD! JUST KEEP THEM OFF ME!›
‹TAKE THE SHOT!›
TUD!
‹DON'T HAVE IT... CAN'T GET... A CLEAR LINE OF FIRE...›
BLUK!
‹OH. WAIT.›
BASH!
‹THERE HE IS.›
‹YEEAGH!›
PFT!
VOIT!

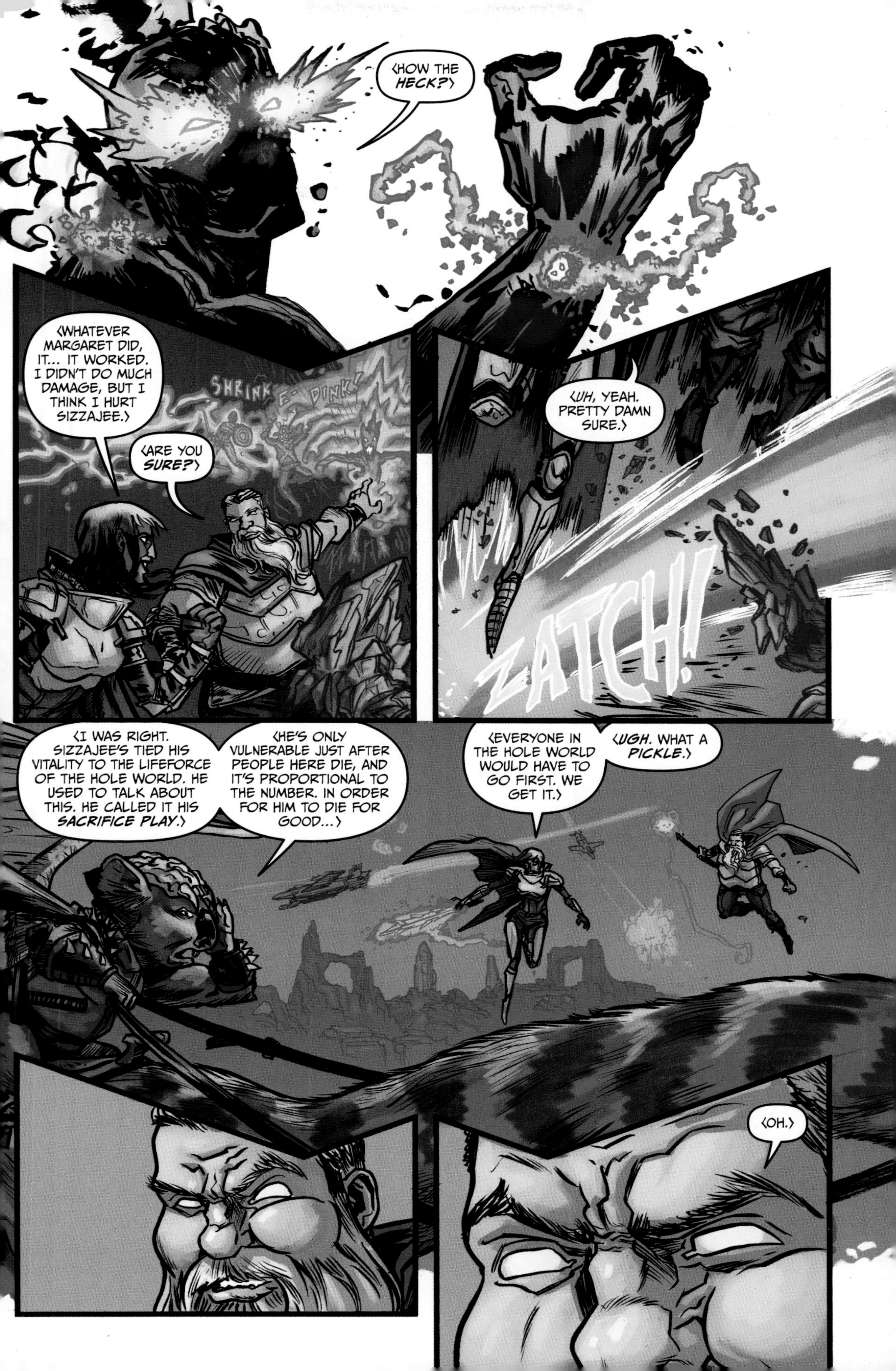
‹HOW THE HECK?›
‹WHATEVER MARGARET DID, IT... IT WORKED. I DIDN'T DO MUCH DAMAGE, BUT I THINK I HURT SIZZAJEE.›
SHRINK E-DINK!
‹ARE YOU SURE?›
‹UH, YEAH. PRETTY DAMN SURE.›
ZATCH!
‹I WAS RIGHT. SIZZAJEE'S TIED HIS VITALITY TO THE LIFEFORCE OF THE HOLE WORLD. HE USED TO TALK ABOUT THIS. HE CALLED IT HIS SACRIFICE PLAY.›
‹HE'S ONLY VULNERABLE JUST AFTER PEOPLE HERE DIE, AND IT'S PROPORTIONAL TO THE NUMBER. IN ORDER FOR HIM TO DIE FOR GOOD...›
‹EVERYONE IN THE HOLE WORLD WOULD HAVE TO GO FIRST. WE GET IT.›
‹UGH. WHAT A PICKLE.›
‹OH.›

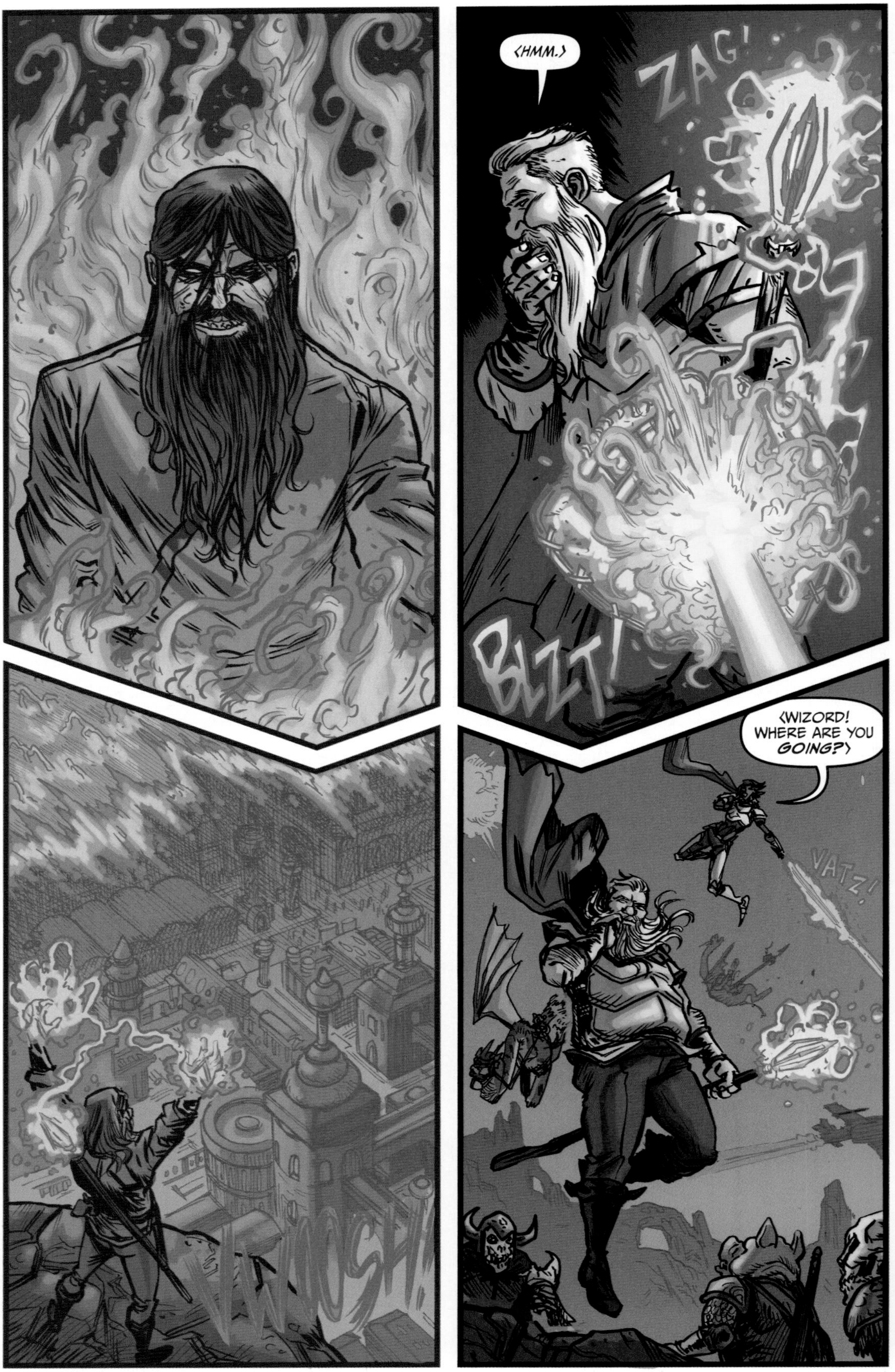

‹HMM.›
ZAG!
BZZT!
WOOSH!
‹WIZORD! WHERE ARE YOU GOING?›
VATZ!

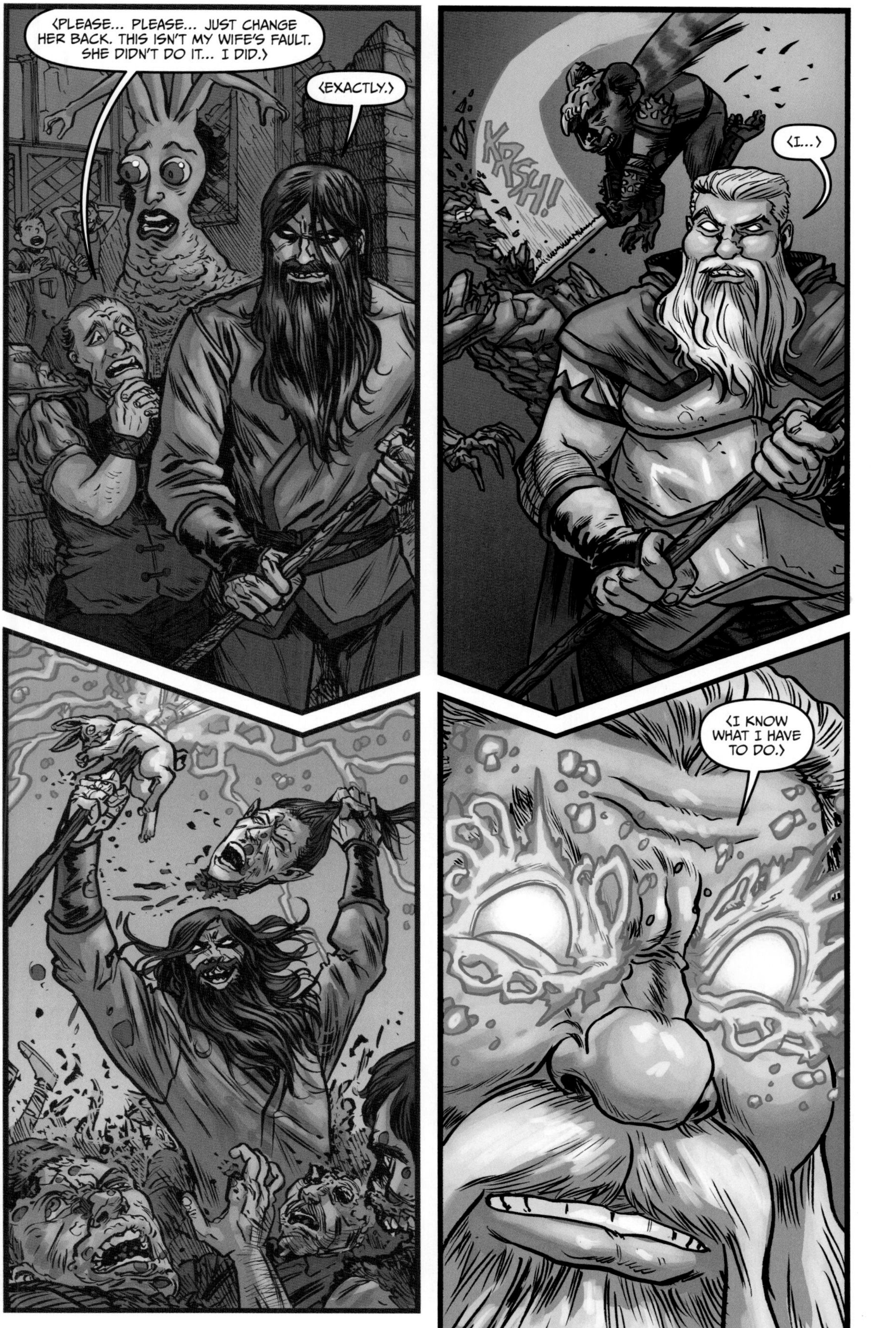

‹PLEASE... PLEASE... JUST CHANGE HER BACK. THIS ISN'T MY WIFE'S FAULT. SHE DIDN'T DO IT... I DID.›
‹EXACTLY.›
KRSH!
‹I...›
‹I KNOW WHAT I HAVE TO DO.›

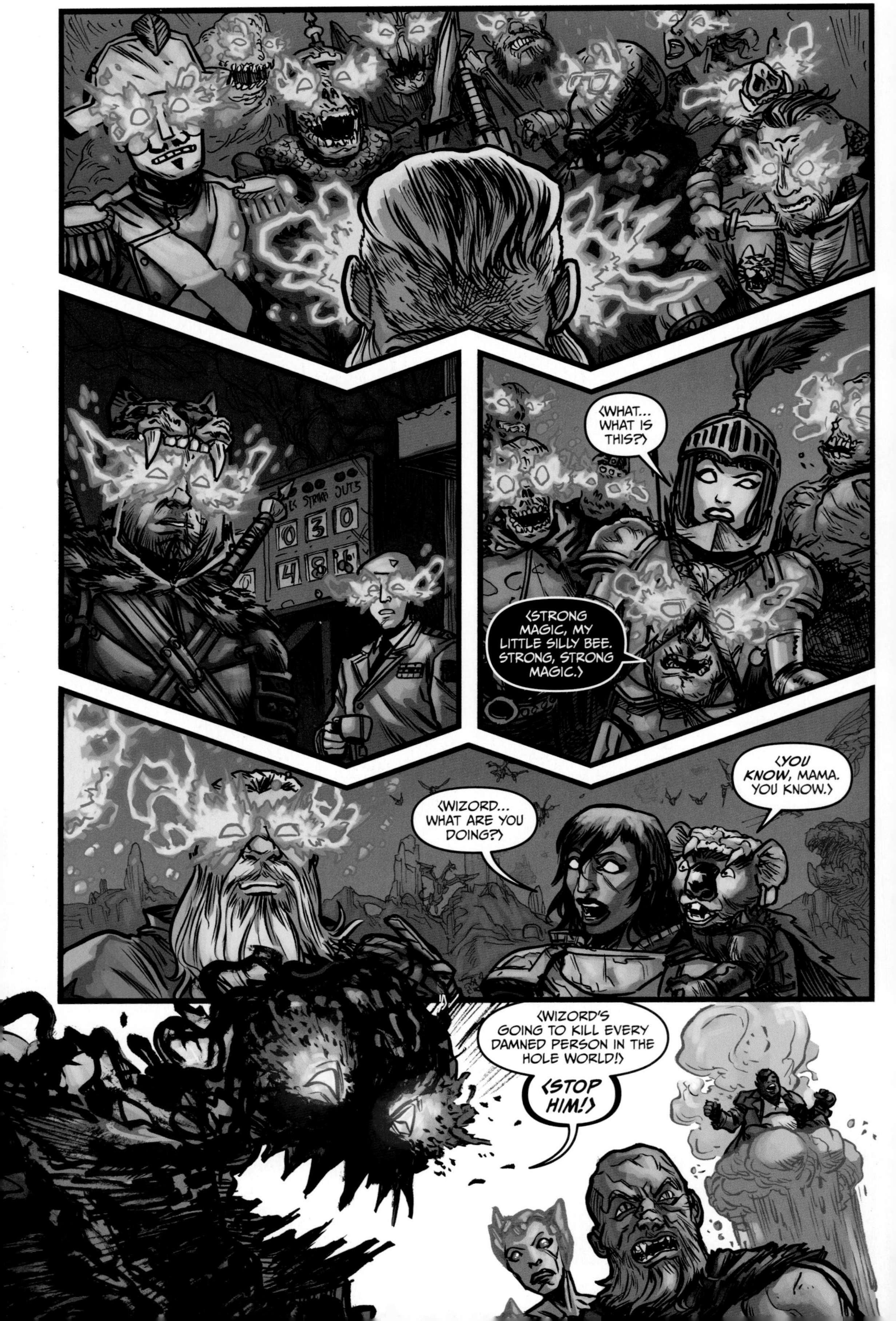

⟨WHAT... WHAT IS THIS?⟩
⟨STRONG MAGIC, MY LITTLE SILLY BEE. STRONG, STRONG MAGIC.⟩
⟨WIZORD... WHAT ARE YOU DOING?⟩
⟨YOU KNOW, MAMA. YOU KNOW.⟩
⟨WIZORD'S GOING TO KILL EVERY DAMNED PERSON IN THE HOLE WORLD!⟩
⟨STOP HIM!⟩

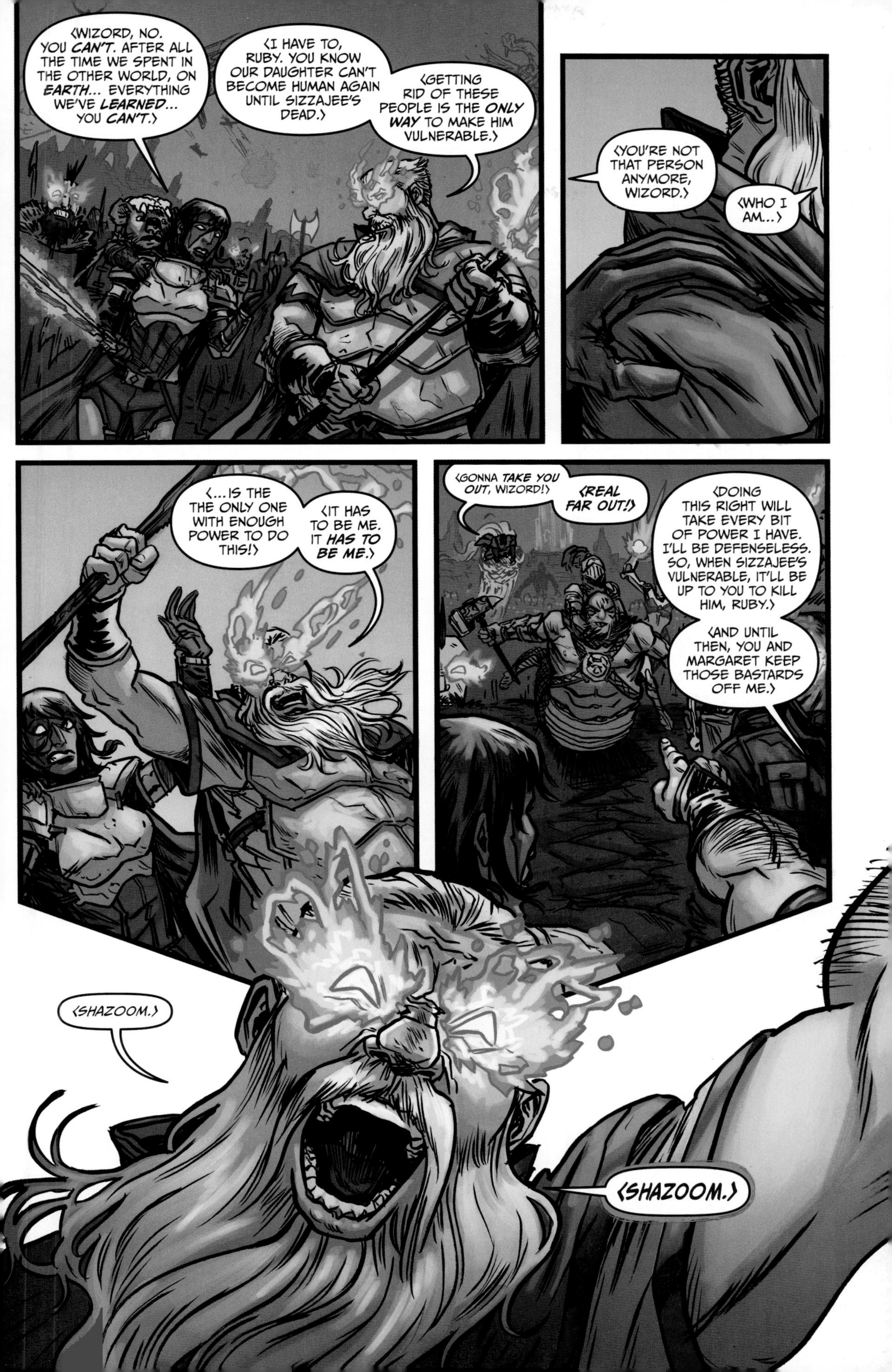

‹WIZORD, NO. YOU CAN'T. AFTER ALL THE TIME WE SPENT IN THE OTHER WORLD, ON EARTH... EVERYTHING WE'VE LEARNED... YOU CAN'T.›
‹I HAVE TO, RUBY. YOU KNOW OUR DAUGHTER CAN'T BECOME HUMAN AGAIN UNTIL SIZZAJEE'S DEAD.›
‹GETTING RID OF THESE PEOPLE IS THE ONLY WAY TO MAKE HIM VULNERABLE.›
‹YOU'RE NOT THAT PERSON ANYMORE, WIZORD.›
‹WHO I AM...›
‹...IS THE THE ONLY ONE WITH ENOUGH POWER TO DO THIS!›
‹IT HAS TO BE ME. IT HAS TO BE ME.›
‹GONNA TAKE YOU OUT, WIZORD!›
‹REAL FAR OUT!›
‹DOING THIS RIGHT WILL TAKE EVERY BIT OF POWER I HAVE. I'LL BE DEFENSELESS. SO, WHEN SIZZAJEE'S VULNERABLE, IT'LL BE UP TO YOU TO KILL HIM, RUBY.›
‹AND UNTIL THEN, YOU AND MARGARET KEEP THOSE BASTARDS OFF ME.›
‹SHAZOOM.›
‹SHAZOOM.›

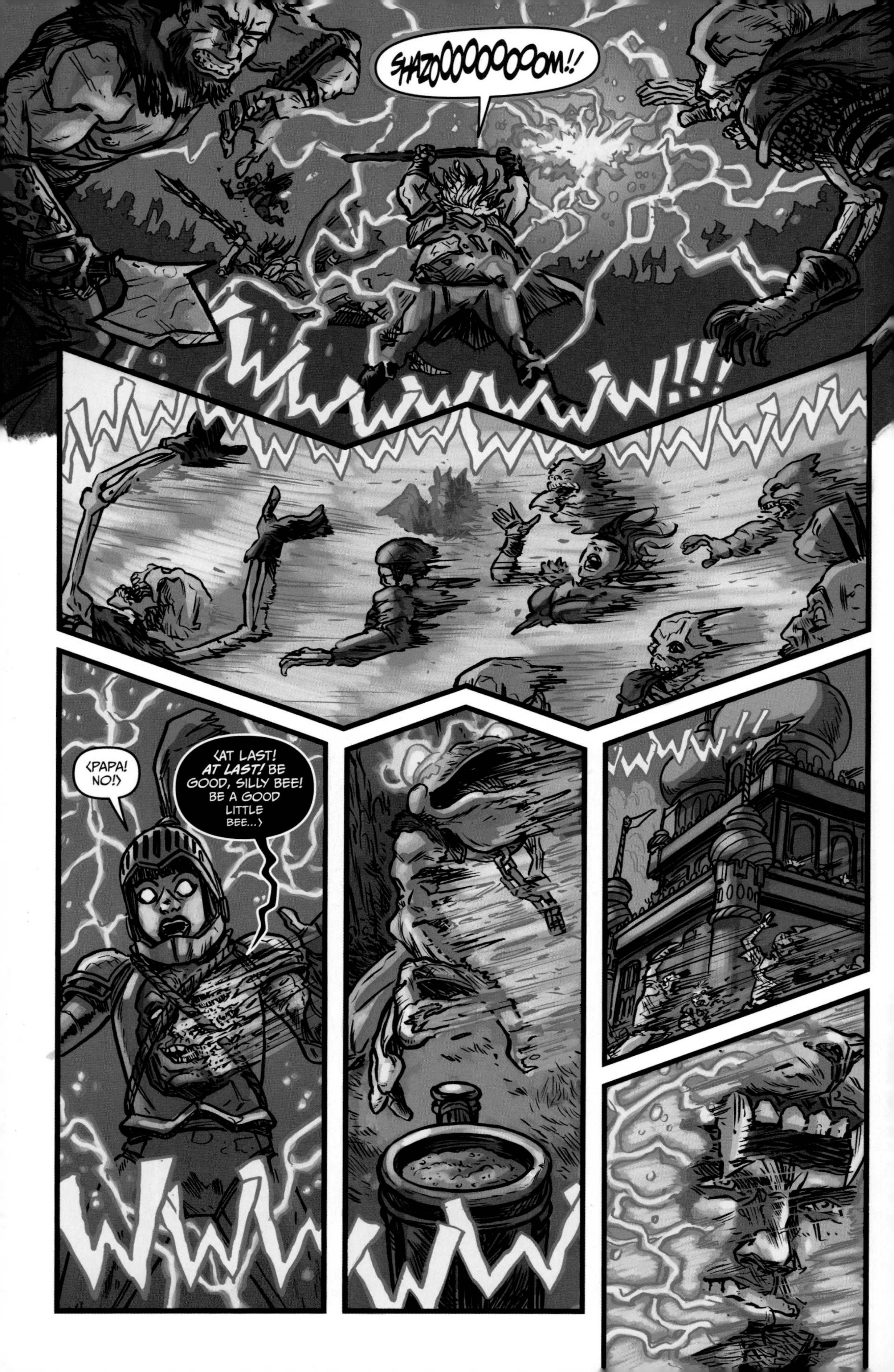
SHAZOOOOOOOOM!!
WWWWWW!!!
WWW!!
<PAPA! NO!>
<AT LAST! AT LAST! BE GOOD, SILLY BEE! BE A GOOD LITTLE BEE...>

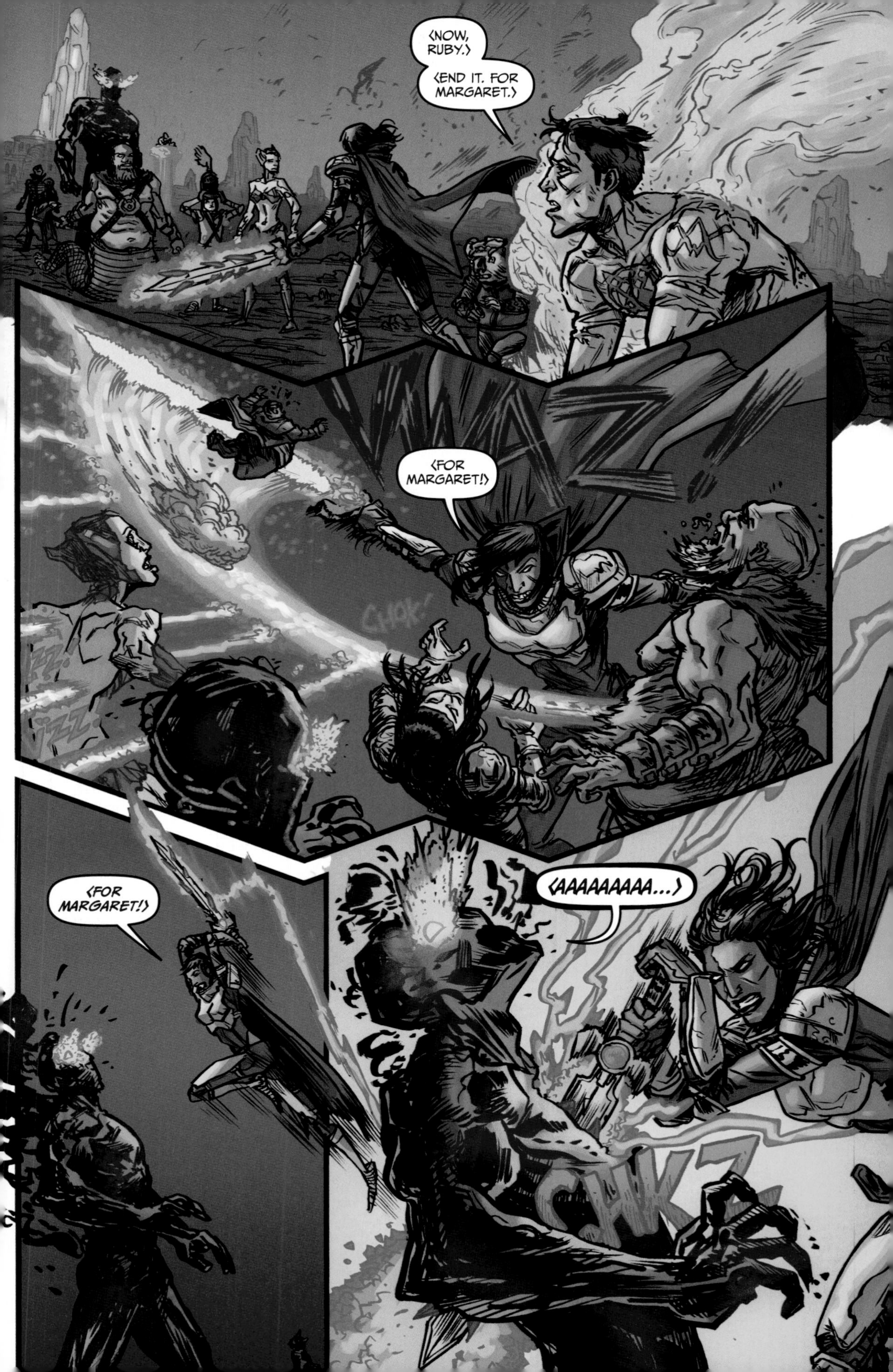
<NOW, RUBY.>
<END IT. FOR MARGARET.>
VWAZZ
<FOR MARGARET!>
CHOK!
ZZZ
<FOR MARGARET!>
<AAAAAAAAA...>
CHKZ

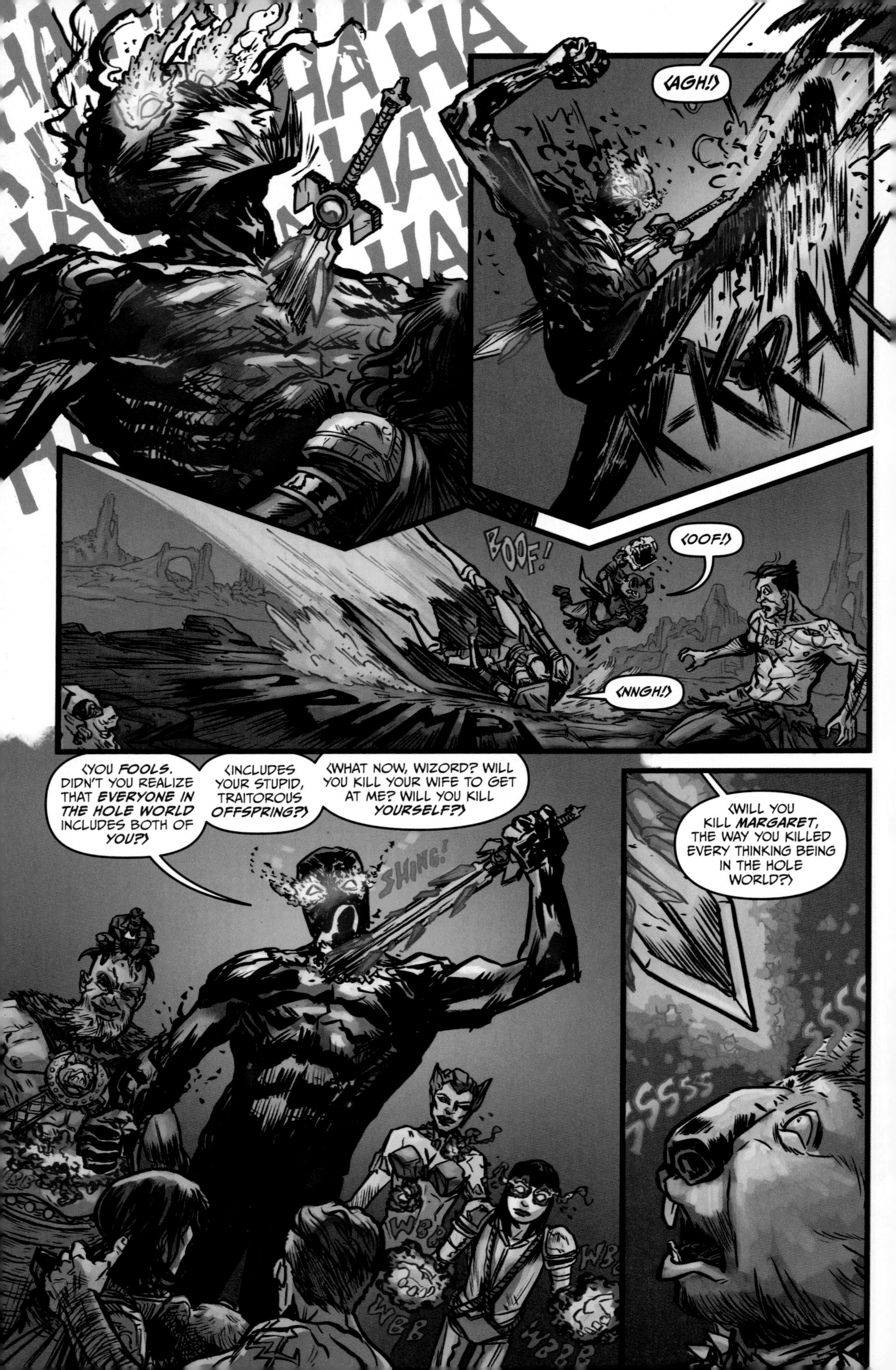
HA HA HA HA HA HA HA HA HA HA
‹AGH!›
KRAK
BOOF!
‹OOF!›
‹NNGH!›
‹YOU *FOOLS*. DIDN'T YOU REALIZE THAT *EVERYONE IN THE HOLE WORLD* INCLUDES BOTH OF *YOU*?›
‹INCLUDES YOUR STUPID, TRAITOROUS *OFFSPRING*?›
‹WHAT NOW, WIZORD? WILL YOU KILL YOUR WIFE TO GET AT ME? WILL YOU KILL *YOURSELF*?›
SHING!
WBB
‹WILL YOU KILL *MARGARET*, THE WAY YOU KILLED EVERY THINKING BEING IN THE HOLE WORLD?›
SSSSS

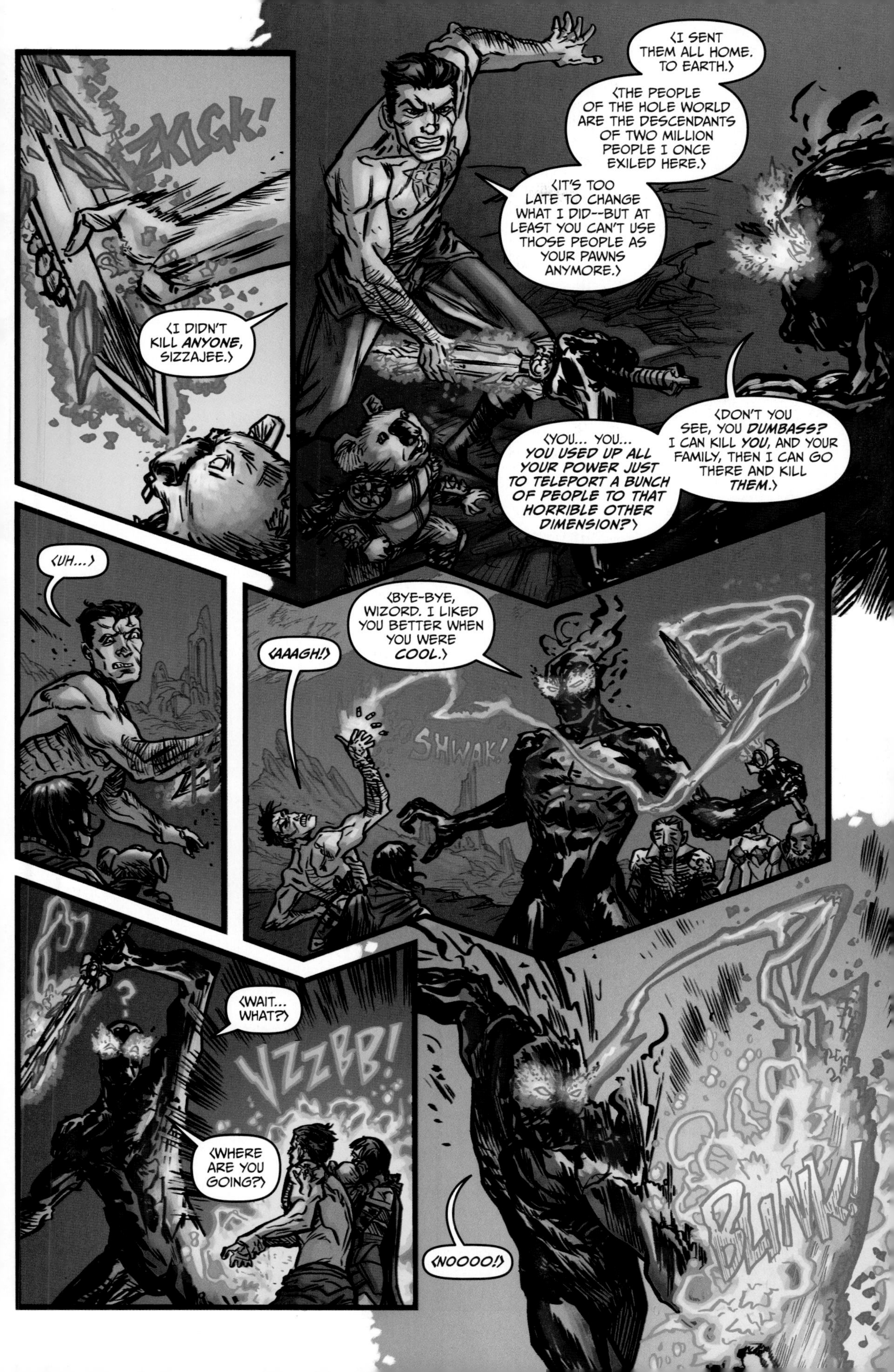
ZKLGK!
‹I SENT THEM ALL HOME. TO EARTH.›
‹THE PEOPLE OF THE HOLE WORLD ARE THE DESCENDANTS OF TWO MILLION PEOPLE I ONCE EXILED HERE.›
‹IT'S TOO LATE TO CHANGE WHAT I DID--BUT AT LEAST YOU CAN'T USE THOSE PEOPLE AS YOUR PAWNS ANYMORE.›
‹I DIDN'T KILL *ANYONE*, SIZZAJEE.›
‹YOU... YOU... *YOU USED UP ALL YOUR POWER JUST TO TELEPORT A BUNCH OF PEOPLE TO THAT HORRIBLE OTHER DIMENSION?*›
‹DON'T YOU SEE, YOU *DUMBASS?* I CAN KILL *YOU*, AND YOUR FAMILY, THEN I CAN GO THERE AND KILL *THEM*.›
‹UH...›
‹BYE-BYE, WIZORD. I LIKED YOU BETTER WHEN YOU WERE *COOL*.›
‹AAAGH!›
SHWAK!
‹WAIT... WHAT?›
VZZBB!
‹WHERE ARE YOU GOING?›
‹NOOOO!›
BLINK!

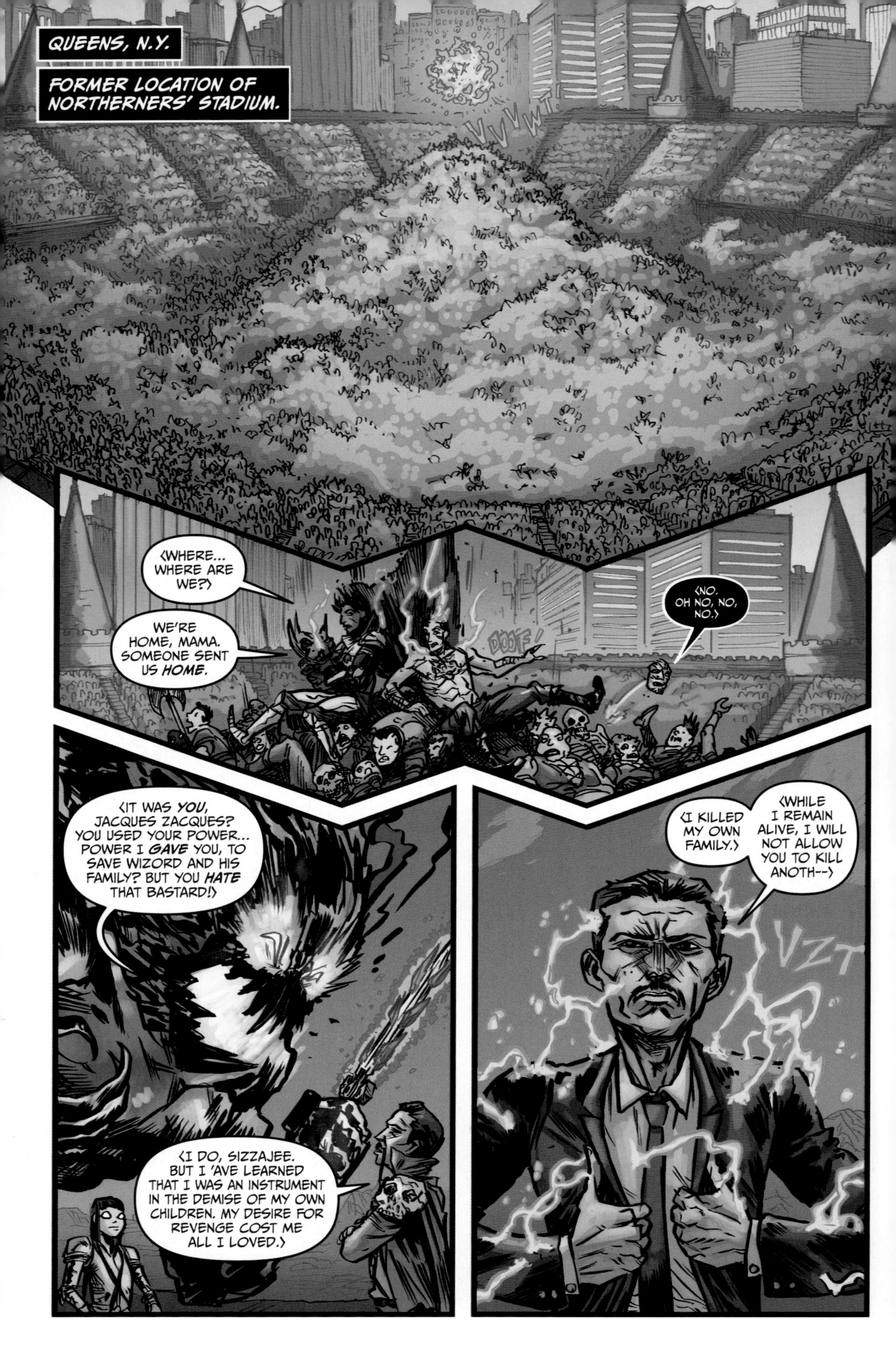

QUEENS, N.Y.
FORMER LOCATION OF NORTHERNERS' STADIUM.
VVVWT
‹WHERE... WHERE ARE WE?›
WE'RE HOME, MAMA. SOMEONE SENT US HOME.
DOOF!
‹NO. OH NO, NO, NO.›
‹IT WAS YOU, JACQUES ZACQUES? YOU USED YOUR POWER... POWER I GAVE YOU, TO SAVE WIZORD AND HIS FAMILY? BUT YOU HATE THAT BASTARD!›
‹I DO, SIZZAJEE. BUT I 'AVE LEARNED THAT I WAS AN INSTRUMENT IN THE DEMISE OF MY OWN CHILDREN. MY DESIRE FOR REVENGE COST ME ALL I LOVED.›
‹I KILLED MY OWN FAMILY.›
‹WHILE I REMAIN ALIVE, I WILL NOT ALLOW YOU TO KILL ANOTH--›
VZT

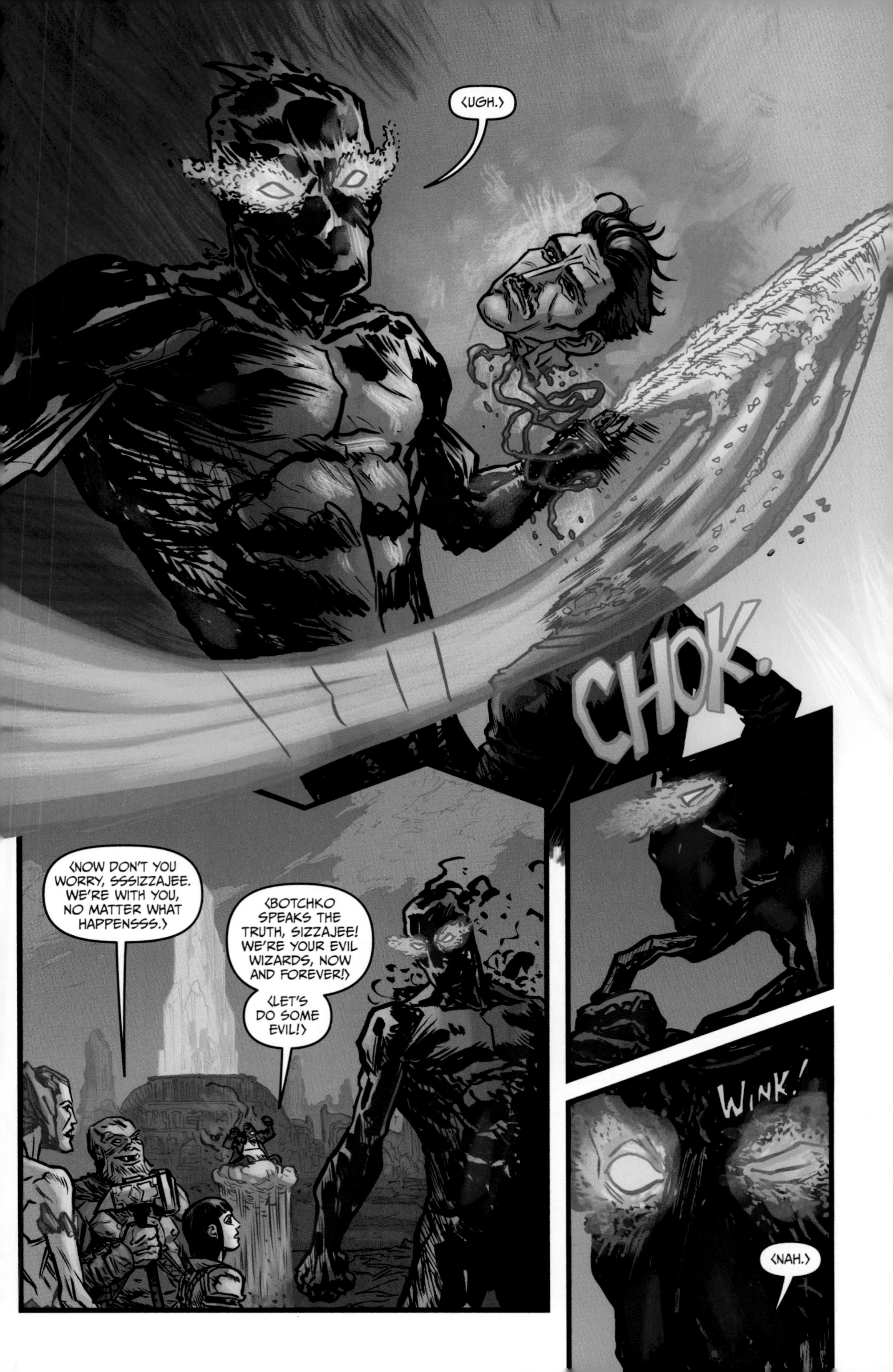

<UGH.>
CHOK.
<NOW DON'T YOU WORRY, SSSIZZAJEE. WE'RE WITH YOU, NO MATTER WHAT HAPPENSSS.>
<BOTCHKO SPEAKS THE TRUTH, SIZZAJEE! WE'RE YOUR EVIL WIZARDS, NOW AND FOREVER!>
<LET'S DO SOME EVIL!>
WINK!
<NAH.>

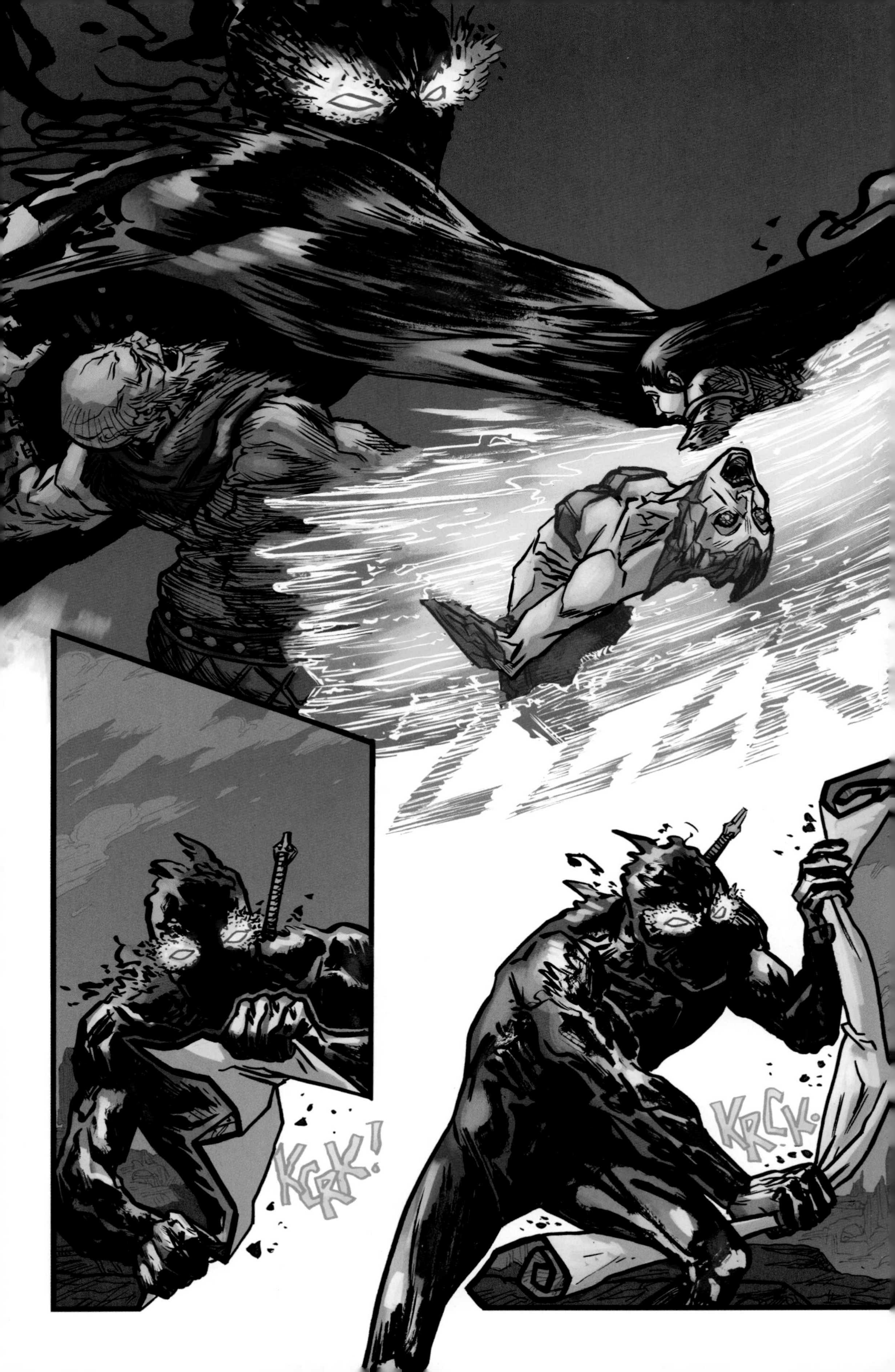
KCRK!
KRCK.

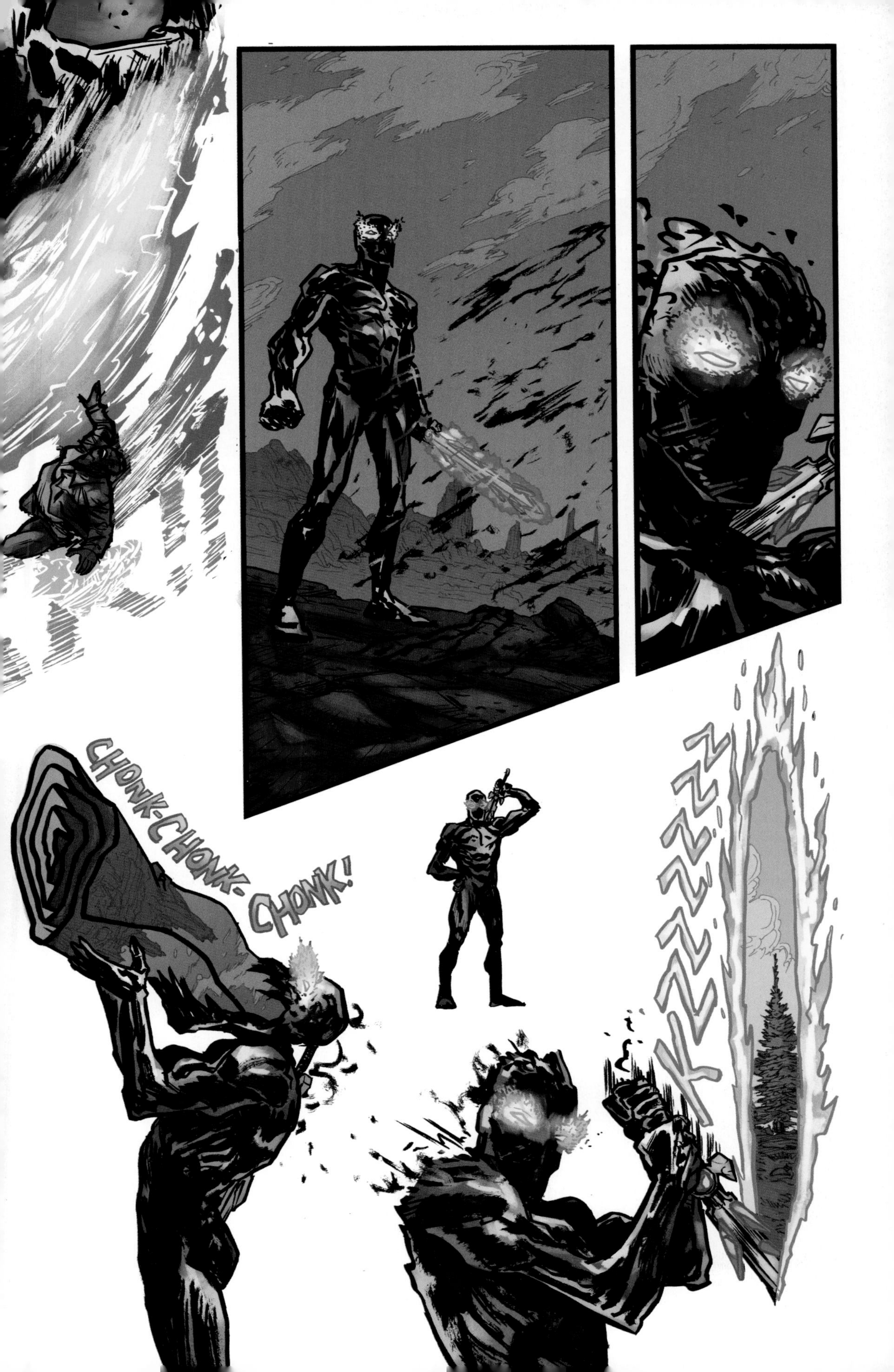
CHONK-CHONK-CHONK-CHONK!
KZZZZZZZZ

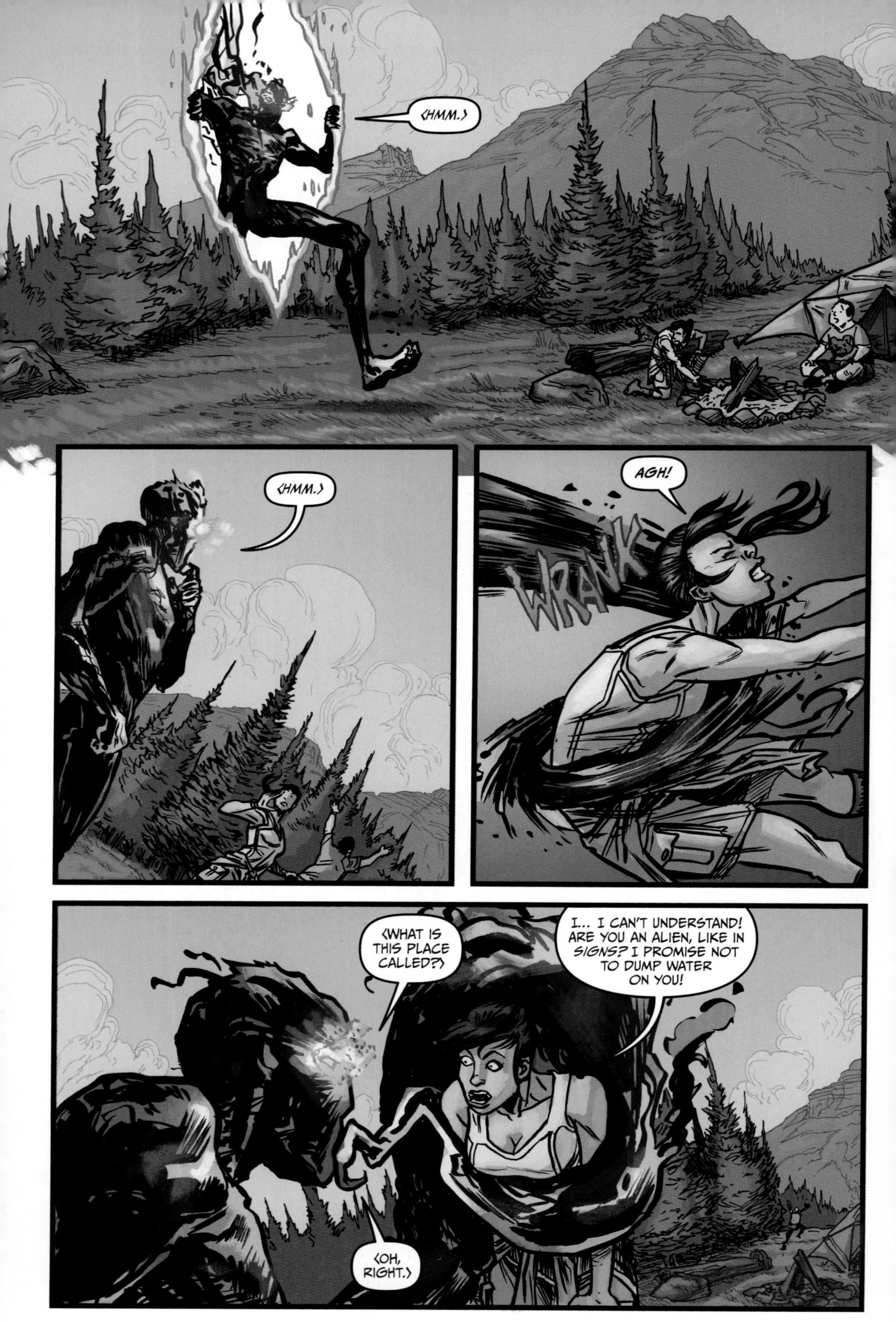
<HMM.>
<HMM.>
AGH!
WRANK
<WHAT IS THIS PLACE CALLED?>
I... I CAN'T UNDERSTAND! ARE YOU AN ALIEN, LIKE IN *SIGNS?* I PROMISE NOT TO DUMP WATER ON YOU!
<OH, RIGHT.>

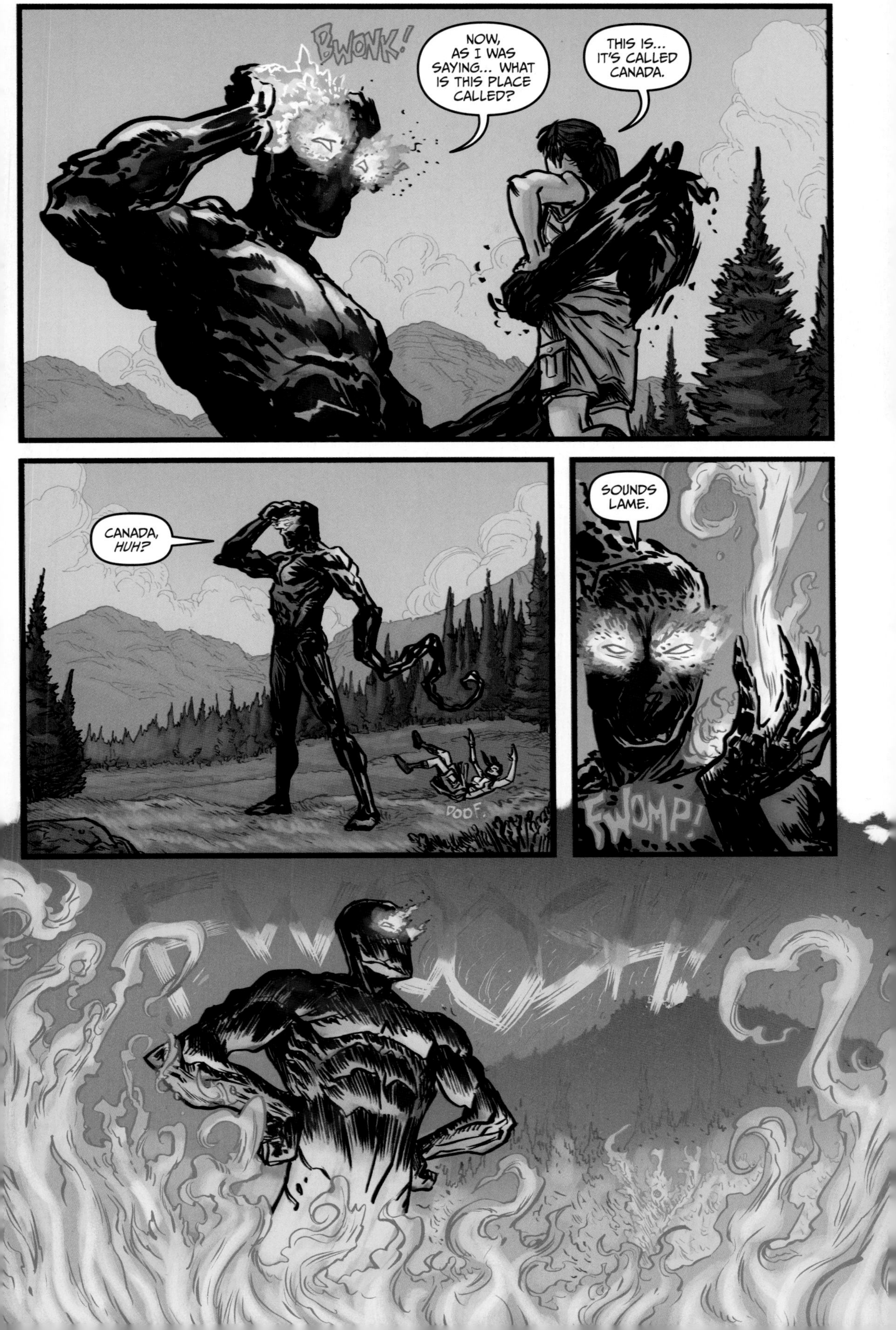
BWONK!
NOW, AS I WAS SAYING... WHAT IS THIS PLACE CALLED?
THIS IS... IT'S CALLED CANADA.
CANADA, HUH?
DOOF.
SOUNDS LAME.
FWOMP!

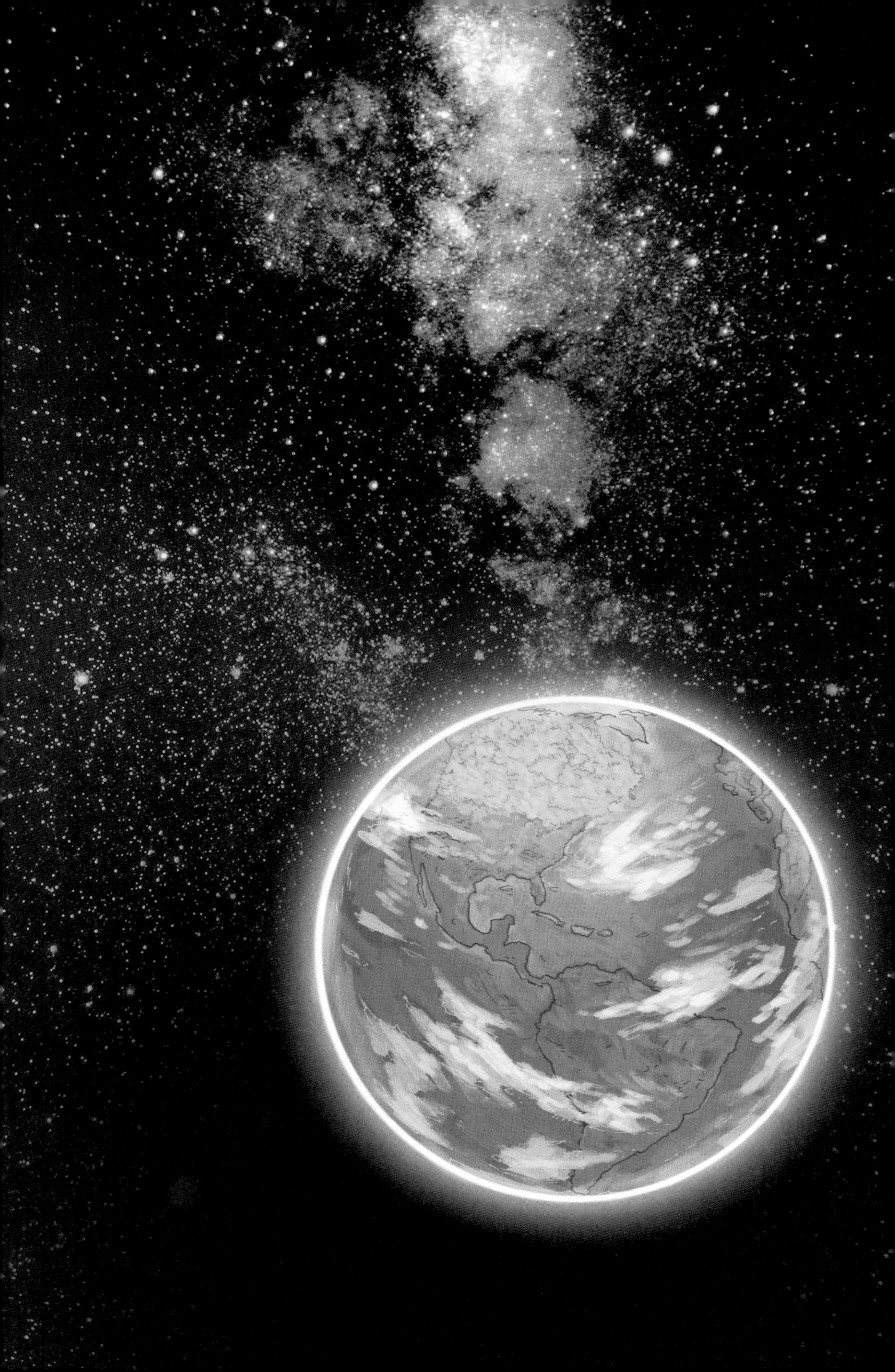

TWENTY-FIVE

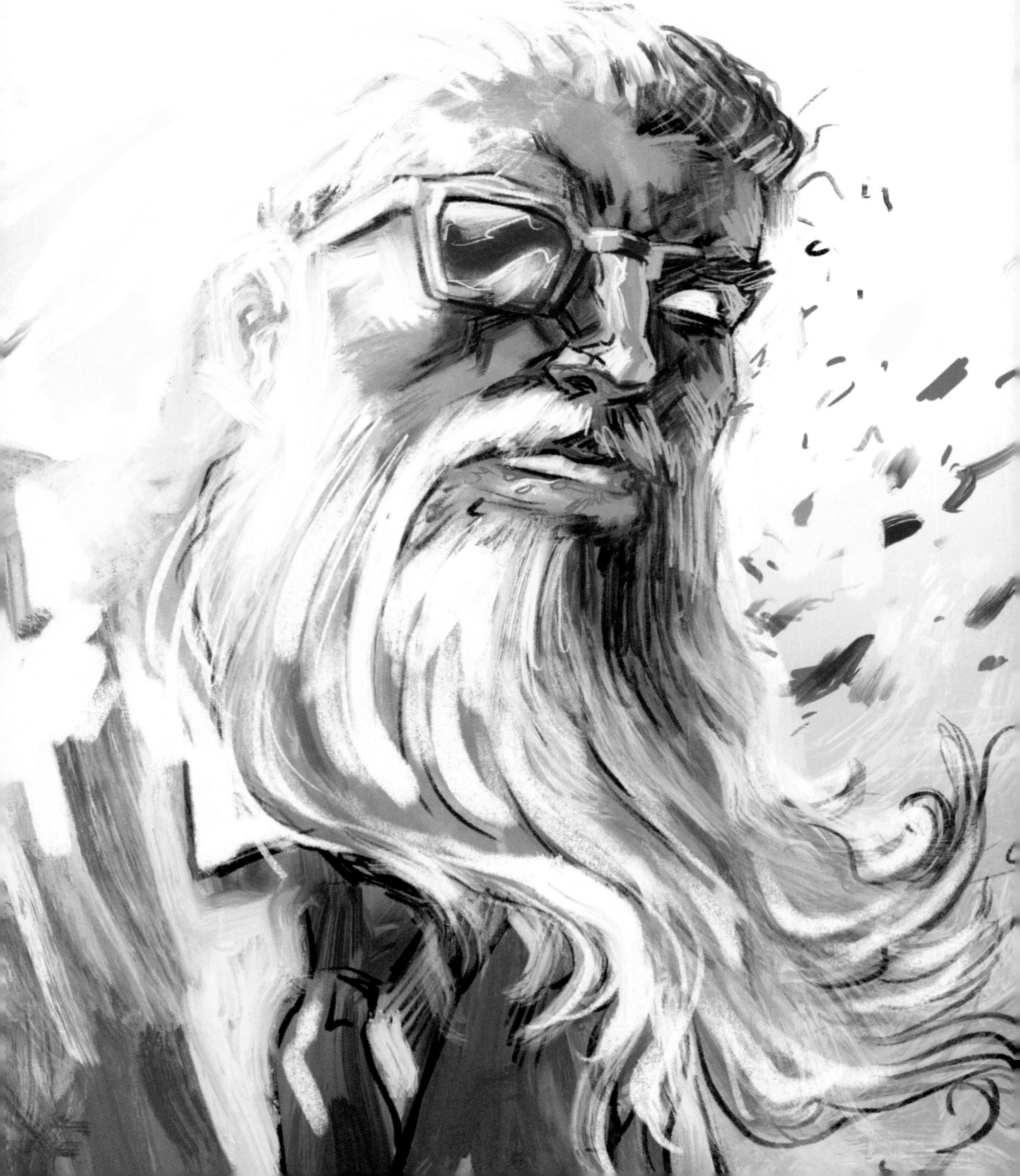

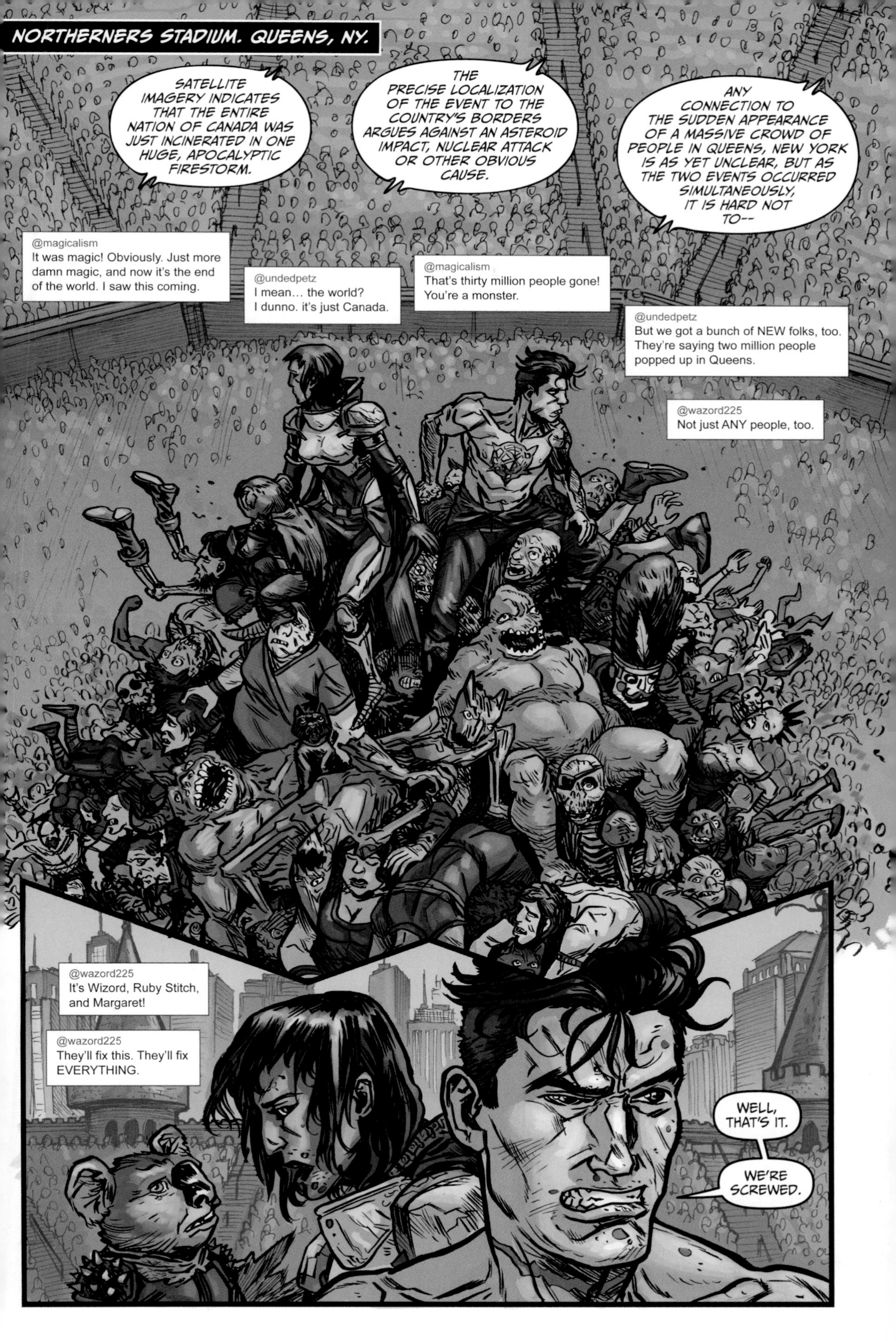
NORTHERNERS STADIUM. QUEENS, NY.
SATELLITE IMAGERY INDICATES THAT THE ENTIRE NATION OF CANADA WAS JUST INCINERATED IN ONE HUGE, APOCALYPTIC FIRESTORM.
THE PRECISE LOCALIZATION OF THE EVENT TO THE COUNTRY'S BORDERS ARGUES AGAINST AN ASTEROID IMPACT, NUCLEAR ATTACK OR OTHER OBVIOUS CAUSE.
ANY CONNECTION TO THE SUDDEN APPEARANCE OF A MASSIVE CROWD OF PEOPLE IN QUEENS, NEW YORK IS AS YET UNCLEAR, BUT AS THE TWO EVENTS OCCURRED SIMULTANEOUSLY, IT IS HARD NOT TO--
@magicalism
It was magic! Obviously. Just more damn magic, and now it's the end of the world. I saw this coming.
@undedpetz
I mean… the world? I dunno. it's just Canada.
@magicalism
That's thirty million people gone! You're a monster.
@undedpetz
But we got a bunch of NEW folks, too. They're saying two million people popped up in Queens.
@wazord225
Not just ANY people, too.
@wazord225
It's Wizord, Ruby Stitch, and Margaret!
@wazord225
They'll fix this. They'll fix EVERYTHING.
WELL, THAT'S IT.
WE'RE SCREWED.

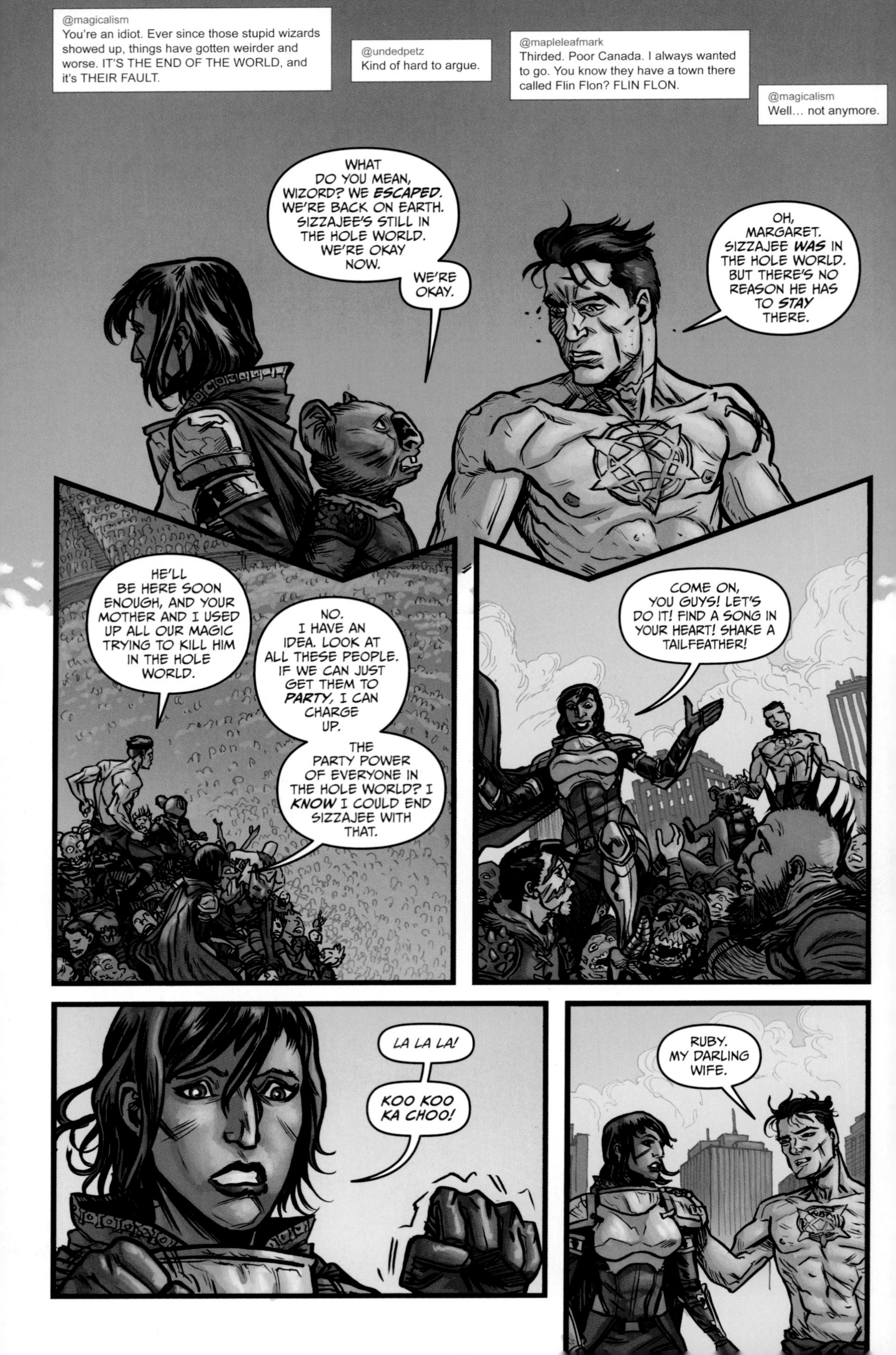

@magicalism
You're an idiot. Ever since those stupid wizards showed up, things have gotten weirder and worse. IT'S THE END OF THE WORLD, and it's THEIR FAULT.
@undedpetz
Kind of hard to argue.
@mapleleafmark
Thirded. Poor Canada. I always wanted to go. You know they have a town there called Flin Flon? FLIN FLON.
@magicalism
Well… not anymore.
WHAT DO YOU MEAN, WIZORD? WE ESCAPED. WE'RE BACK ON EARTH. SIZZAJEE'S STILL IN THE HOLE WORLD. WE'RE OKAY NOW.
WE'RE OKAY.
OH, MARGARET. SIZZAJEE WAS IN THE HOLE WORLD. BUT THERE'S NO REASON HE HAS TO STAY THERE.
HE'LL BE HERE SOON ENOUGH, AND YOUR MOTHER AND I USED UP ALL OUR MAGIC TRYING TO KILL HIM IN THE HOLE WORLD.
NO. I HAVE AN IDEA. LOOK AT ALL THESE PEOPLE. IF WE CAN JUST GET THEM TO PARTY, I CAN CHARGE UP.
THE PARTY POWER OF EVERYONE IN THE HOLE WORLD? I KNOW I COULD END SIZZAJEE WITH THAT.
COME ON, YOU GUYS! LET'S DO IT! FIND A SONG IN YOUR HEART! SHAKE A TAILFEATHER!
LA LA LA!
KOO KOO KA CHOO!
RUBY. MY DARLING WIFE.

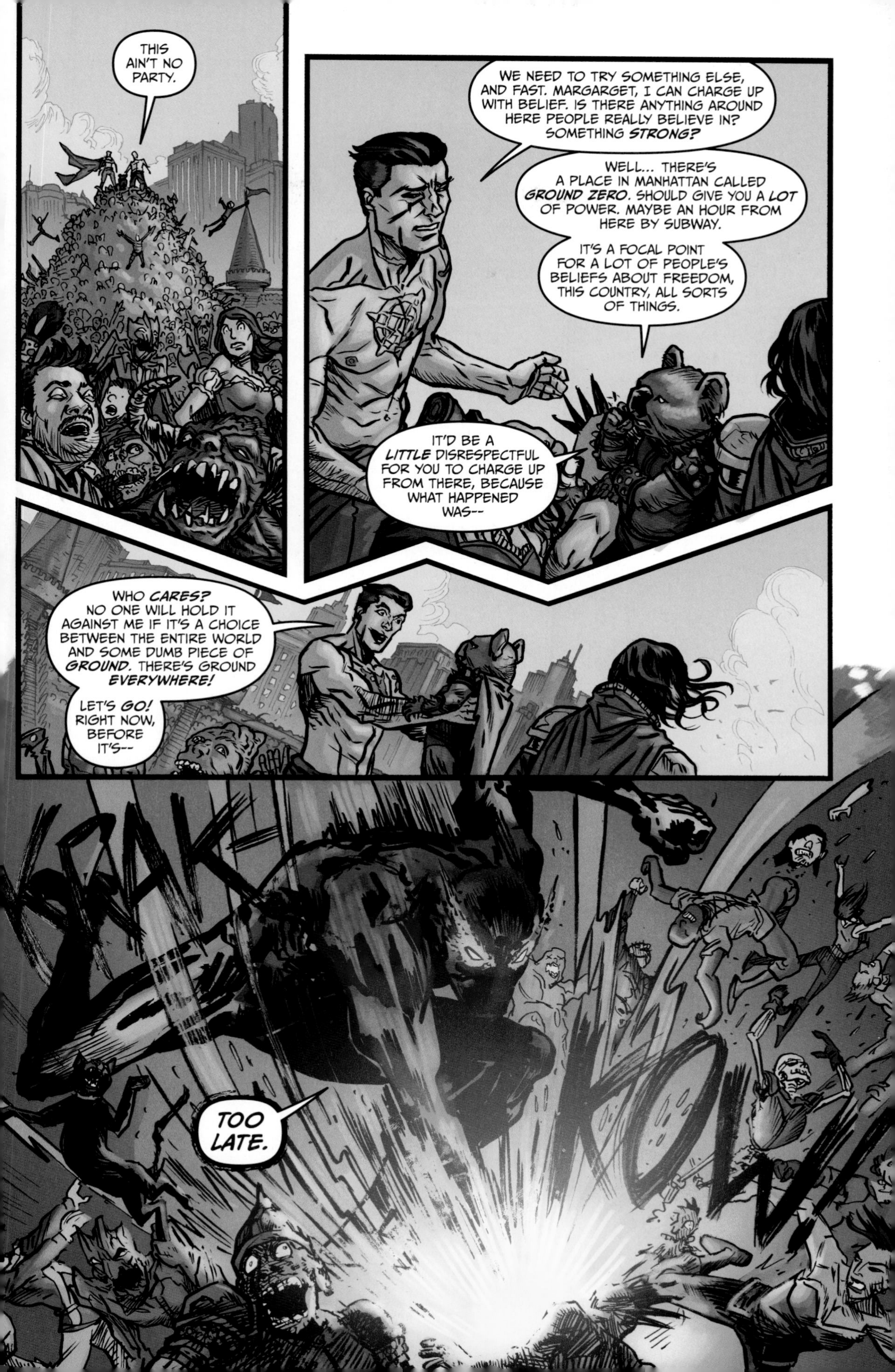
THIS AIN'T NO PARTY.
WE NEED TO TRY SOMETHING ELSE, AND FAST. MARGARGET, I CAN CHARGE UP WITH BELIEF. IS THERE ANYTHING AROUND HERE PEOPLE REALLY BELIEVE IN? SOMETHING STRONG?
WELL... THERE'S A PLACE IN MANHATTAN CALLED GROUND ZERO. SHOULD GIVE YOU A LOT OF POWER. MAYBE AN HOUR FROM HERE BY SUBWAY.
IT'S A FOCAL POINT FOR A LOT OF PEOPLE'S BELIEFS ABOUT FREEDOM, THIS COUNTRY, ALL SORTS OF THINGS.
IT'D BE A LITTLE DISRESPECTFUL FOR YOU TO CHARGE UP FROM THERE, BECAUSE WHAT HAPPENED WAS--
WHO CARES? NO ONE WILL HOLD IT AGAINST ME IF IT'S A CHOICE BETWEEN THE ENTIRE WORLD AND SOME DUMB PIECE OF GROUND. THERE'S GROUND EVERYWHERE!
LET'S GO! RIGHT NOW, BEFORE IT'S--
TOO LATE.

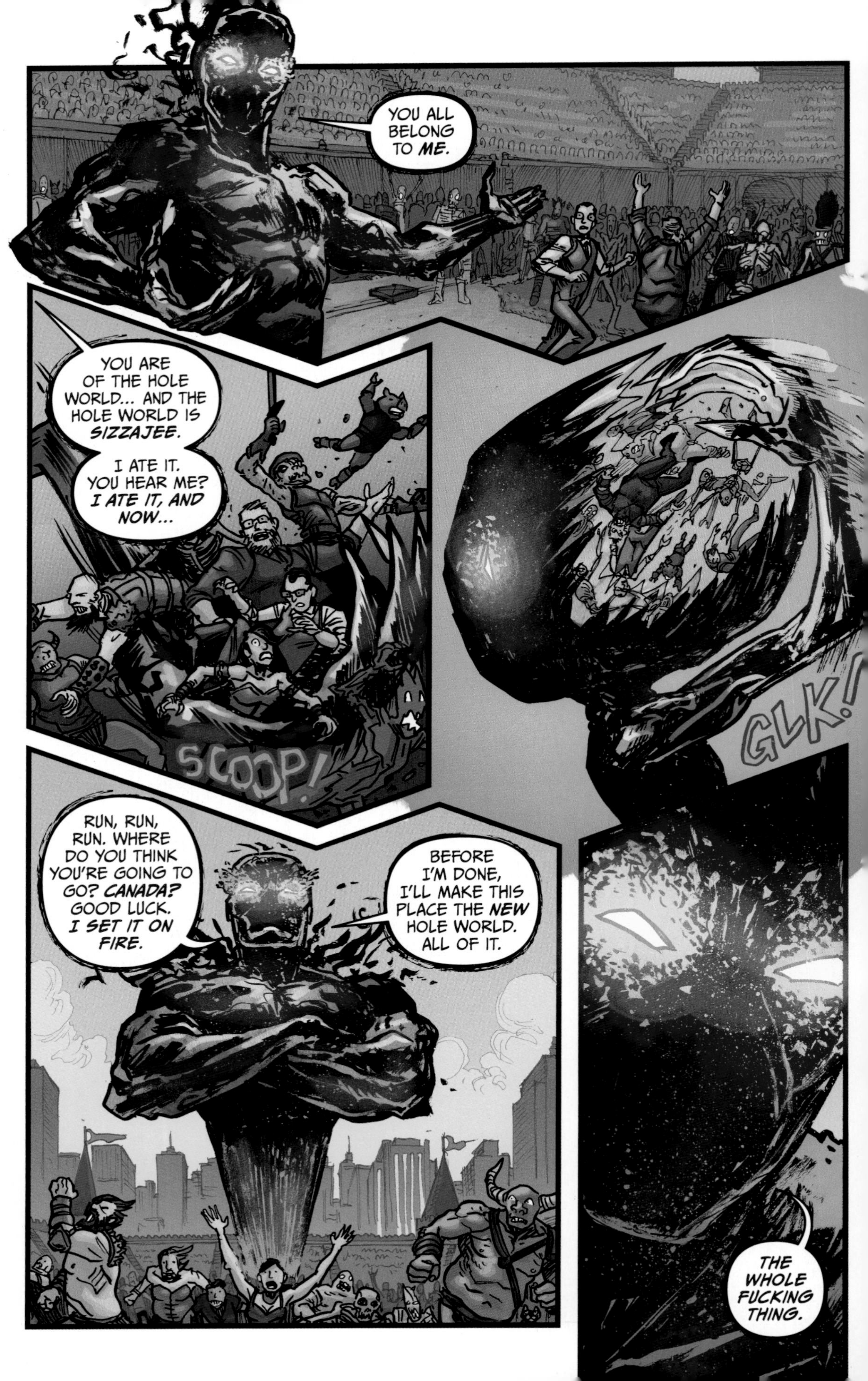

YOU ALL BELONG TO *ME*.
YOU ARE OF THE HOLE WORLD... AND THE HOLE WORLD IS ***SIZZAJEE***.
I ATE IT. YOU HEAR ME? ***I ATE IT, AND NOW...***
SCOOP!
GLK!
RUN, RUN, RUN. WHERE DO YOU THINK YOU'RE GOING TO GO? ***CANADA?*** GOOD LUCK. ***I SET IT ON FIRE.***
BEFORE I'M DONE, I'LL MAKE THIS PLACE THE ***NEW*** HOLE WORLD. ALL OF IT.
THE WHOLE FUCKING THING.

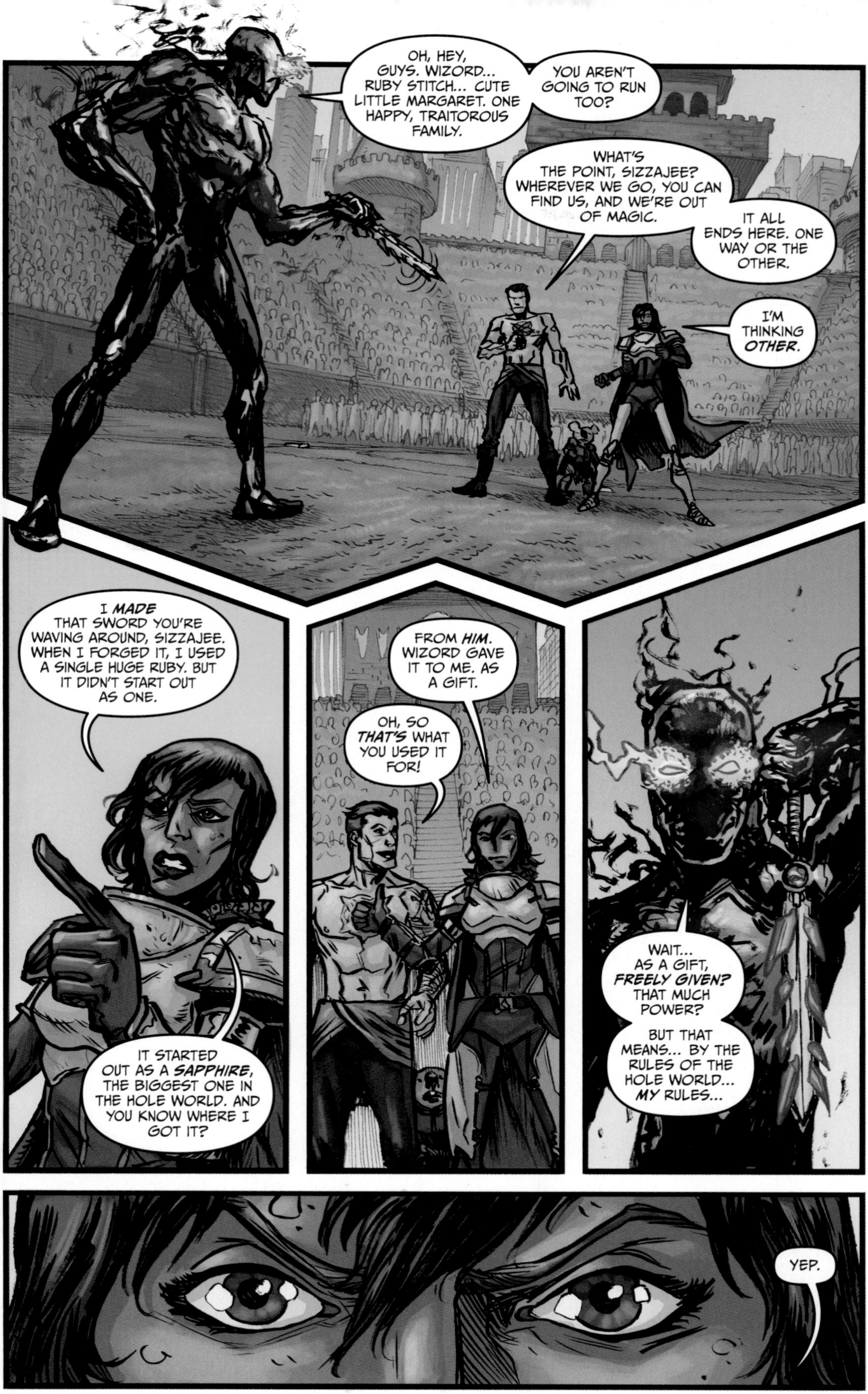
OH, HEY, GUYS. WIZORD... RUBY STITCH... CUTE LITTLE MARGARET. ONE HAPPY, TRAITOROUS FAMILY.
YOU AREN'T GOING TO RUN TOO?
WHAT'S THE POINT, SIZZAJEE? WHEREVER WE GO, YOU CAN FIND US, AND WE'RE OUT OF MAGIC.
IT ALL ENDS HERE. ONE WAY OR THE OTHER.
I'M THINKING *OTHER*.
I *MADE* THAT SWORD YOU'RE WAVING AROUND, SIZZAJEE. WHEN I FORGED IT, I USED A SINGLE HUGE RUBY. BUT IT DIDN'T START OUT AS ONE.
IT STARTED OUT AS A *SAPPHIRE*, THE BIGGEST ONE IN THE HOLE WORLD. AND YOU KNOW WHERE I GOT IT?
FROM *HIM*. WIZORD GAVE IT TO ME. AS A GIFT.
OH, SO *THAT'S* WHAT YOU USED IT FOR!
WAIT... AS A GIFT, *FREELY GIVEN?* THAT MUCH POWER?
BUT THAT MEANS... BY THE RULES OF THE HOLE WORLD... *MY* RULES...
YEP.

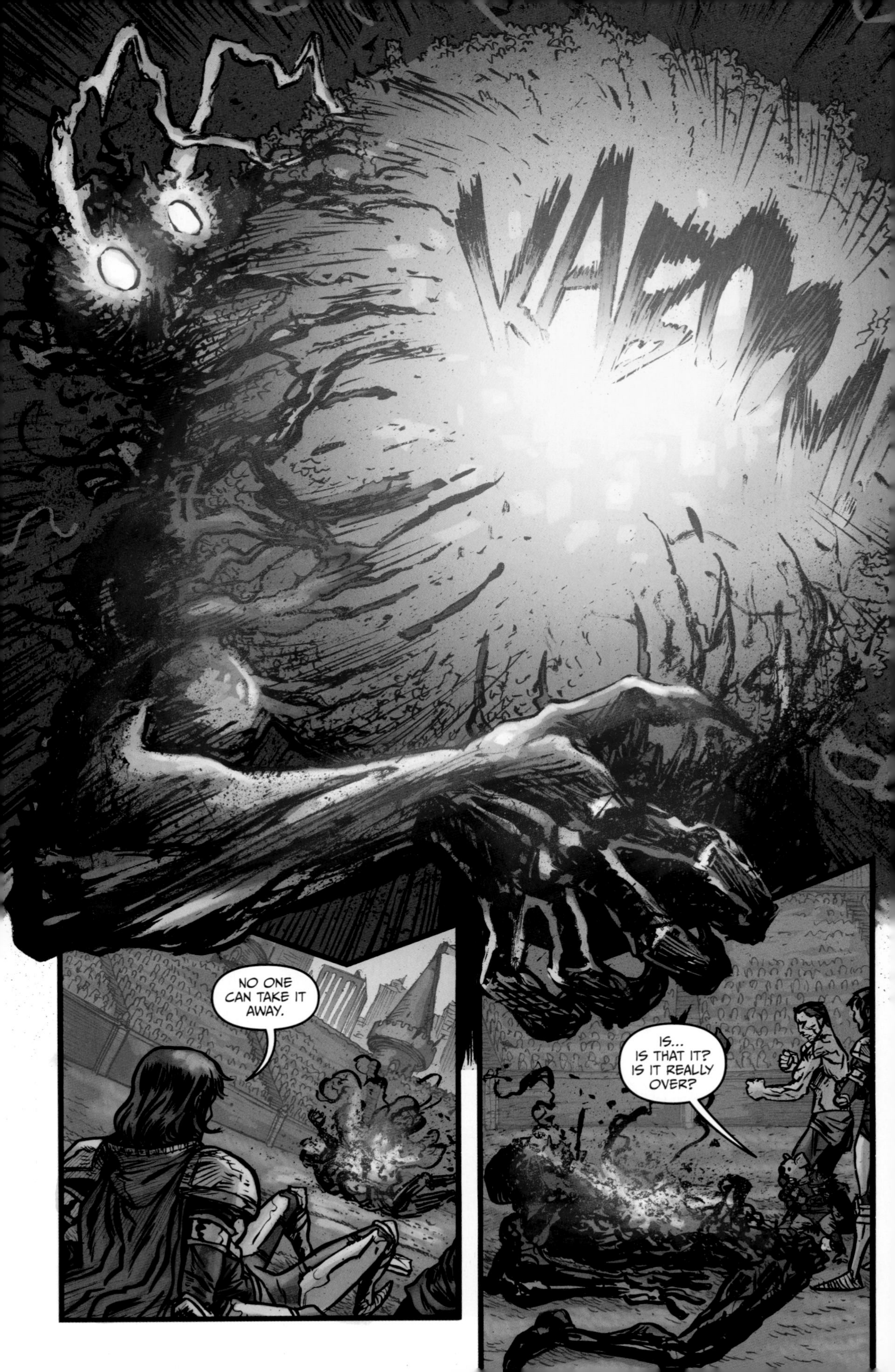
NO ONE CAN TAKE IT AWAY.
IS... IS THAT IT? IS IT REALLY OVER?

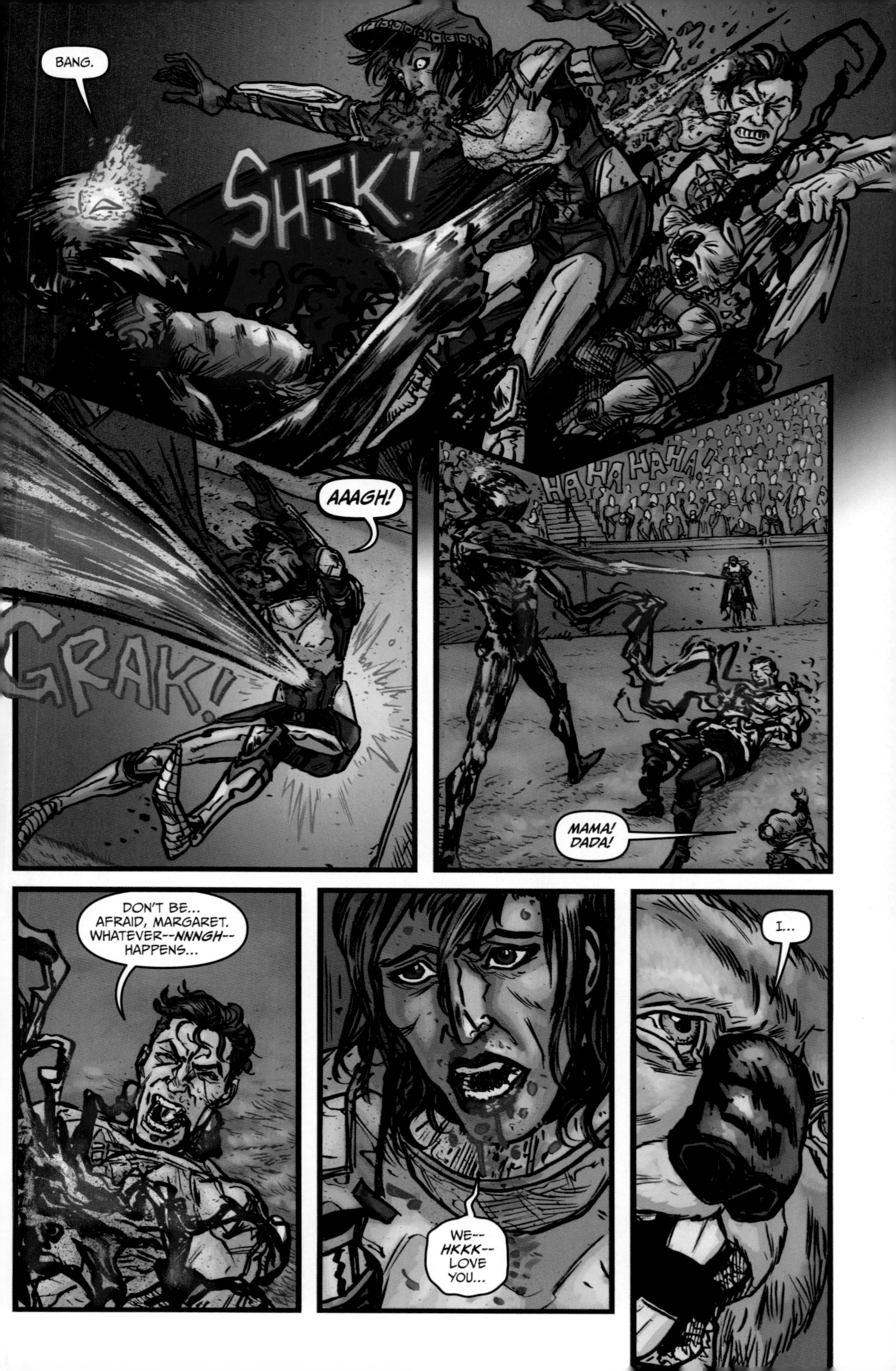

BANG.
SHTK!
AAAGH!
GRAK!
HA HA HA HA HA!
MAMA! DADA!
DON'T BE... AFRAID, MARGARET. WHATEVER--NNNGH--HAPPENS...
WE--HKKK--LOVE YOU...
I...

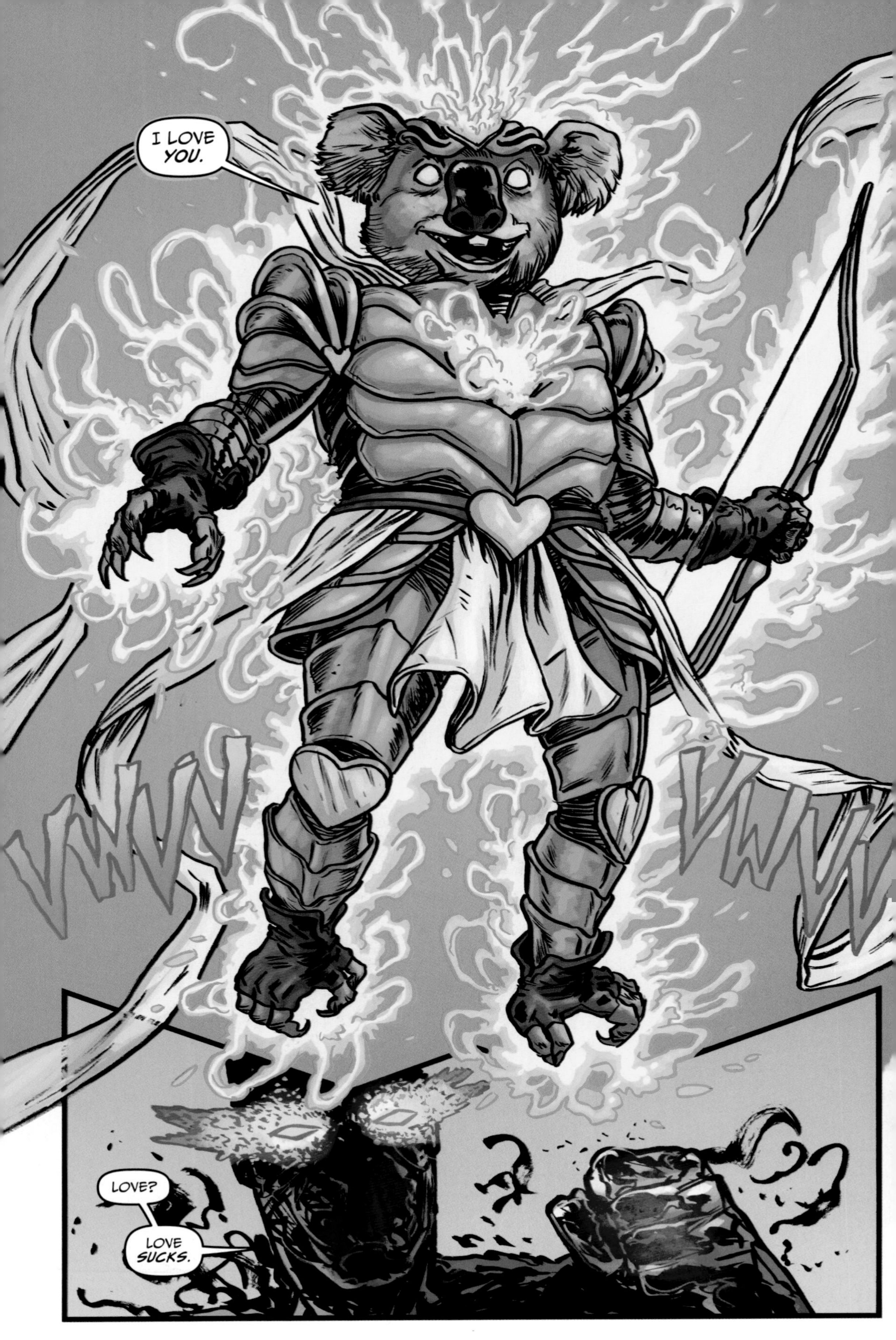
I LOVE YOU.
VWVV
VWVV
LOVE?
LOVE SUCKS.

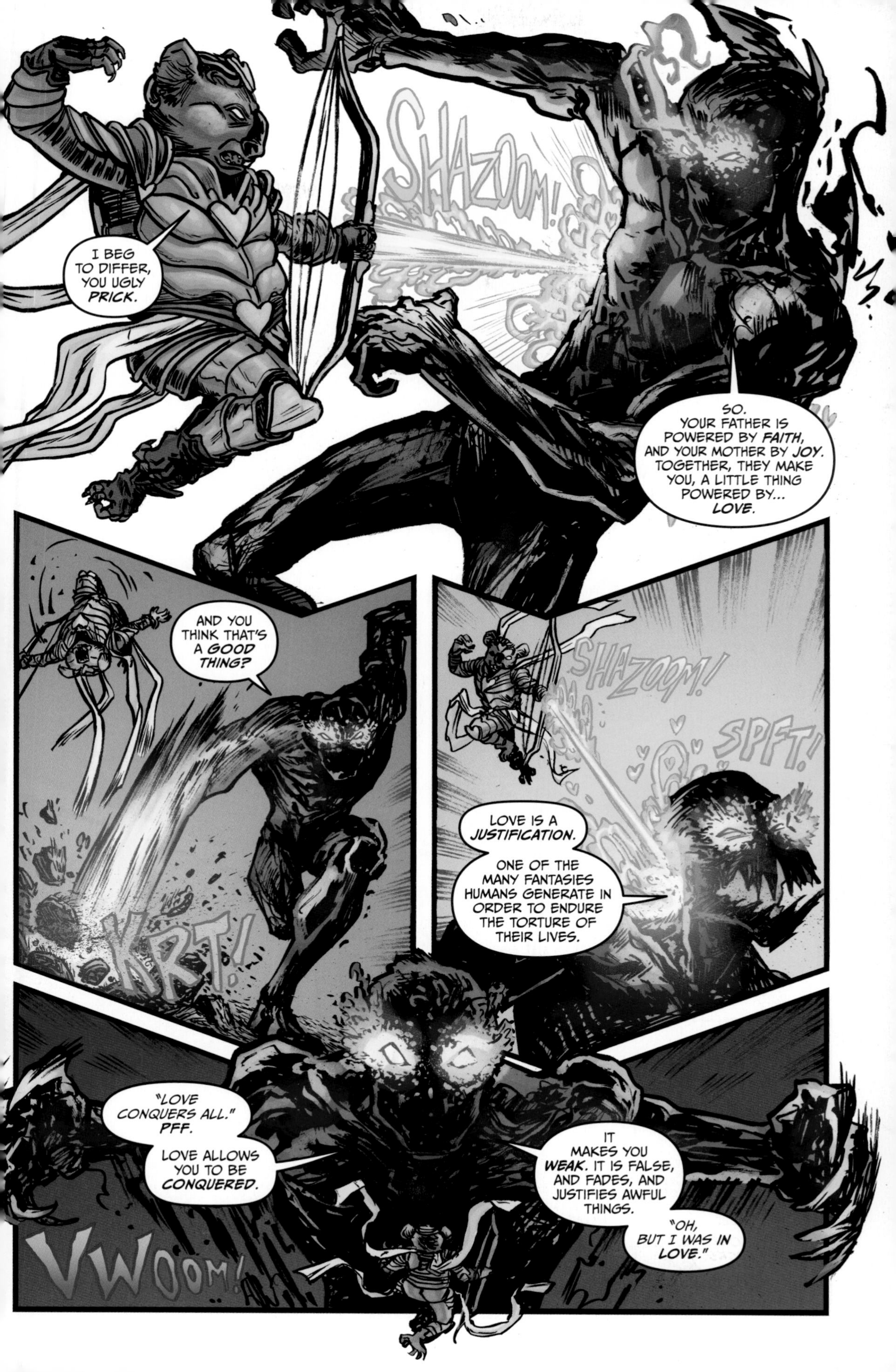
SHAZOOM!
I BEG TO DIFFER, YOU UGLY *PRICK*.
SO. YOUR FATHER IS POWERED BY *FAITH*, AND YOUR MOTHER BY *JOY*. TOGETHER, THEY MAKE YOU, A LITTLE THING POWERED BY... *LOVE*.
AND YOU THINK THAT'S A *GOOD THING?*
KRT!
SHAZOOM!
SPFT!
LOVE IS A *JUSTIFICATION*.
ONE OF THE MANY FANTASIES HUMANS GENERATE IN ORDER TO ENDURE THE TORTURE OF THEIR LIVES.
"LOVE CONQUERS ALL." PFF.
LOVE ALLOWS YOU TO BE *CONQUERED*.
IT MAKES YOU *WEAK*. IT IS FALSE, AND FADES, AND JUSTIFIES AWFUL THINGS.
"OH, BUT I WAS IN *LOVE*."
VWOOM!

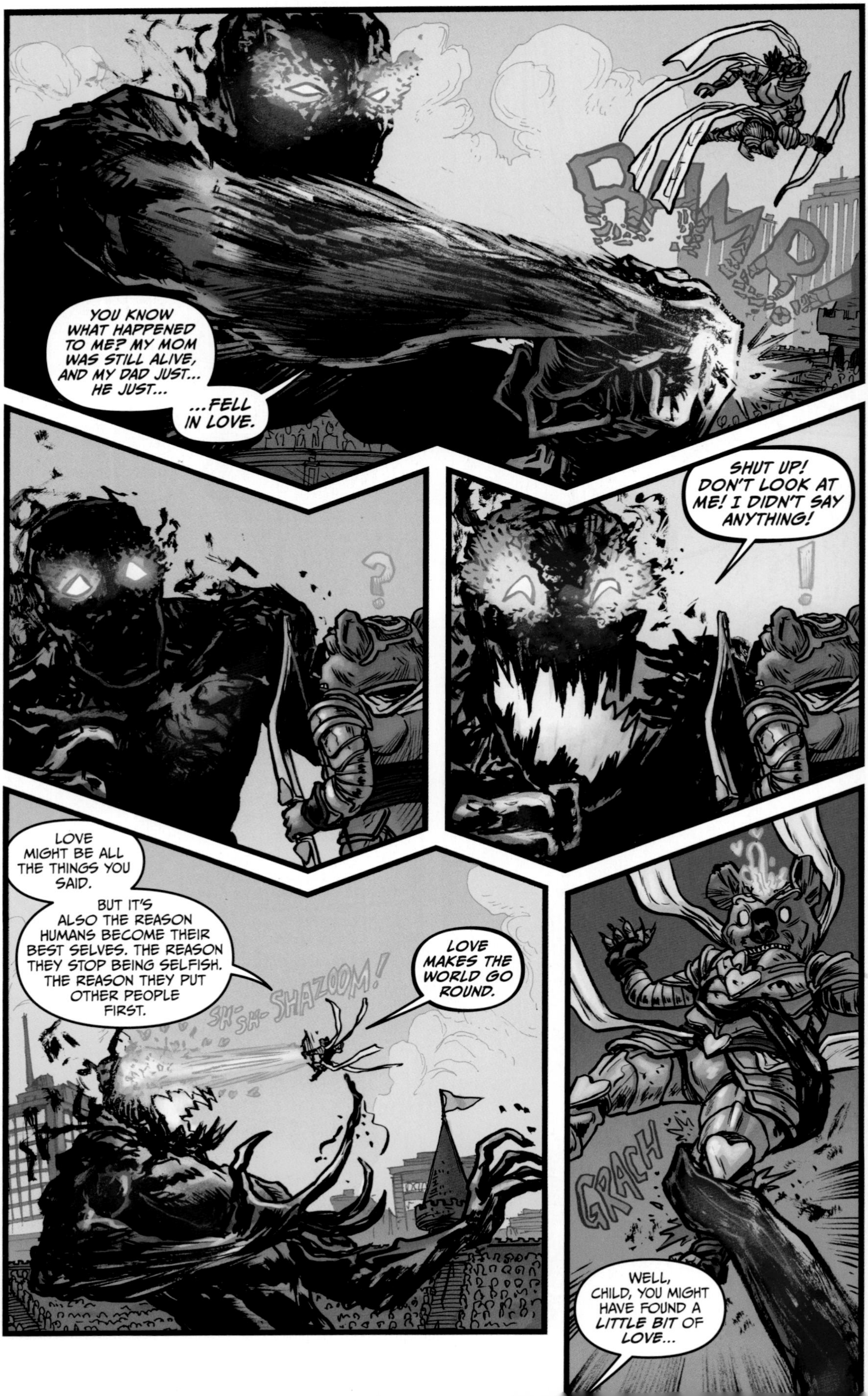
RUMP
YOU KNOW WHAT HAPPENED TO ME? MY MOM WAS STILL ALIVE, AND MY DAD JUST... HE JUST...
...FELL IN LOVE.
?
!
SHUT UP! DON'T LOOK AT ME! I DIDN'T SAY ANYTHING!
LOVE MIGHT BE ALL THE THINGS YOU SAID.
BUT IT'S ALSO THE REASON HUMANS BECOME THEIR BEST SELVES. THE REASON THEY STOP BEING SELFISH. THE REASON THEY PUT OTHER PEOPLE FIRST.
SH-SH-SHAZOOM!
LOVE MAKES THE WORLD GO ROUND.
GRACH
WELL, CHILD, YOU MIGHT HAVE FOUND A *LITTLE BIT* OF LOVE...

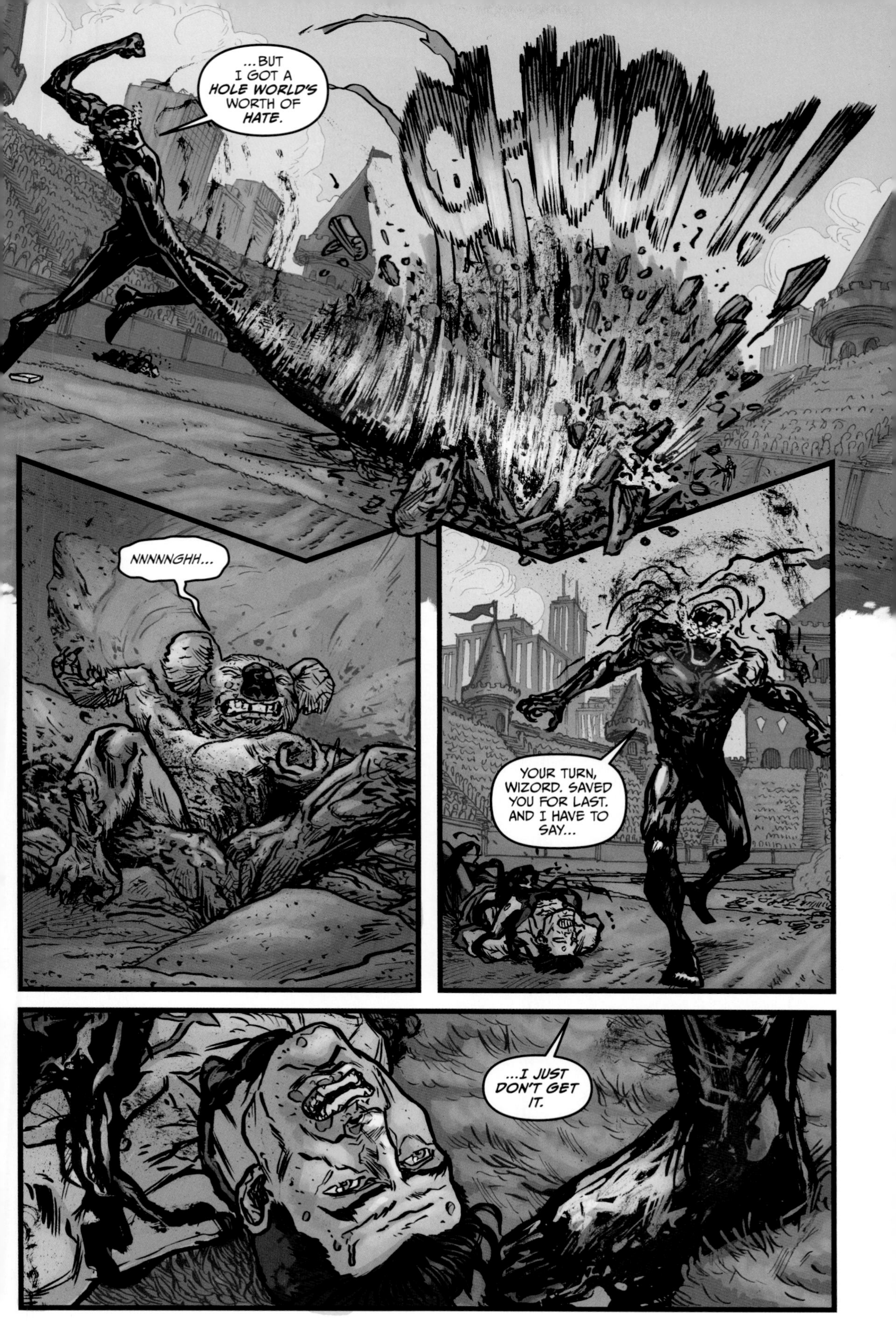
...BUT I GOT A HOLE WORLD'S WORTH OF HATE.
CHOOOM!!
NNNNNGHH...
YOUR TURN, WIZORD. SAVED YOU FOR LAST. AND I HAVE TO SAY...
...I JUST DON'T GET IT.

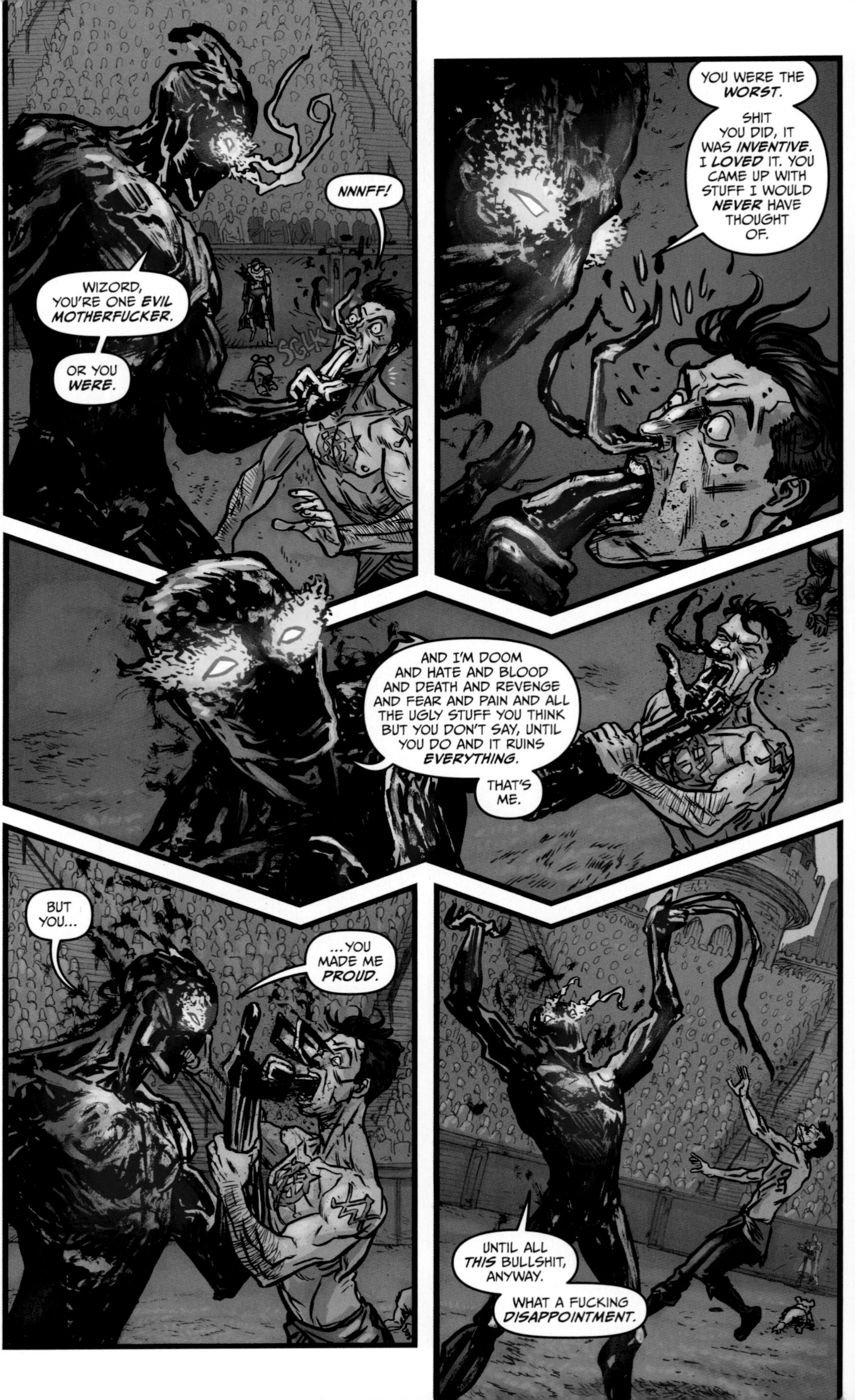
NNNFF!
WIZORD, YOU'RE ONE EVIL MOTHERFUCKER.
OR YOU WERE.
SCLK
YOU WERE THE WORST.
SHIT YOU DID, IT WAS INVENTIVE. I LOVED IT. YOU CAME UP WITH STUFF I WOULD NEVER HAVE THOUGHT OF.
AND I'M DOOM AND HATE AND BLOOD AND DEATH AND REVENGE AND FEAR AND PAIN AND ALL THE UGLY STUFF YOU THINK BUT YOU DON'T SAY, UNTIL YOU DO AND IT RUINS EVERYTHING.
THAT'S ME.
BUT YOU...
...YOU MADE ME PROUD.
UNTIL ALL THIS BULLSHIT, ANYWAY.
WHAT A FUCKING DISAPPOINTMENT.

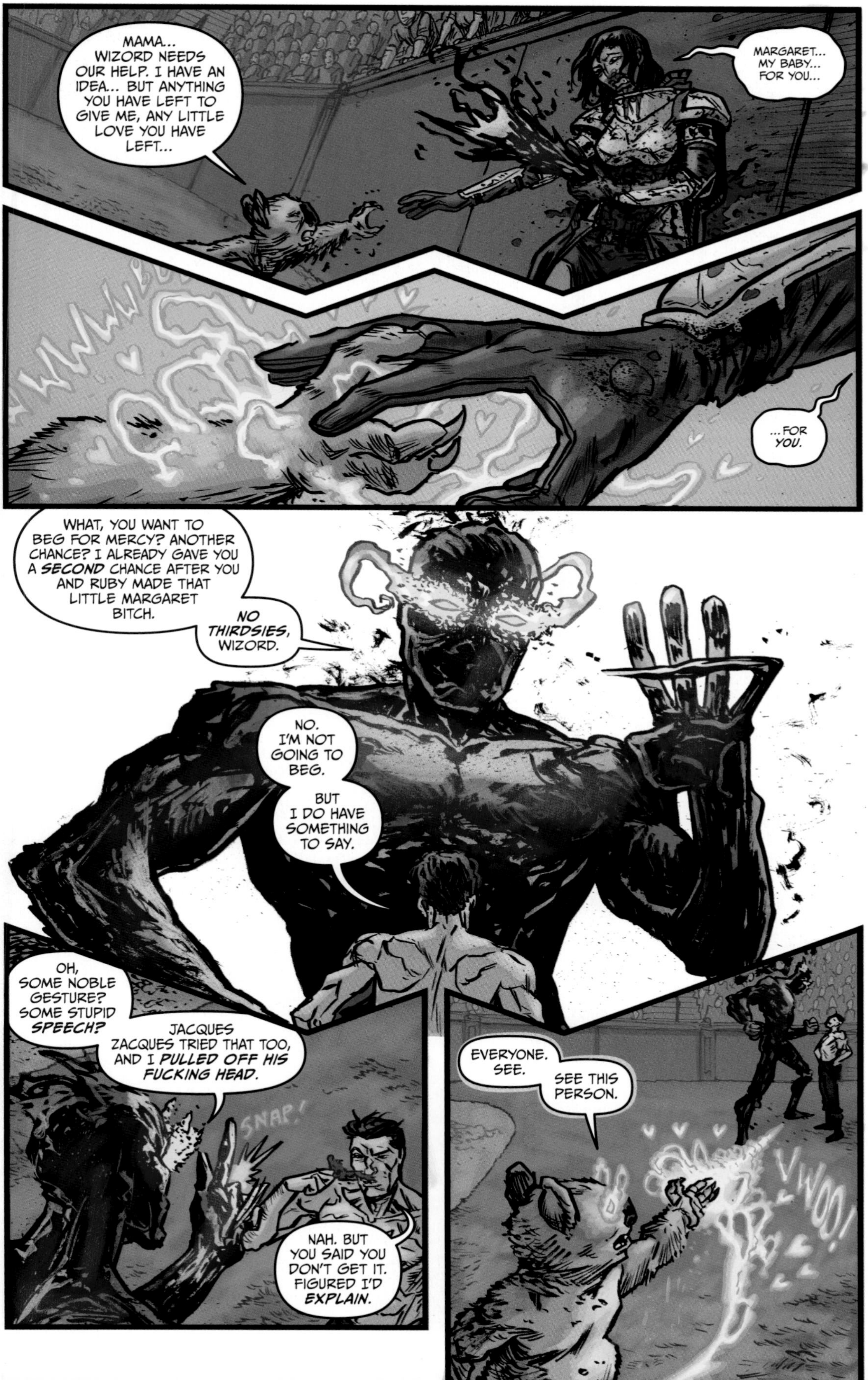
MAMA... WIZORD NEEDS OUR HELP. I HAVE AN IDEA... BUT ANYTHING YOU HAVE LEFT TO GIVE ME, ANY LITTLE LOVE YOU HAVE LEFT...
MARGARET... MY BABY... FOR YOU...
...FOR YOU.
WHAT, YOU WANT TO BEG FOR MERCY? ANOTHER CHANCE? I ALREADY GAVE YOU A SECOND CHANCE AFTER YOU AND RUBY MADE THAT LITTLE MARGARET BITCH.
NO THIRDSIES, WIZORD.
NO. I'M NOT GOING TO BEG.
BUT I DO HAVE SOMETHING TO SAY.
OH, SOME NOBLE GESTURE? SOME STUPID SPEECH?
JACQUES ZACQUES TRIED THAT TOO, AND I PULLED OFF HIS FUCKING HEAD.
SNAP!
NAH. BUT YOU SAID YOU DON'T GET IT. FIGURED I'D EXPLAIN.
EVERYONE. SEE.
SEE THIS PERSON.
VWOO!

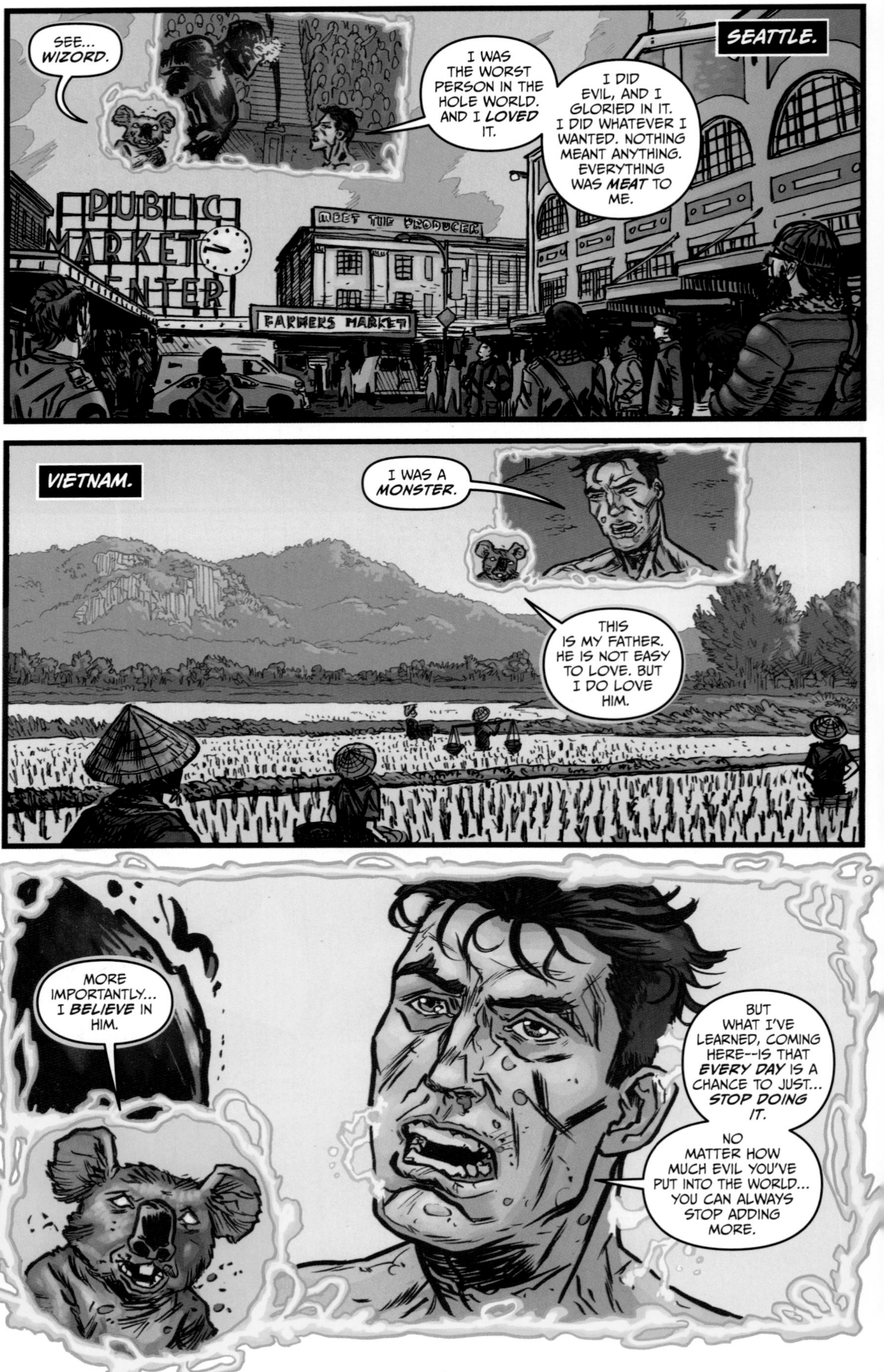
SEATTLE.
SEE... WIZORD.
I WAS THE WORST PERSON IN THE HOLE WORLD. AND I LOVED IT.
I DID EVIL, AND I GLORIED IN IT. I DID WHATEVER I WANTED. NOTHING MEANT ANYTHING. EVERYTHING WAS MEAT TO ME.
PUBLIC MARKET CENTER
MEET THE PRODUCER
FARMERS MARKET
VIETNAM.
I WAS A MONSTER.
THIS IS MY FATHER. HE IS NOT EASY TO LOVE. BUT I DO LOVE HIM.
MORE IMPORTANTLY... I BELIEVE IN HIM.
BUT WHAT I'VE LEARNED, COMING HERE--IS THAT EVERY DAY IS A CHANCE TO JUST... STOP DOING IT.
NO MATTER HOW MUCH EVIL YOU'VE PUT INTO THE WORLD... YOU CAN ALWAYS STOP ADDING MORE.

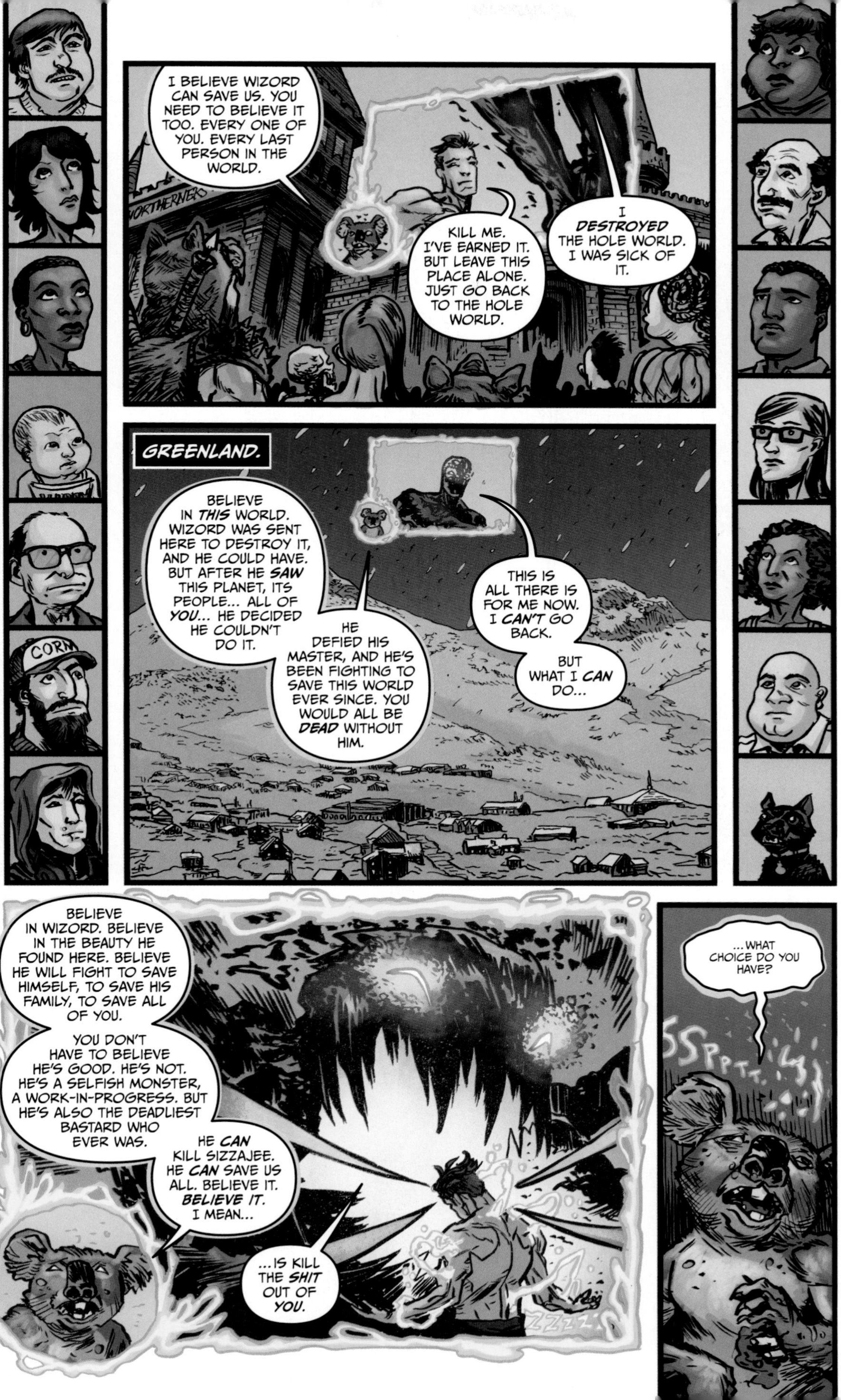

I BELIEVE WIZORD CAN SAVE US. YOU NEED TO BELIEVE IT TOO. EVERY ONE OF YOU. EVERY LAST PERSON IN THE WORLD.
NORTHERNERS
KILL ME. I'VE EARNED IT. BUT LEAVE THIS PLACE ALONE. JUST GO BACK TO THE HOLE WORLD.
I *DESTROYED* THE HOLE WORLD. I WAS SICK OF IT.
GREENLAND.
BELIEVE IN *THIS* WORLD. WIZORD WAS SENT HERE TO DESTROY IT, AND HE COULD HAVE. BUT AFTER HE *SAW* THIS PLANET, ITS PEOPLE... ALL OF *YOU*... HE DECIDED HE COULDN'T DO IT.
HE DEFIED HIS MASTER, AND HE'S BEEN FIGHTING TO SAVE THIS WORLD EVER SINCE. YOU WOULD ALL BE *DEAD* WITHOUT HIM.
THIS IS ALL THERE IS FOR ME NOW. I *CAN'T* GO BACK.
BUT WHAT I *CAN* DO...
CORN
BELIEVE IN WIZORD. BELIEVE IN THE BEAUTY HE FOUND HERE. BELIEVE HE WILL FIGHT TO SAVE HIMSELF, TO SAVE HIS FAMILY, TO SAVE ALL OF YOU.
YOU DON'T HAVE TO BELIEVE HE'S GOOD. HE'S NOT. HE'S A SELFISH MONSTER, A WORK-IN-PROGRESS. BUT HE'S ALSO THE DEADLIEST BASTARD WHO EVER WAS.
HE *CAN* KILL SIZZAJEE. HE *CAN* SAVE US ALL. BELIEVE IT. *BELIEVE IT.* I MEAN...
...IS KILL THE *SHIT* OUT OF *YOU.*
...WHAT CHOICE DO YOU HAVE?
SSPPTT

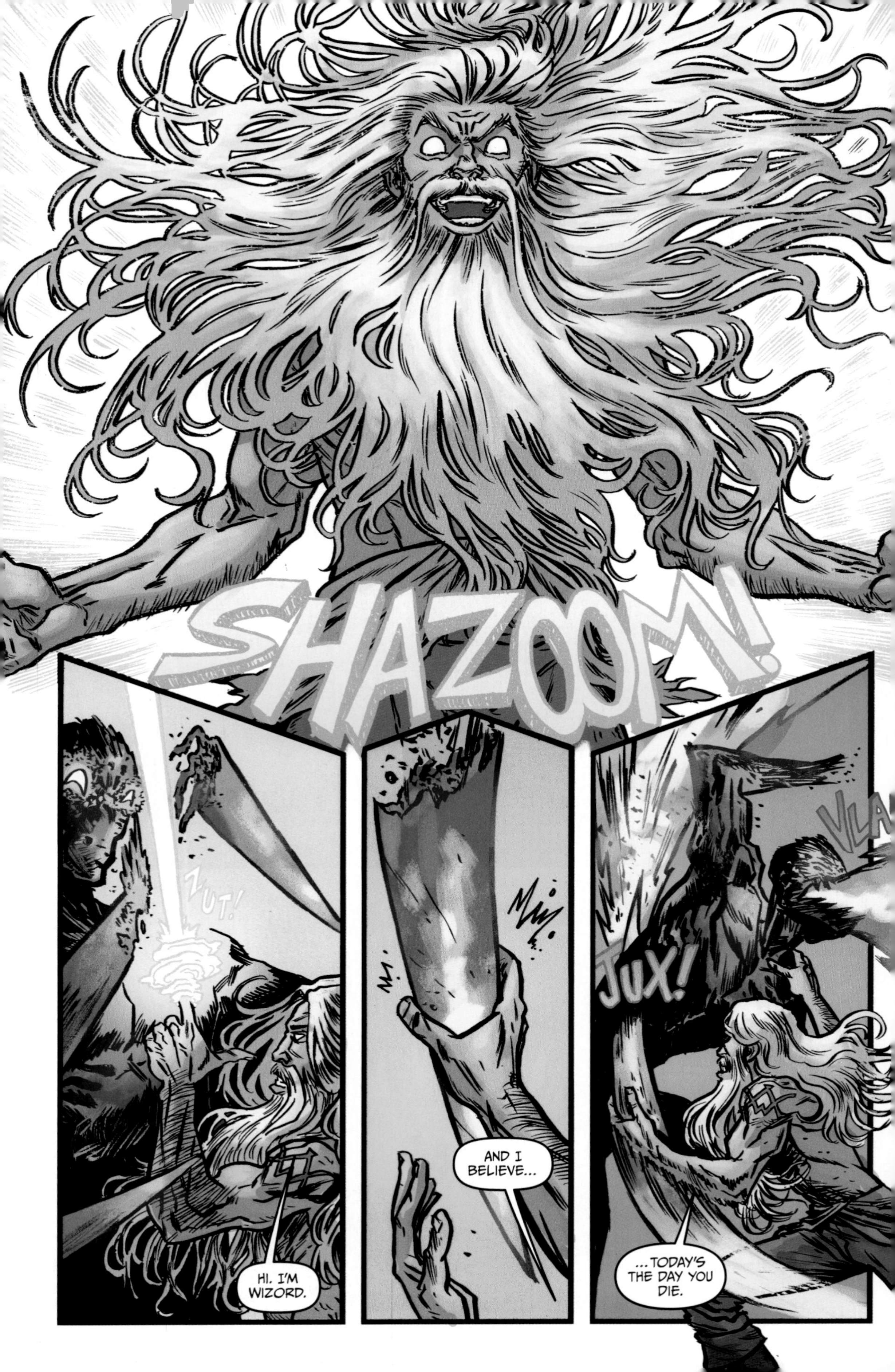
SHAZOOM!
ZUT!
HI. I'M WIZORD.
AND I BELIEVE...
...TODAY'S THE DAY YOU DIE.
JUX!
VLA

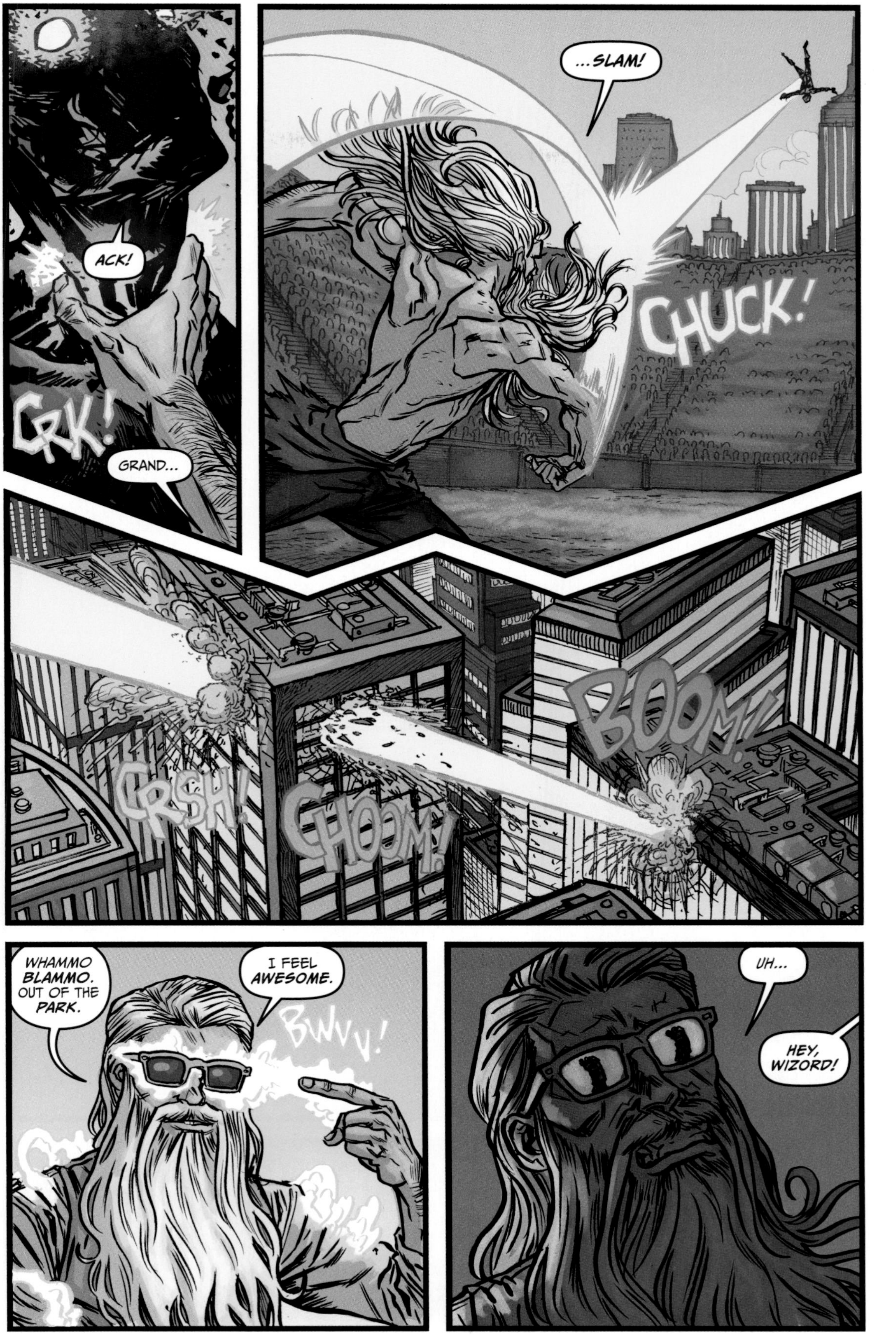
ACK!
CRK!
GRAND...
...SLAM!
CHUCK!
CRSH!
CHOOM!
BOOM!
WHAMMO BLAMMO. OUT OF THE PARK.
I FEEL AWESOME.
BWVV!
UH...
HEY, WIZORD!

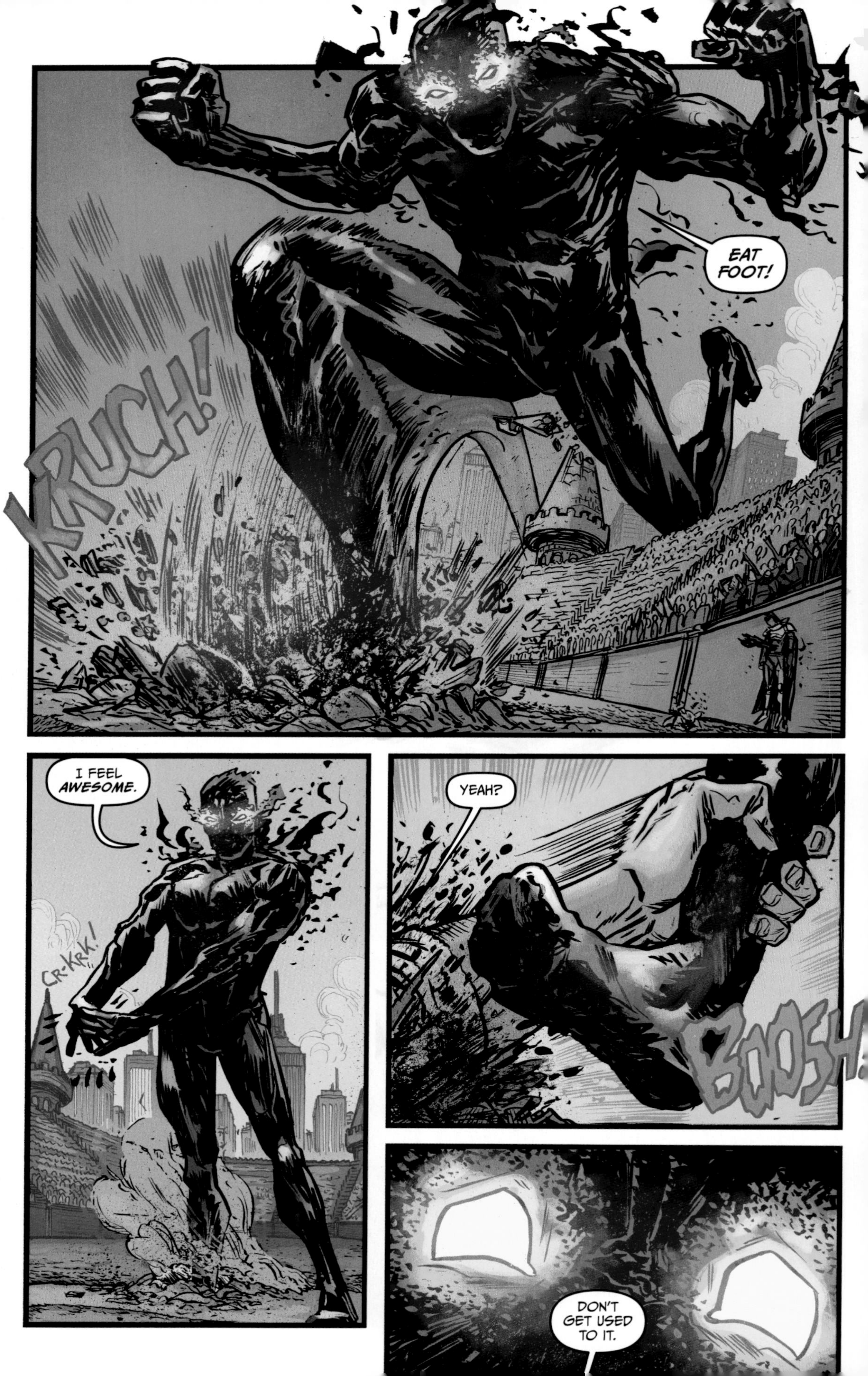
EAT FOOT!
KRUCH!
I FEEL AWESOME.
CR-KRK!
YEAH?
BOOSH!
DON'T GET USED TO IT.

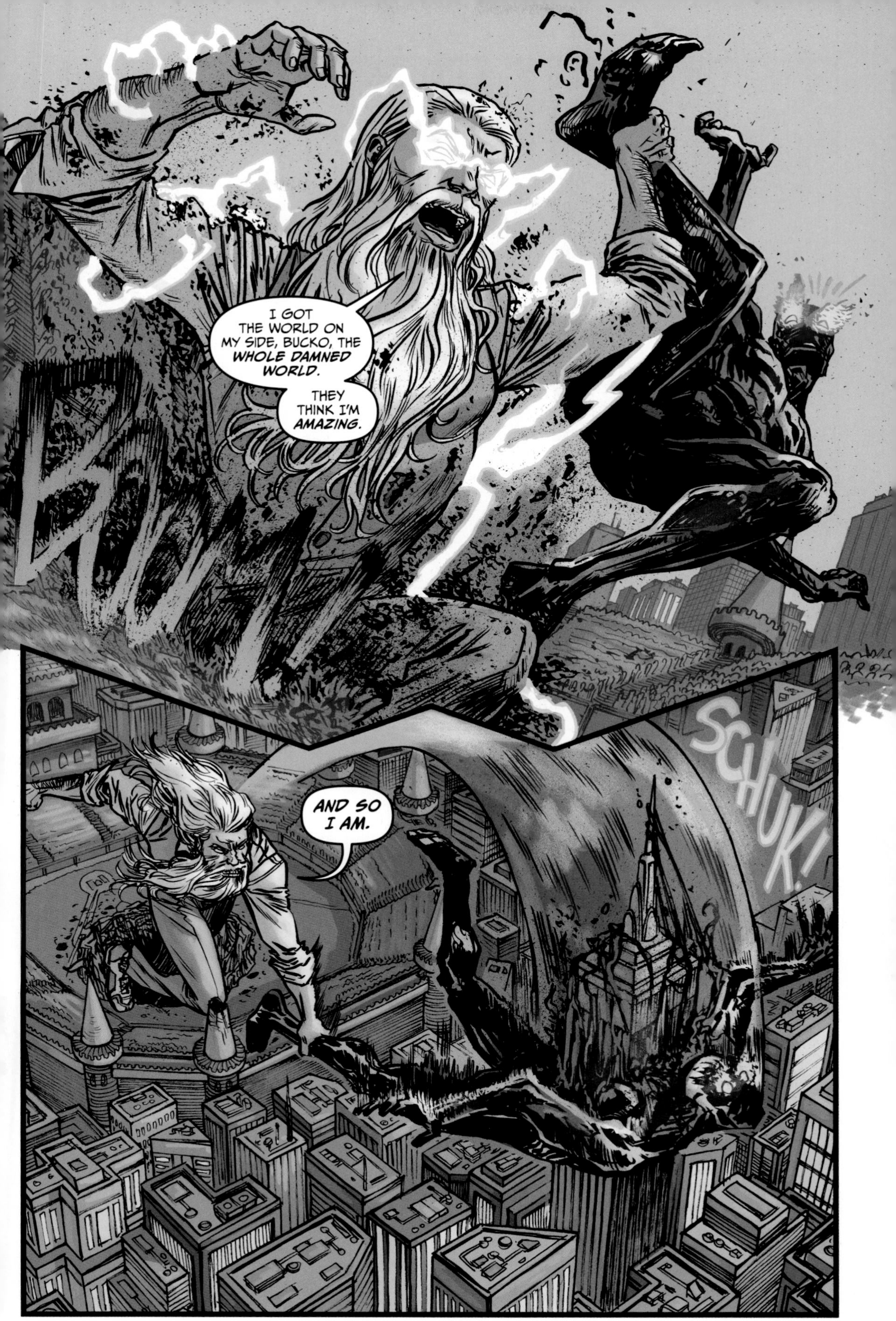
I GOT THE WORLD ON MY SIDE, BUCKO, THE WHOLE DAMNED WORLD.
THEY THINK I'M AMAZING.
SCHUK!
AND SO I AM.

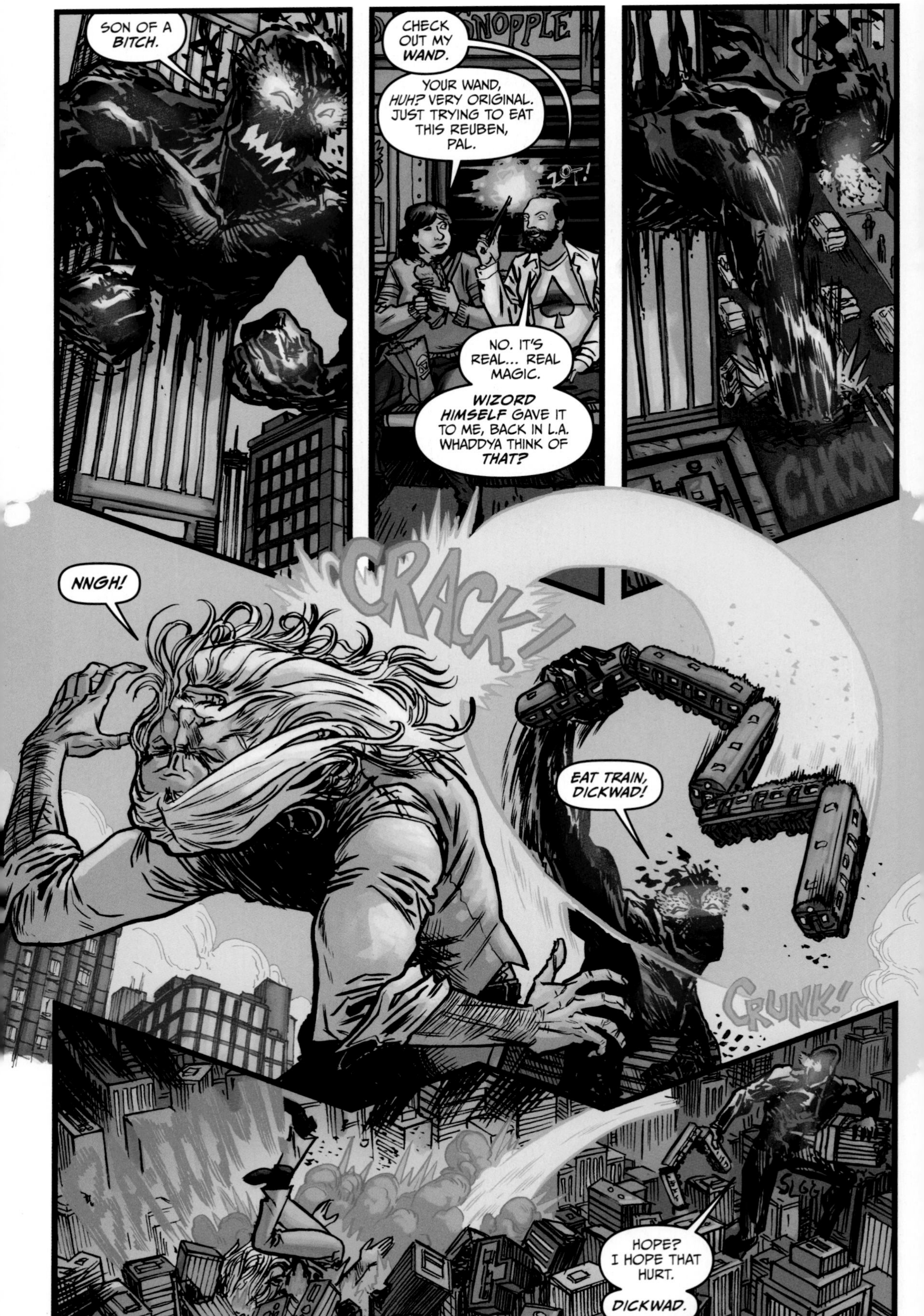

SON OF A BITCH.
SNOPPLE
CHECK OUT MY WAND.
YOUR WAND, HUH? VERY ORIGINAL. JUST TRYING TO EAT THIS REUBEN, PAL.
ZOT!
NO. IT'S REAL... REAL MAGIC.
WIZORD HIMSELF GAVE IT TO ME, BACK IN L.A. WHADDYA THINK OF THAT?
CHKK
CRACK!
NNGH!
EAT TRAIN, DICKWAD!
CRUNK!
HOPE? I HOPE THAT HURT.
DICKWAD.

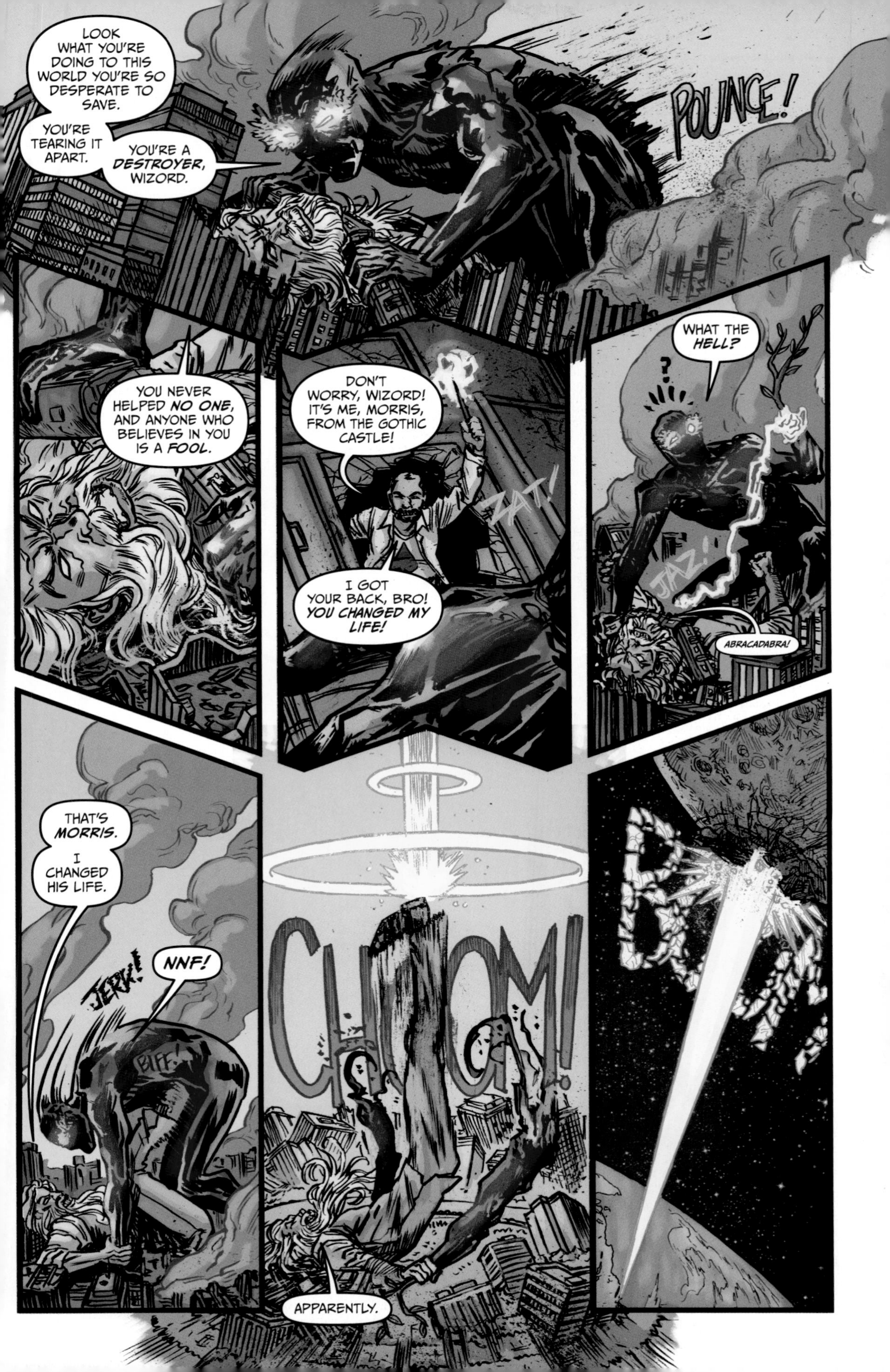
LOOK WHAT YOU'RE DOING TO THIS WORLD YOU'RE SO DESPERATE TO SAVE.
YOU'RE TEARING IT APART.
YOU'RE A *DESTROYER,* WIZORD.
POUNCE!
YOU NEVER HELPED *NO ONE,* AND ANYONE WHO BELIEVES IN YOU IS A *FOOL.*
DON'T WORRY, WIZORD! IT'S ME, MORRIS, FROM THE GOTHIC CASTLE!
ZAT!
I GOT YOUR BACK, BRO! *YOU CHANGED MY LIFE!*
WHAT THE *HELL?*
?
JAZ!
ABRACADABRA!
THAT'S *MORRIS.*
I CHANGED HIS LIFE.
JERK!
NNF!
BIFF!
APPARENTLY.

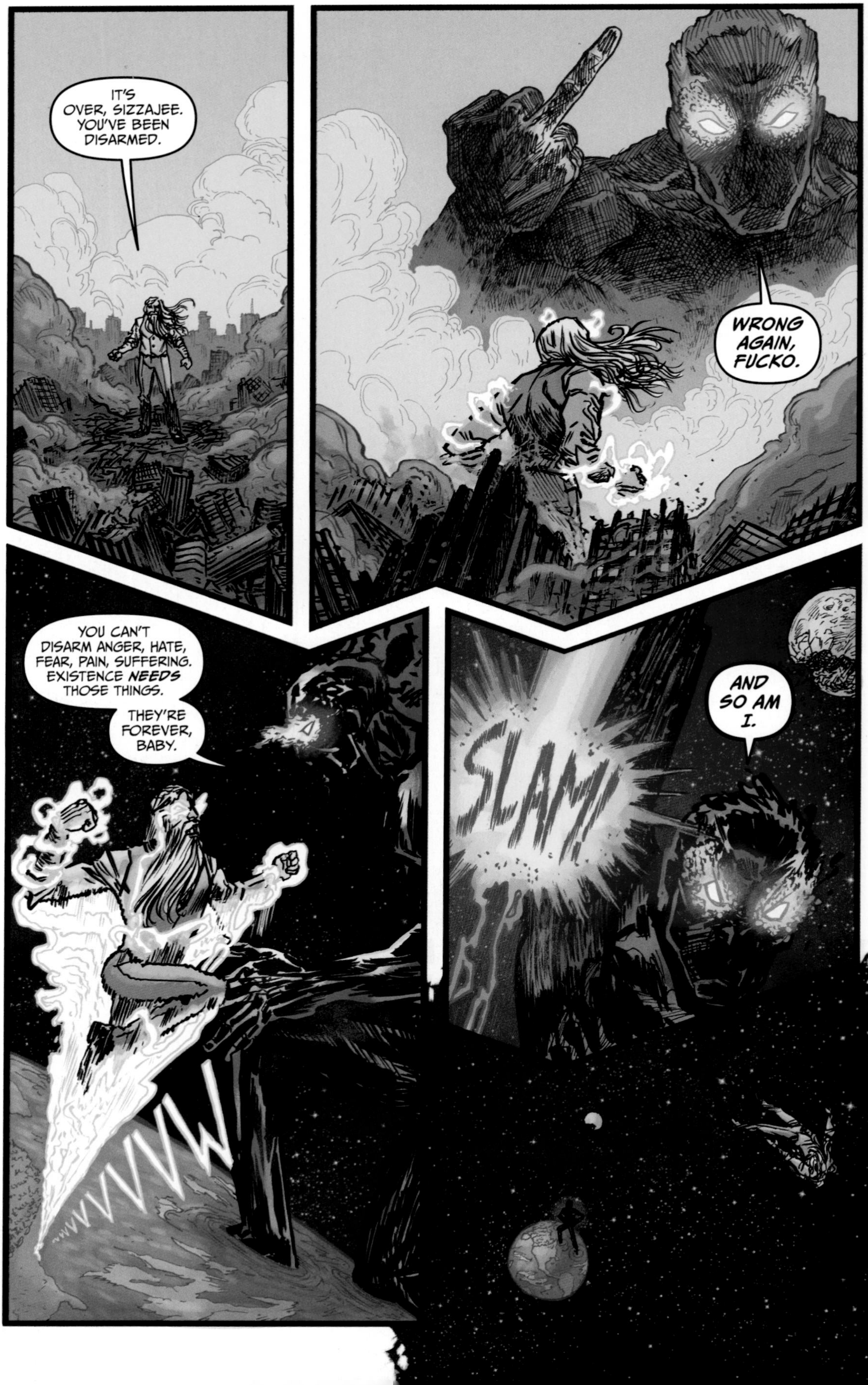
IT'S OVER, SIZZAJEE. YOU'VE BEEN DISARMED.
WRONG AGAIN, FUCKO.
YOU CAN'T DISARM ANGER, HATE, FEAR, PAIN, SUFFERING. EXISTENCE NEEDS THOSE THINGS.
THEY'RE FOREVER, BABY.
VVVVVVW
SLAM!
AND SO AM I.

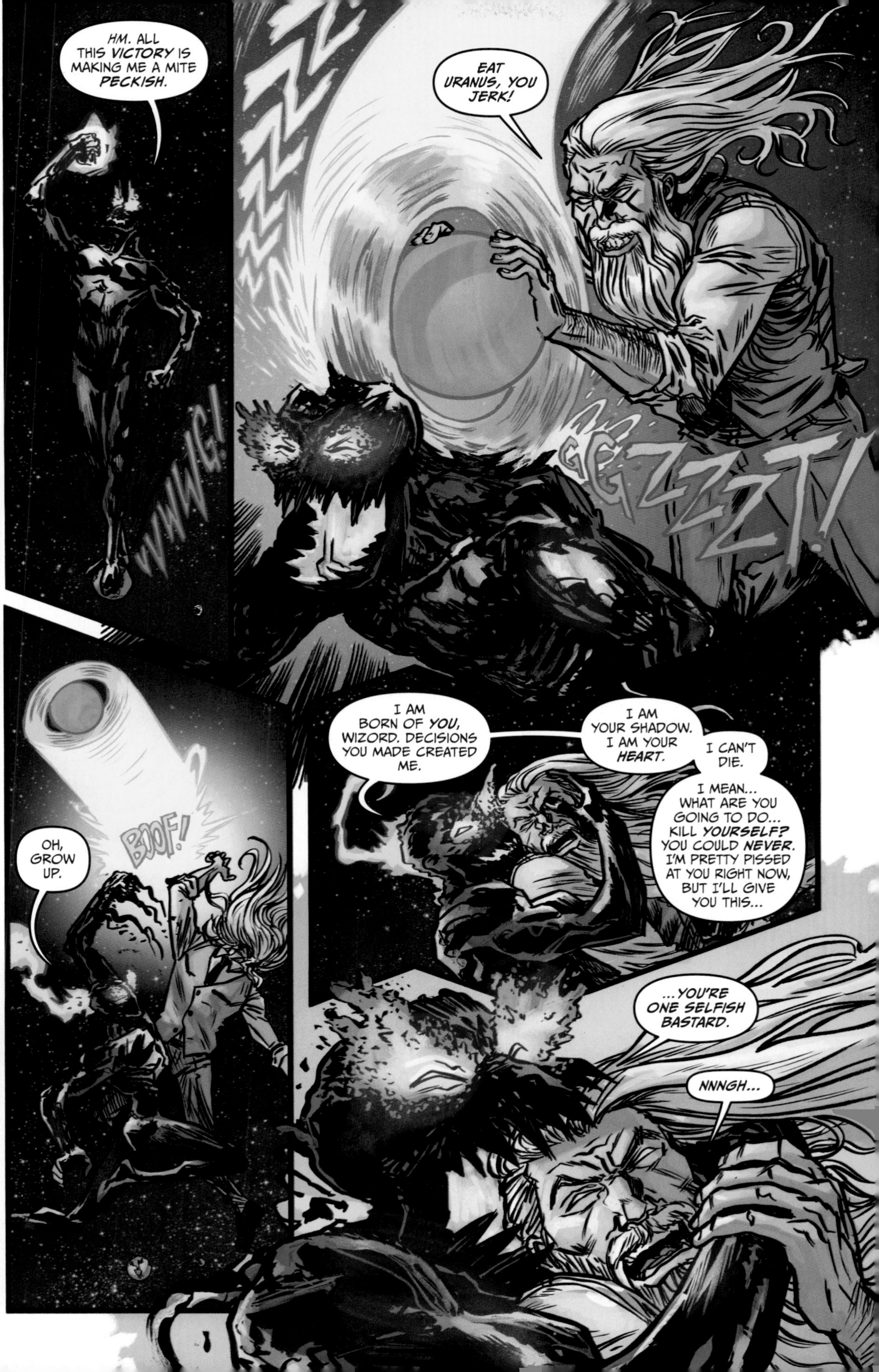
HM. ALL THIS VICTORY IS MAKING ME A MITE PECKISH.
EAT URANUS, YOU JERK!
GGZZZZT!
BOOF!
OH, GROW UP.
I AM BORN OF YOU, WIZORD. DECISIONS YOU MADE CREATED ME.
I AM YOUR SHADOW. I AM YOUR HEART.
I CAN'T DIE.
I MEAN... WHAT ARE YOU GOING TO DO... KILL YOURSELF? YOU COULD NEVER. I'M PRETTY PISSED AT YOU RIGHT NOW, BUT I'LL GIVE YOU THIS...
...YOU'RE ONE SELFISH BASTARD.
NNNGH...

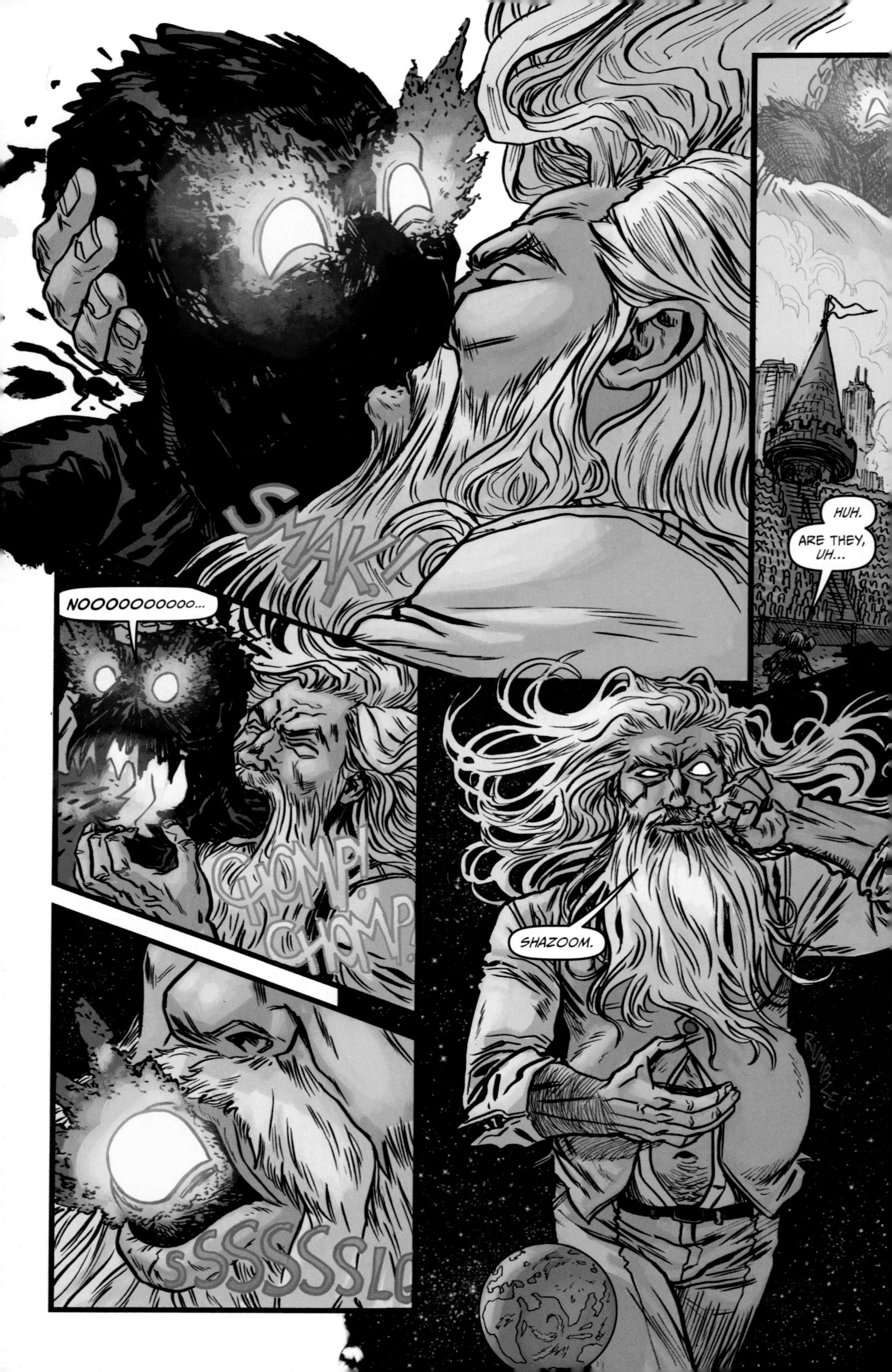
SMAK!!
HUH.
ARE THEY, UH...
NOOOOOOOOOO...
CHOMP! CHOMP!
SHAZOOM.
RUMBLE!
sSSSSSLG

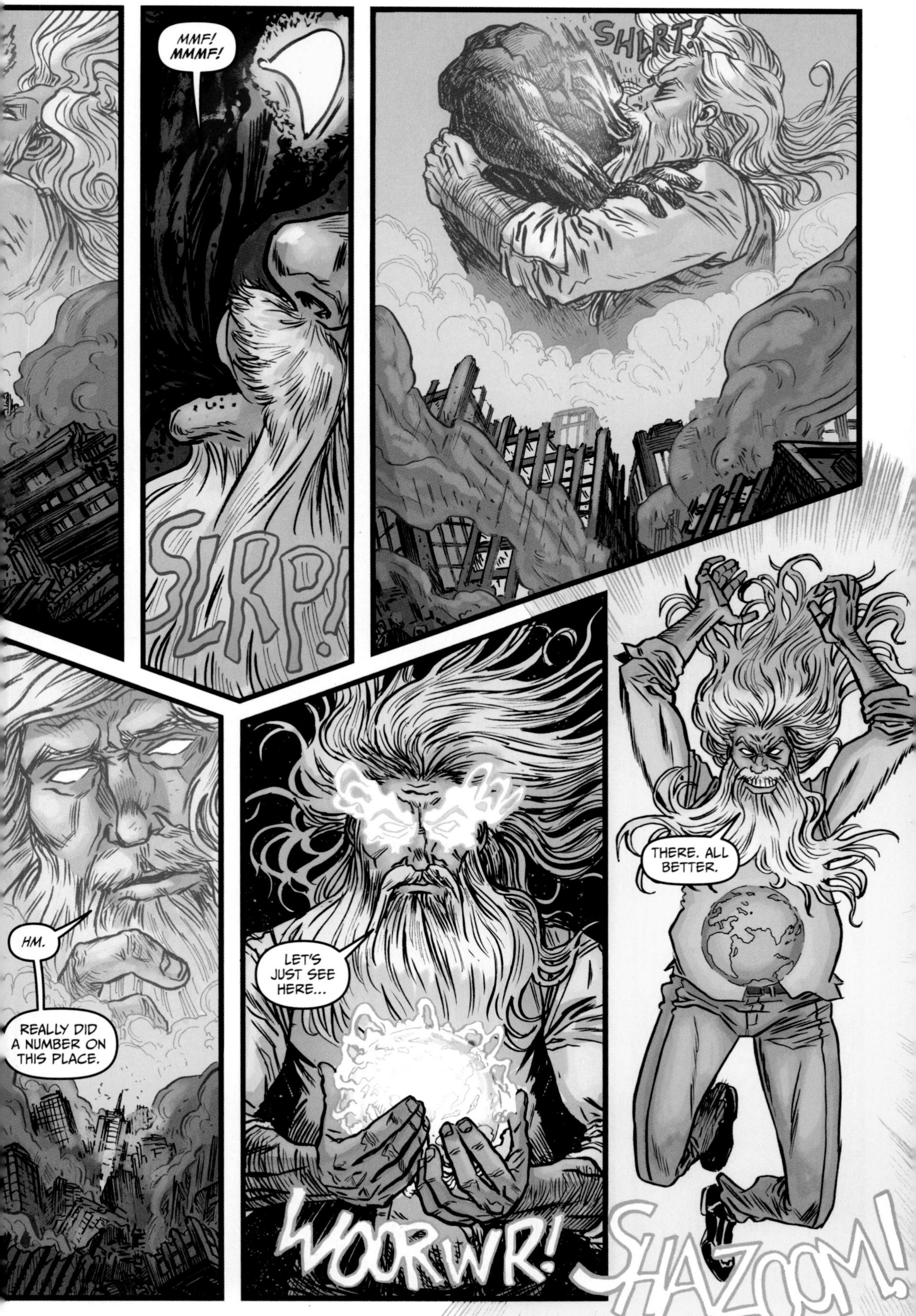
MMF! MMMF!
SLRP!
SHLRT!
HM.
REALLY DID A NUMBER ON THIS PLACE.
LET'S JUST SEE HERE...
WOORWR!
THERE. ALL BETTER.
SHAZOOM!

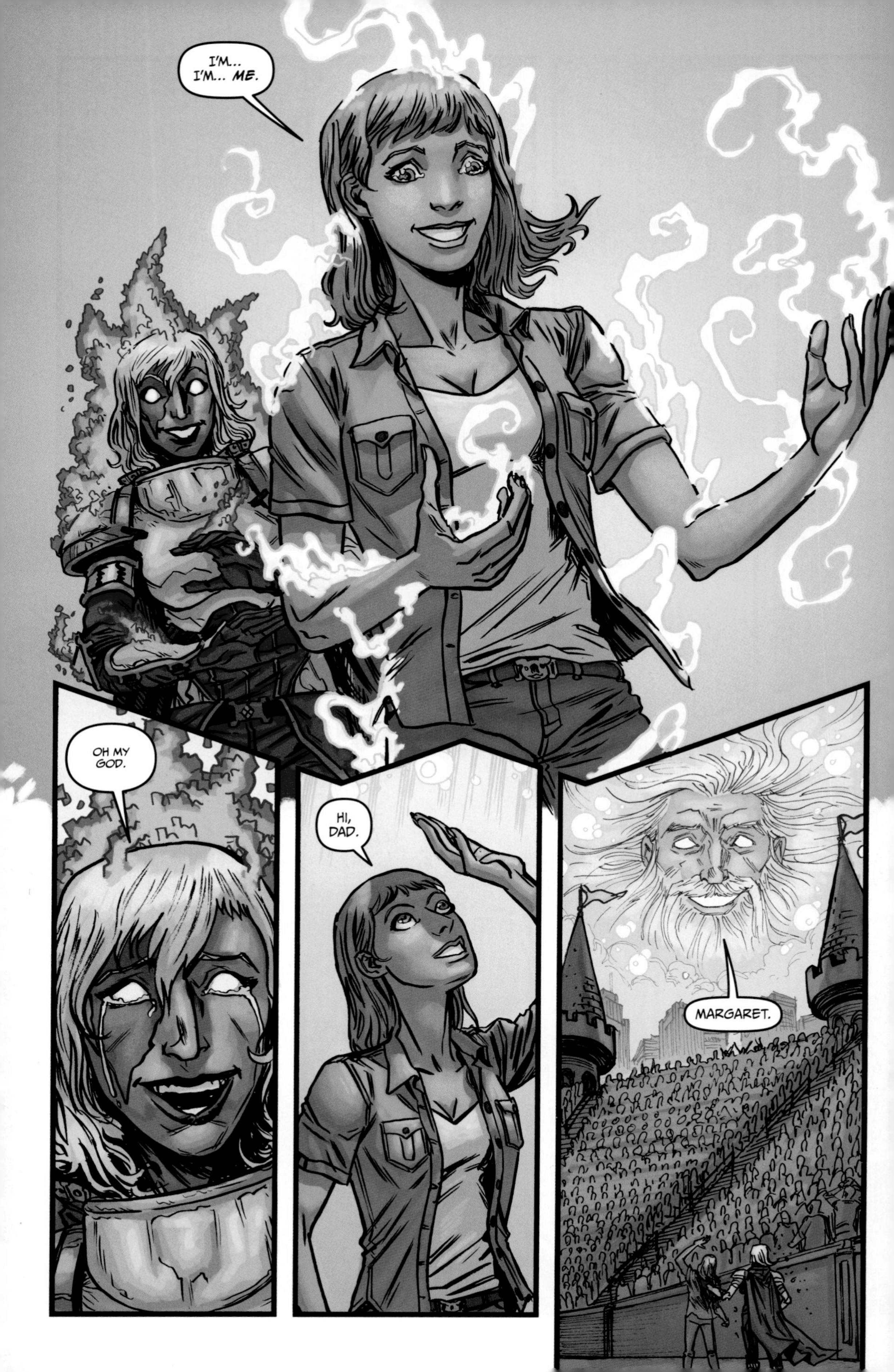

I'M.. I'M... ME.
OH MY GOD.
HI, DAD.
MARGARET.

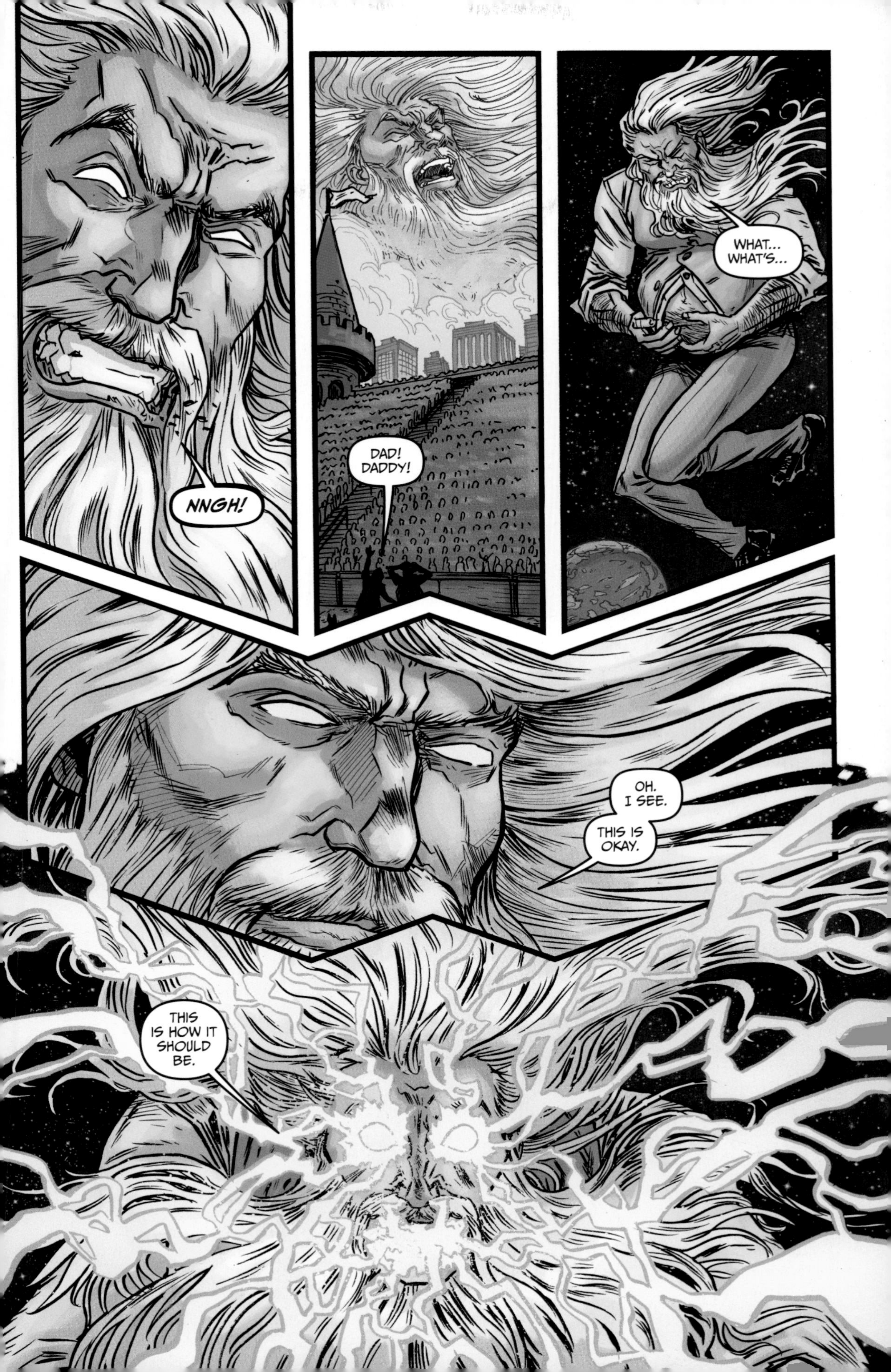
NNGH!
DAD! DADDY!
WHAT... WHAT'S...
OH. I SEE.
THIS IS OKAY.
THIS IS HOW IT SHOULD BE.

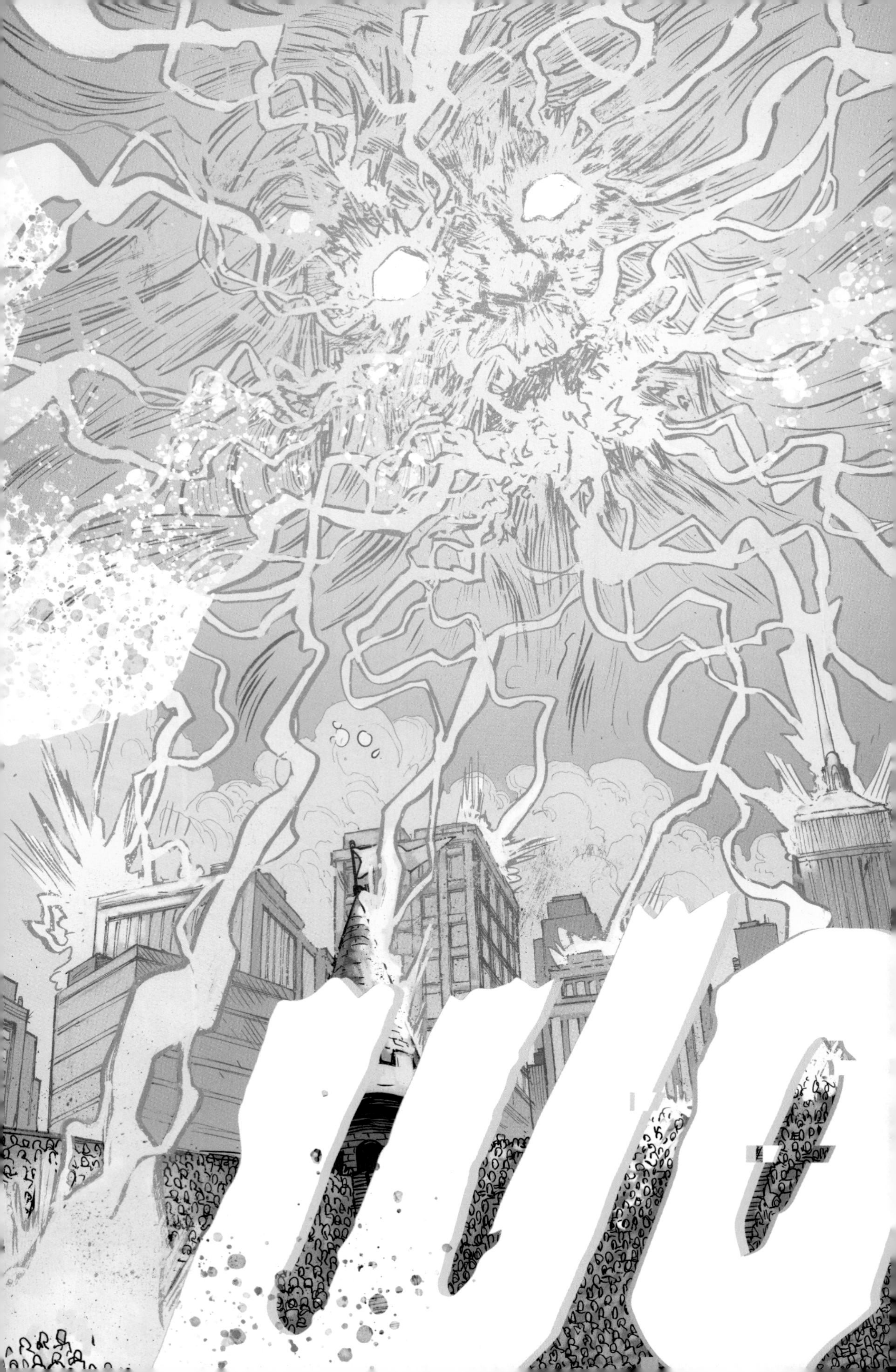

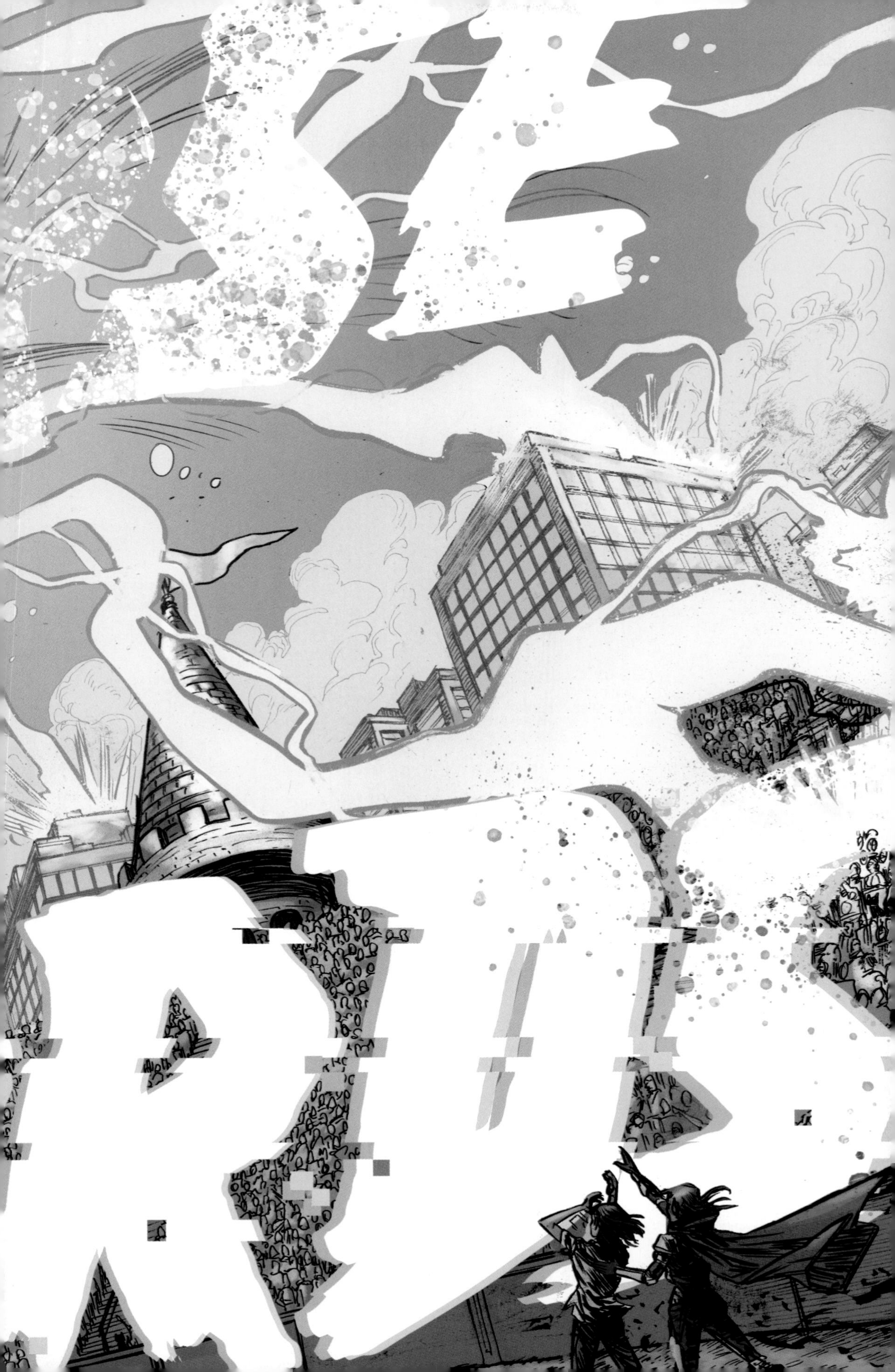

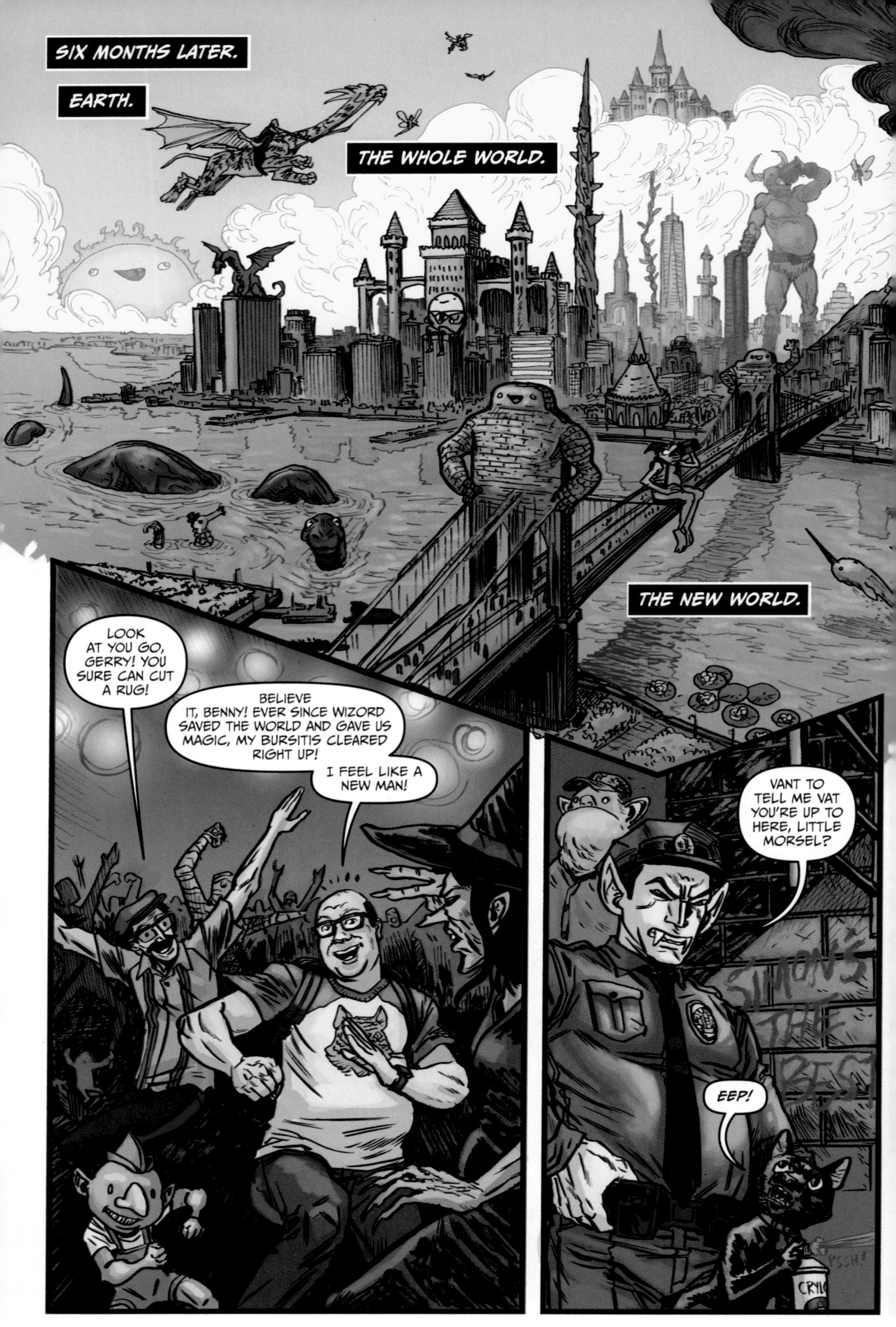
SIX MONTHS LATER.
EARTH.
THE WHOLE WORLD.
THE NEW WORLD.
LOOK AT YOU GO, GERRY! YOU SURE CAN CUT A RUG!
BELIEVE IT, BENNY! EVER SINCE WIZORD SAVED THE WORLD AND GAVE US MAGIC, MY BURSITIS CLEARED RIGHT UP!
I FEEL LIKE A NEW MAN!
VANT TO TELL ME VAT YOU'RE UP TO HERE, LITTLE MORSEL?
EEP!

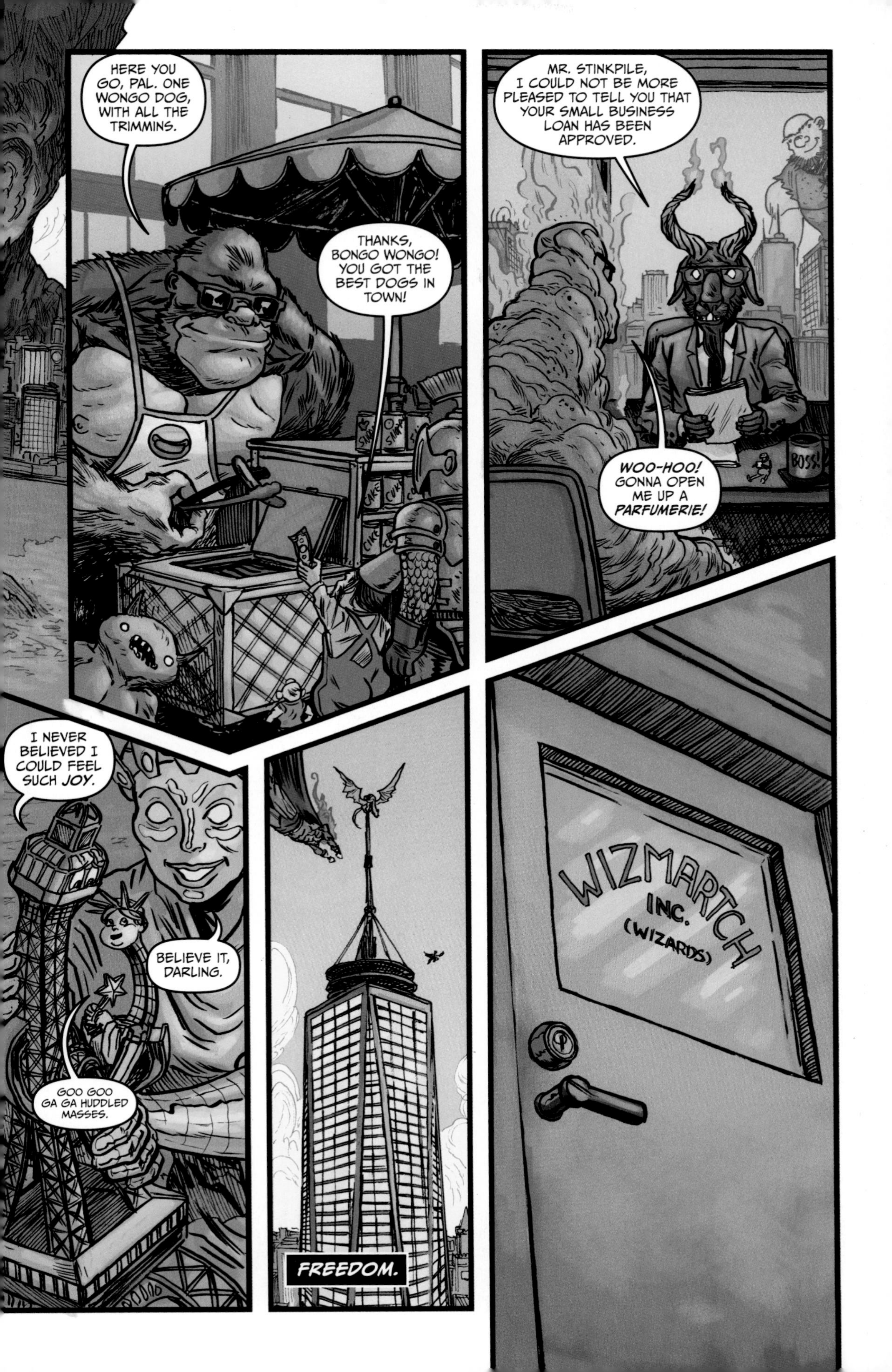
HERE YOU GO, PAL. ONE WONGO DOG, WITH ALL THE TRIMMINS.
THANKS, BONGO WONGO! YOU GOT THE BEST DOGS IN TOWN!
MR. STINKPILE, I COULD NOT BE MORE PLEASED TO TELL YOU THAT YOUR SMALL BUSINESS LOAN HAS BEEN APPROVED.
WOO-HOO! GONNA OPEN ME UP A PARFUMERIE!
BOSS!
I NEVER BELIEVED I COULD FEEL SUCH JOY.
BELIEVE IT, DARLING.
GOO GOO GA GA HUDDLED MASSES.
FREEDOM.
WIZMARTCH INC. (WIZARDS)

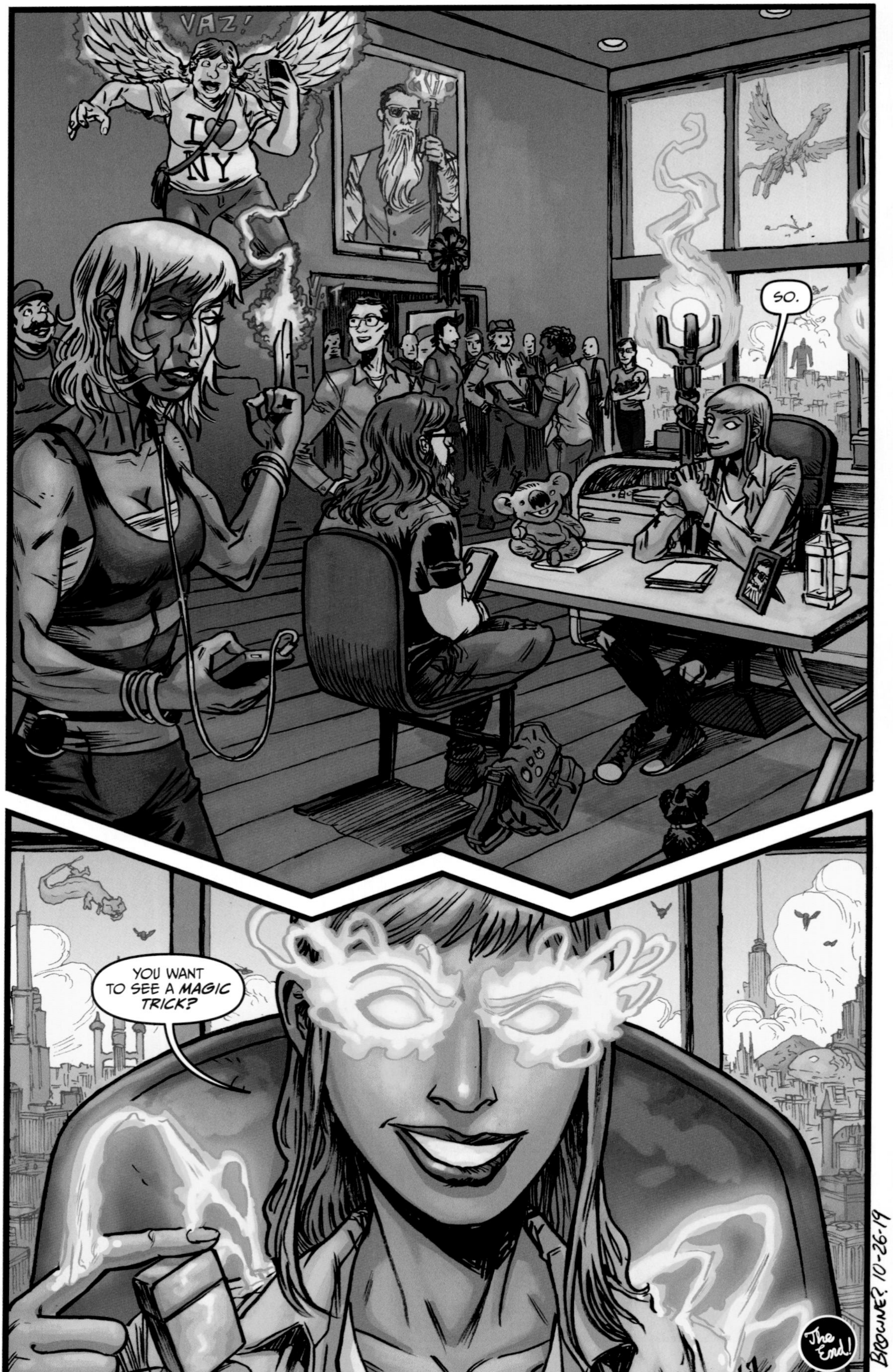
VAZ!
I NY
SO.
YOU WANT TO SEE A *MAGIC* *TRICK?*
BROWNE? 10-26-19
The End!

SPRING HAS SPRUNG SPECIAL VARIANT
BY **MIKE NORTON** AND **RYAN BROWNE**

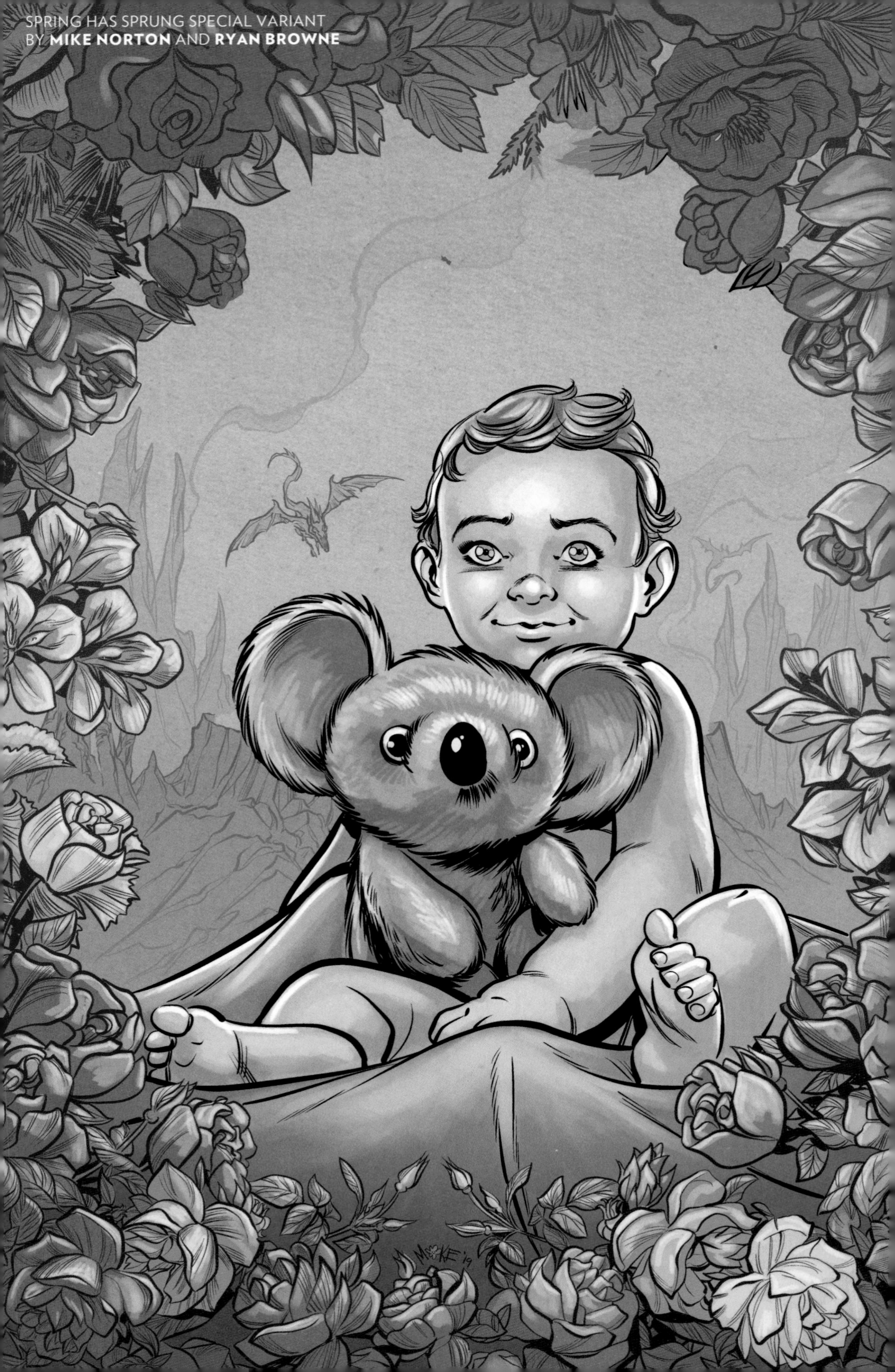
MIKE '19

ISSUE 21-25 CONNECTED VARIANTS
BY **RYAN BROWNE**

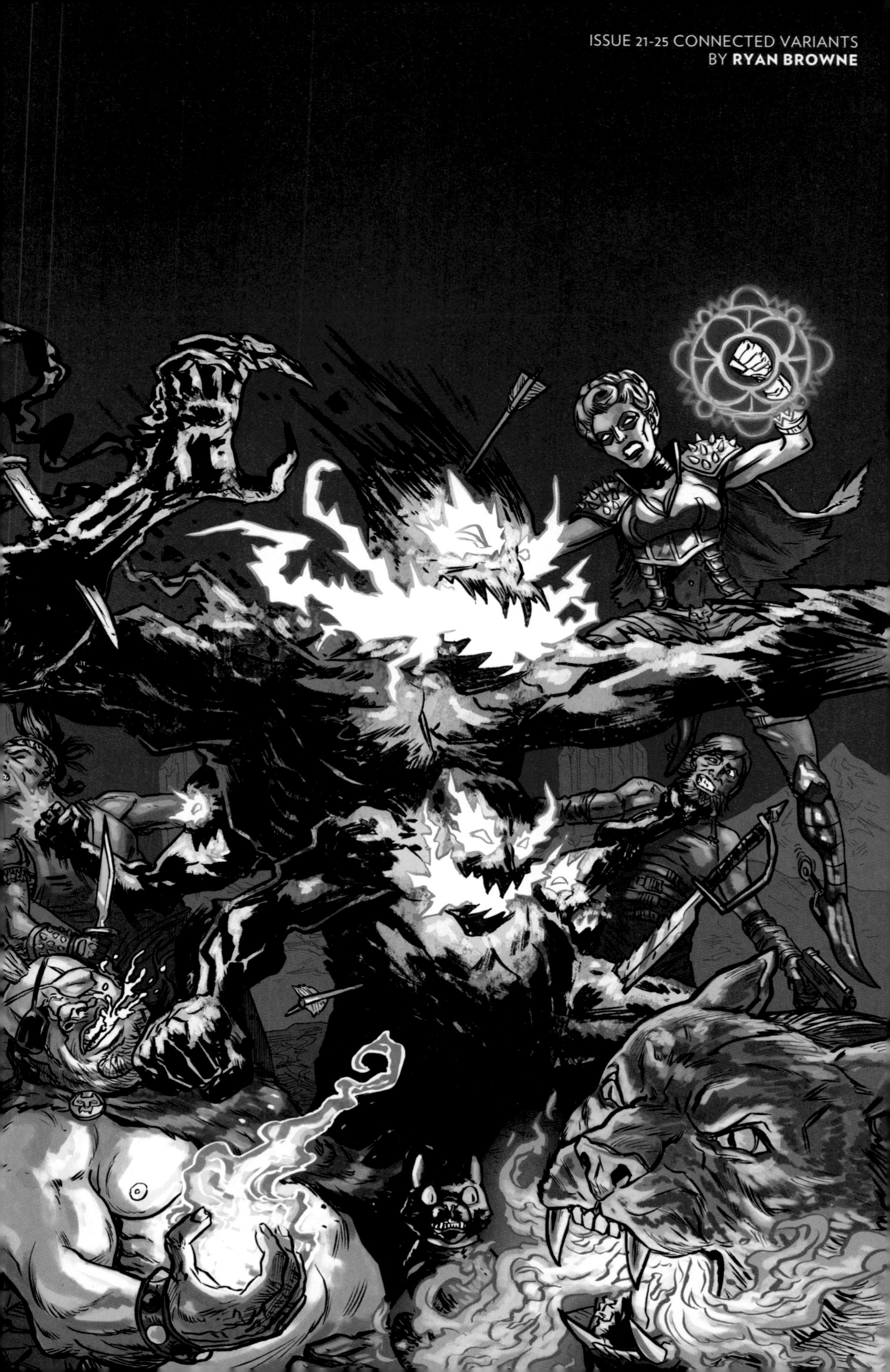

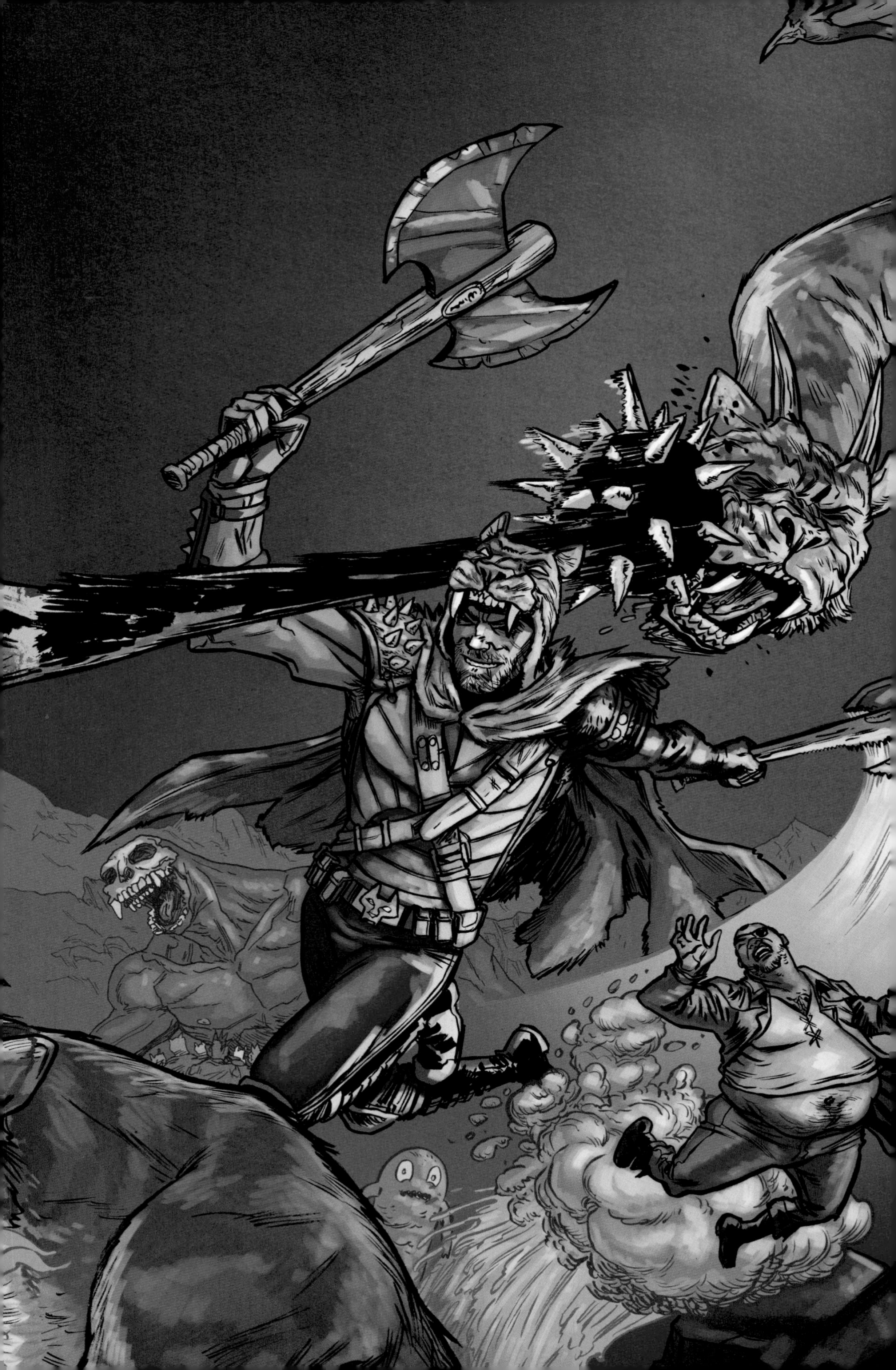

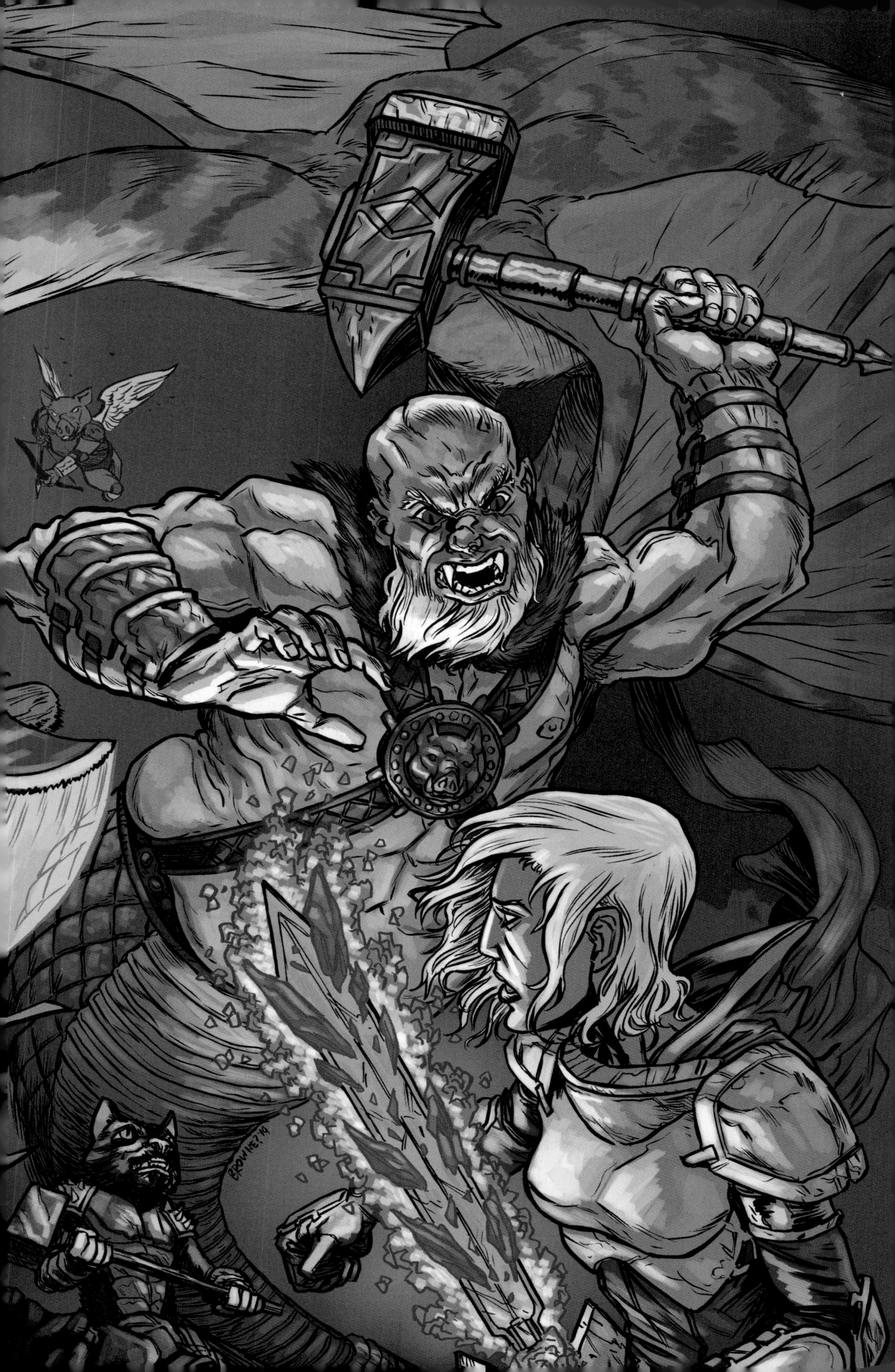

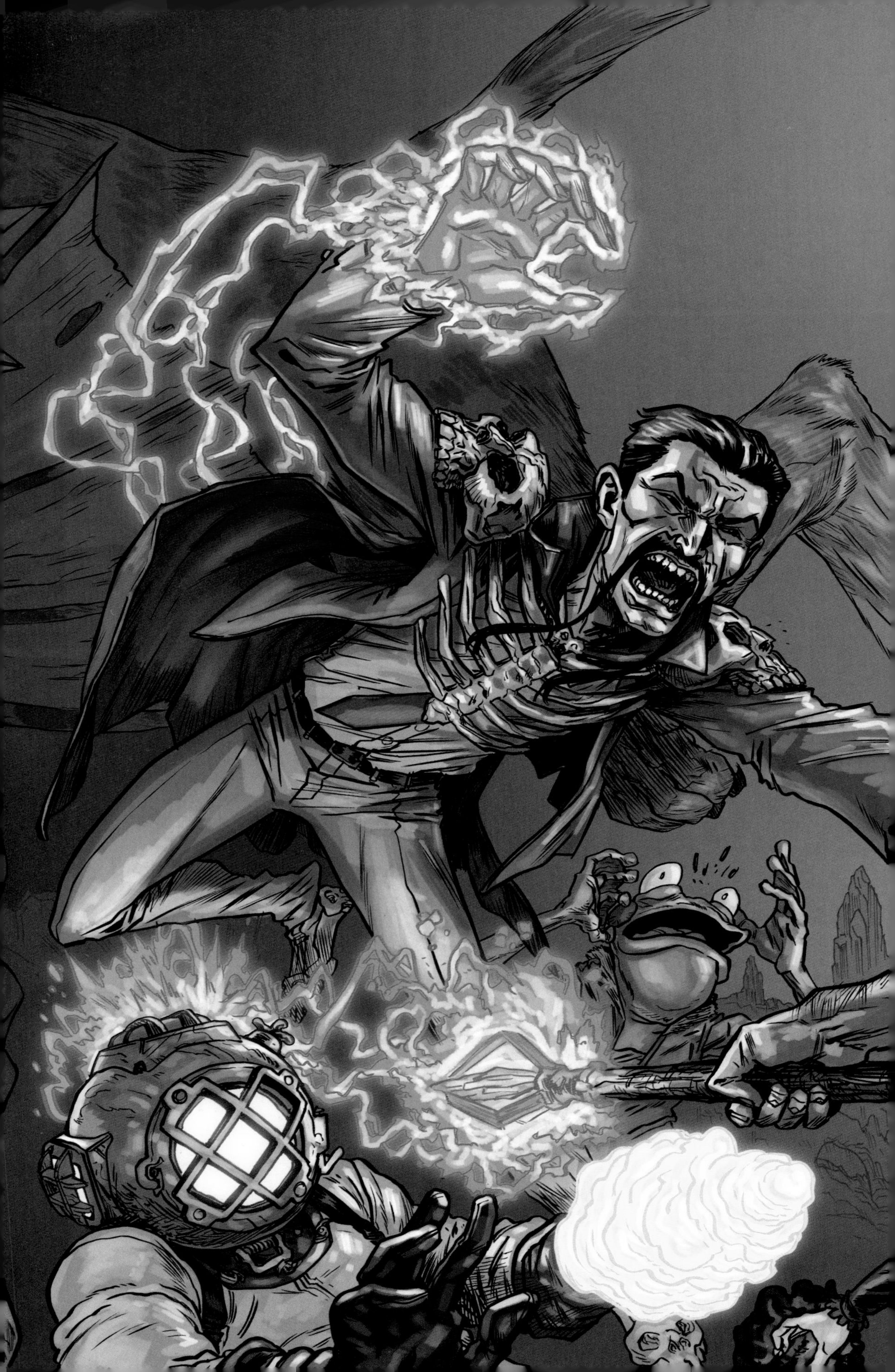

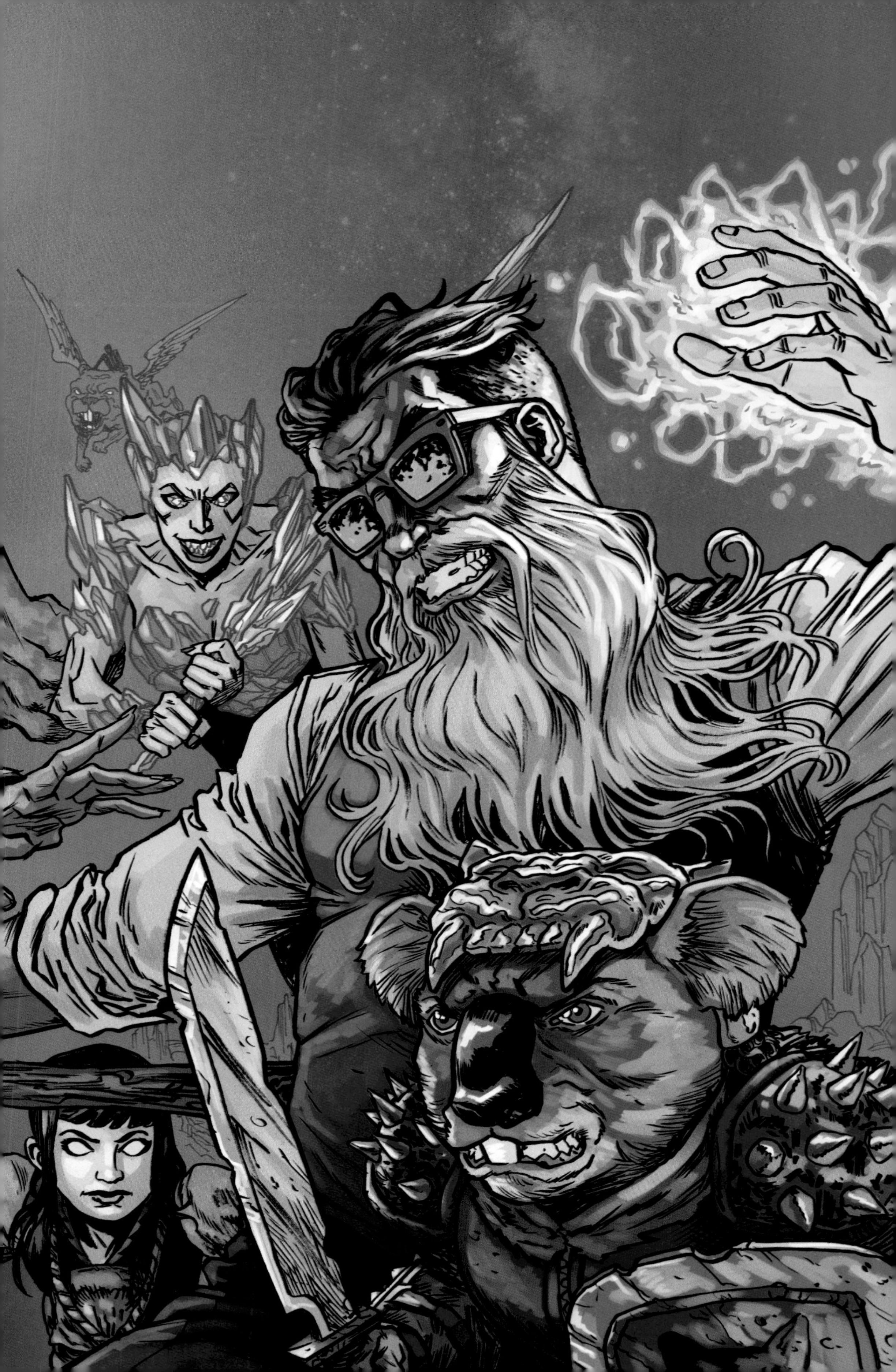

Good-bye, Wizord. Good-bye Margaret and Ruby Stitch. Adios, Sizzajee, au revoir Jacques Zacques, sayonara to Botchko and Lady Violet and all the rest of the Nine.

Smell you later, *Curse Words*.

In the beginning, this book was for Ryan Browne and me. Nothing more complicated than that. We adore each other (I know, emotion, eww, cool dudes aren't supposed to say things like that, and Ryan and I are very cool dudes.) We have almost the same sense of humor, though that "almost" leaves a lot of room for us to surprise each other in our storytelling.

For years prior to this book, young Master Browne and I would bum around in bars at conventions just riffing out stories to make each other laugh. Most of those stories were very dumb. Some were obscene. One of them became *Curse Words*.

We wanted to tell a big, cool ongoing series of our very own at Image Comics, the best home for big, cool ongoing series of your very own. We settled on magic as a theme, because magic meant we could do literally anything storytelling-wise. Ryan's visual humor is very much about anything goes – he's a comics surrealist, and very, very funny. If you haven't, read his *God Hates Astronauts*, which is like *Curse Words* but with superheroes and even stranger, if such a thing seems possible. On my side, I like stories with a strong

emotional core and high-level hook that have no restraints on possibility. My series *Letter 44* is like that, or my new Image series debuting this very month – *Undiscovered Country* (or, if we're doing this, my novels *The Oracle Year* and *Anyone*.)

We went from those basic guidelines to what's more or less the logline for *Curse Words* – "What if there was a wizard... but he was a dick!"

The book was originally called *"WIZSWORD"* but literally everyone said that was impossible to pronounce and also stupid, so we shorted it to *"WIZORD,"* which was less impossible to pronounce but also stupid, at which point we, after many months of trying, finally came up with *Curse Words*. We started a company – SILENT E PRODUCTIONS, LLC (get it?) and buckled down.

Here we are today, over six hundred pages of storytelling later. Some milestones for the book:

--A wizard party to introduce the world to the book at New York Comicon 2016!

--Variant covers by some of our bestest friends in the biz, whom we were honored to have help us bring the book to life and also Chip Zdarsky did one too.

--THE WIZARD VAN TOUR, in which Ryan and I drove around the US promoting the book in a sweet wizard van (that's why we called the tour that).

--The much-smaller one-stop summer 2018 Wizard Van (without a van) Tour to Salt Lake City!

--The mysterious trip to Los Angeles in which we optioned the book for television!

--Ryan and his awesome wife Carrie made a very small new person named Kirby!

--So many fabulous fans. SO MANY.

This book wasn't Saga or Walking Dead... and that's okay. It's an idiosyncratic story that largely exists to make Ryan and me laugh, and gave us an excuse to talk almost every day for years. But the fact that we got to do that is because of you. The book was always financially healthy. Everyone got their page rate plus a bit more when we could. We know that for many people, it became a treasured part of their comics reading life. What more can you ask, as creators? You make something, you put it out in the world, and you hope people like it. If anyone loves it? Wow.

Well. That's it. That response and support from fans, retailers, social media, all of it meant we could make twenty-eight issues, some oversized like this very pamphlet you're reading, exactly the way we wanted.

We told the full story of Wizord and his pals, and did it exactly as we wanted. Hot damn. Thank you.

So, what now? Well, Ryan's off to draw comics for someone else for a bit (boo), and I'm off to tell other stories that won't be drawn by Ryan (double-boo). But, there's good news – we have another story we're dying to tell, which I think we'll begin working on in 2020, hopefully in the spring. That should, in theory, mean that you could start reading it in late 2020 or early 2021, which isn't so far away. It's a complex premise, with possibilities for everything we like to do – for both of us, it'll be a real workout.

We also want to do a big oversized hardcover omnibus edition of *Curse Words*. If we do that, we'll create a new story for it. Beyond that, who knows? I already miss this book, and I could absolutely see us revisiting this world over and over again over the years.

But hey, we should count our blessings. After all, who gets to make a world? Well, Wizord, I suppose. Actually, he made two, if you think about it. Not bad, for an unrepentant jerk.

See you in the New World, friends.

Charles Soule,
Beacon, NY, October 29, 2019

ABOUT THE AUTHORS

CHARLES SOULE has written many comics for Marvel, DC and others-- *DAREDEVIL, STAR WARS, THE DEATH OF WOLVERINE, INHUMANS, SWAMP THING*... all kinds of stuff. He's also the creator of the award-winning epic sci-fi series *LETTER 44* for Oni Press, and his first (hopefully not last?) novel, *THE ORACLE YEAR*. (Don't tell any of those other projects, but *CURSE WORDS* is his favorite.)

He lives in Brooklyn, where he also plays music of various kinds and practices law from time to time.

Follow him on Twitter @CHARLESSOULE.

RYAN BROWNE is an American-born comicbookman who is co-responsible for *CURSE WORDS* (which you just read) and wholly responsible for *GOD HATES ASTRONAUTS* (which you should go read if you haven't). He currently lives in Chicago with his amazing wife, super amazing son Kirby, and his considerably less amazing cat. Also, he was once a guest on *The Montel Williams Show*-- which is a great story and you should ask him about it.

Catch him on Twitter and Instagram @RYANBROWNEART.